HUNT THE DARKNESS

"Witches don't mate," she muttered.

"Perhaps not, but demons do." His thumb skimmed down her cheek to tease the corner of her mouth. "And you, my love, are most definitely demon."

Their eyes clashed. The air sizzled with that ever-ready hunger.

His thumb slipped between her lips . . . and just that quickly, she was desperate for his kiss.

She needed the hungry press of his mouth, the dangerous scrape of his fangs, the intoxicating heat that scorched through her body. . . .

Published by Kensington Publishing Corporation

HUNT THE
DARKNESS

ALEXANDRA
IVY

ZEBRA BOOKS
KENSINGTON PUBLISHING CORP.
http://www.kensingtonbooks.com

ZEBRA BOOKS are published by

Kensington Publishing Corp.
119 West 40th Street
New York, NY 10018

All Kensington titles, imprints, and distributed lines are available at special quantity discounts for bulk purchases for sales promotion, premiums, fund-raising, educational, or institutional use.

Special book excerpts or customized printings can also be created to fit specific needs. For details, write or phone the office of the Kensington Special Sales Manager: Attn.: Special Sales Department. Kensington Publishing Corp., 119 West 40th Street, New York, NY 10018. Phone: 1-800-221-2647.

First Mass-Market Paperback Printing: June 2014
ISBN-13: 978-1-4201-2515-3
ISBN-10: 1-4201-2515-X

First Electronic Edition: June 2014
eISBN-13: 978-1-4201-3514-5
eISBN-10: 1-4201-3514-7

10 9 8 7 6 5 4 3 2 1

Printed in the United States of America

Prologue

Styx's lair
Chicago, IL

Styx was fairly certain that hell had frozen over.

Nothing else could explain the fact that in the past year he'd become the Anasso (King of All Vampires), moved from his dank caves into a behemoth of a mansion that contained acres of marble, crystal and gilt—gilt for Christ's sake—and mated with a pure-blooded Were who also happened to be a vegetarian.

Then, as if fate hadn't had enough laughs at his expense, he'd been in an epic battle against the Dark Lord, which meant he'd been forced to make allies out of former enemies.

Including the King of Weres, Salvatore, who was currently drinking Styx's finest brandy as he smoothed a hand down his impeccable Gucci suit.

Of course, if it wasn't for the fact that their mates happened to be sisters, he would never have allowed the bastard over his doorstep, he pacified his battered pride. His own mate, Darcy, was very . . . insistent that she be allowed to spend time with Harley, who was growing heavy with her first pregnancy.

Or was it litter?

Either way, Styx and Salvatore were forced to play nice.

Not an easy task for two über-alphas who'd been opponents for centuries.

Settling his six-foot-plus frame in a chair that had a view of the moon-drenched gardens, Styx waited for his companion to finish his drink.

As always, Salvatore looked more like a sophisticated mob boss than the King of Weres. His dark hair was pulled to a tail at his nape and his elegant features were cleanly shaved. Only the feral heat that glowed in the dark eyes revealed the truth of the beast that lived inside him.

Styx, on the other hand, didn't even try to appear civilized.

A towering Aztec warrior, he was wearing a pair of leather pants, heavy shitkickers, and a white silk shirt that was stretched to the limit to cover his broad chest. His long black hair was braided to hang down to his waist and threaded with tiny turquoise amulets. And to complete the image, he had a huge sword strapped to his back.

What was the point in being a badass if you couldn't look like one?

Setting aside his empty glass, Salvatore flashed a dazzling white smile. A sure sign he was about to be annoying.

"Let me see if I have this right," the wolf drawled.

Yep. Annoying.

Styx narrowed his dark eyes, his features that were too stark for true beauty tight with warning.

"Do you have to?"

"Oh yes." The smile widened. "You asked the clan chief of Nevada to babysit a witch you had locked in your dungeons?"

Styx silently swore to have a chat with his mate once their guests were gone.

He hadn't intended Salvatore to know that one of his most powerful vampires had been magically forced into a mating.

Hell, he'd had a hard enough time divulging the info with

Jagr, his most trusted Raven. It was only because he needed the vampire to do research that he'd revealed the secret.

A mating was the rarest, most sacred, most intimate connection a demon could experience.

To think for a second that it could be inflicted on a vampire against his will was nothing less than . . . rape.

You didn't reveal that kind of weakness to your enemies. Even if you did have a peace treaty.

Darcy, however, was a genuine optimist who blithely assumed that Salvatore would never abuse privileged information.

Now Styx was stuck revealing the truth to the mangy mutt.

"Sally Grace was not only a powerful witch who was capable of black magic, but she worshipped the Dark Lord," he grudgingly explained, not about to admit that it had been more habit than fear that had led him to lock the female in his dungeons. Sally Grace was barely over five feet and weighed less than a hundred pounds. She hadn't looked like a threat. And she probably wouldn't have been if she hadn't been so scared. "Of course I wasn't going to take any chances."

"Why Roke?"

Styx shrugged. "I was busy dealing with the ancient spirit that was trying to turn vampires into crazed killers."

Naturally Salvatore wasn't satisfied.

"And?" he prodded.

"And the prophet had warned that Roke would be important to the future," he muttered. He'd truly thought keeping Roke in his lair would protect him. Ah, the best laid plans of mice and vampires. "How the hell was I supposed to know Sally Grace was half demon?"

Salvatore grimaced. "It must have been quite a shock to poor Roke to discover himself mated to a witch."

Styx's humorless laugh echoed through the library at the memory of Roke's fury.

"Shock isn't the word I'd used."

"She's lucky he didn't kill her on the spot."

Frustration simmered deep inside Styx. Roke might be an arrogant pain-in-the-ass, but he was a brother. And more importantly, he was a clan chief who had a duty to his people. They had to find a way to break the mating.

And how to make damned sure it never happened again.

"He might have killed her if the magic she used didn't feel as real as any true mating."

Salvatore's amusement faded. "That bad?"

"Worse." Styx surged to his feet. "Without her knowing who or what fathered her, the witch doesn't even know how to reverse the damage."

"You're certain this isn't some trick?"

"I'm not certain of anything beyond the need to find a way to break the bond."

Salvatore poured another shot of brandy. "Do you have a plan?"

Plan? Styx grimaced. The closest they'd had to a plan the past year had been to charge from one disaster to another.

Why would this be any different?

"Sally left almost three weeks ago to search for any clues that would reveal who her father might be," he said.

"And Roke?"

"He's trying to catch her."

Salvatore arched a brow. "You let him go alone?"

"Of course not." A slow smile curved Styx's lips. "I allowed Levet to go with him."

Salvatore choked on his brandy at the mention of the tiny gargoyle who'd attached himself to both Darcy and Harley. Like a freaking barnacle that couldn't be scraped off.

A three-foot pest with delicate fairy wings in shades of blue and crimson and gold, Levet could drive a sane man to gargoyle-cide in three seconds flat.

"You are a bad, bad vampire," Salvatore murmured.

"I try."

Chapter One

Roke hadn't yet given in to his overwhelming desire to commit gargoyle-cide.

But it was a near thing.

Roke was antisocial by nature, and having to endure endless chatter from a stunted gargoyle for the past three weeks had been nothing short of torture.

It was only the fact that Levet could sense Yannah, the demon who'd helped Sally flee from Chicago, that kept him from sending the annoying twit back to Styx.

His mating connection to Sally allowed him to sense her, but Yannah's ability to teleport from one place to another in a blink of an eye meant by the time he could locate her, she was already gone.

Levet seemed to have a more direct connection to Yannah, although they still spent their nights chasing from one place to another, always one step behind them.

Until tonight.

With a small smile he came to a halt, allowing his senses to flow outward.

The sturdy cottage tucked on the western coast of British

Columbia was perched to overlook the churning waves of the North Pacific Ocean. Built from the gray stones that lined the craggy cliffs, it had a steep, metal roof to shed the heavy snowfalls and windows that were already shuttered against the late autumn breeze. A garage plus two sturdy sheds surrounded the bleak property, but it was far enough away from civilization to avoid prying eyes.

Not that prying eyes could have detected him.

Leaving his custom-built turbine-powered motorcycle hidden in the trees, Roke was dressed in black. Black jeans, black tee, and black leather jacket with a pair of knee-high moccasins that allowed him to move in lethal silence.

With his bronzed skin and dark hair that brushed his broad shoulders, he blended into the darkness with ease. Only his eyes were visible. Although silver in color, they were so pale they appeared white in the moonlight, and rimmed by a circle of pure black.

Over the centuries those eyes had unnerved the most savage demons. No one liked the sensation that their soul was being laid bare.

On the other hand, his lean, beautiful features that were clearly from Native American origins had been luring women to his bed since he'd awoken as a vampire.

They sighed beneath the touch of his full, sensual lips and eagerly pressed against the lean, chiseled perfection of his body. Their fingers traced the proud line of his nose, the wide brow, and his high cheekbones.

It didn't matter that most considered him as cold and unfeeling as a rattlesnake. Or that he would sacrifice anything or anyone to protect his clan.

They found his ruthless edge . . . exciting.

All except one notable exception.

A damned shame that exception happened to be his mate.

Roke grimaced.

No. Not mate.

Or at least, not in the traditional sense.

Three weeks ago he'd been in Chicago when the demon world had battled against the Dark Lord. They'd managed to turn back the hordes of hell, but instead of allowing him to return to his clan in Nevada, Styx, the Anasso, had insisted that he remain to babysit Sally Grace, a witch who'd fought with the Dark Lord.

Roke had been furious.

Not only was he desperate to return to his people, but he hated witches.

All vampires did.

Magic was the one weapon they had no defense against.

Regrettably, when Styx gave an order, a wise vampire jumped to obey.

The alternative wasn't pretty.

Of course, at the time none of them had realized that Sally was half demon. Or that she would panic at being placed in the dungeons beneath Styx's elegant lair.

He absently rubbed his inner forearm where the mating mark was branded into his skin.

The witch claimed that she was simply trying to enchant him long enough to convince him to help her escape. And after his initial fury at realizing her demon magic had somehow ignited the mating bond, Roke had grudgingly accepted it had been an accident.

What he hadn't accepted was her running off to search for the truth of her father.

Dammit.

It was her fault they were bound together.

She had no right to slip away like a thief in the night.

"Do you sense anyone?"

The question was spoken in a low voice that was edged with a French accent, jerking Roke out of his dark broodings. Glancing downward, he ruefully met his companion's curious gaze.

What the hell had happened to his life?

A mate that wasn't a mate. A three-foot gargoyle sidekick. And a clan that had been without their chief for far too long.

"She's there," he murmured, his gaze skimming over the creature's ugly mug. Levet had all the usual gargoyle features. Gray skin, horns, a small snout, and a tail he kept lovingly polished. It was only his delicate wings and diminutive size that marked him as different. Oh, and his appalling lack of control over his magic. Roke turned back to the cottage where he could catch the distinctive scent of peaches. A primitive heat seared through him, drawing him forward. "I have you, little witch."

Scampering to keep up with his long, silent strides, Levet tugged at the hem of his jacket.

"Umm . . . Roke?"

"Not now, gargoyle." Roke never paused as he made his way toward the back of the cottage. "I've spent the past three weeks being led around like a damned hound on a leash. I intend to savor the moment."

"While you're savoring, I hope that you will recall Sally must have a good reason for—"

"Her reason is to drive me nuts," Roke interrupted, pausing at the side of the nearest shed. "I promised her that we would go in search of her father. Together."

"*Oui*. But when?"

Roke clenched his teeth. "In case you've forgotten, she nearly died when the—"

"Vampire-god."

Roke grimaced. The creature that they'd so recently battled might have claimed to be the first vampire, but that didn't make him a god. The bastard had nearly killed Sally in an attempt to break the magic that held him captive.

"When the ancient spirit attacked her," he snapped. "She should be grateful that I was willing to wait for her to regain her strength."

Levet cleared his throat. "And that is the only reason you tried to keep her imprisoned?"

"She wasn't imprisoned," he denied, refusing to recall his panic when Sally had lain unconscious for hours.

Or his fierce reluctance to allow Sally to leave Styx's lair.

"*Non?*" Levet clicked his tongue, seemingly oblivious to how close Roke was to yanking that tongue out of his mouth. "I would have sworn she was locked in the dungeons."

"Not after Gaius was destroyed."

"You mean after she saved the world from the vampire-god?" the gargoyle taunted. "Generous of you."

Oh yeah. The tongue was going to have to go.

"Don't push me, gargoyle," he muttered, allowing his senses to spread outward.

He would deal with the aggravating gargoyle later.

Testing the air, he caught the scent of salty foam as waves crashed against the rocks below, the acrid tang of smoke from the chimney, and the distant perfume of a water sprite playing among the whales.

But overriding it all was that tantalizing aroma of warm peaches.

A potent aphrodisiac that once again compelled him forward.

Levet grabbed his back pocket. "Where are you going?"

Roke didn't miss a step as he swatted the pest away. "To get my mate."

"I do not believe that is a good idea."

"Thankfully I don't give a shit what you think."

"*Très bien,*" the gargoyle sniffed. "You are the panty boss."

"Bossy-pants, you idiot," Roke muttered, heading directly for the back door.

He'd officially run out of patience twenty-one days and several thousand miles ago.

Which would explain why he didn't even consider the fact Sally might be prepared for his arrival.

Less than a foot from the back steps he was brought to a painful halt as an invisible net of magic wrapped around him, the bands of air so tight they would have sliced straight through him if he'd been human.

"What the hell?"

Levet waddled forward, his wings twitching as he studied Roke with open curiosity.

"A magical snare. *Sacrebleu.* I've never seen one so strong."

Roke flashed his fangs, futilely struggling to escape.

Damn, but he hated magic.

"Why didn't you warn me?" he snarled.

"I did," the gargoyle huffed in outrage. "I told you it was a bad idea."

Okay, he hated magic *and* gargoyles.

"You didn't tell me there was a trap."

"You are chasing a powerful witch. What did you expect?" The damned beast dared to smile. "Besides, it's such a fine spell. It would have been a pity to spoil Sally's fun."

"I swear, gargoyle, when I get out of here—"

"Are all vampires always so bad-tempered, or is it just you?" a light female voice demanded, the scent of peaches drenching the air.

Roke swallowed a groan, a complex mixture of fury, lust, and savage relief surging through him.

None of it showed on his face as he turned to study the tiny female with shoulder-length hair that was a blend of deep red tresses streaked with gold. She had pale, almost fragile features with velvet brown eyes and full lips that begged to be kissed.

"Hello, my love," he said in a low, husky voice. "Did you miss me?"

* * *

Sally Grace had been well aware that she was being hunted.

Not only hunted . . . but hunted by a first-class, grade A, always-get-my-man predator.

And she should know all about predators.

She'd been prey since her mother had tried to put an end to her existence with a particularly nasty spell on her sixteenth birthday. No one understood the difference between an okay hunter and one you didn't have a hope in hell of shaking off your trail better than she did.

Still, she'd managed to elude him for the past three weeks.

Twenty-one days longer than she'd expected.

Now she intended to hold her ground.

No one was putting her back in a cell.

Planting her hands on her hips, she pretended a confidence she was far from feeling.

"Why are you following me?"

His beautiful eyes shimmered a perfect silver in the moonlight.

Of course, everything about him was perfect, she acknowledged with a renegade rush of awareness.

The exquisitely carved features. The dark hair that was silky smooth. The hard, chiseled body that should only be possible with Photoshop.

And the raw, sexual magnetism that pulsed in the air around him.

There wasn't a woman alive who wouldn't secretly wish he'd handcuff her to the nearest bed.

A pity he was a coldhearted vampire who would happily kill her if her magic hadn't tied them together as mates.

She shivered despite the heavy sweatshirt and jeans she wore to combat the cold.

"Is that a joke?"

She tilted her chin. "There's nothing funny about our situation."

"I agree."

"Then why don't you return to Chicago?" she demanded in frustration. "I'm perfectly capable of tracking down my father without you."

A dark brow arched. "Really?"

"Yes, really."

"The last time you went rogue we ended up mated." His lips twisted as he stopped struggling and instead stood there with his head held high, pride etched onto his beautiful face. As if he was above noticing her tedious spell. "Forgive me if I don't entirely trust you."

Sally flinched, her eyes narrowing. Dammit. She didn't need any reminders that she was a major screwup.

Not when she was tired and frustrated and in the mood to punch something.

Really, really hard.

"*Sacrebleu,*" a voice rasped, drawing Sally's attention to the tiny gargoyle standing at Roke's side. "You may have a death wish, vampire, but I do not. I believe I will speak with Yannah."

Sally blinked, effectively distracted by the question.

Yannah had been a strange travel companion. The small demon had happily zapped Sally to each of her mother's properties so Sally could search for clues of her father, but she'd rarely spoken and had spent most of her time zoned out as she mentally communicated with her mother, who also happened to be an Oracle.

Sally had been almost relieved when Yannah had abruptly announced she had to go home.

She was used to being on her own.

It was . . . comfortable. Familiar.

Tragic, achingly lonely, but familiar.

"She left," she informed Levet.

"Left?" His heavy brow furrowed. "What do you mean left?"

"One minute she was standing next to me complaining about the dust, and the next—" She waved a hand.

"Poof," Levet finished.

"Exactly."

Without warning the gargoyle was stomping away, his tail twitching and his tiny hands waving in the air as he muttered to himself.

"Aggravating, unpredictable, impossible female."

"I feel his pain," Roke drawled.

She turned back to stab him with a glare. "Not yet, but keep it up and you will."

The silver eyes shimmered. "Release me."

Sally wrapped her arms around her waist. She could feel his anger through their bond, but more than that she could feel a seething frustration that was echoed deep inside her.

That scared her more than his irritation.

"Why should I?" she bluffed. Yeah, look at her. All badass just so long as Roke remained trapped in her spell. "You're trespassing on my property."

He glanced toward the cottage. "Yours?"

She shrugged. "It was my mother's, and since I'm her only heir, I assume her various houses are now mine."

"She had more than one?"

"What do you think I've been doing the past three weeks?"

The silver gaze returned to sear over her pale face. "Running."

She sniffed, refusing to admit that running had been a large part of what she'd been doing.

There had been a little method to her madness.

"I've been searching through my mother's belongings," she said. "I hoped that she would have left some clue to my . . ."

She bit off the word *father*. Did a donation of sperm actually earn the title of father? "To who impregnated her."

He frowned. "I thought you said that witches had a spell so their private papers were destroyed when they died?"

It was true that many witches had binding spells attached to their most sensitive possessions. It gave a whole new meaning to taking "secrets to the grave." And her mother had been more secretive than most.

Still, she had to cling to some small fragment of hope. Dammit.

"They do," she grudgingly admitted. "But she wouldn't have destroyed everything. There has to be a clue somewhere."

"Release me and I'll help you search." He studied her stubborn expression, silently compelling her to obey. "Sally."

"Don't growl at me. You locked me in a cell—"

"And I let you out."

"Only because I forced you to."

A dangerous chill blasted through the air at her foolish reminder that he'd briefly been under her complete control.

"Sally, like it or not we're stuck together," he rasped between clenched teeth.

"I don't like it."

The silver eyes narrowed. "If that were true, then you would be eager for my help."

She snorted. "Nice try."

"You know that vampires are the finest hunters in the world," he continued, ignoring her interruption. "And I'm one of the best."

"And so modest."

"If you were as anxious as you claim to end our mating, you would be begging for my . . . services."

His gaze deliberately lowered to take in her slender body, making Sally tremble in reaction. Blessed goddess. The blast of sexual arousal that jolted through her made her feel like she'd been struck by lightning.

And the worst part was, she couldn't blame the intense reaction on the faux mating.

She'd been aching for Roke from the moment she'd caught sight of those dark, male features and the astonishing silver eyes. Not to mention the tight ass that filled out a pair of jeans with oh-my-god perfection.

"Jeez, could you be any more annoying?" she muttered, reluctantly releasing the spell that bound him. The magic was draining her at a rapid rate, and the last thing she wanted was to collapse in front of this man. Better that she pretended to be bored with the game. "You're free. Now go away."

The words had barely left her lips when Roke was flowing forward at a blinding speed.

"Gotcha."

"Roke." His name was a muffled protest against his chest as he lashed his arms around her and flattened her against his body.

"Don't move," he growled, pressing his face into the curve of her neck, his fangs lightly scraping her skin.

"What are you doing?"

He shuddered, his hands running a compulsive path down her back to cup her hips.

"You feel it," he whispered against her neck.

And she did.

Not just the tidal wave of sensual pleasure at being in his arms, but the strange sensation of something settling deep inside her.

An easing of the nagging sense of "wrongness" that had plagued her since leaving Chicago.

His lips moved to press against the thundering pulse at the base of her throat.

"Do you have any idea what you did to me when you disappeared?"

Her lashes slid downward as she absorbed the stunning pleasure of his touch.

"I thought you would be happy to be rid of me," she whispered, breathing in the scent of leather, male, and raw power.

His fingers gave her hips a small squeeze. "You wouldn't have snuck away if you believed that."

The fact he was right only pissed her off.

"Just because I didn't ask for your permission doesn't mean I snuck away."

"Sally, whether this mating is some demon magic or not, it feels real to me," he rasped. "To have you disappear . . ." He shuddered, revealing the genuine pain he'd been forced to endure. "Christ."

Sally grimaced, her anger abruptly being replaced by overwhelming regret.

The mating truly had been an accident.

At the time she'd been scared and desperate or she would never have released her inner demon.

She wasn't stupid. She knew that messing with magic she didn't understand was dangerous. And until she had discovered the truth of her ancestry, she'd usually stuck to the human spells she'd learned from her witch mother.

But accident or not, she'd physically, perhaps even spiritually, bound this proud loner to her.

It was a sin she could never erase.

"I'm sorry," she husked.

His tongue traced the line of her jaw. "Are you?"

"I know this mess is partially my fault."

He jerked his head back in disbelief. "Partially?"

She was instantly on the defensive. "If your precious Anasso hadn't thrown me in the dungeons, I wouldn't have needed to use my powers to escape."

He muttered a curse, returning to nuzzle a searing path of kisses down the side of her neck.

"Let's go back to your apology," he commanded.

Somehow her hands were on his shoulders, her fingers tangled in his silken hair.

"Fine. I regret any discomfort I've caused you," she managed to say, excitement jolting through her as he allowed her to feel the tips of his fangs.

Crap. What was wrong with her? She'd never been one of those freaks who wanted to be dinner for a vampire.

Even if their bite was orgasmic.

Now she was shaking with the need to feel those fangs sliding through her tender flesh.

"And you promise not to disappear again?" he demanded, his hands slipping beneath her sweatshirt.

She shuddered, struggling to think through the haze of lust clouding her mind.

"Not unless I believe it's absolutely necessary."

He made a sound of resignation. "Have you always been so stubborn?"

"Have you always been so arrogant?"

He pressed a hard, hungry kiss to her lips. "Yes."

Chapter Two

Roke felt Sally tremble, her fingers tangled in his hair as her body arched against him.

A groan was wrenched from his throat. Christ, the very air was scented with her desire.

But even as his hands skimmed beneath her sweatshirt to find the soft curve of her bare breasts, she pulled back with a startled gasp.

"Roke . . . stop."

He hissed, burying his face in the soft cloud of her wind-swept hair.

"You're my mate."

"No." She sucked in a shaky breath, her eyes dark with a need she couldn't hide. "It's an illusion."

He lowered his hand from the temptation of her breast, but he kept his arms firmly around her.

She wasn't going to disappear again.

Not even if he had to handcuff her to his side.

He swallowed a low growl.

Having Sally and handcuffs in the same thought wasn't doing a damned thing to help him gain control of his raging libido.

"It doesn't feel like an illusion, does it, my love?" he murmured.

"It's not real." She licked her lips. "It can't be real."

Logically Roke agreed.

Physically? Not so much.

His body was ready and eager to accept that she was created to be in his arms.

His gaze shifted to the tempting curve of her neck, his fangs aching with a savage instinct to mark her as his own.

A damned shame that Styx had warned taking Sally's blood might very well turn the mating from a magical illusion to a bond that couldn't be broken.

Battling against his primitive urges, Roke was distracted by the whiff of granite as the gargoyle waddled back into view, his wings shimmering in the moonlight.

"I see the two of you have kissed and made up."

He sent the pest an annoyed glare. "Go away, gargoyle."

"No." Sally shoved out of his arms, her face flushed and her eyes still dazed with their mutual lust. "He can help search the cottage for clues."

His brows snapped together. "You run from me, but you'll ask a three-foot gargoyle for help?"

She met his fierce disbelief without flinching. "Unlike vampires, gargoyles are sensitive to magic. He might find something that I've missed."

"*Oui,* I am very sensitive." Levet turned toward Roke, sticking out his tongue. "It is the reason women find me irresistible."

With a flick of his tail, Levet waddled toward the cottage. Roke clenched his hands.

So much for a little one on one time with Sally.

"Shit, that gargoyle needs a muzzle," he muttered.

"He's not the only one," Sally informed him, turning to follow the tiny demon into the cottage.

Roke briefly hesitated.

If he had any sense he'd get on his motorcycle and never look back.

Sally was right.

Magic was a vampire's true weakness.

There was nothing he could do when it came to breaking the spell that bound them together. Why not head back to his lair in Nevada and wait for Sally to contact him when she had the means to break the mating?

But the thought had barely time to form before it was forgotten as he headed into the cottage.

He'd spent three hellish weeks chasing after his witch.

Until the bond was broken, he wasn't letting her out of his sight.

Entering through the back door, he passed through the small mudroom that opened into a large kitchen equipped for a witch, not a chef.

There was a massive, stone fireplace with a cast-iron cauldron hanging over a pile of wood. The open rafters were lined with bronze pans and bundles of dried herbs. And in the center of the floor, a circle had been carved into the flagstones that was large enough for two or three witches to sit in without touching.

He followed the scent of peaches into the main room of the cottage, discovering Levet flitting around the sparsely furnished space and Sally standing beside the empty fireplace, her spine rigid.

He grimaced, assuming she was trying to give him the cold shoulder. Then, slowly he realized it wasn't annoyance she was feeling.

It was a dull, bitter pain he could feel through their bond.

With two long strides he was standing at her side, gently tucking her hair behind her ear so he could study her pale profile.

"There's something here that bothers you?"

"You could say that." Her lips twisted as her gaze lingered on the scorched mark on the wall. "This is the precise spot where my mother tried to kill me."

The image of a young Sally lying lifeless on the floor seared through Roke's mind and he struggled to contain his burst of fury. His temper had the unfortunate effect of destroying the structural integrity of any building he happened to be standing near.

Instead he concentrated on the pleasant knowledge that Sally's mother had died a painful, probably even gruesome death at the hands of a fellow vampire.

Levet crossed the room to study Sally with a sympathetic expression on his ugly face.

"Why would your mother try to kill you?"

Sally shivered. "She didn't know my father was a demon. Not until my sixteenth birthday when my powers started to kick in." She gave a humorless laugh. "It was an unpleasant surprise, to say the least."

"Ah. My mother tried to kill me as well." Levet shrugged. "Families are always difficult."

Sally managed a small smile that didn't disguise the wounds that festered in her heart.

"She's dead," she said in grim tones. "She can't hurt me anymore."

Roke's fingers brushed her cheek. "No one is going to hurt you."

She awkwardly stepped away, her expression wary.

Despite their bond she still didn't trust him.

Hell, the woman had been taught she couldn't trust anyone.

"My mother's room is this way," she muttered, leading them out of the front parlor down a short hallway.

Pushing the door open, she stepped aside as the gargoyle entered the small bedroom and began investigating the dust-coated furnishings.

"Do you sense anything?" she demanded as Levet stuck his head in the closet.

"*Non.*"

Roke moved across the hall to the second closed door. "What's in here?"

"Stop," Sally rasped, a hint of embarrassment in her voice.

"Your room I assume?" Roke smiled with wicked amusement as he pushed the door open to take a peek at the pink bedspread on the narrow bed and lace curtains. "It's very . . . frilly."

She sent him an evil glare. "Not all of us sleep in moldy crypts."

He wandered forward, studying the poster hung over the bed. "The Backstreet Boys?"

"I've always preferred my men cute and sexy."

He glanced over his shoulder, the memory of her melting beneath his kisses shimmering in his eyes.

"Not anymore."

She rolled her eyes, but even as she searched for the words to deflate his ego, Levet was scooting past her and heading directly to the bed.

"What do I sense?" he asked, opening the nightstand to pull out the plain wooden box she'd kept hidden from her mother.

"It's just a music box," she readily answered. "I found it here not long after we arrived at this cottage."

The gargoyle glanced at her, his tail twitching. "You found it or it found you?"

Sally blinked. "I don't understand. It was tossed in a pile of rubbish behind the shed. If I hadn't been hiding from my mother, I would never have seen it."

Roke's momentary amusement was snuffed out. "Why were you hiding from your mother?"

She wrinkled her nose. "I was playing with her favorite crystal and set the curtains on fire."

"And you were afraid you were going to be punished?"

"It wasn't that. I was used to being punished."

Roke's jaw clenched. If the witch wasn't already dead, he would take great pleasure in skinning her alive.

"Then why were you hiding?"

"I had to get rid of the crystal. I didn't want her to know—"

"The level of your talent," he finished for her.

"Exactly." Sally unconsciously rubbed her arms as Roke's anger dropped the temperature in the room. At least he hadn't brought the ceiling down on their heads. "My mother liked to believe that she was the most powerful witch ever born."

"How old were you?"

"Six."

Six? Christ. She'd been a baby.

Levet cleared his throat. "Tell me exactly how you found the box."

Sally furrowed her brow as she shifted through her memories.

"I intended to hide the crystal until the spell wore off so I went behind the shed and stumbled over the pile of rubbish."

"Was the box dirty?" Levet prodded. "As if it had been there a long time?"

She shook her head. "No, but it could have been tossed out by the previous owners."

"Did you feel drawn to it?"

Sally lifted her hand in confusion. "Any six-year-old girl would be enchanted by a music box."

Levet wasn't satisfied, his wings fluttering with a sudden emotion.

"Did you ever feel compelled to keep it with you?"

Sally hesitated and Roke stepped toward her, a very bad feeling in the pit of his stomach.

"Sally?" he urged.

"I suppose I thought about the box over the years, but I never felt *compelled* to retrieve it," she admitted. "Why are you asking me these questions?"

Levet pointed a claw toward the box. "There's an illusion wrapped around it."

"Impossible," Sally breathed. "I would have sensed a spell."

"It is demon magic, not human," Levet explained.

"Oh."

Roke instinctively moved closer to Sally. Why the hell did it always have to be magic?

He'd braved the battles of Durotriges to become a clan chief.

He'd killed an entire tribe of full-grown orcs with a kitchen knife.

He could crumble a building to rubble with the force of his anger.

But magic?

He shook his head in frustration.

"Can you break it?" he demanded.

"Do you mean to insult me?" the gargoyle huffed. "There is none greater in destroying magical illusions than *moi*."

Roke made a sound of disgust even as he wrapped an arm around Sally's shoulders and tugged her away from the bed.

"Stand back," he warned.

Sally sent him a worried frown. "Why?"

"That gargoyle is a menace."

"Hey," Levet protested.

Roke pointed an impatient finger toward the box. "Just do your thing."

With a sniff the gargoyle turned back to the box, his tail stirring the dust on the floor as he waved his hands dramatically in the air.

Roke clenched his teeth.

If it wasn't for the fact that Levet was the only one around who could reveal the magic surrounding the box, Roke would have him tossed over the cliff.

Three weeks was longer than any rational man should have to endure with the aggravating pest.

There was another wave of his hands, then a faint pop as the illusion was destroyed.

"*Voilà*," Levet murmured, turning around to offer a small bow.

Sally watched the gargoyle in silence, not quite certain what to think of the tiny creature.

He'd always been kind the few times their paths had crossed in Chicago. But he worked with the vampires.

Which meant she wasn't prepared to fully trust him.

She sighed. What was she thinking?

She wasn't prepared to trust anyone.

Period. End of story.

Still, when Levet moved aside to reveal the once-smooth box now covered with intricate markings, she couldn't help but be impressed.

"How beautiful," she murmured, moving forward to lean over the nightstand.

"Sally, wait," Roke commanded.

Naturally she ignored him.

The man was way too fond of tossing out orders and expecting them to be obeyed.

Besides, the box belonged to her. It was her duty to discover the truth of its origins, no one else. Even if that meant putting herself in danger.

Whispering a soft spell, she studied the intricate carvings.

They were fascinating. Delicate swirls that were connected by various lines and dots that combined to make an exotic design that seemed to call to some part of her.

She frowned, disturbed by the sensation the markings were somehow familiar.

"They're not magical," she said.

"That doesn't mean they're not dangerous," Roke snapped, clearly annoyed that she'd ignored his command.

She turned to send him a glare. "Thank you, Captain Obvious. I'm not stupid."

The silver eyes seemed to glow in the gloom of the room, holding a power that was almost hypnotic.

"No, you're impulsive, unpredictable, and a magnet for disaster," he countered.

Magnet for disaster?

Why the . . . ass.

"Forgive me. I'm only thirty years old," she mocked. "You can't expect me to be a stodgy bore like someone who's been around four or five centuries."

Levet chuckled. "Oh, snap."

Roke sent the gargoyle a warning glare. "Don't you have somewhere else to be?"

"*Non.* Unless . . ." Levet tilted back his head, sniffing the air. "Is that shepherd's pie I smell?"

"And sweet and sour pork, and spaghetti, oh, and apple pie," Sally added. "I left them on the counter in the kitchen."

"Ah. *J'adore* apple pie," the gargoyle sighed, heading out of the room with a happy wiggle in his waddle.

Roke moved to stand beside her, the annoyance fading from his expression as he studied her with a piercing intensity.

She shifted uneasily, always more comfortable when they were sniping at each other.

They both understood the attraction that smoldered between them. And the danger that it could combust the second they lowered their guard.

The spark had ignited the minute he'd strolled into Styx's dungeon.

And the mating had only intensified the hunger until it was almost unbearable.

Their squabbling was a necessary barrier.

"What?" she demanded as he continued to stare at her.

"I haven't forgotten your impressive appetite."

She blushed, remembering his shock when she'd eaten enough food to feed a football team during her incarceration. Her magic, both human and demon, burned through calories at an accelerated rate.

"I'm a growing girl."

He shook his head, his brows drawing together as his gaze took a slow inventory of her slender body.

"No, you're not," he denied in gruff tones, his hands lifting to cup her face. "In fact, you're shrinking."

She shivered beneath his gentle touch, her hands reaching to grasp his wrists.

"Roke."

"And you have shadows beneath your eyes." He ignored her protest, his thumb brushing the purple bruises that marred her pale skin. "Why haven't you taken better care of yourself?"

She shivered, the cool brush of his fingers sending tiny jolts of pleasure through her.

"I've been busy."

"That's why you should never have run from me."

She scowled, but she made no effort to pull away from the soft stroke of thumbs.

"If you try to tell me you would have done a better job searching for my father, I'll turn you into a toad," she warned.

"I was going to point out that if I had been with you I would have made sure you ate proper meals and rested when you were tired."

"I don't need a babysitter."

"No, you need your mate," he growled. "You allowed your pride to deny the natural instinct to be with me and your body suffered the consequences."

Her breath caught.

Okay, she'd been unreasonably weary. And her enormous appetite had faded. And she hadn't been able to shake the gnawing sense of emptiness.

But that could be stress, couldn't it?

The Goddess knew she had enough of that in her life.

"Witches don't mate," she muttered.

"Perhaps not, but demons do." His thumb skimmed down her cheek to tease the corner of her mouth. "And you, my love, are most definitely demon."

Their eyes clashed. The air sizzled with that ever-ready hunger.

His thumb slipped between her lips . . . and just that quickly, she was desperate for his kiss.

She needed the hungry press of his mouth, the dangerous scrape of his fangs, the intoxicating heat that scorched through her body.

Shocked by the raw, potent yearning, Sally turned away.

"I don't have time for this," she hissed, fiercely trying to concentrate on the music box.

"Denying the truth won't change it. Believe me, I've tried," he muttered, grabbing her arm as she waved her hand over the box and whispered a quick spell. "What are you doing?"

"Don't get your panties in a twist." She sent him an impatient glare.

"Panties?" A dark brow arched. "You think I wear panties?"

She gave a choked sound, the visualization of Roke commando beneath the tight black jeans burning through her brain.

No, no, no. She wasn't going there.

"I . . ." She licked her dry lips. "I put a protective ward around the box."

There was a tense second when Sally was sure Roke was going to throw her on the bed and put them both out of their misery. Then, with an obvious effort, he leashed his hunger and turned toward the nightstand.

"It's safe to touch?"

She swallowed the lump in her throat. "Yes."

With obvious wariness, Roke reached to pluck the box from the nightstand to study the carvings. Sally watched him in silence.

"Fey," he at last pronounced.

Fey? How . . . odd.

"You recognize the artist?"

"This isn't art." His slender finger traced a curving line that resembled a crescent moon. "These are runes."

"You're sure?"

His gaze remained on the box. "My talent is reading glyphs. That's why Styx insisted I come to Chicago in the first place."

She watched his finger move to a swirl that ended with three vertical dots, once again experiencing that tug of almost-recognition.

"What do they say?"

"I'm not sure."

She frowned. "You just said that your talent is reading them."

"These are . . . unusual. Perhaps ancient." He gave a shake of his head. "I need to do some research."

A bad feeling started to bloom in the pit of her stomach.

"And where do you have to do this research?"

"My lair in Nevada."

"Are you screwing with me?"

His smile was slow and decadently beautiful, the hint of fang making her shiver.

"Not yet."

Chapter Three

No one would give the house built on the bluffs that overlooked the Mississippi River a second glance.

It was the same as any other farmhouse in the Midwest. A simple, two-story structure, with a wraparound porch and sharply angled roof. At one time it'd been painted white, although it was peeling in several places and there was mold creeping up the foundation.

Nearly hidden behind the large oak and dogwood trees, it looked abandoned from the distant road and the overgrown path deterred any stray trespassers.

Even the locals had learned to avoid the area, disturbed by the odd silence and strange sense of being watched by unseen eyes.

The location of the house was no accident. Beneath the bluffs along the river was a spiderweb of caves that had been the source of local legends for years.

Some claimed they had been Jesse James's hideout. Or connected to the Underground Railroad. Others said they'd been used by smugglers.

And the always favorite rumor that they were a body dump for the Chicago mob.

The truth was far more dangerous.

The caves had been home to demons since long before the humans had ever arrived.

Standing in one of the deepest caves the small man was lost among the shadows.

Not that he would have stood out even in brightest sunlight.

He was one of those people who were easily overlooked.

Short, with sporadic tufts of gray hair on an almost bald head, he had pale skin that was nearly translucent and a pudgy belly that was hidden beneath a loose brown robe. His eyes were a watery blue, although they were usually covered by a thick pair of reading glasses.

He was insipid. Forgettable.

And if it weren't for his ability to retain vast amounts of knowledge he would never have been invited to become one of the rare Oracles that sat on the Commission.

He was a walking, talking library.

He was also a warning on the dangers of judging a book by its cover.

Speaking a spell of protection that would alert him if anyone approached the isolated cavern, Brandel allowed his spirit to slip from his corporal body, and entered the shimmering portal.

He shivered, despite his lack of a physical form.

The silvery fog that lay between dimensions had always unnerved him.

Perhaps because he understood illusions.

The fog might feel tangible, but the truth was that there was a gaping void lurking just out of sight.

He made a sound of impatience as a large Adonis with a halo of golden curls and bronzed naked body appeared.

Raith was addicted to his current body, refusing to leave it behind even when it meant expending a vast amount of his energy.

Vain moron.

"I told you never to contact me when the Commission is in session," he said telepathically, easily able to communicate his annoyance without speaking out loud.

Raith shrugged one broad shoulder. "There is a disturbance."

Brandel made a sound of impatience. "The danger to the vampires has been contained. There is no threat to our arrangement," he said, referring to the spirit that had so nearly created complete chaos.

"I do not speak of the vampires."

"Then what?"

The perfect features hardened. "A whisper of ancient magic."

Brandel felt a stirring of fear. "Our . . . guest?"

"He remains locked in stasis. But—"

"What?"

"He seeks to connect with someone in your world."

"Damn." Brandel could be arrogant, but he never forgot that their prisoner was a powerful demon who could destroy them if he ever broke free. "The last time he did this he succeeded in luring a witch into his prison."

The wide, guileless eyes that were perfect for the Adonis face briefly flickered to reveal the black eyes slit with red that were Raith's true form.

"Yes, a peculiar waste of his efforts. The witch was powerful, but her dark magic would never have been capable of destroying the barriers that hold him captive." Raith gave a shake of his head, still puzzled by the creature's peculiar behavior. "And he had to have sensed my spell would wipe her mind of their brief encounter as soon as she returned to her own world."

"The bastard no doubt wanted a quickie. He always was an obnoxious, self-indulgent ass."

Raith smiled with mocking amusement. "Still annoyed that he managed to seduce your mate?"

Brandel hissed, his unsubstantial form shivering in fury. Like most of his kind he'd sought his mate among the fey. And he'd found her in a beautiful, red-haired imp who'd made his soul sing. The fact that Glenda had never truly bonded with him had never bothered him.

Not until she'd run off with another.

"I had the last laugh," he reminded his companion, recalling with vicious satisfaction how he'd forced his unfaithful wife to watch her lover being entombed in his eternal prison before he'd ripped her heart from her chest.

"So far," Raith warned. "As you said, he has always been arrogant, but he is also a cunning, lethal adversary who could ruin both of us if he manages to escape."

Brandel didn't need the reminder.

The dangerous game he played was constantly on his mind.

Not only the fear of their prisoner escaping, but the constant dread that the Oracles would discover the truth of his presence on the Commission.

Death would be a welcome escape from what the powerful demons would do to him.

"Have you strengthened the shields that hide your guest?"

"Yes, and I've placed a tracer spell on the magic."

"You seem to have it in hand. What do you want from me?"

Raith frowned. "Obviously I need you to follow my spell and investigate the source of the magic."

"I can't."

There was a low vibration in the air. A resonance that threatened to scramble him on a molecular level.

"You wish to terminate our highly profitable partnership?"

"No, of course not," he hastily soothed the older demon.

"Then you will do as I command."

"Be reasonable." Brandel floated backward, putting some distance between him and Raith. The vibrations hadn't done any real damage, but they'd hurt like hell. "Leaving at this time will attract the sort of attention we can't afford."

Raith's eyes narrowed. "Why?"

"Siljar."

"She is an Oracle, is she not?"

Brandel's anger stirred the fog. Damn but he hated the interfering, busybody of a demon.

"Not only an Oracle, but the Queen Bitch herself."

"Queen?" Raith asked. "I thought the Commission was a democracy?"

"So they claim. We each have a vote, but the majority of the Oracles have allowed themselves to be castrated by their fear of Siljar." There was another stirring of the fog. "They have become nothing more than a committee of ass-kissers."

"And you would prefer that they kiss your ass?"

Of course he did.

He'd always lusted for power, but more than that, he lusted for the respect and admiration of others.

Someday, he silently promised himself.

But not today.

"I would prefer that she would bring an end to our tedious gathering," he answered. The Oracles had been called during the King of Vampires' battle with the King of Weres, but as one disaster had followed another, they'd been forced to remain and contain the damage. "So long as we're stuck in these caves my every move is being monitored."

Raith frowned. "Do you think she is suspicious?"

"Of course not," Brandel swiftly denied. "She is merely drunk on her own power."

"You had better pray to our god you are right. We both have much to lose if we are discovered."

Dammit. Brandel didn't need to be told what they risked.

"You take care of your end of the business and I'll take care of mine," he snapped, mind to mind.

"Very well. Your end of the business is tracking the spell and determining if it is a threat to us," Raith swiftly countered, faint vibrations humming in the air. "Understood?"

Did he have a choice?

"Yes."

Raith chuckled. "I always enjoy our little chats."

Roke frowned as Sally paced the small bedroom, her movements jerky and her face paler than normal.

It wasn't unusual for her to be agitated when he was around.

They'd been striking sparks off one another from the beginning.

In more ways than one.

But this was more . . .

He could sense a true fear that she was desperately trying to hide behind a pretense of anger.

"Why are you being so stubborn?" he at last demanded.

She halted, her glare shifting to the box he held in his hands.

"We don't even know if this box has anything to do with me or my father."

"Do you have a better lead to follow?"

Her lips tightened. "No."

"Then you have nothing to lose in coming to Nevada with me."

She looked less than impressed by his logic.

"The last time I trusted the word of a vampire I ended up in the dungeons."

Thanks a butt-load, Styx, he silently chastised his king.

The Anasso's decision to toss Sally in his formidable prison had made certain she had a perfectly legitimate excuse not to trust the vampires.

"I live in the middle of the desert." He offered a teasing smile. "My only dungeon is a nearby gold mine. You could strike it rich while you were down there."

She gave a humorless laugh. "Is that supposed to be re-assuring?"

Roke took a cautious step forward. She was twitchy enough to bolt if he wasn't careful.

"What are you afraid of, Sally?"

She scowled at the soft question. "I'm not afraid of any-thing."

He shook his head, his fingers lifting to press against the pulse thundering at the base of her throat.

"You know better than to try and lie to a vampire. Even if I wasn't bonded to you I could detect the increased beat of your heart and catch the scent of adrenaline." His fingers lightly traced the faint shadow of her jugular vein, his fangs aching for a taste. "Of course, I could be mistaken."

"You mistaken?" she tried to mock. "Shocking."

He cupped the side of her face, the satin heat of her skin against his palm a sensation he could easily become ad-dicted to.

"It could be lust," he murmured, his gaze lowering to the sensual curve of her lips. "And I know the perfect remedy."

"Fine." She pulled away from his touch, but not before Roke caught the intoxicating scent of her arousal. "Vampires hate witches."

With an effort, Roke allowed her to retreat. It was so very tempting to haul her into his arms and seduce her into soft, melting compliance.

It might even work for a few hours.

But he wasn't so vain as to think that getting her into bed would earn her trust.

Hell, she'd probably use it as another reason to push him away.

"How many times do I have to promise I will do whatever necessary to keep you safe?" he instead asked, holding her wary gaze.

"From your own clan?"

"So long as you're under my protection they wouldn't dare hurt you."

"Even if they believe I have you trapped in a spell? Come on, Roke." She shuddered, as if imagining the horror of being ravaged by crazed vampires. "They would kill me in a heartbeat if they thought it was for your own good."

His lips parted only to snap shut.

Shit.

She had a point.

His clan had spent far too long beneath the rule of a chief who'd been more concerned with pleasing his demanding mate than caring for his people. For over a century they'd floundered, so weakened that they'd nearly lost everything before Roke had traveled to the battles of Durotriges to earn the right to become a chief.

That's why he'd been so infuriated by the magical bonding. He'd already made the decision that his mate would be a rational, loyal female who would dedicate herself to the good of his people.

And why his clan was unreasonably overprotective of him.

They were going to be on the warpath when they discovered he'd been bound by a witch.

"I'll speak with them," he promised.

"And tell them what?" she rasped, her hands clenched. "A nasty witch who used to work for the Dark Lord forced a mating on their beloved clan chief. Yeah, that should go over well. They'll be standing in line for the pleasure of killing me."

His growl rumbled through the room. "So what do you

suggest? That we aimlessly run around the world in the hope that we stumble across your father?"

"You can take the box back to Nevada and I can stay here and question the locals." She shrugged. "Someone must have known my mother."

"No."

She blinked, meeting his ruthless silver gaze with an audible huff of annoyance.

"That's it? Just, no?"

"We stay together."

"Why?"

"Because it's killing you to be apart from me."

The stark words hung in the air for a long, tension-fraught moment, then Sally was instinctively shaking her head in denial.

"Oh, my God," she jeered. "Could your ego get any more bloated?"

"It's not my ego, Sally." He moved to touch the shadows beneath her beautiful eyes. "You're fading away."

She rigidly held her ground. "It's just stress."

"And if it's not?"

"What are you trying to imply?"

He tucked an autumn curl behind her ear, the strands of gold shimmering in the moonlight.

"I'm not implying, I'm saying flat out that there are demons who are bound so tightly to their mates they suffer physical damage when they're apart."

She sucked in a sharp breath. "So you truly believe I was pining for you like some cheesy Victorian bimbo?"

His lips twitched. "Yes."

The dark eyes narrowed. "A toad. No, wait. A cockroach."

"You're babbling," he murmured, his fingers skimming down the side of her neck.

She quivered, her pulse leaping beneath his fingers. "No, I'm deciding what I'm going to turn you into."

He allowed his fingers to circle her throat. Not a threat. An intimate claim.

"Sally, we're in this together," he said, his voice low with a genuine weariness. "I've suffered as much as you have."

The tough-girl façade wavered as she bit her lower lip. "I . . . know," she muttered. "I'm trying to find a way to break the mating."

"And I'm trying to help you." His thumb absently stroked the line of her stubborn jaw. "Why won't you let me?"

She held his fierce gaze. "I've been running from people who've wanted me dead since I was sixteen. I won't walk into a clan of bloodsuckers who will blame me for harming their chief."

He didn't have to see the strength of her determination etched on her beautiful face; he could easily sense it through their bond.

If he wanted to take her to his clan, he would have to physically drag her there.

Always assuming she didn't follow through on her threat to turn him into a toad.

"Oh, hell," he growled, pulling his cell phone from his pocket.

"What are you doing?"

He scrolled through his contacts, then swiftly typed in his message.

"Sending a text to Cyn."

She eyed him warily. "What's a Cyn?"

"Not a what. A who," he explained. "He's clan chief of Ireland."

The wariness only deepened. "Why are you contacting him?"

"He's an expert on the fey."

She glanced at the box he still held in his hand. "Why don't we just find one of the fey?"

He curled his lips to reveal his fangs. "Because I don't trust them."

She folded her arms around her waist, the tug on her sweatshirt molding the fabric against the soft curve of her breasts.

"And I don't trust vampires."

He struggled not to be distracted by the thought of stripping off the sweatshirt to expose the exquisite beauty beneath.

"Do you believe I would deliberately try to hurt you?" he bluntly demanded.

"I—"

"The truth."

She hesitated, clearly reluctant to admit that she might have the smallest faith in him.

"No," she at last muttered.

"Then trust that—"

His soft words were rudely interrupted as the gargoyle stomped his way into the room, his tail twitching.

"Ha."

Roke glowered at the unwelcome intruder. "What now?"

"I have sensed her," Levet announced.

"Sensed who?"

"Yannah."

Sally stepped toward the gargoyle in surprise. "She's returned?"

"*Non,* but I can track her."

Roke's annoyance abruptly faded. *It was about damned time.*

"Don't let the door hit you on the way out," he told the demon who'd been a constant pain in the ass over past three weeks.

Sally sent him a chiding frown. "Roke."

Impervious as always to being insulted, Levet moved to take Sally's hand.

"Au revoir, ma belle," he murmured, kissing her fingers. "I suspect that our paths will cross again."

"Not if I have anything to say about it," Roke growled, trembling as he watched the tiny demon waddle from the room.

Logically he understood the gargoyle was no threat.

Sally had no romantic interest in the aggravating pest.

But the mating wasn't about logic.

It was about raw male possession that couldn't bear to see another man near his woman.

Tossing the music box on the nearby bed, Roke prowled forward. He needed to touch his mate.

To replace the scent of another creature with his own.

Easily sensing his laser focus, Sally inched backward, not halting until she was flat against the wall.

"What are you doing?"

"All alone." He halted a mere breath from her stiff body, his hands gently stroking over her shoulders and down her arms. "At last."

"Roke."

Lost in the heady scent of peaches and warm female desire, Roke almost missed the distant roar of an engine.

Then, realizing there could be only one explanation for the sound, he charged toward the window and threw open the shutters.

"Damn," he hissed.

Sally was swiftly at his side. "What?"

"That winged lump of granite stole my bike."

Chapter Four

Sally watched Roke pace the claustrophobic confines of her childhood bedroom. She shivered. He was like a caged panther.

One that could devour her in one vicious bite.

If she was smart she would keep her mouth shut and wait for an opportunity to once again escape.

But of course, she wasn't that smart.

The impulse to needle the annoyed vampire was simply too irresistible.

"I don't know why you're so upset," she said. "It was just a motorcycle."

His pacing came to an abrupt halt, his expression one of horror.

"Just a motorcycle?" he growled in disbelief. "It was a custom-built, turbine motorcycle that cost half a million dollars."

"A half a million?" She gave a choked cough. Sheesh. Being a vampire obviously paid better than being a witch. She had less than twenty bucks to her name. "You've got to be kidding me."

"Why?" He shrugged. "I like speed."

"Yeah, well I like diamonds, but I wouldn't spend a half million on one," she muttered.

Without warning the silver eyes darkened. "I would."

"You would what?"

"I would spend half a million on diamonds if it pleased you," he said, his voice low, rough.

Her mouth went dry. "I was just kidding."

"I'm not." With a fluid movement he was standing directly before her, his fingers trailing down the curve of her throat. "This satin skin should be draped in the finest gems." His brooding gaze followed his fingers as they traced the loose neckline of her sweatshirt. "And champagne."

Excitement tingled through her body, her nipples tightening with unspoken need.

She struggled to think clearly.

"Champagne?"

"I have a rare bottle of Dom Perignon I intend to lick off your body."

Her gaze lowered to the sensuous promise of his mouth, the vivid image of being stretched on the bed while he licked her from head to toe stealing her breath.

He would be slow, thorough, wickedly skilled.

Oh . . . hell.

This wasn't supposed to be happening.

No sex with the yummy, aggravating vampire.

Even if it was fantasy sex.

With an effort she forced her reluctant feet to take a step backward, breaking contact with his destructive touch.

"I don't suppose there's any reason to linger here," she mumbled, awkwardly tugging at her sweatshirt.

There was a flash of fang as Roke struggled to regain control of his own hungers, assuring Sally that whatever was happening between them wasn't one-sided.

Did the knowledge please or terrify her?

Impossible to say.

"Have you considered the fact that our only means of transportation was my motorcycle you so recently mocked?" he demanded.

Well, of course she hadn't considered that fact. She'd been zapped around the country by Yannah for the past three weeks, she hadn't had to consider transportation.

She frowned. "The village—"

"Is locked up tight for the night," he interrupted.

"Don't tell me you don't know how to hotwire a car."

His brow arched. "And you feel up to walking the fifteen miles in the cold?"

Her lips parted to point out that he could easily carry her that distance only to snap shut.

Roke was as aware as she was of the option.

Which meant that he intended to make her beg for his help.

Yeah. Hell would freeze over first.

"Then what do you suggest?" she instead gritted.

"Cyn will be here by tomorrow night." He glanced toward the window that overlooked the bleak, windswept emptiness that surrounded the cottage. "This is as good a place as any for meeting."

Tomorrow? She shook her head. "I thought you said he was in Ireland?"

"He is."

"Is he a magical vampire?"

He snorted. "No, just one with a private jet that's built specifically to carry vampires even during the day. Once he arrives in Canada he'll use a helicopter to reach us."

She blinked. Somehow she'd never considered vampires jet-setting around the world.

Stupid considering they'd embraced every other technology.

Now she was going to be stuck in the cramped cottage with yet another vampire.

Of course . . .

Her heart gave a sudden leap. There were options.

Sensing Roke's sudden suspicion, Sally grimly slowed her pulse and smoothed her expression.

"The marvels of modern technology," she said in deliberately light tones.

He narrowed his gaze, but thankfully didn't press for an answer.

"Is there anything you need before the sun rises?"

She shrugged. "Where do I start?"

"Food? Clothing?"

"A wooden stake?" she sweetly added.

"I'll take that as a no," he snapped with a sudden burst of impatience. "Have you eaten dinner?"

She hesitated. Had she?

The past days had been a blur.

"I think I had an apple earlier," she at last said.

"Come."

She should have been used to his lightning movements, but it still caught her off guard when he captured her hand and ruthlessly tugged her out of the bedroom.

"What are you doing?"

His pace never faltered. "Making sure you take better care of yourself."

She tried to tug her hand free. "I'm capable of taking care of myself."

"I need to do this, Sally." Coming to a halt in the center of the sitting room he whirled to face her, shoving up the sleeve of her sweatshirt to reveal the intricate crimson tattoo that ran beneath the skin of her inner forearm. "So long as you carry my mark, I'm compelled to protect you."

Her irritation at being yanked around like a misbehaving child faded as the ever-present guilt returned.

Because of her demon powers they both carried the mating

mark. And Roke was instinctively forced to fulfill his role as her own personal champion.

She heaved a rueful sigh. "Even from myself?"

"Especially from yourself," he dryly agreed.

"Fine." She waved a hand toward the kitchen. "I don't think Levet could have eaten all the food."

He gave a bark of laughter. "Clearly you underestimate the appetites of the stunted creature."

She was struck by a sudden thought. "Yannah insisted that we bring extra. Do you think she knew Levet was coming?"

"More than likely. She's a strange demon." He grimaced, giving her hand a gentle tug as he steered her toward a nearby chair. "Sit and I'll serve you."

She sank onto the worn cushion, telling herself that it was easier to give in to the stubborn man than to continue a worthless fight. But deep in her heart she knew that wasn't the entire reason for her capitulation.

The truth was that she *was* hungry.

Ravenous.

For the first time in three weeks her mouth was watering and her stomach growling at the mention of food.

Crap. Was Roke right?

Was she one of those demons who couldn't physically tolerate being away from their mates?

No. She shook her head in fierce denial.

Not even her luck was that crappy.

Was it?

Refusing to contemplate the hideous thought, Sally pretended she didn't notice the satisfaction on Roke's face when he returned to the room and she nearly snatched the plate loaded with shepherd's pie and apple pie from his hand.

Instead she polished off the mound of food while he efficiently added logs to the fire she'd started when she'd first arrived at the cabin.

Setting aside the empty plate, Sally covertly watched as Roke straightened and wiped his hands on his jeans.

As always his dark, brooding beauty was like a punch to her gut.

The clean, perfect lines of his male profile.

The rich luster of his dark hair.

The sculpted hardness of his body.

"What about you?" she asked before she could halt the words.

Turning, he studied her with his piercing silver gaze. "I have no craving for apple pie."

The air prickled with the smoldering awareness that never truly went away.

"If you need to feed—"

"Are you offering?" he overrode her words, his voice rough.

A shudder of eagerness shook her body at the thought of his fangs sinking deep into her flesh, her blood heating as if preparing to feed her mate.

The sheer intensity of her reaction made her shake her head in horrified denial.

"Of course not."

His jaw tightened at her blunt refusal.

"Don't worry, little witch, as I said earlier, as much as I hunger for the taste of you, I'm not going to risk making this permanent."

Ridiculously, Sally was instantly offended by his equally blunt response.

"Good," she snapped. "Because I can't think of a worse fate."

Roke swallowed a growl as he watched Sally surge to her feet and jerkily move across the room.

The woman was a menace.

One minute she was looking at him as if she wanted him

to devour her and the next she was acting as if he'd crawled from beneath a rock.

Was it any wonder he didn't know if he wanted to shake some sense into her or jerk her off her feet and wrap those slender legs around his waist so he could plunge deep into her body?

Still seething, he frowned in confusion when she came to a halt in front of a blank wall. It was only when he noticed the charred darkness that marred the wood that he was struck by a sudden pang of regret.

"Damn." He shoved frustrated fingers through his hair. "I'm sorry, I didn't think."

"Think about what?"

"This cottage holds nothing but nightmares for you." He grimaced. "It's no wonder you can't relax."

She slowly turned, her expression oddly puzzled.

"You're right, I can't relax," she muttered. "But, it's not the memories that bother me."

He stiffened, assuming she was once again insulting him. It was, after all, her favorite pastime.

"I'm not leaving."

She absently shook her head. "For once, it's not you either."

He moved to stand directly in front of her. "Tell me."

"I am . . ." She struggled for the words. "Not really sure."

He placed a hand on her forehead, sensing her barely leashed unease.

"Are you ill?"

"No."

"Talk to me, Sally," he urged.

"It's difficult to explain." She furrowed her brow. "I didn't even realize I was being affected until you said something."

He tensed, his senses on full alert as he caught the scent of her subtle fear.

"Affected how?"

"It feels like there's been a change in the air." Her fingers absently stroked the mating mark that he'd exposed when he'd shoved up her sleeve. It was a habit he'd formed himself. Comfort? Confusion? Usually it was a combination of both. "Something that's nagging at me."

He forced himself to concentrate on her concern. "How do you feel it?"

"I don't understand."

"Is it a taste, a sound, a premonition?"

"Oh." She considered. "It's magic," she at last concluded.

He grimaced.

Of course it was.

"Your magic?"

"No." The denial was emphatic. "It's not human."

Roke glanced toward the window, allowing his powers to flow outward. He could pick up a few distant water sprites and an even more distant pack of hellhounds, but none of them were close enough to disturb Sally with their magic.

So what could be . . .

The answer struck without warning.

"Fey?" he demanded.

Sally was too intelligent not to instantly follow his train of thoughts.

"You think it might be the box?"

"When did you start to feel the change? Before or after the spell was broken?"

She chewed her bottom lip, silently searching her memory.

"After," she finally pronounced. Roke whirled away, headed for the bedroom. "Hey, where you going?"

"To get the box."

She was directly behind him as he reached the bed and plucked the box off the quilt.

"Do you think it might be dangerous?"

He wasn't idiotic enough to admit he thought anything to do with magic was dangerous.

He'd already made his opinion of witches painfully clear when they first met.

Now wasn't the time to remind her of his initial prejudices.

"I think that if you can feel the magic, then so can others," he said. "Thankfully this place is isolated enough that it shouldn't attract too much attention."

"We could toss it off the cliff."

He met her worried gaze. "I have a nasty suspicion it would find a way back to you."

She shivered, clearly considering the perfectly logical tactic of running the hell away, before calling on that remarkable courage that alternately impressed and infuriated him.

"I suppose I could try to put a dampening spell around it," she suggested.

"That might help." He studied her pale face. "Do you have what you need?"

She gave a slow nod. "I think so. Let's go to the kitchen."

In silence they made their way through the cottage, Roke stepping aside as she began bustling around the large room, with an efficiency that spoke of years of practice. Soon she had a small chalice filled with dried herbs and strange ingredients. She filled a second chalice with a potion she pulled from one of the cupboards then took both to the center of the circle.

Next she gathered a dozen candles, carefully spacing them around the circle before she walked toward him and held out her hand.

Reluctantly he handed over the box.

It wasn't just his dislike for magic that made him edgy. He understood that it was necessary to try to muffle the fey magic.

But while she was performing her spell, she would be cut off from him.

Completely and utterly.

It was the sort of thing that made any mate crazy.

In an effort to distract his growing discomfort, he moved to watch her set the box in the center of the circle and then slowly begin to light each candle.

"Why can you speak some spells and others you have to cast?"

"Like vampires, every witch has her own strengths," she answered even as her attention remained on completing her delicate task. "My talent lies in molding the environment."

He recalled her earlier words. "That's how you set the curtains on fire?"

"Yes." An absent nod as she grabbed the chalice filled with the dark potion and walked along the inner perimeter of the circle, dribbling the potion on the flickering flames. "And how I put the protective bubble around the box."

He grimaced as the candles hissed and a strange stench filled the air.

"A bubble of what?"

She shrugged. "Weaves of air."

He shifted nervously, his gaze clinging to the delicate perfection of her profile and unconscious grace of her movements. Any second he was going to snap and yank her out of that circle. Distraction. He needed a distraction. Pronto.

"How is a dampening spell different?"

She completed the ritual and set aside the bowl.

"I'm going to try to blend the glyphs in a stew of magic."

"Stew?"

"Stew is a mixture of tastes so it's difficult to pick out one ingredient."

"Ah." It made an odd sort of sense.

She knelt beside the box, sending him a warning glance. "I'm going to raise a protective shield around the circle now. Don't try to come near me."

She lifted her hands, but as she began to chant soft words Roke went rigid with an unexpected alarm.

"Sally," he hissed.

She frowned with impatience. "I'm just starting."

"There's something outside."

Her eyes widened. "Levet?"

"No."

"Then who?"

He concentrated on the vague presence that had arrived outside the cottage without warning.

The intruder was demon, but the scent kept shifting, as if it weren't entirely stable.

"I can't . . ."

He gave a frustrated shake of his head, reaching to pull the large dagger he kept holstered beneath his leather jacket. Then, turning toward the back door, he braced for an assault.

Not that being prepared did a damned bit of good when the attack came.

How did you fight a wave of sonic vibrations that shuddered through the air?

Clenching his teeth, he ignored the damage to his soft tissue that was already healing, whirling to discover Sally bent over, blood running from her ears and nose.

"Shit."

Forcing herself back to a kneeling position, Sally waved an impatient hand.

"Get in the circle."

He didn't hesitate. Sally might want to strangle him, but she wouldn't put the protective shield until he was safely beside her.

Leaping over the candles, he knelt next to her trembling body.

"Now."

Chapter Five

Sally hastily finished casting the spell of protection, not for the first time appreciating her mother's sadistic habit of forcing her daughter to the very limit of endurance then making her perform spell after spell.

On one memorable occasion, she'd even beaten Sally until she was barely conscious and then demanded she levitate a boulder that weighed almost a ton.

At the time Sally had violently hated her mother for her ruthless training, but she couldn't deny that it had kept her alive on more than one occasion.

Now she had to hope it came to the rescue once again.

Blocking out the ringing in her ears and the sluggish beat of her heart, Sally concentrated on the magic that stirred in the air.

This magic was different from her demon powers.

It wasn't an organic release of the magic that flowed through her body.

No, it was a fierce battle that demanded total focus to leash the elements that surrounded her.

Muttering the last of the incantation, Sally tipped the potion onto the floor, releasing the magic.

With an audible hiss the power spread like a dome over the

circle, the shimmering spiderweb invisible to all but her eyes and impenetrable to almost any weapon.

The candles flickered and Roke tensed, the air inside the circle frosty as his power surged.

"You have the barrier up?" he demanded, unable to sense magic.

"Yes." She grimaced, already feeling the drain on her inner resources. "It won't hold up for long."

The pale eyes flared with fury as he reached to gently touch the blood running down the side of her face before moving to brush away the similar drip of blood from her nose.

"You're hurt," he rasped.

"I'll be fine," she assured him. Although she was only half demon, she still healed far faster than a mere human. Thank the goddess. If she'd been mortal that strange blast of vibrations would have turned her insides to goo. Not the most pleasant way to die. "What the hell was that?"

He grimaced. "Magic?"

"None that I've ever encountered before." She pushed back her hair, feeling a layer of perspiration on her forehead despite the chill in the air. "Can you sense how many are out there?"

His attention shifted toward the back door, a dagger that was the size of a small sword in his hand.

"Just one."

"Demon?"

"Yes."

She frowned at his absent tone. "You don't sound very certain."

"My senses tell me that it's a male Miera demon."

"But?"

"But that species of demons are pacifist. They don't have any offensive weapons." He paused, his gaze still focused on the door. "At least none that are natural."

Well something had nearly liquefied several of her vital organs.

"Could he have a human weapon?" she demanded.

Who knew what the humans were secretly building at Area 51?

Death rays . . . photon guns . . . light sabers.

"Anything's possible," he muttered.

"Great."

Abruptly he turned to face her, his expression hard.

"Listen to me, Sally, I want you to—"

"No," she interrupted.

His brows snapped together. "Can I at least finish?"

"No."

"Dammit, Sally."

"I know what you're going to say." She lowered her voice to mimic his sexy growl. "Sally, run away like a good little witch while I play the conquering hero."

He made a sound of annoyance. "You read too many romance novels."

True. She loved romance novels.

Why not?

It wasn't as if she were ever going to have a real-life Prince Charming sweep her off her feet.

"I'm right, aren't I?" She pointed a finger in his face. "You want me to run and hide while you stay and fight."

He muttered a low curse, leaning forward until they were nose to nose.

"Would you rather I asked you to stay and fight while I run away?"

She held her ground, meeting him glare for glare.

"I'd rather you accept that I might be able to help. I'm not completely worthless, you know."

"I never . . ." He pulled back, a nerve twitching at the edge of his mouth. "Christ. There's no winning this argument."

"Then don't waste time on it," she suggested. "We need a plan."

"Too late," he muttered, grabbing the music box as the back door was thrust open.

Sally held her breath as a shadow fell across the floor and a delicate creature stepped into the kitchen.

She gave a choked sound of surprise as she studied the chubby demon with a round head and translucent skin that was nearly hidden beneath the brown robe.

Expecting a towering troll-like figure, or even a cyborg, Sally blinked in shock.

"Is that a Miera demon?"

He shifted close enough for her to feel the rigid tension of his muscles.

"Yes."

"He looks like a banker," she muttered, but despite the creature's bland appearance, she found herself pressing against Roke's shoulder as he crept near.

The entire room was overwhelmed with a choking menace that made her hair stand on end.

Moving with a fluid ease that seemed odd for the pudgy body, the Miera slowly walked around the edge of the circle, flicking out a forked tongue as if it could sense the magic.

"Lower your shields," the demon at last commanded, his human English remarkably polished.

Like a posh Englishman.

Sally shook her head. "I don't think so."

He halted directly before them, his tongue still flicking. "I mean you no harm."

"That would be easier to believe if you hadn't just tried to kill us," Roke drawled.

"All I want is a box," the creature said. "Give it to me and I will walk away."

Sally hissed in shock.

Stupidly she hadn't actually considered why they would

suddenly be attacked by a strange demon. And even if she had, she wouldn't have immediately guessed it had anything to do with the box.

It had, after all, sat in this abandoned cottage for years without attracting attention.

Beside her Roke smiled, clearly having suspected why the demon had attacked. He held up the box so the glyphs etched in the polished wood were visible in the candlelight.

"You mean this box?" he taunted.

A flick of the tongue. "Yes."

"Why?" Roke prodded. "Is there something special about it?"

"It belongs to me."

"Odd. You don't look fey."

The pale, round face remained emotionless, but the sense of malevolence thickened in the air.

Sally frowned. Somehow she suspected that the demon wasn't deliberately trying to frighten them with the heavy atmosphere of evil.

Instead it was as if it was . . . leaking out of him.

"It was a gift," the demon smoothly countered.

Roke tapped the top of the box with his dagger, his gaze noting the intruder's most subtle reaction.

Vampires were masters at detecting weakness in their enemies.

"What does it do?"

"Nothing." The creature lifted a hand. "It's merely a decoration."

Roke shook his head. "You don't risk war with the vampires over a trinket."

Genuine confusion rippled over the Miera's face, his body seeming to smudge and flicker at the edges. What the heck? Was it an illusion?

"I have no fight with the vampires."

"You will," Roke assured him. "Styx takes it quite personally when someone tries to kill one of his clan chiefs."

There was a hesitation and Sally belatedly understood Roke's tactic.

He was judging the desperation of the creature not only by revealing that he was a clan chief, but also by tapping the box with the dagger. It would prove just how important the box was to the Miera and how anxious he was to get his hands on it.

"As I said, give me the box and there will be no need for bloodshed," the demon at last commanded, clearly worried his box might be damaged by the dagger.

"You haven't said what it does," Roke countered, his attention focused on the Miera who was once again walking around the circle even as he spoke directly into her mind.

Be ready to run. . . .

Sally swallowed a tiny gasp. Hadn't she told him not to do that?

And if she hadn't, then that was something that needed to be taken care of ASAP.

Well, just as soon as they were out of trouble.

"The shield is weakening," the Miera pronounced, flicking his tongue with obvious satisfaction.

Roke covertly slid his dagger back into the holster at his lower back.

"If you attack us you risk destroying the box," he reminded the demon, reaching to grasp her hand.

"There are some risks worth taking," the demon hissed, his pale eyes abruptly morphing to a startling black that was slit with red.

Sally might have been wigged out by the strange eyes if she hadn't been desperately struggling to maintain the shield.

The past three weeks had taken their toll.

Her magical tank was running on empty.

The cracks in the shield were beginning to form when she felt a warning blast of frigid air.

Roke's power.

Familiar with the bad, bad things that could happen when the vampire released his innate talent, she made no protest when he yanked her to her feet and shoved her toward the door.

"Sally, now," he barked, trusting her to lower the shield in time for them to leap over the candles.

The demon gave an eerie growl of fury, but before he could react there was a shower of splinters as the overhead beams shattered beneath Roke's power. In the next second Sally was tossed out the door and the cottage that had withstood a century of violent storms, a rare earthquake, and an attack by a rival witch, collapsed into a pile of rubble.

Holy shit.

Roke clutched Sally's fingers in one hand and the box in the other as he headed straight for the nearby shed.

"That was quite a trick," she muttered, her steps shaky as she struggled to keep pace.

"It won't hold him for long," he said in absent tones, his gaze skimming the barren landscape.

"What are you doing?"

"Looking for a vehicle." He hissed in frustration as he realized they had no easy means of escape. He hadn't heard the approach of a car, but that was hardly surprising. It might be humiliating to admit, but when Sally was near he tended to be dangerously distracted. "How did the bastard get here?"

"On foot?" she suggested.

"Possible, but Mieras aren't as physically strong as most demons. They rarely travel more than a few miles beyond their lair." He muttered a curse. There were way too many questions with no answers. "We're going to have to make a run for it."

She staunchly squared her shoulders despite her obvious weariness.

"Okay."

His lips twisted. He didn't doubt she would drive herself until she collapsed into a coma. And all without once asking for help.

She'd been alone too long.

Been hurt too many times.

What she needed was a kind, patient man who could tenderly heal the wounds that life had inflicted.

Not an ill-tempered, loner of a vampire who'd made a vow to devote his life to his clan.

Unfortunately he was all she had.

"Will you trust me to keep you safe?" he abruptly demanded.

There was a predictable hesitation, but after a long pause she gave a nod.

"Yes."

Something moved deep inside him.

A seismic shift that cracked open a vulnerable fissure he had no idea how to repair.

And no time to consider the long-term consequences.

Instead, he swept her off her feet, cradling her against his chest as he flowed silently through the night.

"Hold on," he warned, leaping over a wide culvert.

She threw her arms around his neck, anxiously trying to glance over his shoulder.

"Do you sense we're being followed?"

His arms tightened protectively around her slender body, his fangs fully exposed as he made a direct path toward the trees that filled the small valley below them.

Anything that tried to stop them, he'd rip out their throat.

"No, but there was something off about that demon," he said. He wasn't intimately familiar with Miera demons, but he knew damned well the one that attacked them wasn't natural. "For all we know the creature might be capable of disguising his presence."

She shivered, but her courage never faltered.

"We can't keep running. It'll be dawn soon."

He brushed a kiss over the top of her head, so light she couldn't sense the fleeting caress.

"Don't tell me you're concerned I might be sizzled into a pile of ash?"

"Of course I am," she muttered. "I'm the only one allowed to make me a widow."

His lips twitched. "I'm touched. Unfortunately, there aren't many hotels in this area. Unless you know something I don't?"

He leaped over a large boulder, briefly debating the possibility of taking the direct path over the edge of the cliff, only to instantly dismiss it. There might be caves they could use to wait out the daylight hours and the surging tide would hopefully wash away their trail, but Sally was only half demon and he wasn't about to risk injuring her.

"Maybe."

Not expecting a response to his teasing, Roke came to an abrupt halt to study her guarded expression.

"Are you going to share?"

She refused to meet his searching gaze. "My mother was paranoid to the point of obsession. Probably because she was hated by most people who met her." She grimaced. "She has at least half a dozen safe houses in the area."

Safe houses? Anger surged through him. "Why didn't you mention them earlier?"

"I forgot about them."

"No," he snapped. Dammit. He'd known that she was hiding something from him earlier. Now it was obvious what she was plotting. "You intended to run from me as soon as the sun rose."

She knew better than to try to lie, but a stubborn expression settled on her delicate face.

"I won't be forced to go to your clan."

"I told you . . ." He bit off his furious words. It was less than an hour before sunrise and they were on the run from a demon who could make the very air a weapon. Now wasn't the time for this particular argument. "Which way?" he demanded through clenched fangs.

She kept her gaze averted. "Just keep heading south."

In silence, he carried her down the steep bluff, entering the thick grove of trees. Sally shivered and he wrinkled his nose at the frost coating the underbrush and the sharp stones that cut into his moccasins.

He might be annoyed as hell with the female in his arms, but he couldn't halt his instinctive concern. A vampire was impervious to the elements, but Sally was clearly uncomfortable in the chilled air.

"I don't suppose your mother's safe house is a penthouse suite at The Ritz-Carlton?"

She lifted her brows. "This from the vampire who lives in the middle of the desert?"

He shrugged, in no mood to admit his concern was for her welfare.

Sometimes she annoyed the shit out of him.

"I wouldn't say no to a hot shower and a bottle of Remy Martin Louis XIII Black Pearl cognac."

She grimaced. "Let's just say that it has more of a Bear Grylls vibe to it."

He swallowed a curse, silently reassuring himself that it would only be for a few hours. As soon as night arrived he intended to take her far away from this frigid, desolate spot.

"At least tell me that it's sunproof."

"You won't roast. I promise." She pointed toward an overgrown trail between the trees. "Follow that path." They traveled over a mile before she pointed again. "There."

Roke lowered Sally to her feet, frowning as he searched the small clearing.

"Is it an invisible safe house?"

"Something better," she assured him, lifting a warning hand. "Stay back."

"Why?"

"There are spells we have to avoid."

He watched as she cautiously inched her way forward, her eyes closed as she concentrated on the invisible magic surrounding the small clearing.

"What kind of spells?"

"Most of them are simply to repel stray trespassers. But there are a couple that are dangerous." She held up a hand, speaking soft words that carried a power even he could feel. After several tense minutes she finally opened her eyes. "I've created a small pathway. Follow my footsteps."

She was forging forward before he could halt her, leaving behind Roke to mutter his opinion of impulsive witches who charged into dangerous situations without concern for the sanity of the poor vampire who was stuck trying to keep her alive.

Carefully following in her path, he battled his way past the relentless weaves of revulsion that managed to leak through Sally's barriers. The spell was strong enough that he had to physically fight the urge to turn and flee, reminding him just how much power Sally had to expend to keep them from being harmed.

She needed rest and food.

Two things he intended to ensure she had plenty of once they were safe.

Concentrating on the slender form in front of him, Roke pressed forward until they were at last through the magical barriers.

He shook off the lingering strands of magic, moving to stand at Sally's side as she knelt in the middle of the clearing.

She muttered another spell and the ground parted to reveal a large hole.

"This is it?" he muttered.

"Yep." She swung her legs over the edge of the hole. "Let me go first."

"Why?"

"I haven't been here since I was sixteen and I can't be sure whether or not my mother left behind any painful surprises."

"Sally," he growled.

"I'll be careful." The promise had barely left her lips before she was dropping into the hole.

"Dammit," Roke hissed in horror, swiftly leaping behind her.

He landed in a surprisingly large room that was lined with thick walls of cement.

"Ta-da." Sally sent him a mocking smile. "You see, sun-proof enough for the fussiest vampire."

Stepping forward, Roke lifted his brows as he took in the towering shelves that held cans of food as well as bottled water. There was a narrow bed shoved against a far wall and an open cabinet that held row after row of ceramic pots filled with potions, dried herbs, and copper pans for mixing spells. On the top of the cabinet were kerosene lanterns, basic tools, and a first aid kit.

"Your mother built this?"

She shrugged. "Actually, I think it was a bomb shelter before she decided it suited her purposes and claimed it for herself."

"It will do. At least for today," he murmured, moving forward to touch the pallor of her cheek. "First dinner. And then bed."

Chapter Six

Levet surveyed the tangled mass of steel and chrome and rubber that had once been Roke's motorcycle. A petulant scowl marred his forehead.

It wasn't his fault.

How was he to know that anyone would be stupid enough to put such a sharp curve in the road? Or that the motorcycle would acquire a mind of its own and fly off the road to smash into a tree?

"*Mon dieu*. What an absurd machine," he muttered, well aware that Roke was bound to blame him for the wreck. Vampires were so unreasonable. "Who would build a vehicle with only two wheels? Roke should be happy that I rid him of such a faulty piece of equipment. He might have been seriously injured."

Brushing the dust from his wings, Levet wrinkled his snout, considering the possibility of a long vacation in the Bahamas.

Sand, palm trees, and drinks with little umbrellas in them.

What more could a gargoyle want?

And perhaps in a few centuries Roke would have forgotten all about his silly motorcycle.

It was the scent of brimstone that yanked him out of his broodings, making his tail twitch in warning.

"Yannah?" He searched the darkness, confused when there was no sign of the tiny demon who kept his life in constant chaos. Then, without warning, he felt a familiar tug that started deep inside him spreading outward until he was consumed by a sudden darkness. "Eek."

Only seconds passed, but Levet knew he was being jerked through space. How often had Yannah taken his hand and smiled sweetly before zapping them halfway around the world? And this felt exactly the same, although this was the first time he'd been alone when he was being zapped.

It only made the terrifying experience worse.

Coming to a gut-wrenching halt, the darkness abruptly parted and Levet spread his wings as he struggled to keep his balance.

Mon dieu, he would never get used to that.

Never.

Waiting for the dizziness to clear, Levet glanced around the large cave.

There wasn't much to see, but his gargoyle senses could detect the vast spiderweb of caverns beneath his feet and catch the scent of river water that wafted on the breeze.

Ah. He recognized his surroundings.

This was the hidden lair south of Chicago and where the Oracles were staying.

Which, of course, made sense.

Yannah's mother, Siljar, was a piggly-wiggly, no wait . . . was it big-wit? Wig? Bah. Whatever. Siljar was an Oracle who carried a lot of power on the Commission and Yannah was her most trusted ally. The two would never admit that Yannah carried out secret duties for her mother, but Levet was not entirely blind.

Yannah would abruptly travel to strange places and skulk about areas he considered far too dangerous, then without warning would be halfway around the world, feverishly digging through ancient manuscripts.

Not that she ever discussed her mysterious duties with him. *Non.*

He was just the male she wished to keep tucked in her private lair with his wings firmly clipped.

Scowling at the thought, Levet was preparing to go in search of the aggravating female when a demon stepped into the cave from a hidden entrance.

The small man was swathed in a heavy robe that covered him from head to toe, making him look like a monk with his bulge of a belly, his round face, and his nearly bald head.

But his pale, translucent skin marked him as a Miera demon.

"You," Levet called, making a sound of impatience when the creature pretended he hadn't heard him. "*Sacrebleu.* Are you deaf?"

The male Miera came to a reluctant halt, his expression carefully bland.

"Are you speaking to me?"

"But of course." Levet glanced around the empty cavern. "There is no one else about."

There was a beat before the man managed a smile. "Have you come to petition the Oracles?"

"*Moi?*" Levet's wings fluttered in disbelief. "Do you not recognize me?"

"Should I?"

"But of course. I am, Levet, recently reinstalled member of the Gargoyle Guild and savior of the world."

The man offered a stiff bow. "And I am Brandel, Historian for the Commission."

"You are an Oracle?"

"Yes."

"Oh. . . ." Had Levet been a lesser demon he might have

been frightened by the information. There were Oracles who would destroy entire villages for an imagined insult. Levet, however, had promised himself that he would never be intimidated again. "Very well. I have been brought here by Yannah. I wish to see her."

"Then I suggest you locate a servant to alert her to your presence."

The man turned, as if he were intent on escaping, but Levet was waddling forward to block his path.

"Wait," he said, leaning forward, sniffing the thick robe. "What is that scent?"

A strange humming filled the air as the demon shoved Levet away with a surprising strength.

"Stay back."

Levet frowned, recognizing that precise scent of salty air that clung to the fabric of Brandel's robe.

"Have you been to Canada?"

The humming intensified, creating a vibration in the air. Levet stepped back in concern.

He didn't know what was causing the peculiar hum, but he didn't think it could be a good thing.

Not when it was making his insides feel . . . icky.

Then as swiftly as the humming had started it disappeared and Levet was distracted by the scent of brimstone.

Spinning on his heel, he expected to see Yannah standing in the arched entrance that led deeper into the caves. Instead he discovered a female demon who was almost her exact double.

The same short stature and slender body covered by a white robe. The same oblong eyes that were a solid black, the same delicate features and sharp, pointed teeth. They even had the same long braid that nearly brushed the floor, although Yannah's was a pale blond, while her mother's was gray.

Siljar also carried with her the sort of power that blasted through the air like a freight train.

Yannah didn't yet possess her mother's strength.

Dieu merci.

"Is there a problem?" the tiny demon demanded, her black gaze focused on Brandel.

"Siljar." The Miera lowered his head in a respectful nod. "This . . . creature is searching for your daughter."

Siljar's gaze never wavered.

"Are you just returning?"

Brandel kept his head lowered, his fingers nervously plucking at the hem of his sleeve.

"Yes, I heard a rumor that a rare manuscript had been discovered in a harpy nest near Singapore," he explained in timid tones. "Unfortunately it turned out to be a fake."

Levet stepped forward. The demon was lying. He'd bet his favorite Fabergé egg.

"But . . ."

"You must be tired," Siljar gently overrode his words.

Brandel lifted his head high enough to give a relieved smile.

"Exhausted, actually. If you will excuse me?"

"Certainly."

Siljar stepped to the side so Brandel could scurry from the cavern, her expression distracted.

Levet clicked his tongue. "I may not be an Oracle, but I do have a highly sensitive nose." He turned his head to one side, allowing Siljar to admire his snout. "In profile I am told it resembles Brad Pitt's."

"Ah, so I see." Siljar cleared her throat. "And what did your magnificent nose tell you?"

Levet turned back to meet the Oracle's steady gaze. "Brandel the Historian has not been to Singapore."

"No?"

"*Non.*"

"Then where has he been?"

"Canada."

A slow blink was Siljar's only reaction to the information one of her fellow Oracles was liar-liar-pants-on-fire.

"Interesting."

Levet shrugged. *Eh bien.* If she did not care, then neither did he.

"And odd," he muttered.

"Why do you say that?"

"I, myself, was in Canada before I was so rudely transported here."

"Indeed." Siljar smiled. "Why were you in Canada?"

Now she was interested?

He grabbed his tail to polish the tip, attempting to appear modest.

A difficult task for a gargoyle as formidable as himself.

"As usual the vampires were in need of my considerable skills."

She nodded, naturally eager to learn of his bravery. "Any skills in particular?"

He dropped his tail back to the ground. He needed champagne to get a true gloss.

"The clan chief of Nevada was searching for his missing mate."

"The witch?"

"*Oui.*" Levet heaved a sigh. "Lovely Sally. I hope that she can find the truth of her past. I sense it might be important."

"As do I," Siljar said, so softly Levet barely caught the words.

"Levet." The female voice came without warning, and Levet flinched as Yannah stormed into the room, her long braid swaying and her white robe brushing the ground. "What are you doing here?"

Levet scowled, caught between the familiar sense of delight and annoyance as the female halted directly in front of him.

"How can you ask such a ridiculous question?" he demanded. "You are the one who brought me here."

The black, oblong eyes flashed with fire. "I most certainly did not."

Levet waved his hands in the air, his tail twitching. "Then how do you explain the fact that I was in one place and then . . . poof . . . I was in another?"

"Mother," Yannah muttered and they both turned to discover Siljar had silently slipped away. "She must have brought you."

Perversely, Levet didn't care why Siljar would have gone to the effort to bring him to the caves. He was too annoyed by the fact it hadn't been Yannah.

If he was going to be zapped and poofed and yanked from one location to another, he should at least be rewarded with a kiss and a snuggle.

Where was his snuggle?

"Why do you keep running from me?" he abruptly asked the question that had been bothering him for weeks.

Yannah tilted her tiny nose in the air. "I am not the only one to run."

Oh.

Busted.

Levet grimaced. Perhaps she had a point. He had traveled to Paris without explaining where or why he was going.

"I had to confront my past," he said, defending his hasty escape from her lair. "It was a spiritual journey."

Yannah wasn't impressed. "And when you returned you took every opportunity to be apart from me."

Levet spread his fingers in a helpless motion. "I am a male."

Yannah frowned. "And?"

"And I am not supposed to make sense."

"You . . ." She appeared to have trouble speaking. Strange. She'd never had trouble before. Then she lifted her hand and Levet felt that weird tugging in the middle of his belly. "Go away."

Darkness closed around him.

"Eek."

When Roke had promised he was going to make sure she was well fed, he hadn't been kidding.

Sally had been too weary to protest when he'd urged her to sit on the edge of the cot. And if she were completely honest, she couldn't help but enjoy the sight of the badass vampire fumbling with the unfamiliar task of opening various cans of food to heat them over the kerosene hotplate.

The man was ruthlessly powerful, impossibly beautiful, and so sexy he made her ache with longing.

Who could blame her for the knowledge he wasn't perfect?

But as he brought her dish after dish, carefully testing the temperature before he placed the plate in her hands, her petty amusement was replaced by an unexpected stab of pain.

Which was ridiculous.

So what if Roke was only pampering her because he was compelled by magic? Or that if he was in his right mind, he'd sooner be stuck in this hidden lair with a rabid pit bull than her.

She didn't need to be coddled.

Her mother had taught her that only the strong survived and that a woman stupid enough to depend on anyone was destined to be betrayed.

A lesson that had only been reinforced during her brief stint as a disciple of the Dark Lord.

She didn't want or need anyone to be fussing over her.

She grimaced. Okay. Maybe in her deepest dreams she'd imagined a future where she found a man who could see beyond her training as a witch in the dark arts, and her desperate decision to gain protection from those who worshipped evil, and even her mongrel blood.

But that man would never be Roke.

No.

He was looking for some perfect Xena warrior who he could introduce to his clan with pride.

Not a tarnished witch who was universally reviled.

That unexplainable pain once again slashed through her, and with a jerky motion she rose to her feet to toss the disposable plates into a small trash can.

Instantly Roke was at her side, his expression filled with a concern that threatened to tug at her heart.

Stop it, Sally, she silently warned herself.

It wasn't real.

None of this was real.

"You didn't finish," he chided softly.

"Roke, I'm not a turkey that needs to be stuffed for Thanksgiving."

"You've burned through a lot of energy," he said, his fingers gently tracing the shell of her ear. "You need to replenish your strength."

She took an awkward step away, refusing to meet the stunning beauty of his silver eyes.

"Any more replenishing and I won't fit into my pants."

His gaze slid down her body to linger on the tight fit of her jeans across her slender hips.

"I'll give your mother credit for following the Boy Scout motto," he muttered in absent tones.

She licked her dry lips.

Had the room shrunk?

Suddenly he seemed to fill every inch of it, his frigid power pulsing through the air to brush her skin with an enticing caress.

"What motto?" she managed to ask.

He stepped forward, his gaze returning to her guarded expression.

"Always be prepared."

She made a sound of disgust. Oh yes. Her mother had been all about "an ounce of prevention."

Except when it came to getting pregnant.

Maybe if the powerful witch had done more thorough research on Sally's father before hopping into his bed, Sally wouldn't have spent her life running from people who wanted her dead.

Her futile broodings were shattered as he cupped her cheek in his hand, his thumb tracing the curve of her lower lip.

The cool touch sent shockwaves of pleasure zinging through her body, but this time she didn't pull away.

She told herself she was too tired to fight him, but she knew that she was lying to herself.

Roke only had to be in the same room for her to melt with longing.

Dammit.

"You're not going to try to convince me you were ever a Boy Scout?" she asked, trying for a distraction, but the words came out as a breathless invitation.

He moved in close, lowering his head to speak directly in her ear.

"No, and before you ask, I never ate one for breakfast." His lips brushed the curve of her ear. "I prefer peaches."

Her hands lifted, somehow slipping beneath his leather jacket to explore the wide chest covered by nothing more than the thin tee.

"Roke."

He growled in satisfaction as his seeking lips found the pulse that beat at her temple.

"This isn't the mating."

Her fingers grasped his shirt, her brow furrowed in confusion as tingles of excitement raced down her spine.

She could barely breathe; how was she supposed to think? "What?"

"This heat that burns between us." He pulled back, the candlelight reflected in his pale eyes. "It has nothing to do with the mating."

She shook her head, refusing to admit that she'd been in lust with this man since she caught sight of him.

She needed to cling to the pretense that there was nothing but the spell between them.

Otherwise . . .

She slammed the door before the dangerous fear could form.

"Of course it does."

There was a hint of fang as he trailed his mouth over her flushed cheek, his fingers sliding down to circle her throat.

"You can lie to yourself, but you can't lie to me," he growled. "This desire ignited the moment we met."

The denial died on her lips.

He was right.

The scent of her stirring arousal had to be blatantly obvious to Roke. Her short time in captivity had taught her there was no hiding anything from a damn vampire.

Just one of the countless reasons they were such pains in the ass.

Instead she did what every witch trained in the dark arts did when backed into a corner.

She went on the attack.

"You mean the same moment I was locked in a cell and you told me how much you hated witches?"

He stiffened, unable to deny her accusation. "I didn't claim our first meeting was particularly romantic."

"You wouldn't know romantic if it smacked you in the face."

"Probably not," he grimaced. "My social skills are questionable."

"You think?" she snapped, trying to ignore the unexpected emotion that flared through the silver eyes.

That hint of the stark loneliness did something dangerous deep inside her.

"But I do recognize when a woman wants me," he stubbornly warned, his hand slipping to cup her nape. With a tug he had her pressed against the unyielding width of his chest. "And you, Sally Grace, want me."

"Why you arrogant . . ." He swooped down to steal a kiss. She jerked her head back to glare at him. "Ass . . ." He kissed her again, his lips unexpectedly tender. "Roke . . ." she pleaded, shivering as a honeyed heat flooded through her. "Stop that."

"Why?" he rasped, blatantly rubbing his fully erect cock against her lower stomach.

She sucked in a strangled breath, a fierce need jolting through her and for a dazed second she couldn't remember why.

She'd wanted this aggravating vampire with a fierce craving that was making her nuts.

Why not rip off the tee and lick her way down his body? A few tugs and she could have him stripped of his clothes, then she could take that cock in her mouth and bring the proud vampire to his knees. From there it would be a simple matter to press him backward and climb on top of him and . . .

The vivid fantasies refused to be banished, even as she kept her hands from straying over the chiseled muscles beneath her palms.

"We're supposed to be finding a way to get rid of each other, not making things worse."

"How could this make things worse?"

He lowered his head and nuzzled a path of destruction down the curve of her neck. Sally trembled, raw heat flaring through her at the erotic feel of his fangs scraping against her tender flesh.

"I—"

"Yes, my love?"

She struggled to hold on to the unraveling thread of her protest.

"I don't have sex with men who hate me."

He jerked his head back, as if genuinely surprised by her words.

"You think I hate you?"

"Don't you?" she accused.

"No."

"You blame me for the spell that forced you to become my mate."

His lips twisted, his brooding gaze sweeping over her tense body.

"I feel a lot of things, but hate isn't one of them."

"If the spell was broken—"

Stark hunger flared through his eyes. Oh . . .,goddess.

"I'd still want you," he growled, lowering his head, to allow his fangs to scrape down the curve of her neck. "Like this."

"Roke," she breathed.

A tiny voice warned that she should be terrified by the threat of those enormous weapons so close to her veins, but her body instinctively arched to rub against the hard thrust of his erection.

Roke groaned, his hands slipping beneath her sweatshirt to tug it up and over her head.

The cool air brushed over her skin, but it did nothing to ease the feverish heat that flowed through her veins. A heat that only intensified as he cupped her bare breasts in his hands, his thumbs teasing her nipples to tight beads.

Sally squeezed her eyes closed, savoring the agonizing

pleasure of Roke's touch at the same time she could feel the hunger that pulsed through him.

Perhaps their bond was an illusion, but there was a heady sensation in experiencing their mutual reaction as his lips traced the line of her shoulder and then down her inner arm, sketching the intricate crimson scrolling with the tip of his tongue.

Sally's startled gasp echoed through the shelter.

She'd never realized a mere brush of his lips over her mating mark could be so . . . erotic.

Her skin tingled, electric darts of anticipation arrowing straight to her womb.

She released a shaky groan as his cool, clever fingers skimmed down her body, tugging at the zipper of her jeans.

How many nights had she fantasized about this vampire? His touch . . . his kiss . . .

The feel of his fangs striking deep into her flesh.

Lost in the cascading pleasure, Sally arched her back in silent encouragement.

Roke growled in appreciation, turning his attention to her naked breasts. His tongue tortured the sensitive tip as his hands skillfully slid the jeans down her slender hips, pausing long enough to yank off her shoes before the jeans were removed and tossed across the floor.

Slowly his fingers explored the slender curve of her hip, as he trailed kisses over her opposite breast. Sally forgot to breathe as she restlessly ran her hands over his chest, her body trembling with need.

"This is insanity," she moaned.

"No." He nibbled a path to the tip of her breast. "Insanity is trying to fight this."

A part of her agreed. The part that was shivering with a breathless anticipation that made her heart pound and her knees weak.

Another part, however, understood that this was more than a casual quickie.

The mating mark on her arm still tingled from his light caress, emphasizing their unnervingly intimate connection.

Did she really want to take the chance of becoming even more tightly bound to a vampire who was desperate to get rid of her?

"Roke . . . wait."

With a soft curse, he lifted his head, his expression tight with frustration.

"I can feel your desire, Sally," he rasped. "You ache with your need."

She flushed. It was awful enough he could scent her arousal without having a direct peek into her inner fantasies.

"Which is precisely why this is such a bad idea."

His eyes flashed with silver fire. "It's not an idea. It's fate. We both know it."

"And if it somehow interferes in the magic binding us together? There are demons who use sex to complete their mating."

Without warning, he had her scooped in his arms and stretched across the narrow bed.

"Right now, I'm willing to take the risk."

She shuddered as he leaned over her, burying his face in the curve of her neck.

"Roke—"

"Ssh." He nuzzled soft kisses down the line of her chin. "There is more than one way to share pleasure."

His fingers gently traced the curve of her breasts, as his mouth sought her lips in a kiss of stark need.

She moaned, her toes curling as his tongue penetrated her lips, a flood of melting desire rushing through her.

She knew she should fight.

There were a thousand reasons this could be put in the worst-decision-ever category.

But hell, who was she fooling?

It hadn't only been her appetite that had suffered when she'd been apart from Roke. Her restless nights had been plagued by a craving for his touch.

Now her body was responding to him with a fierce joy that couldn't be denied.

Maybe he was right.

Maybe this was fate.

As if sensing her capitulation, his fingers circled the tight buds of her breasts, learning what made her gasp in delight before he lowered himself to capture a sensitive tip between his lips.

Sally gave a choked cry of pleasure, her fingers tangling in the silken strands of his hair.

She'd always heard that vampires made the best lovers.

Perhaps predictable since they used seduction to feed. But her intense reaction as he sucked her nipple wasn't the result of skill. It was the response of a woman completely enthralled by one specific man.

Roke.

Only Roke.

"So sweet," he murmured, his lips traveling between her breasts as his hands gently tugged her legs apart.

Vaguely aware he was still fully dressed while she was stark naked, Sally was too aroused to feel embarrassment as he trailed his fingers down the curve of her waist and cupped her hips in his hands.

With delicious care his mouth followed the path of his fingers, planting soul-melting kisses down her quivering stomach.

Sally undulated beneath his teasing touch, glancing down to meet the smoldering silver gaze that monitored her with a searing intensity.

A slow wicked smile curved his lips, exposing his snow-white fangs. She groaned, the dampness between her legs flooding the room with the scent of her arousal.

His smile widened.

"Peaches," he growled.

Then, before she could brace herself, he was sliding off the edge of the bed so he could tug her legs over his shoulders and nibble a path up her inner thigh.

She closed her eyes, dropping her head back on the mattress as he at last found the center of her aching need, licking his tongue through the wet heat.

Oh. Yes. Yes, yes, yes.

Her hips tilted upward, silently encouraging the slow, steady stroke of his tongue, her hands gripping the blanket beneath her.

The exquisite pleasure was building at a rapid rate.

Too rapid.

She wanted to prolong the pleasure. To drown in the ripples of delight that shimmered through the very core of her.

But it'd been so long. And it felt so damned good.

His hands loosened their grip on her hips, sliding up her body to caress her stiffened nipples.

"Roke, I—"

Her words were lost as his tongue dipped into her body, thrusting in and out with a rhythm that destroyed any hope of savoring the moment.

She hissed between clenched teeth, reaching down to shove her fingers through his hair, pressing his wicked tongue even deeper.

"Yes, sweet Sally," he growled between strokes. "Come for me."

As if his words were magic, the pleasure swelled to a critical level and with a last thrust of his tongue, Roke catapulted her into ecstasy.

Stunned in the aftermath of her cataclysmic climax, Sally lay in a boneless daze as Roke kissed his way back up her stomach, lingering to lavish her sensitive breasts with detailed attention before he covered her with his hard body.

"I think I'm addicted to peaches," he teased, his fangs scraping lightly over her throat.

Sally shivered, her hands sliding beneath his heavy leather jacket to shove it away from his shoulders.

"Off," she murmured.

With liquid grace he shrugged the jacket off and tossed it on the floor. The leather garment landed with a thud, revealing he had a weapon tucked in a pocket. Probably more than one.

He gazed down at her with smoldering silver eyes. "Happy now?"

She slowly shook her head, her hands tracing the smooth planes of chest. Beneath her fingers she could feel his muscles flex at her touch, his body shuddering in pleasure.

"Not yet."

He smiled. "More?"

"My turn."

She yanked the tee up and over his head, her breath catching as she stared at the width of his naked chest.

She'd expected the chiseled muscles and smooth, bronzed skin. What made her breath catch was the magnificent dragon that had been tattooed over one pectoral muscle and down his rib cage.

Softly, she traced the outline of the golden, mythical creature before moving to the brilliant crimson wings and dark jade body.

"The mark of CuChulainn?" she asked. She'd heard of the mark given to those vampires willing to endure the battles of Durotriges to become clan chief, but she'd never actually seen one.

He made a choked sound of pleasure at her light touch. "Yes."

She stroked to the tail that curled around his side. "Is it sensitive?"

He held her gaze as he slowly extended his arm. "Not as sensitive as this."

She shivered at the sight of the mating tattoo that ran beneath the skin of his inner arm, the memory of his lips tracing the crimson marks stirring the desire she'd assumed to be well and truly sated.

Holding his gaze, she lifted her head to use her tongue to trail over the intricate curves of the crimson lines, her heart racing as his eyes darkened to a beguiling smoke.

"Shit . . . that feels good," he muttered.

She continued to nuzzle the marking, her fingers moving to skim over the curve of his ribs and then down the hard ridges of his stomach. Reaching the waistband of his jeans, she popped the snap and unzipped his jeans.

Immediately his cock sprang free.

"And what about this?" she teased, curling her fingers around his impressive width. "Does that feel good?"

"Oh, hell yes." He shoved himself up to perch on his knees, straddling her as he watched her explore his rigid length. "But, this isn't—"

"This is what I want."

She inwardly shrugged off the premonition that this . . . this intimacy was every bit as dangerous as full-out-interlocking-parts sex.

They weren't hurting anyone, were they?

Besides, there was a thrilling pleasure in knowing this aloof, frigidly controlled vampire was in her power.

Not because of a spell.

Or a trick.

But because her touch set him on fire.

Refusing to contemplate why his fierce passion felt like some sort of victory, Sally stroked her fingers down his straining cock, amazed by the cool smoothness of his skin. Satin over steel.

Excitement curled in the pit of her stomach as she reached

the soft sack, giving him a squeeze that made him choke out a strangled groan before she was exploring back to the blunt tip.

Roke squeezed his eyes shut, hissing as she pushed downward again.

"Oh, gods. I'm not going to survive."

She chuckled as she wiggled until she could sit up, angling downward so she could take the fully engorged erection into her mouth.

"Sally." He cupped her face to pull her back, his harshly beautiful features tight with need.

She met his smoky gaze. "Let me."

He gave a slow nod, his lips curling back to reveal his massive fangs as she took him back into her mouth, her fingers circling his base as she swirled her tongue over his tender tip.

His fingers shifted to tangle in her hair, the ground shaking and a frost coating the ceiling as his power flowed through the room.

"Yes," he groaned, his entire body trembling as he jerkily surged in and out of her mouth. "Perfect. So perfect."

Chapter Seven

Roke had been a vampire for more centuries than he could remember.

Which meant he'd assumed that he'd seen and done just about everything possible in the world.

An assumption that had been blown to hell by the tiny witch who was tucked next to him with her glorious autumn hair spilling over her pale, satin skin.

Christ almighty.

He'd expected pleasure. He'd even expected it to be explosive. A man couldn't lust after a woman with such painful intensity and not be blown away by when he at last got her naked.

But what had happened between the two of them . . .

It went beyond pleasure.

The mere touch of her hand had been enough to set him on fire, the resonating feel of her own arousal pulsing through their bond until he couldn't tell where his passion ended and hers began.

And when she'd taken him in her mouth . . . holy hell, it'd been nothing less than sensual ecstasy.

Now he was perched on his side with Sally lying next to

him, her fingers lightly tracing the dragon tattoo that marked him as a clan chief.

Yet another first.

He hid a rueful smile.

His image of a loner wasn't just an act. He didn't do "cuddling." Hell, unless he was in the middle of sex, he didn't want anyone touching him. Period.

This shared moment was even more astonishing than the tiny quakes of pleasure that continued to vibrate through him.

Why wasn't he pulling away to leave her alone on the narrow cot?

It was his usual modus operandi.

Instead he held himself perfectly still, afraid the slightest movement might break the spell.

"Was it terrible?" she murmured, the brush of her fingers down his ribs sending sparks of euphoria through him.

"Was what terrible?"

"The battles of Durotriges."

He shrugged. Terrible didn't begin to describe the gladiator-style games. The weeks he'd been locked in the arena had passed in a blur of blood and pain and death. But in many ways it'd been a simple time.

You lived or died.

No in between.

"It's never fun to kill a worthy adversary."

"Then why did you enter them?"

He lowered his lashes, hiding his bleak stab of fury at the memory of his former clan chief, Gunnar, and the female vampire who'd ruined him.

The selfish bitch's only power had been her beauty, but she'd managed to use it to turn Gunnar from being a strong, influential leader of a clan that was feared by all, to a mind-less fool who spent so much time pandering to her lust that his people had lost everything.

But it wasn't just Gunnar's self-destruction that caused

the raw regret that refused to heal no matter how many years had passed.

He'd deliberately entered the battles of Durotriges to challenge his former friend as chief, but while he was gone Gunnar's lair had been struck by lightning and burned to the ground.

Or at least that was the story he'd been given.

He'd never been able to shake the suspicion that his beloved sire, Fala, had been responsible.

The female vampire might not have her memories of life as a human, but she'd clung to her beliefs as a wise woman, searching for mystic portents in nature. Including an omen that she'd read the night Roke was turned.

She'd been convinced that it meant that Roke would one day be a great leader.

After Gunnar's death he couldn't help but wonder if the ancient vampire had taken matters into her own hands.

It was the only way to be certain that he wouldn't lose the challenge to become chief.

Aware that Sally was beginning to frown at his continued silence, Roke struggled to speak.

This was not a subject he discussed.

With anyone.

"The previous clan chief . . . was difficult."

She studied his clenched expression, no doubt sensing his instinctive retreat.

"Cruel?"

"Worse." His voice was cold, flat, his rare sense of peace shattered by his unwelcome memories. "He was indifferent."

There was a pause, as if she was struggling between the knowledge she was touching a raw nerve and curiosity.

Unfortunately, curiosity won out.

"How could that be worse?"

His jaw clenched, his thoughts veering toward the sheet of

paper he kept locked in his lair. On it were written what had been lost after Gunnar's mating.

The silver and gold mines that had been the source of their wealth.

The acres of territory that had been claimed by rival clans.

The weaker members who'd been stolen from their lairs and sold to slavers.

He stood at his sire's grave and read from the list, promising her that her sacrifices wouldn't be in vain. He would regain everything they'd lost.

"Vampires are by nature savage creatures." He pointed out the obvious. "Without a strong leader a clan splits apart or becomes victims of more aggressive demons."

She grimaced. He didn't have to explain what happened to the victims.

"Why did the previous chief bother forming a clan if he didn't want to be a leader?"

"He did, at first." Roke had still been a fledgling when his sire had joined Gunnar's clan, but he'd heard enough horror stories to realize how fortunate he was to be trained by the honorable warrior. "He was a rare clan chief who was willing to kick the ass of anyone who got out of line, but was fair in his judgment."

"What happened?"

"He mated."

She blinked at the clipped explanation. "That's it?"

"The female was jealous of the time that Gunnar devoted to his people."

She studied his tight expression. "You didn't like her?"

The temperature dropped at the mere thought of the bitch.

"I hated her for destroying a vampire I once considered my friend."

Sally shivered. "What happened to him?"

He glanced down to where her fingers continued to trace

the dragon tattoo, his body savoring her gentle touch even as he twitched with the need to pull away.

The dark memories were crowding through his mind, a sharp reminder of the people who depended on him. The people who were once again left without a chief, despite his promises.

With a sudden shove he was off the bed and pulling on his jeans.

"That's not my story to tell," he rasped. "You should rest."

There was a sharp, startled silence followed by the sound of Sally turning on her side and yanking the covers over her naked body.

"Got it."

He lifted his gaze to study the rigid line of her back visible through the thin blanket.

"Sally."

"I'm tired, Roke."

And pissed, he silently added, ruefully using his powers to extinguish the candles.

Combined with a large dollop of hurt.

Dammit. He hadn't meant to . . .

What?

Lure her into a sense of intimacy and then slam the door in her face?

He grimaced, moving to take a position where he could keep watch over Sally while making sure nothing tried to slip through the entrance. The spells should be enough to repel any intruder, but he was still bothered by the strange demon who'd attacked them.

There'd been something off about the creature and until he knew exactly what the demon was capable of, he wasn't about to let down his guard.

Not when his mate depended on his protection.

Keeping his gaze trained on the female who was rapidly turning his well-ordered life into chaos, Roke leaned against the cement wall, allowing the day to creep past as he leashed his painful memories and tucked them into the back of his mind.

They'd done enough damage, thank you very fucking much.

The sun was setting when Sally at last stirred, looking adorable with her gorgeous hair tumbled around her flushed face and her eyes velvet dark with lingering sleep.

She sat up, the blanket dipping down to give a peek of smooth satin skin and the gentle swell of a breast.

Roke clenched his jaw, resisting the urge to cross the room and pull her into his arms.

Would she actually turn him into a toad? He didn't think so, but now didn't seem the time to push her.

As if to emphasize the point, her head swiveled to discover him standing near the waist-high counter, her expression instantly smoothing to a cool mask.

"What are you doing?" she demanded, wrapping the blanket tight around her body.

He nodded his head toward the water that he'd poured into a large pan and placed on a kerosene heater.

"I thought you would prefer to wash in hot water."

Her lips thinned, as if considering where she wanted him to shove his hot water; then, with an extreme effort she rose to her feet and gave a regal nod.

"Yes. Thank you."

He bristled at her brittle composure, while his lips twisted at the irony.

Since he'd become clan chief, he'd been convinced that his mate would be a replica of himself.

Controlled. Aloof. Detached.

Now he wanted Sally to lash out at him. To storm around the small space, her eyes sparking with temper and her hair swinging around her beautiful face. Hell, he'd be happy if she threw something at him.

Sally Grace was a bundle of impulsive, unpredictable emotions. It was just . . . wrong to see her so contained.

And he had no one to blame but himself, he acknowledged with a pang of regret.

Still, maybe it was for the best, the voice of reason whispered.

This mating, no matter how real it might feel, was an illusion. His responsibility to his people was a duty that was real.

A damned shame it didn't feel like it was for the best.

In fact, he wanted to grab her and kiss her until her icy composure melted and her arms wrapped around his neck. . . .

Shit.

"I've called Cyn," he abruptly announced, adjusting the various weapons he had strapped to his body. Anything to keep his hands to himself. "He'll meet us at Pandora's Box in an hour."

She frowned. "What's Pandora's Box?"

"One of Viper's numerous bars."

A hint of fire threatened to break through the ice. "You arranged a meeting and didn't think you should discuss the decision with me?"

He shrugged. He wasn't going to compromise when it came to her safety.

"It'll be well guarded."

"By vampires."

"Not exclusively," he said, having visited more than one of the clan chief of Chicago's clubs. "Viper is an equal opportunity employer."

She arched a brow. "Is that supposed to be reassuring?"

It shouldn't be. Viper's clubs tended to be shocking even by demon standards.

Blood, sex, and violence were always on the menu.

They also happened to be guarded by Viper's most loyal warriors.

He nodded his head toward the music box that was set on the floor next to the bed.

"We need to find someplace where you'll be safe while we figure out what is so important about your box."

"Right." Another flash of fire in the dark eyes. Thank the gods. "Would you go to a witch's coven?"

He ignored her question.

"We'll meet Cyn there and you can get something decent to eat." He held up a hand as her lips parted to protest. "If you're not comfortable, we'll leave. Okay?"

Her lips snapped together, the ice returning. "Fine."

He bit back a curse. The sun had barely set and it already promised to be a long night.

He shoved impatient fingers through his hair. "Is there anything else you need?"

She met his gaze. "Privacy."

His lips twisted. A direct hit.

"You want me to turn my back?"

"The spells are woven to keep intruders out." Her chin tilted. "Not to keep people from leaving."

A low growl rumbled through Roke. The primitive urge to remain and make sure his mate was taking proper care of herself was a ruthless compulsion that beat through him even as he forced his feet to carry him toward the front of the room.

She needed space.

He could at least give her that.

"I'll wait for you at the entrance."

Not waiting for a response, he leaped upward, landing on the edge of the hole.

His feet barely touched the grass when he was yanking his dagger from its sheath.

Fey.

The scent was all around them.

Fairy. Imp. Even a few wood sprites.

He scanned the darkness, sensing the gathered crowd scurrying away at his abrupt appearance.

Concentrating on their rapid departure, Roke nearly missed the stack of items that had been piled at the edge of the clearing.

Flowers, ceramic pots filled with fresh honey, carved wooden figurines, and exquisite golden jewelry set with priceless gems had been left behind.

"What the hell?"

Sally quickly scrubbed herself clean with the hot water and soap that Roke had prepared, telling herself that she didn't care if it was the first time anyone had ever considered her comfort. Had he scented the water with dried lavender? No . . . it didn't matter.

Just as it didn't matter that her body still tingled with the pleasure of his skillful touch.

He was an ass.

First clouding her mind with his deceitful-sneaky-vampire seduction and then leaping off the bed as if she were carry-ing the plague.

Pulling on her clothes, she suddenly blushed.

Okay, maybe he hadn't actually seduced her. She recalled being a fairly willing participant.

Still, there'd been no reason to insult her.

Not unless he was afraid that she might start to believe this mating was real.

Two souls eternally entwined . . .

It was that humiliating thought that had given her the abil-ity to face him with a composure she was far from feeling.

She'd be damned if she would let him know how easily he could wound her.

Fully dressed, she pulled her hair into a ponytail and grabbed the music box. Then, extinguishing the candles, she made her exit by the more mundane method of the steps built into the cement wall.

Crawling over the edge of the hole, she straightened, startled to discover that Roke was standing nearby, his gaze trained on the edge of the clearing.

She'd expected him to be out doing . . . what?

Vampire things.

Hunting. Sucking blood. Pissing off witches.

Instantly on alert, she moved to his side, at last catching sight of strange objects.

"Blessed goddess, where did those come from?"

The ground trembled with his power. He obviously wasn't pleased with the strange gifts.

Giving her a warning glance to stay put, he moved to walk around the pile of flowers and pots and . . . good Lord . . . was that jewelry?

"It came from the fey," he murmured, his hand reaching to grasp a delicate necklace spun from strands of gold and sprinkled with shimmering opals.

Naturally she ignored his warning, walking to join him. "Why?"

He gave her a frustrated glare before shaking his head.

"I don't—"

She studied the pure, elegant lines of his profile shown to perfection in the moonlight.

"Roke?"

"A tribute."

"A what?" She glanced toward the pile that was clearly filled with items that would be precious to any fey. Why would they leave a tribute here? "Oh." She was struck by inspiration. "Could this be a holy site?"

Roke straightened, dropping the necklace back onto the pile. "It's possible."

Translation: He didn't believe for a minute this was a holy site.

She absently rubbed her inner arm, an unconscious habit she'd developed since the mating mark appeared.

"Tell me what's bothering you."

He turned to meet her worried gaze, his eyes glowing silver in the darkness.

"It could be for some fey deity, or it could be for the box. Or—"

She grimaced. "I'm not going to like this 'or,' am I?"

His expression was grim. "Or for you."

She was shaking her head before the words left his lips. "No."

With a frown he reached out his hand, cupping her cheek with his slender fingers.

"Sally, it's dangerous to stick your head in the sand."

She brushed away his fingers, aggravated as much by her heart-jolting response to his touch as by his implication that she was being deliberately obtuse.

She had enough problems without being accused of being some sort of fey-magnet.

"In case you've forgotten, I used to live here." She waved her hand toward the nearby trees. "I played in these woods for years without being inundated with fairy gifts."

His expression remained stern. "You left the night your powers manifested."

She shuddered. She didn't need a reminder of the night she'd been driven from her home.

"So what?"

"They had no opportunity to sense your true nature."

Her lips parted only to snap shut.

Damn.

She couldn't deny he had a point.

Like most mongrels her demon blood hadn't started to show itself until she hit puberty. Which meant that it hadn't been until her mother had sliced her palm with a knife to perform a simple spell that anyone realized she was anything but human.

"You think I might be a fairy?"

His brooding gaze shifted to take in the glorious highlights that shimmered like flames in her hair.

"I think there's something about you that the fairies consider worth risking dangerous spells and the unmistakable scent of a vampire to leave these gifts."

She took an abrupt step away from the priceless treasures, a sharp fear piercing her heart.

"No . . . it's not me," she rasped, holding up her hand so she could wave the box beneath Roke's nose. "It has to be this."

He studied her a long moment, easily sensing she was on the edge.

"If that's true, then we need to meet with Cyn so he can decipher the glyphs. It's the only way we'll get the answers we need," he said, his tone so reasonable that she began to nod her head in agreement.

Abruptly realizing she'd been cleverly manipulated, she sent him a frustrated glare.

"You're like a dog with a bone."

He stepped forward, wrapping her in a swirl of frigid power.

"Sally, if I wanted to force you to return to the vampires we both know that I could."

She flattened her lips at the blunt words. They were all too true.

And as much as she hated to admit she needed help, she wasn't an idiot.

Whether it was the box or herself that was attracting weird Miera demons and oddly generous fey, she had to make it stop.

How could she search for clues to her father when she was dodging near-death experiences?

"Fine." She hid her surge of dread behind a stoic mask. "How far is it?"

"A few miles south of here." He scowled, as if annoyed by her brittle tone.

Why? He'd gotten his way, hadn't he?

"Does a few miles mean five or fifty?"

"Less than twenty." He held her wary gaze. "We can travel faster if I carry you."

She sucked in a startled breath. She might be pissed at the annoying vampire, but that didn't keep him from being ridiculously gorgeous.

The mere mention of being cradled against the wide chest with his strong arm wrapped around her was enough to stir heated fantasies.

Her lips trailing over the smooth, bronzed skin. Her hands tangled in the silken strands of his hair . . .

"I think I can manage," she muttered, abruptly turning to head out of the woods.

With long strides he was swiftly at her side, the cool scent of powerful male teasing at her senses.

They walked in silence until they reached the path leading south along the cliffs, Roke's gaze scanning for any danger.

Then, without warning, he lifted his fingers to lightly touch the exposed skin of her nape.

"Are we going to discuss the elephant in the room?" he demanded, his tones dark . . . compelling.

She grimaced. Crap. Had he picked up her X-rated thoughts? "No."

His frustration hummed in the chilled air. "So you're going to pretend that I didn't strip you naked and kiss every inch of your silken skin?"

Oh . . . hell.

She struggled to breathe.

"Exactly."

His fingers moved to stroke over the frantically pounding pulse at the base of her throat.

"That I didn't taste your climax on my tongue?"

She knocked his hand away, glaring at him as every nerve in her body sizzled with excitement. The precise memory of cresting beneath the stroke of his tongue was almost enough to topple her over the edge again.

"Stop it," she hissed, not sure if she meant Roke or her renegade thoughts.

"Not talking about our mutual attraction won't make it go away."

She didn't bother to try to deny that it was mutual.

What was the point?

"Will talking about it make it go away?"

His gaze returned to the surrounding countryside, scanning the thickening shadows as the path led them to the very edge of the cliffs.

"Do you regret what happened?"

Regret?

Oh yeah. Sally had plenty of regrets. But not for the reason Roke suspected.

It was going to be hard enough to scrub Roke from her thoughts once the mating was broken. It was going to be ten times more difficult now that her body was addicted to his touch.

"It was a mistake."

His profile tensed, as if she'd managed to wound him.

Which was ridiculous.

"A mistake?"

"One that won't happen again."

His lips twisted in a humorless smile. "Just keep telling yourself that."

* * *

Brandel wasn't prepared for the sudden mist that floated in the middle of his private rooms.

If you could call the damp, dismal caves rooms.

They felt far more like crypts just waiting for a corpse.

They were, however, the one place he could go to be completely alone.

Or at least that was the plan.

Still weakened from having a house collapsing on top of his corporal form, followed by an unwelcome encounter with Siljar, the last thing he wanted was another unpleasant confrontation.

Which was precisely why he'd ignored the summons from Raith.

He hadn't expected his partner-in-crime to take the risk of making an actual appearance.

"So, you failed?" The voice spoke directly in his mind.

Brandel remained perched on the edge of his cot, too weary to pretend that he wasn't exhausted.

His journey to Canada had been one unpleasant surprise after another.

He'd expected to find some forgotten temple that had been unearthed by annoyingly curious humans. Hieroglyphs that had been buried for centuries were known to release low-level bursts of magic when first exposed. They were usually harmless and passed as the contained magic spread through the atmosphere.

The last thing he'd expected was to be confronted by a vampire clan chief and one of the most powerful witches he'd ever encountered. And he most certainly hadn't expected to discover a box that pulsed with enough ancient magic to make his mouth water.

So rare.

So precious.

He'd been blinded by his hunger to get his hand on the object.

Which was why he'd blundered so badly.

"It was a temporary setback."

The mist stirred, anger vibrating through the air. "Did you at least determine the source of the magic?"

Brandel gave a reluctant nod. "A box."

"Odd. What's in it?"

"Impossible to say. It was guarded by very powerful glyphs."

Raith wasn't pleased. Brandel felt his companion's anger pulsate through the cave, threatening to reveal his presence to the highly sensitive Oracles spread throughout the sprawling caverns.

"You have to get that box. Its magic is beginning to spread."

"I understand the danger," he hissed. "Better than you."

"Then why are you just sitting here?"

Brandel scowled. How easy it was for Raith to toss out commands while he remained safely concealed.

It was Brandel who was forced to take all the risks.

"I can't just leave." He spoke the protest out loud. "Siljar already knows I traveled away from the caves."

Pain lanced through him, nearly jolting him out of his corporal form.

"That wasn't a request."

Brandel flinched, but he wasn't stupid enough to strike back.

Raith had been in close contact with their prisoner for centuries. His ability to absorb such magic had given him a power that Brandel couldn't hope to match.

Not unless . . .

He deliberately squashed the dangerous thought. At the moment he wasn't alone in his mind.

Instead he held up his hand that was beginning to show a hint of translucency.

"I need to feed."

"Feed, then take care of business."

The words echoed in his mind as the mist disappeared as swiftly as it had appeared.

Brandel studied his fading hand, his thoughts returning to the box that held the sort of magic that offered possibilities he'd never before considered.

Dark, treacherous thoughts.

"Mine," he whispered softly.

Chapter Eight

It took almost two hours to reach the wharf that was built on a bleak stretch of rocky beach and another quarter of an hour for the boat to navigate the rough waves. But at last they reached the small island just off the coast.

Tugging the hand of a reluctant Sally, Roke led her past the weaves of illusion that fooled the human eye into believing there was nothing more than an abandoned lighthouse on the island and entered Pandora's Box.

Instantly they were surrounded by a soaring Greek temple filled with amphitheaters where naked water sprites danced and heated baths came complete with beautiful nymphs.

As they entered the massive foyer, toga-clad slaves appeared before them, offering glasses of champagne or, for him, a sip of blood from their throat. Most vampires preferred their drinks straight from the tap.

Roke hastily waved them away, sensing Sally's swelling fear.

She had every reason to distrust vampires and he'd just brought her to a place filled with dozens of his brothers, all indulging in their most primitive desires.

Unfortunately for her, it was the one place close enough to meet with Cyn where they could be assured of safety.

Nothing would be capable of slipping past the defenses that surrounded the island. Both magical and physical.

As if to prove the point, an exquisite blond vampire sashayed into the foyer, her lush body barely covered by her gold lamé toga and her porcelain face beautiful enough for an angel. But the near-black eyes were hard and merciless as she scanned her surroundings.

Bliss had once worked for Viper in his Chicago club, and the lethal predator had proven a talent for creating an atmosphere that had demons flocking to enjoy the entertainments. She'd also revealed an innate cunning that Viper was swift to appreciate.

He'd given her a small fortune and told her to create a fantasy.

An order she had more than fulfilled.

Crossing the marble floor, Bliss allowed a smile to curl her lips.

"Hello, gorgeous," she murmured, her low voice an invitation to sex as she slid her cold gaze toward Sally. "Did you want your dinner cleaned and put in costume? She would make a pretty enough slave girl."

Sally stiffened, outrage overcoming her fear. "Slave girl?"

He placed an arm around her. Not only from the need to publicly claim her as his property, but to keep her from doing something impulsive.

His mate was just crazy enough to launch a spell that would wreak havoc and end up getting them both killed.

"We aren't here for the entertainment," he informed Bliss, not surprised when she strolled forward to run a crimson-painted nail down the leather of his jacket.

He'd crossed paths with the beautiful vampire several years ago and she'd made it clear she wouldn't say no to some up close and personal attention.

"Are you sure?" She parted her lips to expose her extended fangs. "I do private shows for very special customers."

He grasped her fingers that had roamed beneath his jacket, his expression hard with warning.

"I need a private room and a human dinner," he commanded, glancing toward Sally who was staring at the far wall with a fierce pretense of indifference. "With apple pie."

Bliss scowled, not pleased at being rebuffed.

It didn't happen often.

Probably never.

"I have no idea if we have apple pie or not."

He allowed his power to rattle the priceless marble statues set in shallow alcoves.

"Order out."

Realizing he wasn't playing, Bliss went from offended female to gracious hostess.

"Your wish is our command." Turning with a fluid grace, she headed toward a pair of fluted columns that opened into a hallway. "This way."

"Has Cyn arrived?" he demanded, his arm remaining around Sally's rigid shoulders as he urged her to follow Bliss's brisk pace.

"Yes, he's enjoying the baths."

Roke rolled his eyes. Typical. Cyn was a born hedonist who indulged his varied passions whenever the opportunity presented itself.

He would have to fetch the vampire and bring him to Sally, even if it did mean leaving her alone.

There was no way in hell he was exposing her to the sight of dozens of vampires lost in their bloodlust.

Pushing open a door, Bliss stood aside to wave them into the room that reflected the theme of a Greek villa. A circular space, it had an abundance of marble with fluted columns and a domed ceiling that was painted with a half-naked Pandora opening her box to release chaos.

Thankfully, the stark room was furnished with several

white sofas circling a crackling fire that burned in a pit in the center of the marble floor.

Sally should be comfortable enough while he went in search of Cyn.

Turning toward the female vampire who hovered near the door, he allowed her to glimpse the predator inside him that would destroy anyone or anything that threatened his mate.

"This woman is under my protection. I would be very displeased if anything were to happen under your watch."

"She'll be safe," Bliss promised, sliding a cunning glance toward the pale-faced Sally before returning her attention to him. "You, however, might get a little roughed up before I'm done with you."

The husky promise was still floating in the air as Bliss closed the door, leaving him alone with a female who had already threatened to turn him into something nasty.

Slowly turning, he met her icy glare.

"A friend of yours?" she demanded in overly sweet tones.

"No," he denied without hesitation.

He wouldn't play games, not with this.

"She acts like she knows you very well."

He shrugged. "Our paths crossed several decades ago. I wasn't interested then, and I'm not interested now."

She glanced down at the music box clutched tightly in her hands. "She's very beautiful."

He stepped forward, his fingers cupping her chin to tilt back her head. His brooding gaze swept over her fragile features, lingering with regret on her guarded expression. She wouldn't soon forgive or forget his rejection.

"But she's not you."

Her eyes darkened. "I would think that was a big fat bonus."

"Never." His thumb brushed her lower lip. "I want you. No one else."

She frowned in understandable confusion.

Shit.

He was worse than an angsty teenage girl.

Logic told him to keep her at a distance, but his instincts refused to obey. He was desperate to pull her into his arms and offer her the comfort she needed.

"Roke—"

"You'll be protected here," he interrupted. One disaster at a time. "Bliss might be a pain in the ass, but she wouldn't be in charge of Viper's club unless she was one hundred percent loyal to him."

He turned back toward the door, pulling it open.

"Wait." Sally took a step forward. "Where are you going?"

"To find Cyn."

"Shouldn't I go with you?"

He glanced over his shoulder. "Have you ever been in a vampire club?"

She grimaced. "Of course not."

"Then trust me, you'll be happier waiting here."

"Why?"

"There are . . . activities I doubt you would approve of."

"Oh." Her eyes narrowed. "And that's the only reason you want me to stay here?"

His face hardened to a grim mask, as he abruptly realized that it wasn't just her virtue he was trying to protect. It was his peace of mind.

The mere thought of parading her through a crowd of amped-up vampires was enough to make his inner demon snap and snarl.

"No, I don't want other males to see you."

She looked offended. "Are you ashamed to be seen with a witch?"

"No, I'm damned well not ashamed," he growled. "I'm protecting what's mine."

"What's that supposed to mean?"

"It means that one accidental touch and they would be dead."

"Oh." She blinked, her mouth parting at his brutal honesty. "That's . . . crazy."

His gaze lowered to the sensuous curve of her lips. Lips that had driven him to paradise only hours ago.

And that swiftly he was hard and aching.

"You're mine," he rasped.

"Don't say things like that."

He gave a humorless laugh as he shoved up the sleeve of his jacket to expose his mating mark.

"You claimed me as yours, my love. Now you can deal with the consequences."

Without giving her time to respond, he stepped into the hall and closed the door behind him.

For a long minute he hesitated, caught by the scent of peaches that filled the air.

Had the fragrance grown richer? More provocative?

His fangs extended, his body aching to return to her. He wanted to pull her into his arms and shatter the barrier that he'd placed between them.

Instead, he gestured toward the hovering vampires who'd obviously been sent by Bliss to stand guard.

"Nothing gets past you," he growled in warning, waiting for their nods before he headed toward the back of the long building.

Eventually the marble floor was replaced by beautiful ceramic tiles and the air filled with a damp heat.

Toga-clad servants lined the walls, offering a smorgasbord of food and drinks and nubile young bodies.

At Pandora's Box, everything was on the menu.

He stepped through a double set of columns to enter the formal baths, bypassing the public orgy that was currently occupying the main bath, which was the size of an Olympic pool, and heading toward the more private rooms.

He at last located Cyn in a corner room that offered a view

of the moon-kissed waves that swirled around the island and the star-spangled sky.

In the middle of the orange and black mosaic tiled floor was a shallow pool. At the moment it was surrounded by a hundred candles flickering in the cool breeze that swept through the open windows.

And in the center of the pool was a large vampire surrounded by two buxom nymphs.

Roke halted at the edge of the pool, giving a shake of his head.

Cyn, clan chief of Ireland, was an impressive sight.

Six-foot-three with a powerful chest and the thick muscles of an ancient berserker, Cyn had a thick mane of dark blond hair that flowed halfway down his back except for the front strands that had been woven into tight braids that framed his face.

His features were blunt with a square jaw and high cheekbones. His brow was wide and his jade green eyes heavily lashed. Some might consider his mouth too lush for a warrior and his nose carved in an arrogant line, but few would mistake him for anything but a ruthless killer.

His skin was a perfect alabaster with a series of ancient Tuatha Dé Danann tattoos that curled and swirled in a narrow green pattern around his upper arms.

Leaning against the edge of the bath with his naked body sprawled beneath the blue water, Cyn had his arms around the two equally naked nymphs who pressed their impressive breasts against his chest.

Both females were blond, but one had the usual blue eyes of a nymph while the other had gray eyes.

Never let it be said that Cyn wasn't an equal opportunity hedonist.

The Irish vampire smiled, displaying a set of pearly white fangs.

"Roke, welcome."

"Cyn." Roke shifted his gaze toward the gray-eyed nymph who was batting her lashes in open invitation. "Am I interrupting?"

"Join us," Cyn murmured, his voice deep and laced with an accent that hadn't been heard in Ireland in over a thousand years. "There's plenty to go around."

"A generous offer, but we need to talk." Roke folded his arms over his chest, his expression stoic. "In private."

Cyn rolled his eyes. "You always were a party pooper."

Roke arched a brow. "Party pooper?"

"Stick in the mud. Killjoy. Sourpuss."

"Not all of us enjoy drunken orgies that include glimpses of your hairy white ass."

"I have a fine ass," the vampire protested, smiling toward the blue-eyed nymph. "Fiona here can't keep her hands off it."

Roke shrugged. "I prefer my pleasures be enjoyed with less water and fewer spectators."

Cyn gave a sharp laugh. "Fair enough." Rising to his feet he gestured to bimbo one and bimbo two. "Take a break, lassies." Waiting for the females to reluctantly straighten, he laid a smacking kiss on Fiona's pouting lips. "Don't go far."

With shrill giggles the nymphs hurried from the room, not bothering with clothes.

Roke grimaced. "How do you stand the noise?"

Cyn reached for a heated towel, wiping the water from his massive body.

"Didn't you see those titties? Who the hell cares about giggles when you can have those as your personal plush toys?"

Roke was briefly assaulted by the memory of Sally's slender body and breasts that fit in his hands with delicate perfection. Who wanted plush toys when you could have masterpieces?

He shivered, trying to ignore the hunger stirring deep inside.

"You never change," he muttered.

Cyn narrowed his gaze, his amusement fading. "You have."
Yeah. No shit.

"Get dressed and I'll take you to the box."

"What's the point in putting on clothes?" Cyn shrugged. "I doubt I'll shock anyone in this place and I intend to return to finish what I began with the nymphs once we're done."

Roke stiffened, the ground giving a tiny quake. "The point is you're not getting anywhere close to Sally until you're fully clothed."

"She hasn't seen a naked vampire?" Cyn unwittingly took his life in his hands as he stepped toward the door. "Maybe I should . . ." Roke was moving before he was even aware of what he was doing, pinning the massive vampire to the wall with one hand clenched around his throat. "Bloody hell," Cyn rasped.

"I'm not entirely stable right now," Roke confessed, his bloodlust simmering just below boil. "Don't push me."

Cyn scowled, his own power sending warning sparks of pain through Roke's fingers and down his arm.

"So it's true," he growled. "That witch forced you into a mating."

"It's . . ." Roke dropped his hand, suddenly feeling weary. "Complicated."

Styx's lair in Chicago

Styx hadn't been pleased when his mate had insisted that he leave behind the caves that had been his former lair. Darcy was convinced that he had a duty to his position as Anasso and had swiftly moved them into this house that looked like something Tony Montana in Scarface would own.

The marble, the gilt, and the priceless antiques were bad enough, but it was big enough and comfortable enough to encourage unwelcome visitors to linger far past their use-by date.

The current unwelcome visitors were Darcy's mother, Sophia, and her new mate, Luc.

Styx had yet to forgive his mother-in-law for her participation in trying to force Darcy into the arms of the King of Weres, but for the sake of marital harmony (which was necessary to make sure he wasn't kicked out of his bed) he'd agreed to grin and bear Sophia's presence.

He hadn't, however, agreed to watching the two painting one another's toenails while they gorged on chocolate-covered strawberries.

Instead he retreated to his library hoping to find some peace and quiet, only to discover Viper waiting for him.

The current clan chief of Chicago wasn't as large as Styx, but there was an unmistakable ripple of hard muscles beneath the ruffled white silk shirt and black satin slacks. His pale silver hair was worn long and his eyes were as dark as the night sky.

At the moment his hauntingly beautiful face was distracted as he stood beside the window overlooking the rose garden.

"I didn't expect you," Styx murmured, moving to stand beside his friend. "Is there trouble?"

Viper shook his head, his voice pitched so it wouldn't carry to the various demons who strolled through the vast house.

"Not trouble, but I thought you would want to know that I was contacted by Bliss to tell me that she had an unexpected visitor at Pandora's Box."

Styx frowned. The name was vaguely familiar.

"Is that one of your clubs?"

"The one in Canada."

Styx smiled with wry humor. He'd been to the club once.

Roman baths and half-dressed nymphs weren't really his thing.

He was more a find-an-enemy-and-stab-it-with-his-big-ass-sword kind of guy.

"Only you could take a frozen piece of rock and turn it into a fortune," he said.

"I'm a man of many talents," Viper smugly agreed.

"So who was this unexpected guest?"

"Cyn."

"Not that unusual," Styx pointed out. He'd only run across the path of the clan chief of Ireland on a handful of occasions, but each time Cyn had been draped in naked women. "The bastard has always enjoyed the sort of entertainment you provide."

"Well, who wouldn't?"

Styx snorted. "Do you have a point?"

"He said he was meeting Roke there."

"Why?"

"Something about fey glyphs."

Styx frowned. Fey glyphs? What did they have to do with locating Sally's father?

"Did he say—"

Without warning the stench of brimstone filled the air and Styx was whirling toward the center of the room, cursing Darcy for making him leave his sword locked in their room. She had the ridiculous fear he might stab her mother.

Well, maybe it wasn't entirely ridiculous.

Still, he deeply regretted the lack of a tangible weapon as he flinched beneath the blast of nuclear power that could only come from an Oracle.

"Christ," Viper muttered, both of them staring at the tiny demon covered by a white robe, her long gray braid hanging down her back and her oblong black eyes holding an ancient knowledge.

Siljar might be the size of a small child, but she had enough strength to squash them like bugs.

"Styx." The Oracle gave a small bow toward Styx and then his companion. "Viper."

"Siljar." He leashed his instinct to destroy the unexpected

intruder. Vampires didn't like people popping in. Actually, most pop-ins usually ended up with their heads chopped off. "This is a surprise."

She regarded him with a steady black gaze. "I wished to keep our meeting a secret."

"Ah." Viper made a beeline toward the door. "That's my cue to leave the two of you alone."

"No." Siljar brought a sharp halt to his exit. "You might be of service."

"Yeah, get your ass back here," Styx growled, waiting until Viper had grudgingly made his way back to his side before he asked the question he soooo did not want to ask. "How can we help?"

Siljar lifted her hand, giving a small gesture that shut and locked the door.

"What is said here must not go any further."

Styx's annoyance was replaced by a surge of concern. An appearance by Siljar always meant trouble, but tonight she looked even more grim than usual.

"Understood."

"I am uneasy," she admitted.

Styx shot Viper a worried frown.

"Has something happened?" the clan chief asked.

Siljar folded her hands at her waist. "Several somethings, but nothing I can bring into focus."

Styx touched the amulet that hung from a leather band tied around his neck. Why the hell did Oracles always have to speak in vague warnings?

"I don't understand."

Something that was almost an emotion touched Siljar's childlike features.

"There have been petitioners that have arrived at the caves only to disappear."

"Dead?" Styx demanded in surprise.

Every demon knew that petitioners to the Commission were off-limits.

Not even a battle-raged Orc would defy the Oracles.

Siljar grimaced. "Or worse."

Worse than death?

Shit.

"Is there a pattern?" he demanded.

"They're all fey."

"Fey?" Styx frowned. "If there is someone or something killing the fey shouldn't you be discussing the problem with their leaders?" he demanded only to be hit in the side by Viper's elbow.

"What?"

That'd been diplomatic, hadn't it?

At least for him.

Siljar shook her head. "I can't be certain how far the corruption has penetrated."

Styx hid his grimace. He hated vampire politics, but fey affairs made his own seem tame by comparison.

By nature the fey were cunning, treacherous, and utterly fickle. It was impossible to pinpoint their loyalty.

It shifted like the wind.

"What do you want us to do?"

Siljar paused, her eyes shifting toward a silent Viper before returning to him.

"I think a squabble would be just the thing," she at last murmured.

Styx waited. That was it?

He frowned. "I beg your pardon?"

"Having two alphas in the same city is bound to create tension," she said, as if that explained everything.

Viper blinked. Not a necessary vampire function, but the elders instinctively maintained the image of a living human no matter where they were.

"You want the two of us to fight?"

She offered a smile, flashing her pointed teeth. "It doesn't have to be a physical battle, but it must be convincing enough that it's worthy of petitioning the Commission."

Styx lifted a brow. "At the caves?"

"How else can we discover who is behind the disappearances?"

With the impatient question still ringing in the air, Siljar lifted her hand and . . . disappeared.

Poof.

Gone.

"Shit, I hate when she does that," Viper muttered.

"It could be worse," Styx growled. "She could still be here."

Viper threw his hands in the air, heading toward the door. "Next time I need to speak with you I'm sending you a text."

"At least you get to pretend to be pissed at me," Styx said to the retreating back.

"Who's pretending?"

Chapter Nine

Roke remained on edge as he led Cyn through the club to the room where Sally was waiting for them.

It didn't matter that Cyn was now dressed in a pair of black leather pants and a heavy cable-knit sweater. Or that the older vampire had made his distaste of witches more than clear.

The strange mating was still too new, too . . . raw, to easily allow another male so close.

He hadn't been kidding when he warned Sally he would kill a man who touched her.

Waving aside the vampires who stood guard in the hallway, he pushed open the door and stepped inside. Instantly his gaze went to Sally as she rose from the table, taking careful note of the empty plates and the lingering scent of apple pie.

Good, she'd eaten.

"Sally," he murmured. "This is Cyn."

She warily eyed the large vampire. "Cyn."

Cyn stepped forward, frigid tingles filling the air. "So you're the bitch who abused her powers and—"

Immediately Roke was in his friend's face, his fangs fully exposed.

"Don't."

"I told you this was a bad idea," Sally muttered from behind them.

Roke kept his gaze glued to Cyn. "I'm beginning to agree."

"You can't expect anyone to be happy you were shackled by a witch," Cyn snarled.

"Hey, he isn't the only one shackled," Sally groused, the scent of scorched peaches filling the air. "You think I'm any happier about this?"

Cyn glanced over Roke's shoulder to send Sally a disbelieving glare.

"Any female would be damned lucky to have a vampire as a mate."

"Oh yeah? Well for your information if anyone is lucky it's Roke," Sally countered, as willing as ever to spit in the face of danger. Or in this case, a lethal vampire. "I would make any man a fantastic mate."

Roke smiled wryly at his friend's astonished expression. Cyn could make grown trolls piss their pants with a single frown. He hadn't expected the fragile-looking female to fight back.

"Careful, Cyn. Her temper is like a loaded gun in the hands of a toddler," he murmured.

"You know what? Screw both of you," Sally hissed. "I don't need—"

He caught her as she headed toward the door leading onto the terrace. Gently turning her around, he ran soothing fingers up and down her arms.

"Sally, I know this is difficult, but I think it's important we find out what those glyphs mean."

She held herself stiff beneath his touch, battling against her desire to continue with her dramatic exit.

Typical.

Sally Grace made a habit of striking out and then fleeing.

She was a hit-and-run master.

Then, clearly forcing herself to remember she needed answers, she shoved the box into his hands.

"Here."

He leaned down to brush his lips over her troubled brow before turning to offer the box to the scowling Cyn.

Instantly the vampire's anger was replaced with wonder, his large hand cradling the box with ginger care as one finger lightly traced the glyphs.

"Astonishing."

"What's astonishing?" Roke prompted, knowing Cyn could become lost in his fascination with the carvings.

Few people knew that beneath Cyn's hunger for physical gratification was an even greater hunger for knowledge.

He was one of the few vampires with whom Roke could share his own fascination with history, which was the primary reason for their unlikely friendship.

"These are old," Cyn murmured, turning the box as he studied the flowing curves.

"I could tell that much." Roke leaned forward, a sudden chill inching down his spine at the realization the shimmer that glazed the glyphs had become more pronounced. And they were pulsing, as if they were connected to a heartbeat. "What do they say?"

"No, I mean these are really old." He lifted his head, the beads at the end of his narrow braids rattling as they banged against his chest. "Pre-Morgana."

"Morgana? Morgana le Fey?" Sally said in choked tones.

Roke grimaced, abruptly reminded of just how young she truly was.

For him Morgana le Fey was a part of his history, but to her the Queen of Fairies was no doubt a myth that had been lost in the mists of Avalon. Not that Morgana had ever been lost. Well, not until a few months ago when . . .

He gave a shake of his head, concentrating on Cyn.

"I know very little about fey history," he admitted.

"Few of us do." Cyn returned his attention to the box. "Before Morgana le Fey declared herself Queen of the Fairies they tended to be a secretive race."

Roke made a sound of disbelief. "I never thought I would hear *secretive* and *fey* in the same sentence."

"I said secretive, not shy," Cyn corrected. "I assume they were the same flamboyant exhibitionists in the privacy of their courts."

Roke had, of course, heard of the rumors of the fabulous fey courts that had long ago disappeared, although there had never been tangible proof they were more than legends.

"Why were they secretive?"

"The Chatri—"

"Chatri?" Roke interrupted.

"The original rulers of the fey. They considered themselves above the lesser demons."

"All demons considered themselves above other demons," Roke pointed out in dry tones.

"No shit," Sally added.

Cyn turned the box upside down, as if searching for a clue to its origins.

"The ancient fey took it to the extreme."

"How extreme?"

"Eventually they closed off their courts from the world."

That would explain why no one had proof of them, but it seemed a radical decision even for the fickle fey.

"They abandoned their own people?"

Cyn gave a lift of his shoulder. "Only they know the truth, but from the information I could gather I suspect that they considered themselves above the lesser fey."

Roke considered the large number of fey that populated the earth.

"That's taking elitism to the extreme."

Cyn gave an absent nod. "A decision that left the fey in this world vulnerable once Morgana le Fey took command."

Roke grimaced. Morgana le Fey had been a brutal leader, not to mention a sadistic bitch, who'd held hundreds of fairies and Sylvermysts as her sexual slaves.

"Nature detests a vacuum," he said.

Cyn glanced up, the jade eyes shimmering with curiosity. "Yes, which makes me wonder what sort of power struggle is going on in the fey world now. Do you suppose—"

"Does any of this explain what's written on the box?" Sally broke into their conversation, her expression tight with frustration.

Roke turned, reaching to grasp her hand. "Sorry, we have a mutual fascination with the past."

Cyn snorted. "Even if you're completely wrong about the contributing factors leading up to the troll wars."

Sally didn't look particularly interested in the troll wars. In fact, she looked like she wanted to thump both of them with a big stick.

"I'm a little more concerned with the future."

Roke nodded toward the box. "Cyn?"

The large vampire held out the box to point toward the glyphs that flowed across the lid.

"I can only decipher a few of the glyphs. This stands for king." His finger outlined a spiral with two dots in the center. "This is . . . door. An open door."

The symbol was similar to current fey glyphs. "A portal?"

"That would be my guess." Cyn moved his finger to the next glyph. "It's followed by a closed door. Like a prison."

"Maybe it's the story of the Chatri's retreat in this world," Roke suggested.

Cyn frowned. "Perhaps."

Roke followed his friend's gaze to the bottom of the lid where his finger was tracing symbol resembling a face.

"What?"

"This looks like the word for people, but . . ." The finger moved to a swirling line. "This is mist or fog. Mist people?" Cyn glanced at Roke. "Does that mean anything to you?"

Roke shook his head. "No. Wait—"

A small fragment of memory floated at the edge of his mind. Some piece of research he'd found in an obscure book about demons on the edge of extinction.

Before the memory could fully form there was a sharp knock on the door and Bliss's voice penetrated through the thick wood.

"Roke, I need to speak with you."

Roke yanked a dagger from the sheath at his lower back, not missing the edge of urgency in the female vampire's voice.

Glancing toward Cyn, he waited for the male to give a grudging nod, shifting his bulk between the door and the baffled Sally.

Whatever Cyn's feelings toward witches, he'd just agreed to fight to the death to protect her.

With his dagger clutched in his hand, Roke opened the door just far enough to slip into the hallway, firmly closing it behind him.

"What?" he demanded, frowning at Bliss before his gaze slid over her shoulder to spot the dozen nymphs who were kneeling at the end of the hall. "Shit. What the hell is going on?"

"Like I know?" Bliss waved scarlet-tipped fingers toward the mixture of male and female fey who had rapt expressions on their beautiful faces. "One minute the club was running smoothly and the next I find half my staff kneeling in the hall."

"What do they want?"

"They won't say. They kneel there like they've been enchanted." Bliss deliberately glanced toward the closed door. "Or more likely, bewitched."

Roke's protective instincts roared to high gear. This wasn't just some random coincidence.

Sally.

"Do you have a back exit?"

Bliss narrowed her eyes, clearly offended by the question. "Don't ask stupid questions."

Sally covertly put some space between herself and the behemoth of a vampire.

She was female enough to acknowledge he was a dazzlingly gorgeous behemoth. If a female enjoyed golden-haired warriors with eyes like jade and massive muscles. She happened to prefer slender, raven-haired men with mesmerizing silver eyes. . . .

Wait. No.

The point was, that while Cyn possessed more than his fair share of male beauty, he was also a bloodthirsty predator. And he obviously blamed her for mating Roke against his will.

The more space between them the better.

She'd reached the edge of the fire pit when the door was opened and Roke entered with the floozy female vampire.

Her fingers twitched, the urge to toss a spell that would shrivel Bliss's pale, perfect features like a prune nearly irresistible.

Thankfully, her inner bitch was distracted as Roke stepped toward her, his expression grim enough to warn her that he didn't have good news.

Not that she was surprised.

She couldn't remember the last time there had been any good news to share.

"What is it?" Her alarm spiked as Bliss headed directly to a far wall, touching a hidden lever. With a faint click a panel slid inward to reveal a dark tunnel. "Roke, what's going on?"

Sliding a protective arm around her shoulders, Roke urged her toward the opening.

"The locals have sensed your presence."

She frowned. "What locals?"

"The fey. A dozen nymphs are currently kneeling in the hallway."

Cyn made a sound of surprise while Sally felt a queasy fear roll through her gut.

"It could be the box, you know," she muttered.

"Either way the fey are beginning to attract attention," he said, his ruthless push toward the door saying loud and clear he didn't believe for a second the nymphs were interested in the box.

Her fear ratcheted up another notch.

"Do you think they're a danger?"

"I don't know, and until I'm certain, they're not getting near you."

They stepped into the tunnel only to be halted by Cyn.

"Can you protect her without me?" the large vampire demanded, shoving the box into Roke's hand.

"The day I can't protect what's mine I'll hang up my fangs," Roke growled.

"Good. I'll make sure you're not followed."

Roke placed a hand on Cyn's shoulder. "Thank you, old friend."

Cyn nodded, the thin braids brushing against his cheeks as he leaned down to speak in a low voice that wouldn't carry.

"Be careful, Roke," he warned. "The fey pretend to be brainless fools who think of nothing but pleasure, but there's a darkness just below the surface and powers they rarely reveal."

"I have no intention of taking unnecessary risks," Roke

promised, his gaze sliding toward Sally. "I can't say the same for my companion."

She narrowed her gaze. Jackass.

"Feel free to stay with your friend," she snapped. "I'm happy to be on my own."

The silver eyes flared with an unfathomable emotion. "Never again."

Sally found it oddly difficult to breathe as she became ensnared in his shimmering gaze, losing track of their surroundings until an impatient female voice sliced through the thick air.

"There will be a boat waiting for you."

Roke offered the woman a small dip of his head. "We're in your debt."

Bliss leaned forward to trail her lips down his cheek. "*You* certainly are."

"She—"

Without giving Sally the opportunity to react, Roke was hustling her down the tunnel that led to the edge of the island.

"Don't let her bother you," he muttered.

The very intensity of the need to go back and scratch out the female vampire's eyes made Sally grit her teeth.

She didn't want to feel this . . . insane jealousy.

"She doesn't," she forced herself to say, breathing hard as she struggled to keep up with his swift pace. "If she wants you, she can have you."

He shot her a brooding glance. "Liar."

She was.

But she'd be damned if she would admit it.

Instead, she clamped her lips together and allowed herself to be led to the end of the tunnel in silence.

She even managed to hold her tongue as she was tossed in the waiting motorboat that was swiftly slicing through the waves with a throaty power.

They slowed as they reached the rocky shoreline, but clearly too impatient to wait for the boat to come to a halt, Roke scooped her off her feet.

"Hold on."

It was her only warning before Roke was giving a mighty surge and they were flying through the salt-scented air.

Her arms instinctively wrapped around his neck as they landed on a protruding boulder. She expected a jolt that would send them tumbling back into the water.

Of course, she was in the arms of a vampire.

She barely felt his feet touch the ground before they were leaping upward again, climbing the steep cliff with an ease that a billy goat would envy.

In a matter of seconds they'd reached the top of the cliff and Sally shivered as a blast of icy air hit them. He tightened his arms around her as he raised his body temperature to keep her warm.

A part of her wanted to snuggle into that unexpected warmth. To press her face into the curve of his neck and allow his scent to soothe the lingering irritation that another woman had dared to touch him.

Another part was desperate to regain some sense of control over the mind-numbing chaos that was now her life.

"Roke," she said, angling her head to study his stark profile as he cut a fluid path through the thickening trees. "Wait."

His steps never faltered. Typical.

"We need to hurry."

"Hurry to where?"

His lips twisted. "What choice do we have?"

It took her a confused minute to shuffle through the meaning of his obscure words.

It was only when she noticed the stubborn angle of his jaw that the truth hit her.

"No," she rasped. "I've told you, I'm not going to Nevada."

The silver eyes blazed in the moonlight. "It's the only place we can be safe."

"Yeah, that's what I thought when I went to Styx," she hissed.

He muttered a low curse, clearly annoyed by her refusal to forgive and forget her treatment at the hands of his Anasso.

"You are a stranger. And a witch," he said, his gaze searching the darkness for any hint of danger. "Styx was naturally suspicious."

"And now I'm naturally suspicious," she mutinously countered. "'Fool me once' and all that crap."

"So what do you suggest?" He slowed his pace so he could glare down at her stubborn expression. "That we run around in circles?"

She met his smoldering gaze.

For once, she'd actually given it some thought.

"Obviously we need to find a fey that we can trust to tell us what the hell is going on."

He showed a hint of fang. "There's no such thing as a trustworthy fey."

The whiff of granite was the only warning before the tiny gargoyle fluttered down from the branch of a nearby tree.

"I can, perhaps, be of service."

"Shit." In one dizzying movement Roke had Sally lowered to the ground, shoving her behind him so his hands were free to destroy the latest threat. Even if that threat was only three feet tall. "Where did you come from?"

Levet gave a flap of his wings, impervious as ever to the danger coating the air with ice.

"From there." He pointed toward a claw near the top of the tree. "I have been waiting for you to leave the island."

"How did you . . ." Roke gave a sharp shake of his head, pausing as if he were silently counting to ten. Sally was fairly certain he'd better make it a hundred. Levet seemed to aggravate the vampire without even trying. "I thought you were chasing after your female?"

"Yannah sent me back to you."

"Why?"

Levet sniffed, a petulant expression on his ugly gray features.

"Who knows why a woman does anything? The workings of the female mind are beyond comprehension."

"Preaching to the choir," Roke muttered.

Sally smacked him in the middle of the back.

"Careful," she muttered, glancing around his shoulder to peer at the gargoyle. "You said you could help?"

"*Oui.*" Levet's expression brightened. "I am acquainted with an imp who might be of service."

"What imp?" she asked.

"Troy, the Prince of Imps. He resides in Chicago."

Chapter Ten

Roke once again had Sally in his arms as they dashed over the rocky ground, stoically ignoring Levet who struggled to keep pace beside him.

His first impulse had been to run off the miniature gargoyle.

There was no way in hell he could endure his presence for another road trip.

But, he was vampire enough to admit that Levet's unexpected arrival had worked in his own favor.

After all, there was no way in hell he would ever have convinced Sally to return to Chicago without the gargoyle suggesting the imp could be of assistance. And while he was no happier about the thought of allowing her anywhere near the fey, they would at least have the protection of the King of Vampires and his Ravens.

That Roke would insist on.

They were nearing the edge of a small town when Sally stirred restlessly in his arms.

"We can't run all the way to Chicago."

"I don't intend to." He sent his winged companion a stern gaze. "Gargoyle?"

Levet wrinkled his heavy brow. "What?"

"You took off on our only source of transportation."

"Ah . . . *oui*."

His wings seemed to droop. No doubt the little thief hoped that Roke was too distracted to remember he'd taken off with his precious bike.

"This way."

Surprisingly, Levet headed directly toward the town. Roke assumed he would have hidden the bike in the thick underbrush at the edge of the woods.

Why risk leaving it so close to the humans?

Then, halting at a small house that was nearly hidden in the shadows of an abandoned gas station, the gargoyle stood in front of the attached garage and gave a dramatic wave of his hands.

"Ta-da."

Roke moved forward only to come to a baffled halt at the sight of the battered Fiesta that consumed the cramped space.

"What the hell is this?"

Levet shifted from foot to foot, clearing his throat.

"I should think it is obvious. You desire transportation and I have provided it." He gave another wave of his hands. "Ta-da."

Roke carefully set Sally on her feet, already knowing the gargoyle was about to piss him off.

"Where's my motorcycle?"

Levet managed a sickly smile. "A motorcycle is not precisely built for three. This is far more sensible."

"It's a piece of shit." Roke narrowed his gaze. "Now where is my bike?"

"I can locate another vehicle. . . ." Levet's eyes widened as Roke yanked him off the ground by one horn. "Eek!"

Holding the creature at eye level, Roke spoke with a cold precision.

"Where. Is. My. Bike?"

The gargoyle turned from gray to a strange shade of oyster.

"There might have been a teeny-tiny accident."

The nearby garage creaked as Roke's temper threatened to explode.

Only another bike-man could understand his rising fury.

"If you put so much as a scratch on my bike, I'll rip off your wings."

The idiotic demon folded his arms over his chest, trying to pretend he wasn't dangling by one horn.

"I will have you know I did you a favor. That . . ." He struggled for the proper word. "Death trap was not fit for the road." He waved a hand toward the Fiesta. "While this is obviously a classic."

"I'll kill you—" Roke began, knowing beyond a doubt the jackass had destroyed his pride and joy.

But even as his power swirled through the air there was a light touch on his arm. Instantly he was distracted, his entire being focused on the exquisite woman at his side.

It was . . . unnerving.

As if she had become hardwired to his emotional grid.

"Could we fight about this later?" she asked softly.

"*Oui,*" the gargoyle hurriedly agreed. "Later."

He met Sally's dark gaze, giving a slow nod of his head. "Fine. We'll take this until we can find something better."

He moved to pull open the passenger door of the sorry excuse for a car, settling Sally before moving to the driver's side. He was about to slide behind the steering wheel when he halted to grab the gargoyle who was hopping into the backseat.

"Not you," he growled.

"Roke," Sally chastised.

This time he refused to be distracted. The damned pest had destroyed a quarter-of-a-million-dollar bike.

He was lucky he was still in one lumpy piece.

"He can stay behind and disguise our trail," he said, holding Levet's gaze so there would be no misunderstanding.

"But—"

"I am, as ever, delighted to play the role of knight in shining armor," Levet interrupted Sally's protest, backing away with a speed that revealed he wasn't entirely stupid. "It does appear to be my destiny."

"Christ," Roke muttered, stuffing his six-foot-plus frame into the car.

"*Au revoir, mademoiselle,* I shall rejoin you in Chicago," the gargoyle called as Roke swiped his fingers over the steering column, sparking the engine to life.

They chugged out of the garage, Roke cursing the pathetic vehicle while Sally automatically fastened her seat belt.

Once away from the town, he pressed the accelerator to the floor, not surprised when the car barely managed to hit the speed limit.

Still, they were headed in the right direction, and at least for now there wasn't a fey or weird-ass demon in sight.

Hitting the main road leading south, Roke glanced toward his oddly silent companion, his heart clenching with concern at the tension that tightened her pale profile.

"Sally, are you hurt?"

Her gaze remained trained on the narrow road. "I'm tired."

He resisted the urge to trace the pure line of her throat. He'd always possessed a perfect, ruthless control. It'd been the only way to survive as his clan collapsed around him.

But now he was on edge, his nerves raw and exposed. He wasn't sure he could touch Sally without offering more than simple comfort.

"Then rest," he murmured, his voice thick with a hunger that was increasingly difficult to ignore.

"No." She shivered, waving a hand toward the windshield. "I meant I'm tired of this."

He frowned, scanning the empty countryside.

"Perhaps you should be more specific."

Her hand dropped, as if she were too weary to hold it up.

"The running. The hiding." She rested her head against the side window. "The never feeling safe."

His gut twisted. She sounded so . . . defeated.

Nothing at all like his stubborn, spit-in-the-face-of-death witch.

"Sally, we'll figure this out," he assured her, slowing the car to make sure he didn't hit a bump that would bang her head against the window.

At the moment she didn't look capable of protecting herself from the smallest hurt.

"You think so?" she whispered.

"You don't?"

She gave a lift of one shoulder, silent for so long that Roke thought she had fallen asleep.

Then softly her words filled the small space.

"After my mother tried to kill me I swore that I would never be a victim again. That's why I became a disciple for the Dark Lord. I was convinced I would be protected." She gave a short, humorless laugh. "You know how that turned out for me." Roke watched the pain ripple over her delicate face and he was fairly certain that he knew only a small fraction of what it had cost her to pledge her soul to the evil bastard. "Then I stupidly turned to the vampires for help only to end up locked in the dungeons and mated to you." Her hand shifted to rub her inner arm. The mating mark. "Of course, I couldn't be satisfied with those major screwups. I had to go in search of my father, like I thought I could actually accomplish something." Another of those sharp laughs. "Now look at me. I'm some sort of fey-magnet and on the run again. You were right. I am a walking disaster."

Roke floundered.

He wasn't a touchy-feely guy.

Hell, the thought of touchy-feely made him break out in hives.

But he couldn't bear the wistful resignation that was pulsing through his bond with Sally.

"All those times you were alone," he said, his voice harsh. "You're not alone anymore."

She kept her eyes on the road. "I feel alone."

The words made him flinch. As if she'd hit him dead center with a sledgehammer.

He'd done that.

He wanted her to trust him, but he hadn't been willing to offer his own trust.

Now she couldn't turn to him for the comfort she so obviously needed.

"Sally." She refused to glance in his direction and he bit back a curse. "Close your eyes and relax, this is going to be a long drive," he murmured.

For once she didn't argue. He wished she would. Instead she allowed her lashes to lower and she disappeared into her dark thoughts.

Roke gripped the sticky wheel and forced himself to concentrate on the barren landscape.

Until he had someplace where he could be certain they were safe, his number one priority was protecting his mate.

Sally abruptly wrenched open her eyes as she felt the car come to a halt.

Good lord, had she been asleep?

She'd only closed her eyes to try to block out the aggravating vampire beside her. Roke was disturbing enough when she had her barriers in place. He was overwhelming when her emotions were scraped raw.

Now she struggled to clear the fog from her mind as her door was pulled open and Roke was helping her stumble out of her seat and across the graveled lot.

"Where are we?" she demanded, her gaze taking in the roadside café.

Built of white stone with large windows, it looked like something out of a fifties sitcom. It even came complete with a blinding neon sign that she would swear could be seen from the space station.

She squinted, tilting back her head to meet Roke's watchful gaze.

"You need to eat," he murmured.

"And you chose a human restaurant?"

"Do witches have their own chain of restaurants?" His impassive expression was impossible to read. "Jack in the Cauldron?"

She made a sound of disbelief. "Was that a joke?"

The silver eyes shimmered with a breathtaking beauty. "I have my moments."

Her heart slammed against her ribs, vividly recalling a few of his finer moments.

His strong arms wrapped around her. The press of fangs against her neck. The agonizing pleasure of his tongue stroking her to climax.

She stumbled before stiffening her spine.

Dammit.

She'd promised herself that she wasn't going to let him get under her skin.

Not again.

"If you say so," she muttered.

His lips twisted with rueful humor. "Has anyone told you that you're crabby when you're hungry?"

"I'm even crabbier when I want to kick someone in the nuts."

"Harsh," he murmured, something that might have been . . . satisfaction . . . on his face.

As if he was pleased by her peevish threat.

Lunatic vampire.

Accepting she would never understand the impossible man, she turned her attention to her surroundings.

"Where are we?"

"We're near the border."

She blinked in shock. If they were at the border, then that meant they'd been driving for hours.

"I can't believe I slept so long."

"You've been driving yourself too hard," he said as they reached the café, his smile fading as he studied her upturned face. "Will you eat?"

Her stomach growled before her pride could deny the hunger that was clearly determined to make up for lost time.

She rolled her eyes in resignation. "Yes."

"Good."

Roke pushed open the glass door to the diner, his gaze searching the empty tables arranged around the linoleum floor for signs of danger.

Once assured there was nothing more alarming than a middle-aged waitress with a stout body stuffed into a white uniform and bleached hair pulled into a knot on top of her head, he urged her over the threshold.

Sally caught a glimpse of a long counter with stools at the back of the room, with a glass case that displayed an assortment of desserts.

"No apple pie," Roke murmured softly.

Sally's mouth watered at the scents that filled the air. "No, but on the plus side, there's cheesecake."

"Hello." The waitress sashayed forward, her avid gaze drinking in Roke with open appreciation. Not that Sally could blame the poor woman. Men like Roke didn't stroll into isolated cafés except in porn movies. "Can I help you?"

Roke placed an arm around Sally's shoulders, visibly claiming them as a couple. It should have annoyed the hell out of her, but for some stupid reason, Sally didn't even try to pull away.

"A booth with a view," he ordered.

The woman sent Sally an envious glare before turning to lead them toward a far table.

Roke pulled out a chair, making sure that Sally was comfortable before taking his own seat, which offered a view of both the parking lot and the empty lot next them.

The waitress tossed a laminated menu that offered a handwritten list of the breakfast food on the table.

"Coffee?"

"We'll take one of everything," Roke murmured, his gaze never straying from Sally's face. "Start with the cheesecake and a glass of milk."

The waitress choked on her gum. "Everything?"

Roke at last glanced toward the woman, his gaze glowing with a power that had the woman instantly enthralled.

"Is that a problem?"

"No, no problem," the woman instantly denied, the trance allowing her to fulfill her duties on autopilot while remaining oblivious to what Roke and Sally might say or do.

It was an old vampire trick. Once they left the restaurant the woman wouldn't remember they'd been there.

Waiting until the older woman had moved away, Sally regarded Roke's tense profile as he peered out the window.

"Do you think we're being followed?"

"I always assume there's a possibility for an attack," he confessed. "Besides, we need to keep a watch on the local fey. It's hard to keep a low profile with a dozen fairies kneeling in the parking lot."

She flinched at the reminder they were suddenly being plagued by the fey.

"It's not my fault."

Without warning he jerked his head back to meet her defensive glare.

"No, it's not," he said in a fierce voice. "Neither were any of the other bad things that have happened in your life." He reached to grasp her hand. "So stop blaming yourself."

His unexpected words caught her off guard.

Did she blame herself?

It was a question she'd never truly considered.

She grimaced, struck by an unwelcome memory of hiding in a moldy crypt after she'd run away from her mother, cursing her demon blood.

She'd been convinced that if her father had only been human she would never have been forced from her home or become a persona non grata of witch covens everywhere.

She hadn't been good enough.

She wouldn't ever be good enough.

With a small movement she pulled away from his lingering touch, disturbed by Roke's unnerving ability to see past the walls she'd so carefully constructed.

Being exposed meant being vulnerable to danger.

"You blame me," she accused, stubbornly going on the attack rather than admit he might have a point. "At least for the mating."

"Sally—"

His words broke off as the waitress returned to set a plate of cheesecake on the table along with a tall glass of milk.

Eagerly, Sally lowered her head and dug into the food.

When she had a choice between prodding at unhealed wounds or enjoying silky, creamy cheesecake . . . yeah, no contest.

The cheesecake was going to win every time.

Roke waited for Sally to polish off the dessert and start on the plate of scrambled eggs and bacon that arrived next.

Only when it became obvious she intended to try to block him out completely did he reach across the table to lightly touch her arm.

"Sally, look at me."

She went rigid beneath his touch, grudgingly lifting her head to meet his searching gaze.

"What?"

He held her wary gaze, forcing the words past his lips. "It's difficult for me to discuss the death of my chief."

She blinked, clearly caught off guard by his confession before she was smoothing her expression to one of faux indifference.

"Yeah, you've made that perfectly clear," she muttered. "I understand you were close to him."

"It's not that." He grimaced. "Or at least that's not the whole story."

She shrugged. "You don't have to tell me."

"I don't *have* to, I *want* to."

She stared at him, her dark eyes too large for her pale face and her stoic composure unable to hide the fragility just below the surface.

"Fine."

He turned his head to stare out the window, keeping watch on their surroundings as he struggled past his instinctive need to keep the past locked away.

"My sire, Fala, was unusual for a vampire."

"Unusual?" Sally prompted.

"She believed that she could read portents revealed by nature."

"Could she?"

His lips twisted. Fala had thoroughly enjoyed her role as mystic for the clan. Roke had simply enjoyed knowing his beloved sire was happy.

"She had an uncanny knack of being right more often than not," he said.

"Did she pass the talent onto you?"

"No." The vivid memory of Fala standing in the middle of the desert, her dark hair flowing down her back and her sloe eyes narrowed as she studied the formation of rocks or the precise speckles on a bird's egg, sent a pain slashing through his heart. Their bond had been more than sire and foundling. She had been his teacher, his protector, and in some strange way, his mother. "Fala managed to teach me to decipher glyphs and trained me in most of the known demon languages, but I had no talent for her mystic readings."

He turned back as the waitress returned with a tray of pancakes, biscuits, hash browns, and fried pierogies.

They waited until the woman had once again retreated before Sally buttered a biscuit and studied him from beneath lowered lashes.

"Did her mystic readings involve you?"

He wasn't surprised by her perceptive guess. Sally had spent a lot of years in the shadows, studying the people around her so she would always be one step ahead of the danger.

"On the night Fala sired me, she witnessed a comet shoot through the sky."

She finished the biscuit and started to smear something on the pancakes. God almighty, was that peanut butter?

"What does that mean?"

"She interpreted it as a sign that I would one day be a great leader."

The tiny witch actually began to demolish the large stack of gummy pancakes.

"That seems like a good thing."

"I never gave it much thought," he admitted. "Not until my chief, Gunnar, mated."

She abruptly glanced up. "That's why you went to the battles."

He gave a slow nod.

His first thought had been to simply leave the clan and find another.

It wasn't that he was afraid. Not of the battles or challenging his chief. But Gunnar had become a true friend, before his mating.

It'd been Fala who'd pointed out that by fleeing the territory they would leave the rest of the clan at the mercy of the slavers who made a routine habit of picking off the more vulnerable members.

She reminded him of her vision and insisted it was his duty to take care of those who were too weak to run.

"I had to do something before the clan was completely destroyed," he said. "Once I completed the trials I intended to return and challenge Gunnar to become chief."

She unconsciously licked a dab of peanut butter off her lower lip, and Roke's aversion to the brown paste was suddenly replaced by a compelling vision of spreading it across his body so that tiny, wet tongue could spend an hour or six licking it off him.

"Obviously you succeeded."

"No." His distraction was only momentary as he was forced to remember his shock when he'd arrived home. "When I returned to Nevada it was to discover Gunnar and his mate had died in a fire."

She slowly pushed aside her plate, sensing his long-buried pain through their bond.

"Despite the tragedy, it must have been a relief not to have to challenge him."

He clenched his hand on the table, the force of his bleak emotions making the windowpane tremble.

"It would have been if I hadn't suspected that Gunnar's timely death hadn't been an accident."

Her eyes widened. "Murder?"

He nodded, although a vampire didn't have that particular word in their vocabulary.

Until the previous Anasso had taken command of the vampires they'd been little more than brutal savages who took what they wanted without consequences.

That's why it was imperative that a vampire become a member of a clan with a strong chief who could protect them.

"Yes."

She tilted her head to the side, the threads of bronze and gold in her hair shimmering beneath the fluorescent lights.

"Was there another contender to the throne?"

He shrugged. Only a vampire with the mark of CuChulainn could claim the right to become clan chief.

"None that had survived the battles."

She frowned. "Then it was an enemy?"

"Only one that could have walked past the guards."

There was a long pause as she studied his grim expression. "You know who it was, don't you?"

"Fala."

She sucked in a shocked breath. "Oh."

Fine cracks began to form on the table where his fist rested against the cheap Formica.

"She had convinced herself that my glorious destiny needed a helping hand."

"Were you angry with her?"

"I was disappointed she didn't trust my ability to win a fair fight against Gunnar."

Her well-guarded expression at last softened, her hand reaching to lightly touch his clenched fist.

"Have you considered the fact that might not be about trust?"

He scowled. "Then what?"

"Maybe she wanted to spare you the trauma of killing a man you once respected. That's what a mother does." Her eyes abruptly hardened at the thought of her own mother. "Well, at least, I suppose that's what a mother would do if she wasn't a psychopath."

He inwardly cursed, turning his hand so he could capture her chilled fingers.

He'd revealed his past in an effort to earn her trust, not to bring up old wounds.

"Sally—"

"What happened to her?" she firmly interrupted.

His gaze shifted to where her pale fingers remained in his tight grip, absorbing the tactile connection. Her warmth was the only thing that allowed him to speak past the cold regret that surged through him.

"Not long after Gunnar's death she met her ancestors."

"What does that mean?"

"She greeted the dawn," he said, his tone stripped of emotions. Not that he could hide the intense pain he'd felt when he watched Fala step from their lair into the morning sunlight. He'd never truly forgiven himself for being too far away to save her. "Most assumed that she'd tired of her very long life. It's not that uncommon among the very ancient."

Genuine sympathy darkened Sally's velvet eyes. As much as she longed to be a callous badass, her vulnerable heart would always betray her.

Of course, it was that very vulnerability that constantly managed to unman him, he ruefully conceded.

"But you didn't believe that?" she asked softly.

"I've always feared it was guilt."

Without warning her brows snapped together. "No."

"No?"

She squeezed his fingers. "Fala sounds as if she was a strong woman who firmly believed in fate," she insisted.

He gave a slow nod. "She was."

"Then she would have considered her choice a matter of destiny."

"Or desperation."

"Roke, if she truly had faith in her visions, then she had faith in you." She leaned forward, her expression one of utter certainty. "Whatever led her into the sun, it wasn't guilt."

Roke became lost in the dark beauty of her eyes, the

gnawing fear that he'd been responsible for Fala's death easing at the certainty in her voice.

How many years had he punished himself with the fear that Fala had to betray her own honor to protect him?

It'd been a constant source of shame.

Now, with a few simple words, Sally had given him the courage to remember Fala as a proud, fearless vampire who accepted her duty, just as Roke had accepted his.

It was a gift that was beyond price.

He lowered his head in a gesture of profound respect.

"Thank you."

Chapter Eleven

Sally managed to eat through most of the menu before she at last shoved aside the plates, sighing in relief.

Or at least she told herself that it was the vast mounds of food that had lightened her mood and caused the strange flutters in the pit of her stomach.

Otherwise she'd have to admit that Roke's unexpected glimpse into his tormented past had broken through her defenses with an ease that should terrify her.

She didn't want to ache at the thought of him being haunted by the memory of the woman who had sired him, or blaming himself for her death.

And she certainly didn't want to feel the prickles of electric excitement at his casual touches. Really was there any need to brush a stray crumb from her finger, or tuck a curl behind her ear?

It was much better to pretend that nothing had altered between them.

As if to mock her ridiculous decision, Roke reached across the table, his fingers a soft caress as they touched her face.

"You have some color back in your cheeks," he murmured, a satisfied smile curving his lips.

With a sudden need to distract her odd mood, Sally slid out of her seat and deliberately glanced toward the window.

"It won't be long until dawn. Shouldn't we be finding someplace to stay?"

The silver eyes studied her with a hint of puzzlement as he rose to his feet.

"I called the local clan chief before we reached the café and he offered us a safe house not far from here."

She wrinkled her nose. She'd been on the run most of her life, so it wasn't like she wasn't used to going for weeks without a hint of luxury. That didn't mean, however, she had to like it.

"Another safe house?"

"I have hopes this one will provide a few more amenities," he said in sympathy. "Are you ready?"

She shrugged, rubbing her hands up and down her upper arms as a growing sense of restlessness tingled through her.

"As ready as I'll ever be."

Tossing money on the table, Roke led her out of the café and toward the car parked in the center of the lot.

"Pathetic," he muttered, shaking his head.

With a jolt of surprise, Sally realized that she'd fallen a step behind Roke, her gaze glued to his rock-hard ass shown to perfection in the faded jeans.

Cursing her increasingly strange mood, she jerked her head up and prayed he hadn't noticed her lingering stare.

"What's pathetic?"

"This . . ." He waved a slender hand toward the car. "Piece of shit." He gave another soulful shake of his head. "We need a new ride."

She arched a brow. "Are you one of those men who need an expensive ride to make him feel macho?"

With a fluid motion he turned, his hand cupping her chin as he studied her upturned face.

"I've never had a problem with macho, but I do have a

problem with riding around in a tin can." His gaze lowered to her unsteady lips, perhaps realizing she'd lost track of his words. Awareness sizzled in the air, sending a dangerous, melting heat through her blood. Then, with a hiss, Roke's attention shifted toward the nearby trees. "Get in the car."

She didn't hesitate.

Dashing around the hood of the car, she yanked open the door and slid inside. She managed to get the door shut, but she was still struggling with her seat belt when Roke had the motor started and was shoving the car into gear.

She clenched her teeth as they bounced through potholes large enough to swallow the tiny car.

"What is it?"

"Fairies."

She shivered, shifting to peer out the back window. "Are they following us?"

"No, they're watching from the woods," he muttered, pulling onto a narrow path instead of the main road. "At least for now."

They jolted down the pathway at a speed that threatened to rattle the car into scrap metal, but Sally didn't complain. She was as anxious as Roke to reach the protection of the vampire lair.

Roke took two more turns, each one taking them farther from civilization. Just as Sally was about to accuse Roke of refusing to admit he was lost, they came around a corner to halt in front of a large log cabin nearly hidden in the trees.

"Wait here," Roke murmured, sliding out of the car and disappearing among the shadows.

It took him less than five minutes to make a complete sweep of the area before he was returning to the car and leading her into the house.

Keeping a watch on the nearby trees, Sally hardly noticed the wide terrace or the heavy steel door that swung open after Roke had punched in a series of numbers.

It wasn't until she'd stepped over the threshold that she took stock of the actual house.

Her eyes widened as she took in the large great-room that was paneled in a dark, glossy wood. The floors were made of flagstone, matching the fireplace that towered toward the twelve-foot ceiling. Heavy leather sofas and chairs were arranged throughout the long room with a chandelier made from some sort of antlers spilling a soft glow over the entire space.

And peering down from the walls were a half dozen stuffed animal heads mounted on wood placards.

Yeesh.

It looked like a hunting lodge for one of the Rich and Famous, not a supersecret vampire lair.

"This is a safe house?" she demanded.

He shut and locked the door. "Most vampires enjoy their comforts, although there are a few who still prefer isolated caves and a ban on all technology."

She turned her attention to watch as he moved through the room, touching a keypad on the far wall that turned on the monitors that were obviously connected to the security system.

Although he was dressed in modern jeans and a heavy motorcycle jacket, there was something raw and untamed about his dark beauty.

It was etched into the stark features that were framed by the silken ebony of his hair and the feral grace of his movements.

And those astonishing eyes . . .

He was a hunter who would never be entirely civilized.

"Including you?"

He sent her an exasperated glance. "Why do I sense you're convinced I live in a teepee in the middle of the desert?"

She frowned. Was he offended? Impossible. His skin was as thick as a rhino's.

"You don't seem the type to feel comfortable being surrounded by . . ." She waved a hand around the large room. "This."

He wrinkled his nose. "I'll admit I prefer less wood. And I try to avoid dead animals staring at me from the walls."

"No shit." She glanced toward a moose that was eyeballing her with what felt like accusation. "They're freaking me out."

Roke moved to stand directly in front of her, gently adjusting the neckline of her sweatshirt before smoothing her hair behind her ear, as if he desperately needed the small, unnecessary touches.

"There are bedrooms upstairs," he said, his expression carefully guarded even as his fingers traced the shell of her ear. "I know you're probably not tired right now, but Alexei promised the rooms were fully equipped with TVs and attached bathrooms. There's also a kitchen that's kept stocked with human food."

Sally shivered, nearly overwhelmed by the urge to press herself against his hard body.

Dammit.

She'd done so well keeping her intense need for him locked behind a frosty wall of offended anger. She'd allowed him into her bed once and what had it gotten her?

A door slammed in her face, that's what.

But trying to nurse that sense of injustice was suddenly an impossible task.

Not only because he'd given her a glimpse of the lonely man who'd tortured himself for years, perhaps centuries, over the death of his sire. But because she wanted him.

That simple.

She wanted to shove her fingers into the satin darkness of his hair. She wanted to strip off his clothes and kiss a path over his hard, perfectly chiseled body. She wanted to wrap her lips around his hard cock before he was shoving her flat on her back and plunging so deep into her that she cried out his name.

Abruptly realizing he was studying her with eyes that had gone smoky with an answering need, Sally took a step back and tried to pretend that she wasn't aching to feel those extended fangs plunged into her neck.

"What about you?"

His hungry gaze skimmed over her face before lowering to the exposed column of her neck.

"The sunproof rooms are in the basement."

"No, I meant—" Heat filled her cheeks.

"What?"

She licked her lips. "Dinner."

Her hair was tugged by a burst of chilled air as Roke struggled to contain his fierce need to pounce.

"There will be blood kept in the lower rooms."

Her gaze dropped beneath the scorching need that smoldered in his gaze.

This was insanity.

Just because Roke had allowed her to see past his grim exterior didn't change anything.

How could it?

They were still bound together by magic she didn't understand.

They were still on the run from a crazy-ass demon and fairies who may or may not want her dead.

And he was still a chief who had pledged his loyalty to a clan who would never, ever accept her as his mate.

"Of course," she muttered.

His finger slid beneath her chin to tilt her face up to meet his suddenly worried gaze.

"Sally, what's wrong?"

Wrong? She bit back a hysterical laugh.

What was wrong was that she was being burned alive by a craving that threatened to overwhelm her.

"Nothing." She wiped her damp palms on her jeans, well aware her arousal was scenting the air. "I think I'll check out the kitchen."

His gaze settled on the unsteady curve of her lips. "Hungry already?"

"No, but I want to see if there are enough ingredients to brew a few protective spells."

He frowned. "The spells—"

"Nothing dangerous," she said. "I swear."

He paused, searching her wary expression as if hoping to find . . .

She wasn't entirely certain what he was looking for, but he obviously failed to find it as he dropped his hand and stepped back.

"Don't try to leave the house." He nodded toward the monitors displaying images of the thick trees that circled the house. "The security alarms are set."

Stupidly she found herself disappointed at his easy retreat. What did she want?

For him to ignore her don't-touch-me vibes? To force her to overcome her logic and ease her gnawing frustration?

Christ. She was a mess.

It was a wonder the poor man hadn't dumped her along the side of the road for his own sanity.

She hunched a shoulder. "I'm not going to take off."

"Good. For better or worse, we're in this together."

"For now."

His lips twisted into a humorless smile. "I'll be downstairs." He reached beneath his jacket to pull out the music box. "Do you want me to lock this in a safe?"

She reached to take it, feeling the magic wrap around her with a sense of pleasure.

Perhaps she should be worried by her growing delight in the surge of rich, potent power that raced through her as she traced one of the mysterious hieroglyphs, but it felt so utterly natural it was difficult to imagine it was dangerous.

"No, I'll keep it with me."

Roke hesitated, as if he wanted to say something. Or maybe he wanted her to say something.

Maybe to ask him to stay?

When she kept her eyes averted, he muttered something in a low voice and turned to make his way toward the staircase that led to the lower floors.

As she felt the chill of his presence disappear, Sally heaved a deep sigh and headed toward the kitchen.

She'd hoped Roke's departure would ease the restless frustration that was plaguing her. Instead, it only intensified it.

Unless she intended to follow him to his private rooms and fulfill her vivid fantasies, she needed to keep her hands busy and her mind occupied.

Roke went through the motions.

He fed from the bags of blood kept in a refrigerated safe hidden in the wall. He showered and changed into a black satin robe that had been left in the closet. Then he forced himself to lie on the king-size bed that dominated the wood paneled room.

He was too old a vampire to need sleep, but he did need to rest to replenish his powers.

So while he tended to his physical needs, his mind remained consumed with the female who he could feel moving through the house above him.

Her first destination was the kitchen where the smell of herbs mixed with her intoxicating peach scent that seemed to grow more vibrant and complex with every beat of her heart.

Hours passed before he at last heard her heading up the stairs and stepping into the shower. He growled low in his throat at the thought of her standing naked beneath the cascade of hot water.

He'd been in a constant state of arousal since he'd caught the subtle shift in Sally's awareness of him.

Sitting across the table in that café, he'd been painfully aware the second her pulse had picked up and her eyes had dilated.

And even now, her desire hummed through their mating bond, calling to him like a siren's song.

But as revved as he might be to satisfy their mutual hunger, he hadn't missed her tension.

She wanted him.

But she wasn't yet prepared to trust him.

And between the two, it was her trust he most needed.

How else could he protect her?

All very noble, he acknowledged with clenched teeth, but painful as hell. It was no wonder saints always looked like pious sourpusses in their paintings.

Blue balls would do that to the most heroic man.

Waiting until he felt her crawl into bed and tumble into sleep, Roke rose from the mattress and began to methodically clean his guns.

It was a task that kept his hands occupied, but his mind free to work through his tangled thoughts.

The sun was setting when he felt a tingle of fear race through the mating bond followed by a hoarse female cry.

Instantly he was on his feet, allowing his senses to spread through the house as he raced up the steps.

He could detect no intruders, but that didn't halt him from vaulting up the second flight of steps with a blinding speed, the gun he'd just loaded held in one hand and his fangs fully extended.

Exploding into Sally's room, he came to an abrupt halt, his brows drawing together as he realized that she wasn't being attacked.

In fact, she remained deeply asleep on the large bed.

He grimaced, about to back out of the room when she twisted onto her back, revealing the sweat coating her face.

"No," she moaned in a tortured voice. "Leave me alone. Please . . . please."

Roke moved forward, his heart clenching as he watched her struggle against an unseen foe.

"Shh, my love," he murmured, joining her on the bed and pulling her into his arms. "I've got you."

She thrashed against him, whimpering in fear until he lowered his head and brushed a soft kiss against her forehead.

"Roke?"

"Easy, love," he husked, his hand running a gentling path up and down her back.

"Roke?" Slowly she lifted her lashes to reveal her eyes still dark with terror. "What happened?"

He tucked her tight against his chest left bare by his gaping robe.

"You were having a bad dream."

"Oh." She shuddered, sucking in a deep breath. "I'm sorry."

"Don't apologize," he said, pressing a finger to her lips. "Tell me why you were screaming."

Her lashes lowered, as if hoping to disguise her lingering unease.

"It doesn't matter," she said, her tone fierce, as if she was trying to convince herself. "It's over."

"I shared my nightmare," he reminded her, using the tip of his finger to trace the line of her lower lip. "It won't bring Fala back, but it did allow me to accept her death without the bitterness that has been destroying me. Sometimes a wound has to be lanced before it can truly heal."

Thankfully his low words seemed to offer a measure of comfort, and he could feel her tension easing as she nestled her head against the width of his chest.

"Maybe this wound shouldn't heal."

"I don't believe that." He leaned down to give the lobe of her ear a punishing nip. "Tell me."

She grudgingly tilted back her head to meet his steady gaze.

"The Dark Lord."

Roke brushed the damp strands of her hair from her face, already having expected what tormented her.

"He's dead, Sally. He can't hurt you anymore."

"I know that logically, but—"

He stroked his fingers down her throat. "But?"

Another shiver wracked her slender body. "Do you know why the Dark Lord accepted me as a disciple?"

He settled back against the headboard, cradling her shivering body in his lap.

"I assume it has something to do with the fact that you happen to be one of the most powerful witches ever born?"

"I'm not sure if that's a compliment or an insult."

He brushed his lips over the top of her head. "I'm not sure either," he admitted wryly. "You terrify the hell out of me."

She gave a shaken laugh before she was sucking in a steadying breath.

"I was still on the run, trying to hide from the witches my mother had sent to trace me when the Dark Lord . . . contacted me. He said I possessed a talent that no one else had."

Roke grimaced. He was familiar enough with the evil deity to know the bastard no doubt smashed into poor Sally's mind with the force of a cement truck.

"What was your talent?"

"I was a conduit."

Roke frowned. "What's a conduit?"

Her hand gripped his upper arm, her heart pounding at the memory.

"The Dark Lord could speak directly through me," she

rasped. "I had a direct connection so he could use me like I was his personal cell phone."

"Shit." He slid his lips to her temple, his arms wrapping around her as if he could take away the horror. He'd been wrong. The Dark Lord hadn't been like a cement truck in her brain. He'd been a constant, pulsing, malevolent force. "I'm so sorry, Sally. I wish I could scrub away the memories." His lips moved to her cheek. "Actually, if you weren't so damned powerful I could scrub them."

"No." Her hand unconsciously smoothed up his arm to his shoulder. "I need to remember the danger of putting my fate in someone else's hands."

Roke glanced toward the heavens. Of course she would use the memory of her brutal enslavement by the Dark Lord to try to build an even greater wall between them.

"Putting yourself in someone else's hands isn't always bad," he murmured, deliberately allowing his fingers to trail down her back. Being the good guy clearly wasn't working. Maybe it was time for a more direct approach. "We all need to depend on someone once in a while."

She made a sound of disbelief. "Mister Lone Wolf trying to preach to me about depending on someone else?"

He trailed his lips up the line of her jaw, savoring the scent of peaches as he found the racing pulse just below her ear.

"I depend on others," he assured her.

She swallowed a small groan, her nails digging through the thin silk of his robe.

"Who?"

"My clan." He used the tip of his tongue to trace the large vein on the side of her neck. "My Anasso." He tugged aside the narrow strap that held up her satin nightgown she'd no doubt found in the closet. "You."

"Me?" She sounded genuinely shocked. "What would you depend on me for?"

It was a question he'd been avoiding since the mating first happened.

She was right.

He did like playing the lone wolf. Well, not a wolf. He hated Weres. But, he'd preferred to keep others at a safe distance.

It'd been that way for centuries.

And yet, in the few weeks since their mating, he'd become growingly content with the sense of Sally that was nestled deep inside him.

Not just the glorious sexual heat that flowed through him like molten lava, but the complex combination of fear and joy and aggravation, not to mention his obsessive need to protect her, that seared away the ice he had used to protect his heart after Fala's death.

Now he made no effort to deny the intoxicating brew as he shoved his fingers in her hair, tilting back her head to give him easier access to the delectable line of her collarbone.

"You've reminded me that life isn't just about duty," he admitted, his fangs scraping her delicate skin. "And that I've closed myself off from my emotions for too long."

Her breath came out in a shaky sigh, her firm ass wiggling against his cock with an invitation that made him groan.

"The emotions—" Her words were cut short as he kissed a path between her breasts.

"Hmm?" he prompted.

"They're not real," she moaned.

He chuckled, using a fang to slice through the nightie and expose the perfection of her breasts.

"Oh . . . I'd say they're very real."

Sally jerked as he licked the tip of her breast. "I meant the emotions," she choked out. "*They're* not real."

Roke lifted his head to meet the guarded gaze. His entire body was hard and aching with anticipation.

"They feel real," he muttered, his voice already thick with need. "They feel painfully real."

She briefly stiffened and Roke braced himself for her rejection. Goddammit. Even when he could feel her body trembling with need, she seemed determined to fight her desire.

Then, holding his darkened gaze, she allowed her hand to slip beneath his robe, splaying her fingers over his unbeating heart.

"This is only going to complicate the situation."

His already hard erection gave a painful throb. Her touch was so light he could barely feel it, but it was enough to send an explosion of pleasure through him.

This woman had the power that no other possessed.

Her every touch, every brush of her warm breath, every beat of her heart, made him feel as if this moment was something new. Something so rare and precious that it could only happen between the two of them.

And perhaps that was true.

Perhaps the connection between mates added a depth of intimacy that could never be experienced by two mere lovers.

Certainly there had never been another woman whose hunger was a tangible force that pulsed deep inside him, arousing his own desire with shocking force.

He groaned as he lowered his head to bury his face in her hair, filling himself with the scent of warm peaches.

"The situation has been complicated from the beginning, my love," he murmured. "But this . . ." He traced the shell of her ear with his tongue. "This part is simple."

She shivered. "What if it makes the mating permanent?"

The thought should have been worrisome. Surely nothing was more important than breaking the unnatural bond?

Instead he dismissed her concern without a second's hesitation.

"There could be a dozen ways we might accidentally make

the mating permanent," he muttered, covering her hand to press it hard against his chest. He was so hungry for her touch it was a physical pain. "Besides, if you were a demon who based your powers on sex, we'd know that by now. You would have been compelled to seek out sex, even if it wasn't with me."

She bit her lower lip. "Maybe."

He frowned. He didn't need the mating bond to know she was fiercely aroused.

Her need scented the very air.

But, tilting back her head, he read the hesitation still darkening her eyes.

"What is it, Sally?"

"I feel—" She licked her dry lips, sending a flare of heat shooting straight to his cock.

"What?" he husked.

"Out of control."

Shit. He'd been floundering out of control for weeks. It was becoming a normal state of affairs.

"And that's a bad thing?" he asked.

Her expression remained somber. "For me . . . yes."

Ah. He understood.

Her life had been a desperate fight for survival since she turned sixteen; no doubt the only thing she'd been able to control was her own body.

But, the Dark Lord had even taken that away from her by making her his conduit.

It had been rape at its most basic form.

No wonder she was wary of putting herself in a vulnerable position.

"You want control?" he murmured softly, planting a kiss on her plush lips. "You've got it."

With gentle care, he scooped her off his lap, laying her next to him on the mattress before he stretched out his legs and settled against the pile of pillows.

She blinked in confusion, her hair a tumble of red and bronze and deep gold as it framed her pale face.

"What do you mean?"

"I'm yours. Do what you want."

Her brows lifted, but he didn't miss the covert curiosity in her gaze as it lowered to take in his chest that was exposed by his open robe.

"You're so certain my choice won't be sticking a stake in your heart?"

He held her gaze as he cautiously lifted his hand to trace the curve of her lips.

"We have to learn to trust each other," he murmured. "It's the only way we're going to survive."

She gave a slow, hesitant nod, looking unbearably fragile in the darkness. Their earlier passion had exploded so fast there had been no time for thinking.

Now she had to gather her courage to take control of their lovemaking.

To take control of him.

He swallowed a low groan.

It was an oddly erotic thought.

"Okay," she at last managed to husk. "Don't move."

Roke smiled at her command, folding his arms behind his head. Sally paused another moment, then with a fluid motion she pushed herself off the mattress, and before he could guess her intent, she was straddling his hips and gazing down at him with a tiny smile.

Roke hissed in shock, clutching the quilt to prevent himself from grasping her hips and guiding her onto his aching cock.

He was the one who invited her to take control.

He wouldn't take it away from her.

Even if it killed him.

Tiny quakes of pleasure shook his body and she narrowed her gaze.

"I warned you . . . don't move."

Roke hissed, his fingers nearly ripping through the quilt as she calmly reached for the hem of her satin nightgown and pulled it over her head. He didn't need light to make out the perfect swell of her breasts crowned by rosy nipples or the narrow curve of her waist, or the smooth ivory of her skin.

With a groan his hips thrust upward, rubbing his arousal against the thin strip of satin that was all that covered her moist core.

"My beautiful witch."

"You once told me that Styx should throw away the keys to the dungeon and leave me for the wolves," she murmured, her hands sliding beneath the lapels of the robe and tugging it off his body.

His fangs were fully extended as her fingers explored his bared chest, circling his nipples before heading ever lower. It was the sweetest torture he had ever endured.

"One of the dogs ever lay a hand on you and they're dead," he growled, his hands lifting to run up her bare thighs. "Hell, if any man touches you, they're dead."

She rolled her eyes before slowly leaning forward to press her lips against his neck.

"I don't want any other man to touch me." She found a sensitive spot at the base of his throat, tormenting him with tiny nibbles. "One mate is more than enough."

He arched his back as anticipation swelled through him. "It's not that bad, is it? Mates can be useful on occasion."

"Really?" Her lips skimmed over his chest, her hair an erotic brush against his skin "And how are you useful?"

"I have all sorts of talents," he growled, his fingers slipping beneath the scrap of silk so he could rip off the underwear. "Shall I demonstrate?"

"I don't know." She licked a beaded nipple. "I think it's my turn to demonstrate."

He groaned as she deliberately allowed her breasts to rub against his chest.

"Christ, you're not going to need a stake to kill me."

With a low, throaty chuckle she began crawling down his body, her gaze fixed squarely on his straining erection.

"I like this idea of being the one in control."

So did his cock.

The bastard twitched and throbbed, as if silently pleading for her touch, even as he ruthlessly sought to keep himself from coming.

One touch and he feared he would explode.

"Do you want me to beg?"

She slowly smiled, clearly pleased with her power over him. "The thought is tempting."

Oh hell. He'd created a monster.

"You are tempting, my love," he groaned. "I need to be inside you."

A smile curved her lips.

No, not just a smile.

A wholly wicked smile that spoke of ancient Eve and female enticement.

"But I'm not done."

On the point of assuring her that *he* was going to be done if she didn't hurry things along, Roke gave a strangled shout and nearly shot off the bed as Sally leaned down and licked him from balls to tip.

Holy shit.

She wasn't a witch, she was a temptress.

Swirling her tongue around the very tip of him, she gave him another leisurely lick before she at last parted her lips and took him into the warm wetness of her mouth.

His hips elevated off the bed as she explored every straining inch of him, swiftly learning precisely what earned his most desperate groans.

Finally he had to admit that he couldn't take another second of her delectable torture.

Already his balls were tight with the approaching climax. He wanted to be lodged deep inside her when he came.

Reaching down, he grasped her arms and tugged her up to sprawl on top of him. She sighed as her legs fell on either side of his hips, the heat of her moist core pressed against his shaft.

"Sally, I'm going out of mind," he groaned, his fingers gliding up her inner thighs to stroke through her wet heat. "Put me out of my misery . . . please."

"Yes," she breathed, her eyes filled with a confidence as she leaned forward that was as sweet as the soft kiss she pressed to his lips.

There was no doubt to mar this precious moment.

Only the joy of two people who belonged together.

Stroking through her dampness, he located her tiny bundle of pleasure, teasing her until she was at last pleading for release.

Then, angling her hips over his straining cock, he cupped her ass and with one smooth thrust he entered her.

She gave a soft cry of pleasure and he caught her lower lip between his teeth, careful to keep his fangs from grazing her fragile flesh.

It was true that they couldn't know what would or wouldn't make their mating permanent. But the one certain means for a vampire was the exchange of blood.

He couldn't risk accidentally taking her blood in the heat of the moment.

Not until Sally had the opportunity to decide what she wanted from her future.

Arching his hips off the bed, Roke drove himself even deeper, the intensity of the sensations almost overwhelming.

"Roke," Sally groaned, her tongue dipping between his fangs to tangle with his.

His fingers dug into the softness of her backside. "Am I going too fast?"

"It's perfect," she moaned. "So perfect."

"Do you feel me deep inside you?" he demanded.

"I feel you . . . everywhere." She pulled back, her eyes dark with astonishment. "I feel everything you feel."

"Because we're mated." He threaded his fingers through her hair, stroking in and out of her in a swift rhythm. "We've become one. Heart and soul."

"Roke."

She dipped her head downward, claiming his lips as Roke quickened his thrusts, his entire body surging toward a sense of completion that he never dreamed possible.

Chapter Twelve

There were few people or demons who were more familiar with the complex spiderweb of tunnels where the Oracles were staying than Styx.

Before his mating to Darcy, he'd lived in them for several decades along with the previous Anasso.

Which meant that he knew every secret passage and hidden nook.

A knowledge he put to quick use less than an hour after he and Viper had arrived.

Once they'd formally lodged their petition with a dour-faced Sota demon and been shown to their bleak caverns where they were supposed to wait for an opportunity to have their dispute heard by the Oracles, Styx had led them from the public chambers to the dank tunnels beneath.

Stepping through the illusion of a seemingly solid stone wall, Styx pulled his large sword free of the sheath strapped to his back.

"Bring back old memories?" Viper demanded, ridiculously wearing black chinos and a white ruffled shirt with a brocade vest. His silver hair was braided, emphasizing the beauty of his elegant face, and the sword he carried looked like it should belong to a fencer, not a warrior.

But only an idiot would believe that Viper wouldn't have his heart carved out with a flick of his wrist.

Styx, on the other hand, didn't bother with subtlety.

Leather, shitkickers, and plenty of snarly attitude.

Simple.

"Not so old," he said, leaping over a large boulder that blocked their path. "Although it does seem like another lifetime."

Viper easily kept pace. "Who would have thought just a year later we'd both be mated and saviors of the world?"

Styx snorted. "Be careful, Levet takes full credit for being savior of the world."

"He would," Viper said dryly.

Styx kept his attention on the widening tunnel, well aware there were cracks in the uneven walls where an enemy could hide.

He wasn't about to walk into an ambush.

"I'll gladly allow him to have the glory if it keeps him out of my hair."

Viper gave a short laugh. "Yeah, good luck with that."

"Miracles happen."

"True," Viper drawled. "You found a mate who hasn't stabbed you with a stake."

"Yet," Styx pointed out, an indulgent smile curving his lips.

He wanted this business done so he could return to Darcy. The faster the better.

They turned down another tunnel that ended in the appearance of a dead end. This time, however, when they stepped through the illusion there was an unmistakable scent of decay.

"Viper," he growled, coming to a sharp halt.

His companion moved to stand beside him. "I smell it."

Styx wrinkled his nose. "Fairy."

"Dead fairy."

Styx nodded toward the nearby entrance to a small cavern. "Ready?"

Viper shrugged. "Always."

Together they entered the cavern, discovering the fairy lying in the center of the smooth floor.

Without a sound Viper was sprinting toward the far end of the cavern, searching behind the nooks and crannies that could hide the killer.

Styx knelt beside the body, reaching out his fingers to touch the dead man's throat as he made a physical inventory.

Outwardly the fairy appeared unharmed. His long red hair was untangled, his pale skin unmarred, his lean body in one piece, and there wasn't so much as a drop of blood on the traditional robes that were given to most petitioners.

Rising to his feet, he watched Viper return.

"Anything?" he demanded.

The younger vampire gave a shake of his head. "No, whoever did this is long gone."

Styx glanced back down at the fairy. Most demon bodies disintegrated within a matter of hours, sometimes minutes. It was a necessary precaution to avoid detection by the humans.

"Not long," he corrected. "The fairy was killed less than an hour ago."

Reaching into his front pocket Styx pulled out a cell phone, relieved to discover it was fully functional. His powers had a tendency to destroy electronic devices.

"What are you doing?" Viper asked as he punched in a number.

"I have Jagr posted to keep watch on the entrance to the cave." The leader of his Ravens answered on the first ring. "Report," Styx barked.

Viper stepped away as Styx listened to the clipped response, only returning when Styx returned the phone to his pocket.

"Well?"

"Three people entered the caves," Styx repeated what he'd learned. "The two of us and a male fairy."

Viper arched a brow. "Which means the killer was already in the caves." The clan chief abruptly stilled, clearly recalling his own visits to the caves when he'd been attempting to save the life of his mate. "Unless he used the secret entrance?"

Styx shook his head, already having thought of the possibility.

"I have them covered."

"And no one entered?"

"No, but Jagr said that D'Angelo reported earlier that he spotted a cloaked figure leaving from a side tunnel."

"Did he track him?"

Styx shrugged. "He tried, but a few miles from the caves the figure disappeared."

"Disappeared?" Viper grimaced. "Like poof?"

"Yep."

They shared a mutual gaze of unease. Not only at the thought of demons able to transport from one place to another, which hardly seemed fair, but because it was obvious who was hidden beneath the cloak.

"Siljar?" Viper muttered.

"She's at the top of my list," Styx agreed, his voice pitched low enough to keep it from traveling.

Making wild accusations while surrounded by the most powerful demons in the world seemed a dangerous proposition.

Viper considered a long minute. "Why would she slip out and then disappear? She could have used her private rooms and no one would ever know she'd left."

A good point.

Styx frowned, shuffling through the various reasons a demon would choose to leave the caves.

"I assume translocating would demand the sort of power

that would alert the other Oracles she was leaving," he said, at last suggesting the most logical explanation.

"True." Viper sheathed his rapier. "Of course, it's possible her disappearance might have nothing to do with the fairy's death."

"Or just as likely it wasn't Siljar at all," Styx said, his own sword remaining clutched in his hands. He was still hoping for a chance to stick it into an enemy. If he had to be away from Darcy, then at least he should have the pleasure of a rousing fight. "Which leaves us with the need to discover who is missing."

Viper made a sound of disbelief. "Don't look at me. I'm not going to do a roll call on the Oracles."

"Coward," Styx mocked.

"Damn straight," Viper agreed without apology. "They scare the hell out of me."

Styx had to agree. "They scare the hell out of everyone."

"Then we do this the old-fashioned way." Viper knelt beside the corpse. "Your senses are better suited to tracking," he pointed out. "You check to see who came into the cave and I'll try to figure out what killed the fairy."

Styx didn't hesitate as he headed out of the cave.

He might be the ultimate leader of vampires, but he wasn't an anal ass who always had to be the one to give the orders.

Viper was right. He was the better tracker while Viper had an eye for the finer details he easily overlooked.

Concentrating on his surroundings, Styx made a thorough survey of the tunnels that led away from the cave, traveling until he met the main passageway before doubling back.

Returning to Viper, he waited for the younger vampire to finish his inspection and rise to his feet.

"Did you locate a track?" the younger vampire asked.

Styx scowled. He was never afraid to face an enemy. He'd been in countless battles over the centuries.

What he hated was puzzles.

They always managed to bite him in the ass.

"Too many," he snarled.

"There was more than one?"

His displeasure dropped the temperature by several degrees. "There was one set of tracks and a dozen different scents."

Viper predictably scowled in confusion. "How's that possible?"

Styx clenched his jaw. He'd encountered demons capable of disguising their scent. Or even altering it to throw off a hunter. But he'd never heard of a demon who could smell like a different creature at the same time.

"It isn't." He gave a frustrated shake of his head. "What did you learn?"

Viper glanced back at the dead fairy. "About as much as you, unfortunately," he admitted. "There's no obvious wounds, there's no blood missing and, as far as I can tell, the major organs are still intact."

"No signs of a struggle?"

Viper shook his head. "It's almost as if he just lay down and died."

Styx muttered a curse. There was nothing more they could do.

It was time to turn the information over to someone who might be able to determine what happened.

"I think we've learned all we can here," he muttered. "Let's get out before the killer realizes we discovered the body."

Viper led the way out of the cave. "This isn't going to be as easy as I'd hoped."

Styx rolled his eyes. "It never is."

* * *

Sally lay on her side with Roke spooned behind her, his arms wrapped tightly around her waist and his face buried in her tangle of hair.

She felt . . . shattered.

Not just by the explosive bliss Roke had given her, although that had been enough to leave any poor woman dazed and confused.

But from the sheer intimacy of their connection.

Real or not, the mating had allowed the very essence of Roke to become embedded in her soul. She'd experienced his fierce hunger for her touch. His overwhelming delight in her simplest caress. And most terrifying of all, the unwavering devotion that fed his obsession to protect her.

No one had ever truly cared for her.

Even before her mother had discovered the truth of her tainted blood, the powerful witch had treated her as nothing more than a necessity. She was created to protect the world from an ancient vampire, nothing else.

And certainly none of her fellow disciples of the Dark Lord gave a shit about her.

She was an expendable commodity.

Was it any wonder she was floundering? She was desperately trying to squash the urge to bask in the warmth of his emotions, but it was like offering a buffet to a starving man. Impossible to resist.

Still, she wasn't completely stupid.

This wasn't destined to be a happily ever after and whoever said it was better "to have love and lost" was full of bullshit.

She'd endured rejection, betrayal, and actual torture, but she'd refused to be crushed by what life threw at her.

Now a voice was whispering that losing Roke might very well be her Kryptonite.

Plagued by her dark thoughts, Sally turned her attention to the first thing that caught her eye.

The box she'd left on the night table.

She frowned, studying the hieroglyphs that glowed with a silver light in the shadows.

Earlier, she'd spent hours running her fingers over the delicate carvings while she waited for her potions to brew. Her fascination had been more than just an appreciation for the beauty of the glyphs.

She was growingly convinced that she could actually understand what the box was trying to tell her.

Madness, of course. But she couldn't entirely shake the sensation.

"You're quiet," Roke murmured, his lips nuzzling the side of her neck.

She shivered, startled by tingles of heat that darted through her.

It seemed obscene that such a light caress could make her melt with need.

With an effort, she fought the urge to wiggle her ass against his cock, which was already hardening in anticipation. She'd just accepted that sharing such intimacy with Roke was far too dangerous to her fragile heart. Did she want to make it worse?

Yes, yes, and double yes, a wicked voice whispered in the back of her mind.

"I'm thinking," she forced herself to mutter.

He tensed. "Oh hell, that can't be good."

She glanced over her shoulder. "What's that supposed to mean?"

The silver eyes shimmered with a breathtaking beauty as he swept his gaze over her face.

"I don't want you trying to convince yourself this was a mistake."

Keep it light, Sally.

There was no use in confessing that she was swiftly making a bad situation worse by tumbling head over heels in love with him.

"Don't be a jackass this time and I won't," she said.

"Touché." He grimaced, obviously recalling the last time he had her in bed. "Tell me what you're thinking about."

"This."

Twisting out of his arms, she sat up and reached for the box.

"Not my first guess," he muttered, reluctantly shoving himself up to lean against the headboard. "The glyphs are growing brighter."

She kept her gaze glued to the box, knowing the sheet would have fallen down to his waist, exposing the bronzed beauty of his chest and the dragon tattoo that she'd so recently outlined with the tip of her tongue.

"Yes." She was forced to clear her throat. "I tried to muffle them with another layer of magic earlier, but it doesn't look like it's working."

"Is that what's bothering you?"

"No." She shook her head, her fingers tracing a glyph as the magic pulsed deep inside her. "I was studying it before I went to bed, and I could swear I—"

"What?"

"That I can decipher a few of the symbols."

There was a startled silence as Roke stared at her in blatant confusion.

"You read ancient fey?"

"Of course not, but . . ." She struggled to find the right words. "It's almost as if it speaks to me."

"Shit," he growled, his brows snapping together.

She flinched, startled by his intense reaction. "You think I'm going crazy?"

"No, I think the box has more power than I feared," he corrected in dark tones. "What does it say?"

"It's still mostly garbled. Like a radio station that's not quite tuned in," she said, knowing she wasn't making much sense. "But this is royalty." She pointed to a glyph that resembled an elaborate star, before moving to the one that Cyn had assumed was a closing door. "And this isn't the retreat of the fey."

"Then what is it?"

"A prison."

Roke nodded, accepting her explanation without hesitation.

Sally clenched her teeth against the renegade flutter of her heart. His absolute faith in her was almost as unnerving as his tender concern.

"Royalty in prison," he murmured. "Do the two glyphs go together?"

"Yes, I'm sure of it."

Not that it helped, she ruefully acknowledged.

Even if she was learning how to decipher the glyphs, they weren't giving her the sort of information that could tell her why she was suddenly attracting fey like bees to honey.

"Anything else?" Roke asked, his fingers lightly brushing her shoulder as she hesitated. "Sally?"

The casual contact sent tiny jolts of pleasure through her, threatening to drive any rational thought from her mind.

She turned the box over, grimly ignoring the cool fingers that continued to stroke over her acutely sensitive skin.

"I think this is a map."

Roke leaned forward, the sweep of his hair against her cheek as soft as satin.

"A map to where?"

She breathed in the scent of potent male, soothed by the dark spice even as it stirred her arousal.

"I don't know. But it's important." She wrinkled her nose, glancing to the side to meet Roke's steady gaze. "I'm sorry."

His hand moved to cup her chin, turning her head so he could study her rueful expression.

"Sorry about what?"

"I know you would rather be searching for my father so we

can break our mating," she said. "Not chasing down some imp in Chicago."

His eyes flashed with silver fire, as if annoyed by her words.

"What I want is to know that you're safe, after that . . ." He leaned down to kiss her with a mind-numbing intensity before giving her lower lip a punishing nip. "Nothing else matters."

"Roke—"

Her hand had lifted to touch his cheek, forgetting that she'd just decided it was far too risky to give in to her passions, when the temperature abruptly dropped and Roke was leaping off the bed.

"Get dressed," he commanded in low, urgent tones, moving to yank open the nearby closet and pulling on a pair of faded jeans he found hung inside.

Scrambling off the bed with far less grace, Sally hurried to where she'd left her clothes folded on a nearby chair.

"What is it?"

"Our least favorite demon," he muttered, his expression grim as he grabbed a gun from the floor.

He must have brought it up with him when he heard her cry out.

"Crap," she muttered, hastily pulling on the clothes she'd washed earlier before slipping her feet into her tennis shoes. "What's the plan?"

He moved toward the window, his gaze inspecting their surroundings.

"We need to get to the garage," he at last decided. "There should be something with enough horsepower to outrun even the fastest demon."

"I'm ready," she said, tucking the box in the pocket of her sweatshirt.

Roke led the way to the door, halting on the landing as he

tilted back his head to allow his senses to flow through the silent house.

He leaned down to speak directly in her ear. "We'll go out the back."

"Through the kitchen," she whispered back.

"Why?"

"My potions."

He gave a short nod. "Let's go."

They pressed against the wall as they moved down the stairs, carefully avoiding the splashes of moonlight.

He forced her to pause again as they reached the bottom of the stairs, his muscles coiled to strike as he tested the air for the location of their enemy.

At last he gave a jerk of his head and Sally hurried into the kitchen, gathering the small jars of potion she'd prepared during the long day.

They wouldn't be much help.

One was a disguise spell she intended to use once she'd located the necessary amulets to mask their trail, and the other was a potion to create a small explosion that might help confuse the enemy.

"This is all I have."

He crossed the tiled floor, pulling open the back door. Scanning the darkness, he at last gave a wave of his hand.

"Stay behind me," he growled.

For once Sally didn't argue.

She might be a powerful witch, but Roke was the superior fighter.

She didn't want him hesitating to attack because she was in the way.

The chilled air wrapped around her as Sally stepped out of the house, the scent of pine trees and frost teasing at her nose.

Roke, however, obviously caught a less pleasing odor as his lips curled back to reveal his massive fangs.

Hissing in fury, he turned to the side, his head tilting

backward as a shadow detached itself from the roof of the house to aim straight at his head.

Sally had a blurry glimpse of brown robes flapping around a pudgy body before the creature was hitting the ground as Roke moved to fluid speed to avoid a collision. She took a stumbled step backward, and the Miera demon straightened, a strange narrow stick held between his lips.

Baffled, Sally had no idea what the hell he was doing until Roke made a sound of impatience and tugged the tiny dart from his neck.

A blowgun?

That seemed . . . underwhelming.

"Roke," she cried out.

More annoyed than hurt, Roke emptied his gun into the demon who moved with surprising speed to avoid the bullets. Forced to accept the weapon was worthless against this particular enemy, Roke tossed aside the gun and bared his fangs.

"We end this now," he snarled.

The pale eyes darkened to an unnerving black with a crimson slit as the creature glanced toward Sally.

"Yes, we will."

Roke snarled, leaping forward. The Miera dodged to the side, dropping the stick as he pointed a finger toward Roke. Almost instantly the strange vibrations began to fill the air.

Roke leaped again, managing to slice his claws across the demon's face before he was knocked to his knees by the vibrations.

He growled, forcing himself upright despite the blood dripping from his nose.

Oh . . . hell.

Sally muttered a swift spell beneath her breath, tossing the potion jar directly at the demon. It shattered at his feet, and the Miera glanced downward in surprise.

It was immediately obvious that he wasn't familiar with witches. If he had been, he might have reacted with greater speed. As it was, his momentary hesitation made certain he was still standing in place when the explosion sent him flying backward.

Roke was instantly charging through the debris to land on top of him, pinning him to the ground and sinking his fangs deep in his neck.

It should have been over.

Sally didn't know of any demon who was capable of withstanding the attack of a vampire clan chief.

But even as she prepared for the grisly death, she was caught off guard when Roke was being tossed aside and the demon was rising to his feet.

"Roke."

She stepped forward, wracking her mind for a spell that might help as both men flowed to their feet.

The Miera was looking worse for wear with his face sliced open and his throat mangled, but oddly there was no blood. Roke, on the other hand . . .

She sucked in a startled breath.

He looked god awful.

His bronzed face had been stripped of color until it was a horrifying shade of ash, while the blood now dripped from his eyes as well as his nose.

Was it the strange demon power affecting him?

Or something else?

Whatever the cause it was swiftly weakening him, although he refused to concede defeat.

Surging upright, he swung his fist toward the demon's pudgy face, managing to connect with sickening force. The Miera flew through the air, slamming into a tree. Still, he didn't go down.

Blessed goddess.

What did it take to kill the damned thing?

Clearly wondering the same thing, Roke braced himself

for the demon to attack, his fangs bared and a dagger held in one hand.

Feeling ridiculously helpless, Sally mentally flipped through the spells she could use without a potion or proper preparation.

There were a few. Unfortunately most of them were too weak to hurt a demon, and those that were potent enough were too unpredictable. Casting a spell wasn't like shooting a gun. She could only aim in the general direction and hope for the best.

She wasn't going to risk hitting Roke.

More out of frustration than hope that it would help, Sally lifted her arm and launched her last jar of potion at the aggravating creature.

The disguise spell couldn't hurt the Miera, but it might distract him long enough for Roke to get in another shot.

The jar flew through the air, unnoticed by the two males who were both coiled to strike, shattering at the Miera's feet.

An odd silence followed the crash as they all stared at the mist curling around the demon's feet. Sally frowned, glancing at Roke. She'd expected him to attack while the Miera was preoccupied, but his eyes were glazed and the dagger dropped from his slack fingers.

Oh . . . shit.

His injuries were even worse than she first assumed.

Her wary gaze returned to the demon, wondering if it intended to kill her slow or fast.

She was hoping for the fast option.

The demon, however, remained distracted, his pale eyes widening as if he were shocked.

Sally took a hesitant step forward. If she could get close enough she might be able to hit him with a paralysis spell. It wouldn't hold him for long, but it might be enough to get Roke far enough away that he could recover his strength.

Three feet away she came to an abrupt halt.

There was something . . . weird about the Miera. A strange blurring around him that reminded her of the first time she'd seen the demon.

Only now the faint flickering in and out of focus was becoming far more pronounced, as if he were about to fade from view entirely.

Not sure what was happening, Sally jerked back into motion, this time heading directly toward Roke.

Lowering herself to her knees, she watched as the demon tried to kick away the clinging mist. He was reacting to the simple spell with a fear that was way out of proportion.

Or maybe not so out of proportion, she slowly realized.

The spell continued to crawl up the demon's body, smudging his physical shape, inch by inch.

Could the spell be causing an interruption with his personal demon magic?

Sally didn't know, and she didn't care. All that mattered was the frustration that marred the pudgy face before the demon gave a lift of his hand and disappeared.

Chapter Thirteen

Uncertain if the demon was truly gone, or if he might suddenly reappear, Sally ran a frantic hand over Roke's face, her breath ripped from her lungs at the feel of his icy skin.

He was always cool to the touch. Every vampire was. But not . . . frigid.

There was something seriously wrong with him.

"Roke." She leaned down to whisper directly in his ear, terrifyingly certain he was slipping away from her. "Roke, can you hear me?"

"He's fading."

The sound of the low, musical male voice had her jerking her head to the side to discover a slender imp with emerald eyes and long hair the shade of newly minted copper.

He was dressed in a camouflage robe that blended with the nearby trees, and she never would have noticed him if he hadn't spoken. A knowledge that did nothing to reassure her.

Still on her knees, she held up a warning hand, mentally preparing a spell of revulsion. It wouldn't hurt the imp, but it might convince him to go away.

"Stay back."

The stranger placed a hand over his heart, offering the traditional gesture of peace among the fey.

"I only wish to help," he said, his face impossibly beautiful in the moonlight.

She licked her dry lips. They'd been running from the fey for what seemed like forever, but he didn't act aggressive. After all, there was nothing to stop him from attacking her if that's what he intended.

Of course, he might be trying to lure her into a sense of security to get his hands on the box.

"Who are you?" she asked, remaining on guard.

He surprisingly offered a low bow. "A loyal subject."

"Subject?" she muttered in confusion.

He straightened, meeting her puzzled gaze. "You are a Chatri, aren't you?"

A Chatri?

As in fey royalty?

A cold chill inched down her spine at the unexpected question.

It was the box.

It had to be.

"No." She gave a violent shake of her head. "I'm just a witch."

He looked instantly contrite. "Forgive me. I understand if you want to keep your identity a secret."

Okay, this was going from weird to weirder.

If she hadn't been desperate to help Roke, she'd be fleeing in the opposite direction.

Instead, she forced herself to glance at the vampire who remained unconscious on the ground.

"I just want to help my . . ." Her lips twisted as she said the word she'd been avoiding for the past month. "Mate."

The imp sucked in a sharp breath. "You're mated to a vampire?"

"Yes," she admitted in impatient tones. "Can you help him?"

"May I approach?"

The imp waited for her to give a reluctant nod before

gingerly crossing the ground with a grace that would match a vampire. He lowered himself to his knees, his fingers reaching to touch Roke's ashen cheek.

Sally watched in silence as the imp closed his eyes and appeared to be assessing Roke's injuries.

"What is it?" She at last broke the silence.

The imp opened his eyes, his expression troubled. "I can't determine the precise poison, but it must be something specifically designed to harm vampires."

Sally frowned. How could Roke have been . . . oh. Her hands clenched as she remembered the dart that the demon had shot at Roke.

At the time it'd seemed like nothing more than an irritant. Now it was obvious the demon had used it to administer the poison with the intention of keeping Roke distracted until it could go into effect.

He hadn't counted on Sally's spell to ruin his plans.

Bastard.

"Can you help him?"

The imp shook his head. "No."

"Then who can?"

"Maybe the vampires." The green eyes held a concern that was at odds with his calm voice. "Does he have a clan nearby?"

She had to remind herself to breathe. "No. Why?"

"He's a chief. They can draw power from their clan."

Oh. She didn't know that. Chewing on her bottom lip she tried to calculate how far they were from Nevada.

"How long does he have?"

The imp grimaced. "Not long. I'd say no more than an hour. Maybe two."

"Damn." She tasted blood as her teeth sank into her lip, tears filling her eyes. Even if she drove like a bat out of hell she couldn't reach his people. "It's too far."

A copper brow arched at choked words. "I'm an imp."

Sally blinked. "Yeah, I got that."

"I can create a portal to take you anywhere you want to go," he said slowly, as if realizing she was having difficulty processing anything beyond her savage fear that she was going to fail Roke.

She held the green gaze. "Can you take me to Nevada?"

"Yes," he agreed. "Although I can only travel to a place I've been to before."

"Las Vegas?" she suggested, recalling Roke saying his clan was within easy distance of Sin City.

He gave a dip of his head. "Of course. Are you ready?"

Sally shut down her brain.

It was the only way to halt the shrill voice in the back of her mind that was screaming she couldn't trust a strange imp who just happened to show up when she needed him the most. And that even if the fey could be trusted, she was a fool to willingly put herself in the hands of Roke's clan.

She didn't have a choice.

If she didn't do something quick, Roke was going to die.

She knew it in the very depths of her soul.

"Yes."

The male studied her pale face for a long, silent moment before lifting a hand to weave a pattern in midair. Slowly a shimmer began to appear, growing wider with every pass of his slender hand.

Sally felt an odd sensation bloom deep inside her. Was she reacting to the portal? Or was it the imp magic that was stirring a pulse of power that flowed through her blood?

She shook her head. What did it matter?

Once he was satisfied his portal was stable, the imp held his hand toward Sally, nodding toward Roke.

"Hold on to the vampire."

Sucking in a deep breath, she placed her hand in the imp's and then slid her arm under Roke's neck, leaning down to press her lips to his icy forehead as the imp pulled the portal toward them.

Not sure what to expect, Sally stiffened as the prickles of energy raced over her body, an explosion of colors swirling around her as if she could actually see the magic of the portal.

The imp made a sound of wonderment, his eyes wide as he studied the whirling kaleidoscope.

"Astonishing," he murmured. "It's never been like this."

Sally didn't know if he was referring to the colors or the sensations of being sucked through space at supersonic speed, and she didn't have time to ask as they came to a sharp halt. Holding tight to Roke, she watched as the colorful display slowly dissipated, revealing a vast desert shrouded in darkness.

"This is it," the imp murmured.

Sally nodded, her gaze skimming the distant mountains before turning her attention toward the glowing lights of Vegas that lit the night sky even miles away.

"How far are we from the vampires?"

"Not far enough for my comfort." The imp shuddered, pointing south. "They're rapidly approaching."

She pressed another kiss to Roke's forehead. "Thank the goddess."

Careful not to startle her, the imp crouched beside her, his expression troubled.

"You're certain?"

Nope. Not in the least.

"Roke needs them." Was her only answer.

"You can leave him here and return through the portal with me," the imp said. "A Chatri should not be in the hands of vampires."

"I'm not a . . ." She gave a futile shake of her head. What did it matter? "I'll be fine."

"I hope so." He shot an anxious glance toward the thickening shadows. "They're almost here."

"Go," Sally urged.

The imp hesitated, clearly torn between a desire to stay and offer her protection and a fear of the approaching demons.

It was the burst of frigid power that filled the air that had him performing a hasty bow and stepping back into the portal.

"Take care."

Sally ignored her stab of fear as the imp disappeared. It was too late for regrets.

She was here to keep Roke from dying.

Nothing else mattered.

Bent low over her mate, Sally watched as the two approaching silhouettes solidified into a large male and much smaller female.

Another surge of fear clenched her heart. The male was bigger and bulkier than Roke with long, dark hair pulled into a braid. His features were broad and his eyes a light brown. The woman, on the other hand, looked like a puff of wind might blow her away.

Short and slim, she was wearing spandex bike pants and a sports bra that emphasized her tiny dimensions. She had golden curls pulled from a heart-shaped face and big, blue eyes. She might have looked like a china doll if not for the frigid hate that was etched on her delicate face.

Oh, and the big-ass fangs that glistened in the moonlight.

Of the two, Sally was much more terrified of the female.

"It's him," the woman said, her feral gaze trained on Sally. "What have you done to our chief, witch?"

"Nothing." Sally swallowed the lump in her throat. "I mean—"

"Check the area," the female interrupted, speaking to her companion. "I smell fey."

The male instantly obeyed the command, proving Sally's instincts had been right. The female was the more dangerous.

Which meant, Sally had to convince her that they didn't have time to screw around with the usual preliminaries.

"You must listen to me," she said in urgent tones. "Roke has been poisoned."

"Poisoned?" The vampire frowned. "With what?"

"I don't know. We were attacked by a demon and he shot him with a dart." Sally bit off her words, realizing she was babbling. "That's why I brought him here."

The icy blue eyes narrowed. "He dies, you die. Got it?"

Sally clenched her teeth. This was going about as well as she'd expected.

"Just help him."

There was a chilled breeze as the male vampire returned. "There's no one else in the vicinity."

The female nodded her head toward Roke. "Take Roke to his lair and call for the healer. Tell her that he might be poisoned." The blue eyes narrowed as they remained locked on Sally. "Or it might be a spell."

The male moved obediently forward, scooping Roke off the ground with a gentle care that eased a small part of Sally's thundering terror.

Whatever their fury with her, it clearly wasn't directed at their chief.

"What about the witch?" the male asked as Sally scrambled to her feet, trying to put some distance between them.

The female strolled forward, her lips twisted with disgust. "Unfortunately, we have to keep her alive until we know if she's put a spell on Roke. If she did, she's the only one who can break it."

"A pity," the male muttered.

The female shrugged. "Until then, I get to do something I've waited weeks to do."

Sally parted her lips to assure them that all she wanted to

do was help Roke when the female lifted her hand and with a casual motion slapped Sally with enough force to make the world go black.

Styx watched Siljar as she leaned over the dead fairy, her black, almond-shaped eyes unblinking and her hands folded at her waist.

She'd been in that precise pose for the past ten minutes while Styx impatiently paced the stone floor and Viper kept watch at the mouth of the tunnel.

He still wasn't sure if he'd made the right decision to bring Siljar into the investigation. Sure, she'd been the one to start the ball rolling. But he couldn't deny there were questions of whether she might actually be involved.

It'd only been after he and Viper had discussed every angle of the investigation that he realized they'd come to a dead end.

What choice did he have but to ask the powerful Oracle for help?

At last the tiny demon straightened, her braid nearly brushing the floor.

"His magic has been drained," she pronounced.

"And that killed him?"

"Yes."

Styx frowned. That seemed . . . hideous.

"How?"

"There are demons who feed off magic, but it's a rare talent," Siljar explained.

"Good. That narrows down the field of suspects."

Siljar arched a brow. "*Law & Order* or *NCIS*?"

Styx shrugged, refusing to be embarrassed. "*Law & Order*. Darcy is an addict."

"How very odd."

Maybe it was a little odd for a centuries-old vampire to

snuggle on the couch with his mate and watch *Law & Order,* but he didn't give a shit.

If it made Darcy smile he was fully on board.

"Are there any Oracles who suck magic from their victims?" he asked.

Siljar stilled, her black gaze studying him with unnerving intensity. "You instantly assumed it was an Oracle. Why?"

Styx grimaced. Sometimes he forgot just how perceptive the tiny demon truly was.

A serious mistake.

"I have my Ravens spread through the area."

She appeared unconcerned by his reluctant confession. "I expected as much."

"Only three people entered the caves before we found the corpse. Viper, myself, and the fairy." He glanced toward the fairy who was rapidly disintegrating. Another hour and he would be nothing more than pixie dust. Literally. "Whoever killed him was already here. Unless they have your ability to travel."

"Not without alerting me," Siljar said without hesitation. "No one beyond me and my daughter, Yannah, traveled out of these caves for the past week."

Styx nodded. It's what he expected, considering the effort the demon had expended to try to do his disappearing act in the middle of the woods.

"But there are Oracles who share your talent?" he pressed.

Siljar tilted her head to the side. "Why do I suspect that is more than a casual question?"

"One of my Ravens spotted a cloaked figure leaving the caves and disappearing a few miles away."

"The figure disappeared, it didn't just disguise its presence?"

Styx folded his arms over his chest, offended by the question. "No disguise could fool my Raven."

Indifferent to Styx's icy tone, Siljar tapped a finger against her chin.

"Are your Ravens still out there?"

"Of course."

"Has the creature returned?"

Styx had checked with Jagr only minutes before. "No."

"I believe I will call the Commission into session." Siljar headed toward the opening of the cavern, her pace surprisingly swift for such a tiny demon. "It should prove interesting to see who is here."

"Or not here," Styx added.

"Precisely."

Chapter Fourteen

Brandel hurried through the secret tunnel, still struggling to hold his corporal shape.

Goddamn that stupid witch. She'd ruined everything despite his clever plan.

After the previous fiasco he'd realized he couldn't just charge in and grab the box.

He'd spent hours creating the perfect poison and loading it in the dart, then more time devoted to tracing the ancient magic to locate the box. Time well spent he'd assured himself as he caught sight of his prey trying to escape.

He released his dart and attacked, knowing that the poison would swiftly weaken the vampire to leave the witch unprotected.

Of course he wasn't an idiot.

A powerful witch was never truly helpless.

But he'd been prepared to battle against spells of aggression, not a simple disguise spell that attacked him on his most fundamental level.

Wanting to roar in fury, Brandel instead muffled his emotions and kept to the shadows as he weaved his way through the various passageways that led to his private rooms.

Not only did he want to avoid attracting the attention of his fellow Oracles, but he also couldn't risk his anger warning Raith that he'd failed yet again.

He had just turned into the inner cavern that he'd claimed as his own when a slender Kapre demon appeared behind him.

"There you are, Oracle."

The Kapres were tall, slender creatures with moss green skin that was completely hairless. They were also a passive race with few powers who often hired themselves as servants to more powerful demons.

This particular Kapre was a valet to Recise, a Zalez demon who was one of the most powerful of the Oracles. The position gave the prissy, overly formal twit a sense of superiority over other demons.

Fiercely reminding himself that he was posing as a mild-tempered Miera, Brandel turned, concentrating on holding his form.

"Not now," he said, his tone carefully bland. "I'm busy."

The creature sniffed, his black eyes filled with a malicious amusement.

"What you are is late."

"Late?" Brandel frowned. "Late for what?"

"The Commission has been called into session."

Brandel was forced to turn away, knowing his eyes would reveal his true nature as he struggled against a surge of fear.

"Why?" he asked, pretending to straighten the pillows arranged on a flat outcropping that served as a sofa.

Another sniff. "It's not my place to understand the workings of the Oracles."

He continued to arrange the pillows, barely containing the pulses of vibrations that would destroy the Kapre. He needed information. Unfortunately, the servant was the only one who could give it to him.

"Perhaps not, but I'm sure your position as Recise's most loyal servant has given you access to highly sensitive information." He forced himself to stroke the bloated ego of the Kapre.

He could almost feel the creature preening behind him. "Certainly I am trusted, but my master is quite discreet."

Hmm. Clearly it was going to take more than flattery. Brandel reached behind a pillow to pull out a small bag filled with precious gems. He extracted a small emerald before turning to hold it in his open palm, pretending to study it in the candlelight.

"Not everyone is so discreet, are they?"

"True." The servant licked his thin lips, his gaze locked on the emerald with blatant greed. "I did hear a rumor that the body of a dead fairy was found in the lower caves."

No. It was impossible. He'd hidden the body where it couldn't be found, hadn't he?

"Was he very ill?" he asked with the pretense of innocence.

The servant shrugged with obvious indifference. "No one knows for certain what happened, but Siljar is determined to have a full investigation."

Brandel forced his lips into a stiff smile. Meddlesome bitch.

"Of course she is."

"Can you imagine any demon foolish enough to try to kill beneath the noses of the Oracles?" The Kapre inched forward, his gaze never wavering from the emerald. "The demon would have to be suicidal."

"Obviously." With a flick of his wrist, Brandel sent the emerald flying through the opening to land in the passage outside his chamber. "I must change before I can join the others. Please inform Siljar I will only be a few minutes."

"Yes. Yes, of course." The servant scrambled toward the

small gem, unaware of the invisible barrier that Brandel placed over the opening.

Once assured there would be no further interruptions, Brandel headed into the back chamber allowing his shape to dissipate into mist as he considered his limited options.

He could rush and try to join the Commission with the excuse he'd been out for a stroll. Or even remain in these private rooms and send word that he was sick and unable to attend the council.

But neither would halt Siljar's quest to discover who killed the fairy.

If he remained, there was a very good chance he was going to end up in the Oracles' secret dungeons.

A place where demons went and never left.

Ever.

"Damn," he muttered, knowing he had no choice but to disappear.

Raith would be furious to lose their eyes and ears on the Commission. It'd always been essential to have early warning if the Chatri decided to make a return to the world. And, of course, to halt if the fey approached the Oracles with complaints their people were disappearing.

Still, it was easy for Raith to toss out commands when he remained in the safety of their world.

It was Brandel who was forced to take all the risks, with very few rewards.

Well, no more, he abruptly decided.

He was leaving behind the Oracles and tracking down the witch.

Once he had the box, no one would be giving him orders.

Styx stood at the back of the large cave that had once been the receiving room for the previous Anasso.

Not much had changed in the past months. At least not as far as the scenery.

The dark stone of the floor and walls had been polished smooth over the ages and a shallow stream of water ran through the back of the cavern. Torches were set in brackets along the walls that shimmered in the crystals that had been exposed in the lofted ceiling.

The atmosphere, however . . . yeah, that couldn't be more different.

All hints of the opulent gold and crimson furnishings had been stripped away and replaced with a twelve-foot marble table that consumed the center of the room with twelve chairs set at precise distances apart. And gone were the barely civilized vampires with their raucous parties and bloody brawls.

In their place were a variety of subdued demons attired in matching white robes who settled in their seats with a silent dignity.

With a wry smile, Styx waited for Siljar to step to his side, her expression unreadable as they watched the last Oracle take his seat.

"Is this all of them?" Styx asked.

"All but one."

Ah. Success.

"Who is missing?"

"Brandel."

He turned toward the tiny demon, making certain his voice was pitched low enough to keep from carrying.

"You don't sound particularly surprised."

Her expression remained aloof, but Styx could sense her growing concern. He grimaced.

The thought of an Oracle going rogue was enough to give the entire demon world nightmares.

"I have been . . ." She searched for the proper word. "Troubled by him since our arrival to the caves."

"Anything in particular?"

"I sense there is more to him than meets the eye."

Well that was predictably ambiguous.

God forbid an Oracle just say what she was thinking.

"A secret he's hiding?" he prompted.

She shook her head. "It's more than a secret."

"Then what?"

"I think his very identity is a lie."

Styx blinked, then blinked again.

It was one thing for a human to alter his identity. A new hair color, a pair of colored contacts, and a change of name and—presto—a new person.

But a demon . . .

They would have to modify themselves on a cellular level, or have their essence scrubbed like Gauis, to fool other demons.

Even then he couldn't imagine an Oracle being deceived for long.

"I don't understand," he muttered.

"Neither do I," Siljar slowly admitted, her eyes shifting from the gathered Commission to meet his confused gaze. "But I do know one thing."

"What?"

"Your brother Roke is in danger."

The warning was so unexpected that it took Styx a beat to wrap his head around it.

"Roke?" He was instantly in full Anasso mode. No one screwed with one of his brothers. Not unless they wanted to deal with him. "What does he have to do with this?"

Siljar paused, as if considering her words. "As you are perhaps aware, I am in tune with the universe."

He shrugged, not giving a shit what she was babbling about. He just wanted the info on Roke.

"If you say so."

Her lips thinned, but she ignored his lack of tact.

Thank the gods.

"Which means I am occasionally urged to tug on the threads of fate," she continued.

A polite way of saying she was an intrusive busybody interfering in other people's lives.

This time he was smart enough to keep his thoughts to himself.

See? He could be trained no matter what Darcy might say.

"And you tugged on a particular thread?" he carefully demanded.

"I did." She gave a dip of her head. "It brought me Levet."

Styx shuddered. "That's a thread you can keep."

"Levet was a companion to Roke when they tracked down his mate in Canada."

He bit back his impatient hiss. "That has some connection to Brandel?"

"Levet was here when Brandel returned from a mission he claims took him to Hong Kong." She at last got to the point. "Levet, however, was quite certain he smelled of the same ocean spray he'd just left."

Styx was briefly distracted. "Ocean spray has different scents?"

"So it would seem."

Who knew? Pulling out his phone, Styx punched in Roke's number, willing the younger vampire to answer.

"Damn. Straight to voice mail," he at last growled. "I need to find them."

Siljar lifted her hand, releasing enough of her outrageous power to keep him from charging out of the cavern.

"No, I have a more important duty for you," she informed him.

"But . . ." With a snap of his fangs, he regained control of his severely strained temper. This was one of the few fights he couldn't win. "What duty?"

"We need to discover more about Brandel and why he would be interested in the clan chief of Nevada."

Her words made sense. It would be easier to protect his brother if he understood the nature of the threat.

Dammit.

"And what of Roke?" he snarled.

Siljar flashed her razor-sharp teeth. "I will send him assistance."

Roke struggled to open his eyes, briefly wondering if he'd been on a bender.

His head was throbbing, his mouth was dry, and his bones ached as if he'd been beaten by a rabid troll. Always the signs of a fantastic party.

Then, he at last managed to focus his gaze enough to take in the familiar sight of his private lair.

As always he took comfort in the plain stucco walls and dirt floor covered by simple Navajo woven blankets. The ceiling was open beamed and the furniture hand-carved from sturdy oak.

It was like him.

No fuss, no frills.

As his senses slowly came back online, he turned his head, sensing he wasn't alone.

"Zoe?" He wasn't entirely surprised to discover the small, blond-haired vampire perched on the edge of his mattress. Zoe had been attempting to convince him that she belonged in his bed for the past decade.

Now, however, he shuddered at just how . . . wrong her presence felt next to him.

"So, the dead decides to awake," she murmured, reaching to run her fingers through his hair. "You scared the hell out of me."

He instinctively pulled from her light caress, desperately searching his foggy mind for the cause of his throbbing fear.

He was missing something.

Something that was more important to him than life itself.

Baffled by the strange sensation, he tried to raise his head only to flop back on the pillow with a groan.

"What happened?" he moaned.

Zoe returned her hand to her lap, her expression hardening with a frigid fury.

"You were poisoned."

He jerked in shock. Vampires could be sickened by toxic substances, but their swift regenerative abilities kept poison from being an effective weapon.

"Impossible."

"Not impossible." Zoe lifted her hand, as if to touch him only to return it to her lap. "It very nearly killed you."

"How can I be poisoned?"

"It was a unique combination of a human blood-thinning drug laced with particles of silver." Zoe pointed toward the IV stand with several empty blood bags that was tucked in the corner. "We had to drain your blood and replace it with clean. You're fortunate to be alive."

Jesus. Someone truly wanted him dead.

Nothing surprising in that, of course.

But the rising anxiety that was making his body tremble was new and original. And wholly unwelcome.

He frowned. "How did I get here?"

"We think through an imp portal."

"An imp?"

"That's something we can discuss later," Zoe attempted to soothe. "For now you need to rest."

"No. I need . . ." What did he need? It was there, deep inside him. He could physically feel the raw, aching need. The savage desire to leap from the bed and find what was causing his ruthless pain. Hell, he could even smell . . . peaches? Oh, shit. His roar shook the room. "Sally."

Zoe widened her eyes, leaning forward to pin him to the bed with her hands.

"Shh."

His fury made splinters of wood rain from the ceiling. "Where's my mate?"

"She's fine," Zoe muttered, struggling to keep him flat on his back. "Don't move."

"She's not fine," he snarled, infuriated by his weakened state. His mate needed him, and he was failing her. Again. "I can feel her pain." He grasped Zoe's wrists, trying to pull them off his chest. "Dammit."

"Dyson," the female vampire called, her muscles trembling as she went to her knees to gain leverage.

Any other day, Roke would have already tossed her in the corner and been on his way to Sally. He wasn't clan chief because of his charming personality. But he was even more weakened than he'd first suspected and it was taking everything he possessed to continue the fight.

"Where's Kale?" he demanded, referring to the vampire he'd left in charge of the clan.

The younger vampire didn't have Roke's sheer power, but he was a steady, cool-headed leader who could be trusted not to allow his emotions to overrule his logic.

Unlike Zoe who was temperamental, and dangerously obsessed with claiming a place at Roke's side.

"He's in Las Vegas negotiating a new treaty with the local curs."

"Call him," he commanded, his gaze shifting to the large vampire who hurriedly entered the room and crossed toward the bed. "Dyson release me." Roke snarled in shock when the male instead wrapped a heavy chain over his legs and attached the other end to a bracket beneath the bed. The chain wasn't enough to hold him, but it had been enchanted to prevent his escape, even if he was at his full strength. "What the hell?"

"You're weak," Zoe murmured, climbing off the bed to regard him with a wary expression. "You have to rest."

Roke glared at the bitch and her partner in crime. "I'm your clan chief."

"Yes, which is why we intend to protect you," Zoe insisted.

"I don't need your protection." His hands clenched as he futilely struggled against the unseen spell holding him down. "I need my mate."

Zoe's pale blue eyes darkened with unmistakable envy. "She's bewitched you. Once we break the mating you'll realize we've only done what is necessary."

Damn. Sally had been right to fear his people. He'd suspected that they would be angry with her for forcing a bond with him, but he'd never believed they'd actually harm her.

"I'll destroy anyone who puts so much as a mark on her," he warned, the merciless sincerity in his tone making Dyson pale in fear.

Zoe licked her lips, not entirely impervious to his fury. "You're not thinking clearly, Roke."

"Tell me what you've done to her," he hissed.

"She's being held in the mines."

"Oh, shit." His eyes squeezed shut. They couldn't have found a better way to torture Sally if they tried. After being locked in Styx's dungeon, she'd become terrified of being trapped in a cell. She had to be freaked out of her mind. "Get her out." He sent a blast of power that made both vampires stumble. "That is a command."

Zoe glanced toward the ceiling that threatened to collapse on them. "You must relax."

"Release Sally and we'll discuss this rationally," he ordered.

"There will be no need for discussion," Zoe informed him. "The witch has created the fake mating, with the proper persuasion she'll end it."

Oh, hell.

Sally.

He had to get to her now.

"No," he snarled. "It has nothing to do with a spell. It was her demon blood."

Zoe tilted her chin. "Either way, we'll force her to free you."

"She can't." His fury shattered the windows. "Goddammit. She can't."

Zoe refused to back down. "Dyson can be very persuasive."

Roke bared his fangs. "No."

The male vampire rushed forward as the entire building shook in reaction to Roke's fury. Trapped by the enchanted chain, Roke could do nothing as the massive fist connected with his jaw with enough force to knock him out.

Chapter Fifteen

Sally crouched in the corner of the barren cell, her arms wrapped around her bent knees as she forced herself to breathe.

She didn't know how long she'd been locked in the darkness that was so thick she couldn't see beyond the tip of her nose. Or even how much time had passed since the large male vampire had left after using a whip to strip the flesh from her back.

It had to be several hours since her skin had grown back, although it remained tender to the touch, and she was so hungry her belly was beginning to cramp.

Where was Roke?

She knew he wasn't dead. She could still feel their bond, although it was oddly muffled.

At first the knowledge he'd survived the journey from Canada to his lair had trumped her fear at being tossed into a cell at the bottom of an abandoned gold mine.

Then, as the hours had passed, and she'd been shackled to the wall and beaten like a piñata, her relief had altered to a confused fury.

Where the hell was her supposed mate?

And why was he allowing his people to treat her like an enemy?

Was it possible that he was too ill to insist she be freed?

Or even being held as a captive until the mating could be broken?

She tried to hold on to the belief that any second Roke was going to appear and release her from the prison. It was that or tumbling into madness.

She abruptly stiffened. Wait. Was that . . . roast beef she was smelling? Maybe she'd tumbled into madness after all.

The disjointed thoughts had barely passed through her mind when the candles set outside the cell flared to life and a tiny, golden-haired vampire appeared from a side tunnel.

Sally grimly rose to her feet, wrapping the blanket that she'd found on the narrow bed around her naked body.

Dyson had forced her to strip before beginning his whipping. It was a customary technique intended to amplify her humiliation.

It worked.

But as she watched the female vampire glide toward the cell, sliding a large tray of food underneath the door, she managed to gather the remnants of her tattered pride.

There was something so freaking annoying about the china blue eyes and too-pretty face.

It made Sally want to lob a spell that would splat all over that pale beauty.

Petty?

Yep. But who the hell cared?

"So soon?" she forced herself to drawl, ignoring the delicious scents wafting on the air. God. She wanted to fall on her hands and knees and devour the entire tray like an animal. "A trained torturer knows that you give your prey time to recover before resuming the pain. Otherwise it loses its effectiveness."

"I'm not here to hurt you," the female protested, pointing toward the tray. "I've brought you dinner."

"Ah." She managed a mocking smile. "It's the good cop/bad cop routine."

"I'm not a good enough actress to pull off the role," the female protested, smiling to show a hint of fang. "If I had my preference, you'd be staked in the middle of the desert and left for the vultures to feed on. Unfortunately, Roke refuses to allow you to be put to death."

Sally struggled not to react, her fingers digging into the rough wool of the blanket.

"He's . . . awake?"

The vampire shrugged. "Our healers have managed to save his life, but he remains weak."

Sally swallowed the lump in her throat, still caught between her fierce concern for Roke and the growing anger that he hadn't rescued her yet.

"Then he must have told you that the mating was an accident," she said.

"So he says." The vampire couldn't sound more bored. "He also insisted that you be fed and that a hot bath brought to you later."

Sally blinked. Roke ordered that she be fed and bathed like a damned dog in a kennel?

"And that's it?" she rasped.

"As far as you're concerned."

"I don't believe you." Sally pressed her back against the steel wall of her cell, the pain inflicted by Dyson's whip nothing in comparison to the tidal wave of agony that threatened if she allowed herself to accept the female's filthy lies. "He wouldn't leave me trapped down here."

"For now he's occupied with his clan." The blue eyes narrowed. "He does have duties, you know."

"I have no intention of interfering in his duties."

"But you already have," the woman abruptly hissed.

Sally shivered as the temperature abruptly dropped. Christ, being around vampires was like being shoved in and out of a freezer.

"Not intentionally."

The female made a sound of disgust. "Maybe not, but because of you he's abandoned his people for weeks."

"I told him that he didn't have to stay with me."

"He's a vampire of honor. He unfortunately felt he had no choice but to offer you his protection." The woman's tone indicated just what she thought of Roke's choice. "Now he—"

"What?"

The woman nibbled her lip with her fang, trying to appear as if she were debating whether to finish her thought or not.

Devious leech.

"I'm not sure Roke wants you to know."

"Tell me."

"The clan is concerned that his mating to you has divided his loyalties."

"Concerned?" Sally frowned at the unexpected words. "Why?"

"He can't be an effective chief if he's devoting his time to tending to your constant needs." Her voice was edged with an icy hatred. "We've endured an absent leader before and we won't suffer through it again."

Sally ignored the female's unmistakable jealousy. It was obvious she wanted Roke for herself.

No big shocker.

"What does that mean?"

The vampire grabbed the bars of the cell, her frigid gaze pinning Sally in place.

"There are younger, stronger clansmen who have won the battles of Durotriges and are now prepared to challenge for their right to become chief."

Oh. Sally's stomach churned with a growing horror. Of all the various scenarios she'd envisioned for Roke's return to his clan, this one had never even blipped on her radar.

"He's going to be challenged?"

"If he can't prove he's willing to put you aside."

"That's not fair," Sally whispered. "He didn't create the mating, I did."

"Then break it," the leech abruptly hissed.

"I . . . can't."

The temperature dropped again, coating the bars in a layer of ice.

"Then you're willing to sacrifice Roke?"

"No. Of course not." She clutched the blanket tighter, shaking with a combination of cold and outright fear. How could Roke possibly fight after he'd nearly died? Weren't there any rules about the battle being fair? "I don't know how to undo the bond, but I'm going to discover how."

"When?"

"Let me go," Sally pleaded, unwittingly moving to stand next to the bars. Dammit. She had to convince this female to release her before Roke could be challenged. "I'll find my father and—"

"There's no time." The vampire's voice held a compulsion that was a tangible force. If Sally hadn't been so powerful, she wouldn't have stood a chance against it. "Soon he'll be stepping into battle. He's weakened, barely able to leave his bed. There's no way he'll survive unless you end this."

Sally bit her lip, fear galloping through her. If something happened to Roke, it would be entirely her fault.

How could she live knowing what she'd done?

Oh hell, if something happened to Roke, she wouldn't *want* to live.

"I can't."

"Only you can do it, Sally," the female pressed. "Break the mating."

"It's impossible," she cried.

The compulsion continued to beat at her for a silent minute, then, with a click of her tongue, the leech took a step back and smoothed her hands down her spandex pants.

"A pity." The boredom returned to her tone, the ice on the bars melting. "Roke hoped you would do this the easy way."

Sally blinked in confusion. "What?"

"He was . . ." The woman pretended to consider her words. "Displeased when he awoke to discover that we'd treated you so roughly. He was the one to suggest we try to touch your soft heart to convince you to break the bond. He said it would be far more effective than actual torture."

"No." Sally gave a violent shake of her head, but deep inside a shard of doubt pierced her heart. "He wouldn't."

The vampire's laugh filled the air, grating against Sally's exposed nerves.

"It doesn't matter. If you won't do it the easy way, there's always the hard way. My personal favorite." Blowing Sally a mocking kiss, the woman turned on her heel and headed back out the tunnel. "Enjoy your dinner."

Feeling numb from the emotional beating, Sally sank to her knees and began demolishing the food. She didn't know what she was putting in her mouth, and she didn't care.

All that mattered was regaining her strength.

If the female vampire was telling the truth, then she had no one to depend on but herself to escape her latest prison.

Nothing new in that.

She'd been caged, beaten, and betrayed more than once over the years and managed to survive.

She would survive this.

Pretending she didn't notice the tears streaming down her face or the tiny tremors that shook her body, Sally stoically polished off the roast beef, potatoes, bread, and large glass of milk.

She had to concentrate on regaining her strength and escaping.

Anything else would break her.

Shoving the tray away, Sally slowly rose to her feet, the faint scent of granite replacing the chilled stench of female vampire.

"Hello?" she called, jumping backward as a shape suddenly fell from a small hole in the ceiling. "Levet?"

With a violent shake, the tiny gargoyle sent a cloud of dust flying through the air. Then, with a flick of his wings, he was waddling forward, his expression concerned.

"*Ma cherie?* Are you hurt?"

"It doesn't matter." She grasped the bars of the cell, her heart pounding. "Get me out of here."

"I intend to," Levet assured her, studying the lock on the door with a growing frown. "But the security is *formidable.*"

Of course it was.

Trust Roke to have a prison that was as stubborn and tenacious as he was.

"Can you get me out?"

The gargoyle wrinkled his snout. "Not without assistance."

"Shit."

Reaching through the bars, Levet gave her leg a comforting pat.

"Do not give up. I will return with the chivalry."

"Chivalry?" Sally frowned as the tiny gargoyle gave a flap of his wings and disappeared into the narrow opening in the ceiling. "Oh . . . the cavalry," she muttered, moving to collapse on the edge of the bed.

She wasn't going to depend on the gargoyle to rescue her.

She wasn't going to depend on anyone. Ever again.

But, she had to have a few minutes for the food to kick her metabolism into gear.

After that . . . she was getting out of there.

Even if she had to use her magic to destroy everything around her.

Roke was having a nightmare.

He was trapped in his lair, unable to reach his mate who was in danger. And if that wasn't bad enough, there was something banging against his cheek. It was driving him nuts.

"Wake up," an insistent voice yelled in his ear, at last jerking him out of the clinging darkness.

With a groan he forced his eyes open, grimacing at the sight of the ugly little mug only inches from his face.

"Slap me one more time, gargoyle, and I'll turn you into a bowling ball," he growled.

"And how will you do that?" Levet taunted, ceasing his slaps although he remained far too close. "You are trussed up like a Christmas goose." The gray eyes widened. "*Sacrebleu.* I said that right, did I not?"

"Get out of my face," Roke growled, waiting for the creature to take a step away from the bed before he continued. "How did you get here?"

Levet sniffed, his wings glittering in the candlelight. "Once again I was poofed against my will." He frowned, scratching a stunted horn. "Do you think that's illegal? I should lodge a complaint. Of course, it was an Oracle—"

"Enough." Roke cursed himself for even asking the question. Who the hell cared how he got there? Nothing mattered but getting to Sally. "Just get the chain off me."

The gargoyle pointed a claw in his direction. "Only if you promise you will release Sally from that hideous cell."

"You've seen her?" Roke rasped, desperate for information about his missing mate.

"Unfortunately."

"What have they done to her?"

"There was blood in the cell so obviously she's been beaten, but I believe it is her mental state that has taken the greatest damage." Levet studied him as if he were something that had crawled out of the gutter. "How did you allow this to happen?"

Roke clenched his teeth against the agonizing thought of Sally scared and alone in a dark cell while his people tried their best to break her.

He would never, ever forgive himself.

Not that he was about to admit his seething guilt to the tiny gargoyle.

He had to remain in command if he was to rescue Sally.

"Clearly I didn't allow anything," he snapped.

Levet sniffed. "They are your clan members."

"Trust me, I intend to deal with my people, but first we have to get to Sally," he snarled. "Now release me."

Waddling forward, the gargoyle easily unraveled the chain that had so effectively held Roke prisoner, scurrying backward as Roke surged off the bed and headed toward a heavy armoire at the back of the room.

Still weakened from the poison, not to mention being knocked out by his own clan brother, it took Roke two tries to wrench the heavy piece of furniture out of the way to reveal the opening behind it.

"A secret passage?" Levet muttered in surprise. "Why do you not simply go out and demand that your people release Sally? You are chief, are you not?"

Roke headed into the tunnel that was dug beneath the ground. No vampire was without a secret backdoor.

Usually more than one.

"My clansmen are convinced my mind has been clouded by a spell," he grimly admitted. "I'm not going to waste time trying to convince them of my sanity when Sally needs me."

The scent of granite followed behind him.

"Why did you bring her here if you could not protect her?" Levet accused.

Roke frowned, his mind trying to sort through his clouded memories as he headed away from the collection of lairs that had been wrapped in spells of illusion to resemble an abandoned mining town.

He remembered fighting the demon. And growing weaker with every passing second, although he hadn't known at the time that the dart had contained a poison deliberately concocted to kill a vampire.

And then, as the world had started to go dark, he thought Sally had tossed her last potion at the demented bastard, but he'd been too far gone to know if it had been effective.

After that . . .

It was all a blur.

"I didn't bring her here."

"Then how did you get here?"

"I don't know."

"But—"

"Gargoyle, shut it," Roke growled, pausing to allow his senses to flow through the vast expanse of tunnels that connected the gold mines.

Locking on Sally, he picked up his pace, hoping to leave the aggravating gargoyle behind.

Of course, his luck couldn't be that good.

Dropping down an abandoned shaft, Levet floated down beside him, churning his tiny legs to keep up as Roke resumed his swift pace.

"It seems odd you wouldn't know how you traveled from Canada to this place." Levet refused to leave him in peace.

"I was unconscious."

"Not very sensible of you," the pest helpfully pointed out. "Especially when you had a young damsel depending on you."

Roke bared his fangs in annoyance. Goddammit. Did the gargoyle think he'd deliberately left Sally vulnerable?

"It wasn't a choice."

"Still."

With a flutter of his wings, the gargoyle thankfully shut his mouth, perhaps sensing Roke was close to the edge of snapping.

One more implication he'd intentionally failed his mate and he wouldn't be responsible for his actions.

Slowing his pace as he caught the recent scent of vampires, Roke searched the darkness for any hidden guards.

He wasn't surprised there were none.

Zoe's downfall was always her arrogance.

She never considered that a creature as tiny as the gargoyle could sneak past her defenses to release Roke.

Just as he'd once underestimated a pretty witch who'd managed to turn his life upside down.

Convinced that there was nothing lurking in the shadows, Roke slipped into the bottom cavern and rushed toward the cell.

"Sally," he husked, nearly going to his knees at the sight of the fragile figure wrapped in a blanket huddled on the bed.

Lifting her head, Sally revealed her pale, tear-streaked face and large, wounded eyes.

"Roke?"

"Christ," he hissed, his hands shaking as he struggled to focus his power.

With her hair hanging in tangles and her slender body shaking with obvious fear, she looked dazed, as if she were struggling to simply hold herself together. He'd never seen her so . . . fragile.

Not when she'd been imprisoned by Styx. Or forced to fight the strange vampire spirit. Or even when they'd been attacked by the mysterious Miera demon.

She faced every new challenge with a courage that had been unnerving.

To think that he'd brought her to the point of defeat.

It was unforgivable.

"What are you doing here?" she hissed.

"I'm here to get you out," he assured her, using a concentrated burst of power to destroy the lock.

"Why?" she muttered, her hand lifting as he entered the cell and rushed toward her. "No. Stay back."

Coming to a grudging halt, Roke glanced over his shoulder. "Gargoyle."

Levet eyed him from the door of the cell. "*Oui?*"

"Keep guard."

The gargoyle turned to head toward the opening of the tunnel, his tail twitching.

"I hold you entirely responsible for this mess, bloodsucker."

"So do I," Roke muttered, returning his attention to the woman who regarded him with eyes too large for her pale face. Cautiously he crept forward, indifferent to the knowledge she could easily turn him into something nasty. He almost wished she would. He deserved to be a toad. "I'm not going to hurt you, my love. I only want to help."

The wounded eyes abruptly flared with anger. "And that's why you left me locked up?"

He grimaced, feeling her raw sense of betrayal through their mating bond.

"I would never have allowed you to be locked up."

"That's not what your girlfriend told me."

He frowned. "Girlfriend?"

"Blond-haired, blue-eyed bitch who enjoys causing pain."

"Zoe." He perched on the edge of the bed, moving slowly enough not to startle her. He'd already done enough damage. "I'll kill her."

"Don't blame your minions," she snapped, her chin tilting. "They were only carrying out your orders."

He hid his relief at her display of temper. He doubted she

would appreciate knowing how horrified he'd been to see her with her spirit crushed.

"You don't truly believe that," he murmured softly, allowing his profound need to keep her safe to flow through their bond.

She bit her bottom lip, looking unbearably young. "Then why did you abandon me?"

"Abandon you?" His hands reached to frame her face. "Christ, Sally, I would quite literally walk through the pits of hell to be with you."

Chapter Sixteen

Sally tried to resist the urge to lean against the hard width of Roke's chest.

Dammit. She was pissed at him, wasn't she?

Certainly she'd devoted several pleasurable minutes to imagining the joy of castrating him.

But, the second he'd appeared, the crippling pain of betrayal had abruptly eased, replaced by the comforting sense of him deep in her heart.

Not that she was about to forgive and forget, she fiercely assured herself.

Fool her once, shame on him. Fool her twice . . . blah, blah, blah.

"If that were true, I wouldn't have been left here to rot," she pointed out.

"I've spent the past hours unconscious in my lair. Not that it would have mattered." His voice thickened with anger. "I was chained to my bed."

Was he serious?

Who would chain a clan chief to his bed?

"By your own people?" she asked in disbelief.

"My clan believes my mind has been clouded by a spell,"

he said, his eyes flaring with silver fire. "They're determined to protect me."

"By torturing me?"

"God." Without warning his arms wrapped around her, hauling her into his lap as he buried his face in the curve of her neck. "I'm so sorry," he whispered. "I never, ever wanted you hurt."

She didn't try to fight her way out of his arms.

She told herself it was because it would be a wasted effort. Even though she could sense he was weakened, she still had no chance of overpowering him.

But, that didn't explain why she leaned into his embrace. Or why she absorbed the scent of sexy male and raw power as if it were necessary to her very survival.

It was the shower of dust from the ceiling that alerted her to the potential danger.

"Roke," she murmured, tilting her head back to watch the crack in the stone above her head widen another inch beneath the force of his emotions.

"Shh." His lips pressed to the sensitive skin of her throat, his fangs fully extended. "Let me hold you."

"The ceiling—"

"I know," he muttered, still holding her hard against his body. "I'm trying."

"Perhaps we should finish this later?" Levet's voice echoed from the tunnel.

At last Roke lifted his head, his face grim. "Is someone coming?"

"They are entering the caves above us," the gargoyle warned.

Sally went rigid, her heart lodged in her throat as Roke cupped her chin in his hand and studied her frightened expression.

"Will you trust me?" he asked softly. His brows drew together as she hesitated. "Sally?"

She gave a grudging nod.

Beneath her lingering hurt, she knew that Roke had never meant for her to be caged and tortured. If she hadn't been beaten and starved and imprisoned in the dark, she wouldn't have given Zoe's poisonous words a second thought.

But she was still angry that she'd once again been treated like a piece of worthless trash. And, if she were completely honest with herself, hurt by the undeniable proof that Roke's clan would never, ever accept her as his mate.

Why she would care wasn't something she was going to dwell on.

"Only until we get out of here," she muttered.

"Fair enough," he breathed, reaching for the music box that was set on the mattress beside her. Pressing it into her hand, he gently pulled her to her feet.

In silence they moved out of the cell, Roke tugging her toward a narrow slit in the stone wall that barely looked big enough to squeeze through.

Holding her breath, she fought to keep the blanket wrapped around her body as she wiggled through the opening, relieved when it widened into a passageway leading away from the cavern.

She took a step forward only to be halted when Roke laid a hand on her bare arm.

"Wait."

She watched in puzzlement as Roke turned back toward the opening, his face hard with concentration.

"What are you doing?"

"Making sure we can't be followed."

There was the sound of claws scraping against stone before Levet was squirming through the narrow crack.

"Hey, wait for me."

"Great," Roke muttered, grabbing one of Levet's stunted horns to shove him out of the way. "Stay behind me."

The temperature dropped as Roke released his powers,

the earth shaking beneath Sally's feet as the section of the ceiling abruptly collapsed to block the opening.

Blessed goddess.

Sally coughed at the cloud of dust as Levet gave a squeak of alarm. Roke, however, calmly inspected his handiwork before turning to join them.

"That should keep them out," he said, his eyes shimmering with a breathtaking silver glow as Levet abruptly formed a small ball of magical light.

"Where are we going?" Sally demanded, allowing Roke to lead them toward a fork in the passageway and down a path that looked like it'd been abandoned for years.

"This leads to the older mines," he explained, his voice distracted as his gaze searched the darkness for unseen enemies. "There are a hundred tunnels; they can't guard them all."

It wasn't actually a plan, but Sally didn't have any better solution, so tugging the blanket up to her knees, she followed his swift pace. She was eager to put as much space between her and the approaching vampires as possible.

She wasn't going back in that cell.

Period.

Levet brought up the rear, his light bouncing off the jagged walls of the tunnel, and his low grumbles providing a welcome distraction for Sally.

Roke didn't seem nearly as appreciative, occasionally tossing a dark glower over his shoulder. Thankfully for the health of the tiny gargoyle, the tunnel began to angle upward, branching into a dozen smaller passages that demanded Roke's full attention.

Nearly half an hour later they reached the mouth of the mine, stepping into a wooden building filled with long-forgotten mining equipment.

"Wait here," Roke muttered, silently gliding across the floor to peer out a busted window.

"Well?" Sally prompted when his hands clenched in obvious frustration.

"They're spreading out," he admitted, turning to meet her anxious gaze. "We're going to have to make a run for it."

Her mouth went dry, her palms damp at the very real fear they were trapped.

"I can't outrun vampires."

Slowly he moved toward her, holding her gaze. "I can."

"But . . ." Her words ended in a gasp as he reached down to scoop her off her feet, cradling her against his chest. She instinctively pressed a hand against his chest as the other kept the blanket in place. "No."

His dark face was unreadable, but she could feel the urgency that thundered through his body.

"Sally, let me help you. I . . ." He struggled to speak, his regret at having failed her a tangible force. "I need this."

Levet scurried toward the open door, his tail whipping around his feet in agitation.

"They are coming."

Roke held her gaze. "Sally?"

"Fine." She gave a jerky nod, a rising panic making it difficult to breathe. "Let's get this over with."

His arms tightened, his expression warning of dire consequences for anyone stupid enough to try to stand in his path. Then, gesturing for Levet to go first, they headed out of the shack at a speed that made her eyes water.

Wrapping her arms around Roke's neck, she glanced over his shoulder.

Oh . . . crap.

As fast as Roke might be, he was weakened and forced to carry her while his clansmen were obviously fresh as freaking daisies.

"They're gaining on us," she forced past the lump in her throat.

Roke's pace never slowed, but his head turned toward Levet who had taken to the air to keep up.

"Gargoyle, if you have any magic, now is the time to use it," he growled.

"*Oui.*"

Turning midflight, Levet pointed his finger toward the pursuing vampires, muttering a spell in an ancient language. The air prickled with a surge of magic, making sparks twirl around the gargoyle's hand before it was shooting straight toward the vampires.

Peering over Roke's shoulders, Sally prayed for the desert floor to split open to consume the pursuers. Or at least for a massive explosion that would slow them down.

Instead, what she got was a sputtering shower of sparks that was about as lethal as a firecracker.

"That's it?" Roke rasped in disbelief.

"It is more than you can do," Levet muttered in sullen tones.

"Shit." Coming to a halt, Roke lowered Sally to her feet and stepped in front of her.

Sally pressed a hand to her thundering heart, sweat trickling down her spine despite the chill in the air. There were few things more frightening than watching a half-dozen vampires circle her.

But while she could literally taste the fear racing through her, she fiercely refused to panic.

Not this time.

Grimly, she focused her surge of emotions on the magic that bubbled deep inside her.

She wasn't going to be taken without a fight.

Thankfully ignoring her, the tiny blond-haired vampire strolled toward Roke, her gaze flicking toward Levet with blatant disdain.

"I wondered how you escaped your lair."

Roke folded his arms over his chest, his silver eyes slowly meeting the gaze of a nearby clansman, waiting for him to lower his head in a sign of submission before moving to the next. He continued the process until each of them had silently conceded his alpha status before shifting his attention to the woman who refused to back down.

"You left our lairs unprotected?" he asked, the dark accusation meant as much for the warriors as for Zoe.

Still, it was the female who answered. "No, Dyson remained behind to make sure this wasn't a distraction to leave the clan vulnerable to an ambush."

"At least someone is thinking clearly."

Zoe tilted her chin, her expression defiant. "Just as you will be thinking clearly once we've broken the witch's hold on you."

The earth trembled beneath their feet as Roke released a tendril of his power.

"I don't want to fight, Zoe, but I will."

She spared a brief, hate-filled glare toward Sally before she took a step toward Roke, her hand held out in a gesture of peace.

"Please, Roke," she pleaded. "You know you can trust me."

Roke's eyes were hard and cold as diamonds, his face looking as if it'd been carved from granite.

Sally gave a small shiver. She and Roke had been growling and fighting since they'd first laid eyes on each other, but he'd never, ever looked at her like that.

She hoped to God he never did.

"I'm taking Sally away from here." His voice was soft, but there was no mistaking the lethal intent. "If you try to stop me you'll be hurt. End of story."

Zoe flinched, but her determination never faltered. Sally

might have admired the female's courage if she didn't suspect it stemmed from Zoe's intense desire to claim Roke as her own.

Bitch.

"We can discuss this back at my lair," Zoe said.

"No." There was another mini-earthquake. "Let us go."

"We can't. You know that." Zoe pointed toward Sally, although her gaze never shifted from Roke. "So long as the witch has you in her power, you're in danger."

"In my power?" Sally muttered beneath her breath. "Yeah, right."

Of course the vampire heard her. "Shut up, witch."

Roke growled low in his throat, the sound making Sally's hair stand on end.

"You will speak to her with respect."

"Roke . . . this isn't you. You would never choose a woman over your clan. And certainly never a witch," Zoe tried to soothe, while Sally took a step away.

It didn't take a genius to know that the shit was about to hit the fan. She needed to be prepared.

Returning her concentration to her magic, she frowned as she felt a heat spreading across her stomach. What on earth? Cautiously she held the blanket out just far enough that she could peek down to discover what was causing the strange sensation.

She hastily swallowed her gasp at the golden glow that surrounded the music box clutched in her hand.

This was different from the shimmer that outlined the glyphs.

This light encompassed the entire box and was pulsing like a heartbeat . . . God almighty, it was pulsing in time to *her* heartbeat.

Which meant that whatever magic was happening was directly connected to her.

But what did it mean?

Would the box help to amplify a spell?

Or would it actually interfere?

Only one way to find out, she abruptly decided, lifting her head as Roke's argument with Zoe reached its inevitable conclusion.

"Sally is my mate," Roke was snarling, his hands lifting as the vampires began to press closer. "My loyalty is to her."

Zoe grimaced. "I'm sorry, Roke, but someday you'll thank me." She gave a wave of her hand. "Take them."

It was now or never.

Sally closed her eyes, speaking the words for a stun spell. She'd never tried to use it against vampires, but it was the only offensive spell she would work against such a large number of enemies.

If she could plait the air into a tight enough weave before releasing it, the explosion should be able to stun the vampires long enough for them to try to make another stab at escape.

A long shot, but better than nothing.

Unconsciously stroking her fingers over the box that had warmed until it was almost painful, Sally snapped her eyes open and spoke the word that would release her spell.

At first nothing seemed to happen and Sally's heart stuttered to a horrified halt.

She didn't know if she was strong enough to survive being thrown back into that dark, lonely cell.

Not with her sanity intact.

Then, abruptly the strands of her magic began to form, threading together at a dizzying speed. She clenched her teeth, feeling as if she were being yanked inside out by the swelling power.

This was bigger than a simple stun spell.

The realization had barely formed when the threads began to glow with a dazzling light. It reminded her of something . . . another magic she'd recently seen.

Oh, hell.

It was the portal that the imp had formed to bring her to Nevada in the first place.

She desperately threw out her hand, trying to grasp ahold of Roke before she was sucked into a swirling tangle of colors.

Roke didn't know what the hell was going on.

One minute he'd been bracing himself to fight his own clan and the next he was being jerked through space and slammed into an invisible barrier that nearly knocked him out.

Sprawled on the grass, he struggled to get his bearings.

"Dammit." He turned his head enough to see a lump of gray stone lying next to him. Levet. Perfect. "Did you do this, gargoyle?" he growled.

The lump slowly sat up, exposing the fairy wings that sparkled in the moonlight.

"I cannot create a portal."

Roke pressed a hand to his forehead, feeling like he'd cracked open his skull.

"You've been popping in and out for days."

"It was Siljar who was responsible for my . . . unorthodox travels," he said.

Roke struggled to think. "Then she brought us here?"

"*Non.*"

"How can you be certain?"

Levet gave a click of his tongue. "Because I recognize a portal when I have been thrust through one."

"Christ." With an effort he forced himself to a seated position, his gaze searching the ground beside him. "Sally?" He cursed, jumping to his feet. There was no tiny, autumn-haired witch in sight. "Where is she?" he snapped as Levet waddled toward him.

The gargoyle frowned, his expression concerned. "Do I look like I know?"

Roke muttered a curse, allowing his senses to flow outward. It took less than a second to realize they were at the edge of Styx's property in Chicago. There was no mistaking the sprawling, manicured lawn and the honking-huge house, not to mention the energy pulse from a dozen powerful vampires.

And then there was the barrier against magic that explained why the portal had come to such an abrupt end and why his skull had nearly been split in two.

So where the hell was Sally?

Leashing his rising panic, Roke closed his eyes and concentrated on the bond that connected him to his mate. A surge of relief rushed through him as he felt the steady pulse of her heart. She was alive. But the sense of her was . . . muffled. As if something or someone was trying to disguise her presence.

"She must not have come through the portal," he snarled, pulling out his phone and punching in numbers.

Zoe answered on the first ring.

"Do you have my mate?" he demanded, his anger snapping a nearby oak tree in half. "Don't screw with me on this," he warned as Zoe denied any knowledge of Sally. "Goddammit."

Levet's tail quivered as he impatiently waited for Roke to shove the phone back into his pocket.

"Sally?"

"Zoe claims that she disappeared at the same time we did," he said, pressing a hand to the empty ache in the center of his heart. "She assumed Sally cast some sort of translocation spell."

Levet snorted at the vampire's persistent assumption that

a witch could actually transport people from one place to another.

"You trust her?"

Roke grimaced. He didn't want to. He wanted to believe that Zoe was holding Sally captive and that he had only to return to Nevada to free her.

As much as he hated the thought of his mate alone and terrified in a cell, it was preferable to the fear that she'd been taken by an enemy who intended . . .

Christ, he couldn't even go there.

"If she had Sally, then Zoe would have used her presence to force my return," he grimly admitted.

Levet's wings drooped. "Whoever created the portal must have taken her."

"The fey," Roke said. "It has to be."

The gargoyle nodded. "So how do we retrieve her?"

There was a blast of icy power as a large Aztec warrior stepped through the invisible barrier.

"Roke. Thank the gods," Styx said, his massive body covered by leather pants and a black tee. His hair was braided and his massive sword was strapped to his back. "I've been trying to contact you."

Roke brushed aside his king's concern. Nothing mattered but finding Sally.

Nothing in the entire world.

"I need your help," he rasped.

Instantly realizing something was desperately wrong, Styx was on full alert.

"What happened?"

"We were in Nevada—"

"Being chased by his clansmen," Levet interjected, his tiny arms folded over his chest.

Roke ignored the ridiculous pest. "When we were sucked into a portal and brought here."

Styx arched an ebony brow. "You were being chased by your clansmen?"

"*Oui*," Levet agreed with a sniff.

"That doesn't matter," Roke growled. What kind of fate would steal his beautiful mate and leave him with the stupid gargoyle? "Sally was with us, but she never arrived. We have to find her."

"Easy, amigo," Styx soothed as the eight-foot brick fence surrounding his back garden exploded in a shower of rubble. "We'll find her."

"We need a fey," Roke said between gritted fangs.

Levet abruptly snapped his fingers. "Troy."

Styx scowled. "The imp?"

"He has royal blood," Levet pointed out. "No one has greater power to trace a portal."

Roke shoved his hands in his front pockets, struggling to control his power. He could level a city block if he wasn't careful.

"Can this Troy be trusted?"

"He's fey, but yes, I think he can be trusted," Styx said, his too-perceptive gaze studying Roke's worried expression. "Why?"

"The fey have been chasing Sally since the gargoyle removed the illusions wrapped around her music box."

Levet lifted his hands. "Hey, do not blame me."

"Odd," Styx murmured.

Roke shook his head. "No more odd than the Miera demon who attacked us."

Styx's eyes narrowed. "Did you say Miera?"

"Yes. He attacked us twice. The second time he nearly killed me," Roke admitted in bleak tones. It was his inability to destroy the bastard that had allowed Sally to be put in danger. "Do you know who he is?"

Styx grimaced. "There's a missing Oracle who has been killing the fey."

Oracle?

Well, shit. That would explain the creature's strength if not his weird-ass powers.

"Brandel?" Levet abruptly asked.

Styx nodded. "Yes."

"Bah." The gargoyle wrinkled his snout. "I knew he had been to Canada."

Roke made a sound of impatience. "What does this Brandel have to do with Sally?"

"Actually, we were hoping you could tell us," Styx said.

"He wanted the box. Or at least that's what he claimed." Roke hissed in frustration. "I no longer know if it's Sally or the box that everyone is trying to get their hands on."

"It all has to be connected," Styx said, his brows furrowed.

"I don't care," Roke snapped. "I just want Sally."

Styx nodded in ready agreement. "Levet, get the imp."

Chapter Seventeen

Sally stood in the middle of the sun-drenched field, completely disoriented.

Okay. Just a second ago she'd been in a dark desert surrounded by angry vampires. Then she'd released her spell and there had been a swirl of dizzying colors. And then . . .

Then she was standing in this meadow that was filled with buttercups and daisies and tiger lilies along with lilac bushes to add to the dazzling display. Overhead the sky was a clear, impossible blue with an occasional bird casting a shadow over the endless fields.

Where was she?

And more importantly, where was Roke?

"Hello?" she called, taking a hesitant step forward. The movement abruptly drew her attention to the fact that the itchy blanket had been replaced by a flowing satin gown in a pale ivory.

The spaghetti straps allowed the warm sun to stroke over the skin of her shoulders while the lace around the hem tickled the tops of her bare feet. She might have appreciated the beautiful garment if she hadn't been worried how she'd acquired it between one heartbeat and the next, and who had placed it on her naked body.

As it was, she held the music box in a death grip and took another step forward.

"Roke?" she called.

There was no answer beyond the rustle of the breeze through the flowers, but sudd~nly she caught the scent of a rich full-bodied wine.

It was intoxicating.

"Is someone there?" she called out.

Without warning a marble grotto appeared in the center of the field.

Built of white marble it had fluted columns and a dome roof that glittered gold in the sunlight.

Sally gasped, stunned by the magic that sizzled in the air.

She'd never felt anything so raw, so . . . primal.

And more disturbing, it was stirring a thunderous reaction deep inside her. As if a dam had suddenly burst to release a flood of magic she never knew she possessed.

Blessed goddess. What was happening to her now?

Still trying to process the tidal wave of magic, Sally was distracted as a shadow appeared between the columns of the grotto.

Crap. There was something coming.

That couldn't be a good thing.

Barely daring to breathe, she watched as a tall, elegant form stepped from between the columns, moving down the steps with a liquid grace.

Sally blinked. Then blinked again.

He was . . . beautiful.

Staggeringly, breathtakingly beautiful.

Wearing a robe of purest white, the stranger had long hair the color of spun gold held from his face by a narrow band of silver studded with priceless gems. His eyes were faintly slanted and the color of polished amber flecked with jade. His skin was unblemished and so silky smooth it didn't look real, while his lips were sensuously carved and tinted the shade of ripe strawberries.

He moved toward her with such a regal air she nearly curtsied, his gaze skimming over with a clinical curiosity.

As if she were a wild animal that strayed into his fairy-tale land.

"Ah, Sally," he murmured, his voice brushing over her like velvet. "At last."

He knew her name. How?

Sally licked her lips, trying to think beyond the magic bubbling through her.

"Who are you?"

"Sariel."

Which told her precisely nothing.

"Where am I?"

He seemed to consider. "A difficult question."

Sally grimaced. The fact that Sariel didn't have a straightforward answer wasn't comforting.

"Not usually."

He waved a dismissive hand. "The place does not matter."

"Fine." Obviously he wasn't going to answer the question. Move on. "How did I get here?"

"I called and you came."

"How?"

He smiled. "Your powers grow with every passing hour."

She frowned. "You're saying I brought myself here?"

"Of course."

She had a flashback to magic that seared through her just as the swirl of color had engulfed them. Was it possible that she actually created a portal that had brought her here?

She was shaking her head before the thought could fully form.

"That's impossible."

The amber eyes continued to study her, his exquisite face impossible to read. Had he never seen a witch before?

"You'll discover nothing is impossible once you've fully embraced your birthright."

Embrace her birthright?

She didn't know what that meant and she didn't care.

All she wanted was to be away from this too-perfect place and in the arms of her mate.

"No," she denied. "Where's Roke?"

"The vampire?"

"Yes."

He paused, the magic thickening in the air. "Your portal sent him to the King of Vampires," he at last said.

Sally released a shaky sigh. Relief was flooding through her at the knowledge that Roke was safe, even as she tried to wrap her brain around the idea she'd created a portal that not only sent Roke to Chicago, but brought her to this place.

"Dear goddess." She pressed a hand to her aching head. "This is madness."

"I agree," Sariel surprisingly murmured. "And only you can bring it to an end."

"Me?"

"It's the reason you were created."

She flinched at his unexpected words, then a bitter laugh was wrenched from her lips.

"Newsflash, Sariel, I was created to maintain a sorcery spell I inherited from my mother."

He gave a slow blink, as if wondering why she would bother him with such boring trivialities.

"The spell was inconsequential," he informed her.

"Inconsequential?" she repeated, stupidly offended by his lack of interest. "That . . . vampire could have destroyed the world."

She'd nearly died during the battle. Hardly inconsequential. At least not to her.

"Perhaps, but your mother's need for a daughter was only a minor reason for your conception."

She clenched her teeth. The man might be all kinds of beautiful, but he had the personality of a slug.

"How would you know?"

He easily held her gaze. "Because I am your father."

Roke paced until the grass was trampled and a small groove was worn into the ground.

It was that or crossing the short distance to grab the Prince of Imps by his long red hair and shaking the shit out of him.

Something Styx had made him swear he wouldn't do.

When Levet had returned with Troy, Roke had exploded in fury.

The creature looked like he should be working in a strip club.

Large and muscular with the build of a linebacker, he was wearing zebra striped spandex pants and a see-through shirt that revealed the width of his pale chest and the nipples that had been pierced so he could run a delicate gold chain between them.

The crimson fire of his hair was pulled into a dozen intricate braids that emphasized his delicate features while the emerald eyes smoldered with a sensuality that was almost tangible.

He was a walking, talking invitation to sex.

What the hell good could he do?

But once Styx had briefly explained they needed him to seek out the fey magic, the imp had set to work with an efficiency that helped to ease Roke's initial desire to toss him into the trash.

And it didn't hurt that Levet had stomped toward the mansion, muttering something about visiting Darcy.

There was no way Roke's nerves could endure both Levet and Troy, the Prince of Imps, in the same space.

Still, as the seconds ticked past and the imp continued to

kneel a few feet away, his hands raised as if he could feel something floating in the air, Roke's attempt at patience was about to come to a violent end.

"Well?" he at last barked.

Troy slowly rose to his feet, brushing the dust off his obnoxious spandex pants.

"There has definitely been a portal opened here," he said. "Recently."

Roke hissed in frustration. "We know that much."

Styx stepped next to him, placing a warning hand on his shoulder before speaking directly to the imp.

"Can you identify who opened the portal?"

Troy shrugged, a bemused expression settling on his narrow face.

"It is fey, but . . . more."

"More what?" Roke snapped.

"More everything." The imp once again held his hand toward the empty air, as if he could feel precisely where the portal had opened. "The magic is intoxicating."

Roke bared his fangs. "You're not helping."

"Leeches." Troy slid a hand down his too-tight pants. "Yummy, but always so impatient."

Styx tightened his hand on Roke's shoulder, keeping him from lunging.

"Tell us who opened the portal," Styx commanded.

The bemused expression returned to Troy's face. "If I didn't know better, I would say it was a Chatri."

Roke jerked in shock. "Shit."

Troy's eyes narrowed, revealing a cunning he hid behind his frivolous façade.

"You know fey history?" the imp asked.

"More than I ever wanted to," Roke growled, his hand pressing against the empty ache in the center of his chest. Had a Chatri somehow created a portal that had stolen his mate? Or was the magic merely a residue. "Can fey magic be contained in a box?" he abruptly demanded.

Troy widened his eyes in surprise. "What sort of box?"

"A music box decorated with ancient glyphs," Roke answered.

"How would you know of such an object?"

"My mate has one." Roke clenched his hands at the stab of pain that sliced through his heart. "Is it dangerous?"

Troy shook his head. "No, from what little information we have, the boxes were used by the Chatri to share information, not magic."

The imp acted sincere, but Roke remained unconvinced. Demons were notoriously reluctant to give up secrets about their individual species.

"What sort of information?" he probed.

Troy shrugged. "Family histories, the ingredients for rare spells, occasionally maps."

"Maps?" Roke latched on to the unexpected revelation. "Are you sure?"

"Of course, I have a collection of boxes in my private vault," Troy said. "At least two are maps to entrances of the hidden fey dimensions." The imp studied Troy with a puzzled gaze. "Why are you asking?"

Roke forced himself to give a shake of his head. So Sally hadn't been mistaken when she confessed she thought she was beginning to understand the language of the glyphs. Unfortunately, that wasn't going to help him find her.

"Later," he muttered. "Could a box create a portal?"

"No." Troy's response was emphatic, his hand lifting toward the spot where the portal opened. "This was the work of an extremely powerful fey. One who can call on the talents of the Chatri."

Roke grimaced.

They were wasting time and he hadn't discovered anything

beyond the fact the imp insisted there was some sort of ancient fey magic involved.

"Can you trace it?"

Troy looked confused. "You mean follow it back to where it originated?"

"No." Roke forced himself to count to ten. No sense in killing the one fey who might be able to help him. "I want you to open the portal."

"Why?"

Roke flashed his fangs. "You don't need—"

"Roke believes his mate is stuck inside it," Styx interrupted Roke's furious words, his own voice smooth.

Troy frowned at Roke. "You're mistaken."

Roke growled. Okay. Now the damned imp was just trying to piss him off.

"I'm rarely mistaken," he said, the earth trembling.

"Easy, leech," Troy said, hastily trying to lessen the violence that prickled in the air. "A portal won't close if there's still someone inside it."

Roke cursed. If Sally hadn't been left behind in Nevada, and she wasn't in the portal, then where the hell was she?

"Then why isn't she here?" he snapped, as if Sally's absence was entirely the imp's fault.

Troy took a cautious step backward, clearly having dealt with unreasonable vampires before.

"My only guess would be that she took a detour."

Detour? The ground split open just inches from his feet.

"What the hell does that mean?" he snarled.

Troy paled, taking another step backward. "The truly skilled fey are capable of creating more than one opening. She could have brought you here and continued on to another location."

Styx glanced toward Roke, his expression troubled. "Can she create portals?"

Roke shoved his fingers through his hair. There was no

denying that Sally had been changing over the past weeks. She'd always been a powerful witch, but now her innate demon blood was vying for dominance and there was no telling what talents might spontaneously erupt.

"Hell, I don't know," he muttered, his gaze glued to the imp. "Can you find where she went?"

"No. I'm sorry."

"Then who can?"

Troy gave a helpless lift of his hand and gave the wrong answer.

"No one."

Sally would have laughed if she could have forced it past the lump in her throat.

"Father?" she muttered, staring in horror at the impossibly beautiful creature.

She'd fantasized about this moment since she was old enough to realize other kids had dads who did more than donate sperm.

Late at night, after her mother had forced her to endure hours of unrelenting training and at last locked her in her room, she'd lie on her bed and pretend that her father was just about to arrive and take her away.

Some nights he would be a badass superhero, like a Navy Seal or a storm chaser. She would pretend that he was off saving the world and that was why he hadn't come to visit.

Some nights he would be a kind, comfortable sort of man. Maybe a teacher. Or a doctor. And he didn't yet know that he had a daughter, but as soon as he discovered the truth, he would be rushing to take her to his home, which was filled with all the love a lonely little girl craved.

Then, she'd been forced to accept it wasn't human blood running through her veins and her fantasies had become less idealistic and more resigned.

Obviously her mother's quickie had been with a random demon who'd been competent at disguising his true identity and that was that.

No father rushing to claim her as his daughter.

No Christmas-card family waiting in her future.

Just a common, nameless demon whom she would never have sought out if she hadn't needed his help to end her accidental mating.

Now she struggled to accept this . . . glorious, unnervingly alien being . . . was her father.

"Is that some sort of joke?"

He gave a slow blink. "Why would I jest about such a thing?"

Yeah. That was the question of the day, wasn't it?

She shivered despite the heat of the sun. "I've stopped expecting anything to make sense after I fell down the rabbit hole."

"This is no . . ." Sariel seemed to struggle over the unfamiliar word. "Joke. You are indeed my daughter. Blood of my blood."

Sally licked her lips. This was some sort of trick. It had to be.

"If that's true, then how did you meet my mother?"

His answer came without hesitation. "She was under the influence of a powerful spell that allowed me to pull her through the barriers."

"What spell?"

"A fertility spell."

Sally frowned. How had he known? "You could sense it?"

"Yes. It was like a beacon for me to latch on to."

"So you brought her here and . . ." Sally grimaced. No daughter should have to consider the ins and outs of her mother's sex life. "Seduced her?"

"Not here." He shrugged. "But yes, I did seduce her."

The ick factor doubled in value.

"No." She shook her head, unconsciously pressing the box

against her stomach as if it might whisk her away from this psycho wonderland. "I don't believe you."

Sariel's slender nose flared in outrage. "You accuse me of lying?"

"My mother would have known the second she caught sight of you that you aren't human," Sally informed him, her voice two octaves too high. "She hated demons. She certainly wouldn't have willingly crawled into bed with one, no matter how gorgeous you might be."

The man smiled with pure arrogance. "I can be very persuasive."

"Okay . . ." Sally held up a hand in protest. "TMI."

"Excuse me?"

Sally shook her head. "Even if you did manage to overcome her prejudice, there's no way she wouldn't have aborted me once she discovered she was pregnant."

"Ah." He didn't look particularly concerned that Sally might have died before she was ever born. But then, Sally was beginning to suspect that the demon didn't have many feelings that weren't directly connected to his own survival. "Her memories would have been stripped when she left my bed."

"By you?"

He gave an impatient shake of his head. "No, by the barriers that surround me."

Sally bit her lower lip. It was hard to deny the sincerity in his voice. He truly believed that he was her father.

Was it possible?

She studied the painfully beautiful face, searching for the truth.

"So she didn't remember she slept with you?"

"That is correct."

"Then she must have slept with a human male and assumed I was the result of that hookup," Sally said, grudgingly accepting that Sariel's story made as much sense as anything else.

"If you say." He waved a dismissive hand. "My only concern was for you."

Concern. She made a sound of disbelief.

"Yeah, right. If you actually had any concern for me, you wouldn't have ignored me for the past thirty years."

He looked puzzled by her accusation, the soft breeze stirring his satin gold hair.

"There was no need to attempt to contact you until you came into your powers. You were of no use until then."

She should have been prepared for the callous explanation.

A father who hadn't bothered to send her so much as a postcard in the past thirty years wasn't interested in her as a person, no matter how many fantasies she'd woven about him.

If he suddenly decided to contact her, it had to be about what-can-you-do-for-me.

Just like it'd been with her mother.

Still, she couldn't halt the heavy sense of disappointment that lodged in the pit of her stomach.

"What powers?" she at last forced herself to demand. Might as well get all the bad news over with at once.

Like ripping off a bandage.

"The power to create a portal, first of all," Sariel said, impervious to her thickened voice and slumped shoulders.

"I can't . . ." She gave a shake of her head. She'd worry about who'd created the portal later. "Never mind. What else?"

"Your human blood had to be fully consumed by the pure fey that now runs through your veins," he said. "Only then could you pass through the barriers and release me."

Was that why she was changing? Because the fey blood was overwhelming the human?

And if so, why would that cause her to be a sudden fey-magnet?

"Release you from what?" she obediently asked, her gaze flicking down his tall body.

She couldn't see any shackles, but maybe they were invisible. Or metaphorical.

"I'm being held prisoner," he insisted.

"By who?"

"That is not the point," he said, his velvet voice edged with impatience. "All that matters is that you are the key to my escape. As I said, that is the reason you were born."

Chapter Eighteen

Sally stared at the cool, beautiful face even as she battled back the stupid urge to cry.

"Let me see if I have this right." She was relieved when her voice came out mocking instead of pathetic. Hey, a girl had her pride, didn't she? "You lured my mother into your bed so you could have sex with her and create a child who would grow up to be the magical key you need to release you from your prison."

Sariel dipped his head in agreement. "Precisely."

Sally abruptly turned her head to glance over the meadow filled with fragrant flowers and fluttering butterflies.

"Why am I not surprised?" she muttered.

There was a faint rustle of silk, then her supposed father was standing directly in front of her. As if he was annoyed she might find something more interesting than his glorious beauty.

"I do not understand."

She forced herself to meet his amber gaze. "My mother needed an heir to carry on her legacy. Why wouldn't my father be a desperate imp in need of a magical key?"

He blinked, the jade flecks in his eyes shimmering with outrage.

"Imp?"

Sally frowned in confusion. "Isn't that what you are?"

"Certainly not."

"You said I now have fey blood."

"I said *pure* fey blood," he corrected.

"What's the difference?"

"Only the Chatri can claim to have blood that is pure," he said, giving a dismissive wave of his hand. "Imps, fairies, sprites, and the rest are lesser fey."

Sally felt her chin drop, her breath locked in her lungs as she stared at Sariel in shock.

"You're a . . . Chatri?"

He peered down the length of his regal nose. "I am their king."

Ah. Of course he was.

She didn't know whether to laugh or cry.

"I thought you left the world centuries ago?"

"We returned to our homelands when our children began to seek mates among the lesser fey," he confessed, his nose flaring as if he could smell something nasty. "We could not allow our race to become corrupted."

This from a man who'd slept with a strange witch just to make a metaphoric key?

"Then how did you become imprisoned?"

Something that might have been annoyance darkened his amber eyes. Or was it embarrassment?

"I remained behind to close the doorways. I was distracted and vulnerable to an age-old enemy I had thought we'd sealed off from the world."

"Who?"

He brushed off her question with a shrug. "I will explain all once I am free."

Yep. Embarrassment.

The mighty king clearly didn't want to discuss how he came to be taken by an enemy he considered beneath him.

Of course, Sally sensed this man considered most creatures beneath him.

Including her.

"What am I supposed to do?"

"Use the map on the box."

"Oh." She held up the box in her hand. Foolishly, she hadn't connected the two. "Did you make this?"

"Naturally."

Sally snorted. There was no *naturally* about it.

"How did it end up at the cottage?"

A brilliant butterfly landed on his shoulder, adding to his sense of otherworldliness.

"I hid it among your mother's belongings when she left," he said.

Sally paused, remembering back to the day she'd found the box on the rubbish heap. She'd just assumed that it'd been left behind by the previous owners.

"My mother must have been the one to throw it away," she muttered.

His shrug sent the butterfly fluttering into the air. "It would not matter what she did with it, the magic was bound to you."

She grimaced. How much magic had been attached to her before she'd ever been born?

Her mother's sorcery spell. Her father's GPS spell.

She hoped to hell she didn't have any grandparents who'd gotten in on the action.

"Fantastic," she muttered.

Sariel ignored her sarcasm. "The map is etched on the box. You must follow it to release me."

Sally stilled. Okay. What was she missing?

"Why do I have to follow some treasure map when you're standing right here?"

He lifted a hand to wave it toward the sun-filled meadow. "My powers allow me to create a mirage that appears real to others."

"So this is all an illusion?" Sally demanded in disbelief.

She would have sworn on her favorite book of spells that this was real.

She could hear the sound of birds singing in the distant trees, she could feel the brush of the breeze and the heat of the sun on her skin. She could smell the heady scent of fine wine.

That sort of texture didn't happen in an illusion, did it?

"Rather more than that, but the term will suffice," her father said. "My physical body is trapped in a portal between this world and another."

Her gaze lowered to the box she clutched in her hand. "And the map will lead me to you?"

"Yes."

The glyphs continued to glow, the fluid angles and curves shimmering with magic.

"You realize I can't read the glyphs?" she muttered.

"You will," he said with an arrogant assurance that grated on her already raw nerves.

"You're standing right there, whether you're real or not," she snapped. "Why don't you just tell me how to get to you?"

He was shaking his head before she finished. "The portal is not a human tunnel from one place to another. It is made of magic that . . . floats."

Sally frowned. "What does that mean?"

"It doesn't remain in the same place." He pointed toward the box. "The glyphs are carved with my power. They will always be capable of finding me."

His confidence that she would rush to fulfill her destiny didn't do anything to ease her temper.

As far as he was concerned she was just a tool he'd created to pick the lock on his prison cell.

It didn't matter to him that her life had been a brutal battle for survival. That she'd been fighting one enemy after another . . .

Abruptly reminded of her most recent battle, she narrowed her eyes to glare at the finely carved face.

"And what about the psycho demon who's been trying to get his hands on the box?"

She expected dismissal at her welfare; instead a vibrant anger darkened the amber eyes.

"You allowed another to know about our secret communication?"

"It wasn't a matter of *letting* him know," she said. "I never saw him before Levet removed the layers of illusion from the box and glyphs started glowing like a neon sign."

The scent of wine saturated the air, Sariel clearly not pleased with her explanation.

"Who is Levet?"

"A gargoyle who has helped me more than once."

He was indifferent to her pointed reminder that there were demons who'd actually thought she was worth trying to protect.

Demons like Roke.

Her heart clenched with a sharp, near debilitating need to be in his arms.

"Who else knows of the box?"

She shrugged. "The vampires."

He hissed out a low breath. "You have put me in great danger."

"I've put you in danger?" She shook her head at his total self-absorption. She'd thought her mother was a narcissist, but she was an amateur when compared to Daddy Dearest. "I'm the one who has nearly been killed twice by the lunatic demon. Does he have something to do with you?"

He ignored her question, along with any concern for her safety.

"You must use the map to find me," he commanded, taking a step back, then another. "Until then."

The charming meadow began to fade around the edges, as if it was collapsing on itself.

At the same time her father was growing more and more distant.

Crap.

Her father was about to disappear and she hadn't even asked him how she'd managed to mate with a vampire, let alone how to break it.

If the weird demon didn't kill her, Roke would.

"Wait . . ."

Roke earned his title of being a stubborn SOB.

If someone gave him an answer he didn't like, he simply waited until they gave him the one he wanted.

Even if the waiting included some broken bones, some blood, and a whole lot of tears.

Standing in silence as Troy tried to explain to him all the reasons he couldn't open the portal or use his fey magic to locate Sally, he at last lifted a hand to halt the useless chatter.

"There has to be some way to trace her," he insisted, his arms folded over his chest.

Sunrise was less than an hour away.

He intended to have his mate in his arms before that happened.

Troy heaved a frustrated sigh. "If she's your mate, you should be able to sense her location, shouldn't you?"

Roke hissed, the absence of Sally a raw wound that was slowly destroying him.

"It's being . . . muffled," he admitted in bleak tones.

Troy narrowed his emerald gaze. "Then she's either using a spell to mask her location—"

"No," Roke denied.

Sally wouldn't be hiding from him.

But what if she still believed he'd deliberately abandoned her in the mines, a treacherous voice whispered in the back of his mind.

Maybe she was so pissed she was trying to avoid him.

Or worse . . . frightened.

No. That he couldn't bear.

"Or she's in another dimension," Troy offered, thankfully distracting his dark thoughts.

"Can fey move between dimensions?" he asked.

Troy hesitated before giving a grudging nod. That was no doubt another one of those secrets the fey preferred to keep off the record.

"Only the very powerful," he admitted. "But why would she want to?"

It was a question that made his fangs ache. "She had to have been forced."

Troy looked baffled. "By who?"

"It could be one of the fey," he muttered. "Or the damned Miera demon who's been chasing us."

The imp shook his head. "A Miera can't manipulate portals."

Roke made a sound of impatience, resuming his pacing as he struggled against the tidal wave of frustration.

"This was no normal Miera."

Styx stepped forward, his large body consuming more than its fair share of space.

"Perhaps you can clear up a mystery."

Troy preened, his emerald eyes promising all sorts of sensual pleasures.

"I am an imp of many talents."

Styx ignored Troy's blatant invitation. This was obviously not his first time dealing with the annoying twit.

"What sort of demon feeds off fey magic?" he asked.

Roke halted his pacing at the same time Troy gave a startled grunt of disbelief.

"Are you serious?" the imp rasped, his expression troubled.

"Never more serious," Styx assured him.

"None that I know of," Troy slowly said.

Styx frowned. "You're certain?"

"Let me rephrase that." In the blink of an eye, Troy's act of a frivolous fool was gone and in his place was a cunning fey prince who made an art form of being underestimated. "There are no official demons who admit to feasting on fey magic."

Styx snorted. "There are unofficial demons?"

Troy shrugged. "The humans have their Big Foot and Loch Ness Monster, we have our Nebule."

Roke hissed in disgust, realizing he'd had the answer all along.

Shit. Why hadn't he put this together sooner?

"That's it," he snarled.

Styx turned to eye him in confusion. "What?"

"On the box. The glyphs mentioned mist people," he said, shoving his fingers through his hair. "It struck a memory at the time, but I couldn't pinpoint it."

"Explain," Styx commanded in clipped tones.

It was Troy who answered.

"The fey have a folktale that there were a species of demons who are capable of taking any physical shape they want."

Styx didn't look impressed. "There are a few rare vampires who can alter their shape. They can even mist walk."

Troy shook his head. "These aren't vampires. They're an entire race of people who are made of nothing but mist until they can drain a fey and use their magic to take a physical form."

"That's why they kill fey?" Styx asked.

Troy gave a nod of agreement. "They have no magic of their own. They must steal ours."

Roke had run across a description of the "mist people" when he was doing research on extinct races of demons. There had been little more than a vague reference to a species who were made of mist and hunted the fey.

"What else can they do?" he asked.

Troy grimaced. "It was said that they have a strange power to vibrate the air."

"Shit." Roke glanced toward his king. "That's exactly how he attacked us. Those vibrations nearly turned our insides to mush."

Styx considered a long minute. "That wouldn't be fatal to a vampire."

"No, but it's debilitating," Roke said. "It weakened me to the point that I didn't realize the bastard had shot me full of blood thinner and silver." A muscle in his jaw tightened until he could barely speak. "And it might easily be fatal to Sally."

The Anasso was grim as he returned his attention to Troy. "Where can we find these Nebule?"

"Our stories claim that the Chatri drove the last of them from our world before they returned to their homelands." Troy smiled without humor. "But of course, there are always rumors that a few survived, and that they lurk among us just waiting for an opportunity to strike. I always assumed they were boogeyman tales used to frighten our young."

"That doesn't answer my question," Styx growled.

"Because I have no answer." Troy glanced toward Roke. "Do you know why he was attacking you specifically?"

"He wanted Sally's box."

Troy furrowed his brow. "The box? I don't . . . oh, wait."

Roke stepped toward the imp, desperate for any information that might help him locate his mate.

He needed her next to him . . . in his arms.

And she was never leaving his side again.

Period.

"What is it?" he snapped.

The emerald eyes were sparkling with a barely suppressed excitement.

"Tell me, does the box glow?"

Roke balled his hands into fists. It was that or grabbing the imp and shaking him for answers.

"Yes."

"Oh, my God." Something that looked like wonderment settled on Troy's pale face. "It's the magic."

Roke growled deep in his throat. He should have destroyed the damned thing the minute they realized it was more than just a trinket.

"You said the box didn't have magic."

"It doesn't contain a magical spell. Or the ability to create magic on its own," Troy clarified, appearing far too eager. "But if it's still bound to a Chatri, then a Nebule would be able to suck the magic from the connection."

Fear exploded through Roke. Goddammit. He had to get to his mate. The need was clawing through him with a relentless agony.

"You're saying this box might still be under the control of a Chatri?"

"Yes." Troy tried and failed to disguise his rising anticipation. "My collection has the glyphs that were created by my forefathers, but now they're just scratches in the wood. They no longer channel any magic."

Roke cursed, indifferent to the distant fountain that crumbled to dust as his power spread through the area.

"Why would some Chatri be screwing with Sally?"

Troy's lips parted, then with a startled gasp he was jerking around to stare at the precise spot where Roke had been tossed out of the portal.

"I think we're about to find out."

His words had barely left his lips when there was an odd tingle in the air and Sally tumbled out of midair.

Roke was charging forward and had her in his arms before she could hit the ground.

Chapter Nineteen

Sally felt as if she'd tumbled out of Wonderland, only to be caught up in the tornado from *The Wizard of Oz*.

Only this tornado was named Roke.

She didn't know how he happened to be waiting at the precise spot where she would smack into a barrier and be ripped out of the portal. Or why he was standing there with an imp and the King of Vampires.

And it didn't really matter as she found herself held tightly in his arms while he rushed her into Styx's mansion, growling at anyone who dared to try to help.

She wanted nothing more than a hot shower and an equally hot meal before she collapsed in the first available bed she could find.

As always, Roke was able to sense her need and with minimum fuss he had her in the private room she'd used when she was last in Chicago.

At the time she'd been overwhelmed by the elegance of the suite that was decorated in shades of sea-foam green and silver.

She'd never seen a marble fireplace that consumed an entire wall or walked across a Parisian carpet that she was fairly certain was a priceless antique. Certainly she'd never seen a bedroom that had a coved ceiling with a painting of angels dancing among the clouds.

In the center of the room was a canopy bed with a pale green comforter that was perfectly matched to the chaise lounge set beside the windows. And along a far wall were a hand-carved armoire and a mirrored dressing table.

It all combined to make her feel like an intruder.

But tonight . . . no wait, it had to be nearly morning . . . she didn't give a crap.

So long as it wasn't a freaky illusion or an abandoned gold mine, or a dungeon, she was satisfied.

Allowing Roke to carry her into the bathroom, she was happy to discover the satin gown had been replaced with the itchy blanket. It made it easy to drop it to the floor so she could step beneath the scalding hot water.

Roke murmured something before disappearing from the room. Sally thought she heard something about food, but she was too numb to concentrate on more than one thing at a time. At the moment the winner was the cascade of hot water that felt like heaven.

She stood in the shower until her skin was pruny and her legs threatened to buckle. Then, wrapping a towel around her damp body, she left the vast marble bathroom and made a beeline for the bed.

Crawling beneath the covers, she was prepared when Roke returned with a tray of food that could easily have fed a football team.

Fried chicken, hamburgers, pizza, barbecued ribs, fries, apple pie . . .

He'd obviously hit every fast-food restaurant in the area.

In silence Sally consumed a respectable portion of the feast, replenishing her depleted energy before she set the tray on the nightstand next to her. Then, leaning against the headboard, she watched as Roke paced the floor with barely leashed agitation.

Her heart gave a treacherous leap.

He was just so . . . gorgeous.

Not unearthly beautiful like her father.

Or handsome like a human model.

He was raw and dangerous and so potently male he made every female hormone in her body sizzle with awareness.

Perhaps sensing her gaze, he abruptly glanced toward her with eyes darkened by storm clouds of emotion.

"Are you warm enough?" he asked, never halting his restless pacing. "There are more blankets in the cupboard."

"I'm fine."

His brows drew together. "You're shivering."

With a sense of surprise, Sally realized he was right. She hadn't noticed that her entire body was trembling beneath the covers.

"Delayed shock," she muttered.

His jaws clenched, the priceless oil paintings on the wall rattling as he struggled to control his burst of frustration.

"Tell me what you need."

"You could sit still," she suggested with a grimace. "You're making me dizzy."

"You're not the only one with delayed shock," he muttered, coming to a reluctant halt. His dark face was in full lockdown as the paintings continued to rattle. "I'm on the edge of a full-out rampage."

Sally snorted. "You're always on the edge of a full-out rampage."

His eyes flashed silver fire. "Only since I met you, my love. Until then I was accused of having ice in my veins."

She stiffened at the unfair accusation. "Don't blame me."

"I don't. I blame the irony of fate." He rammed his fingers through his hair. "It just couldn't resist destroying my arrogant assumption I could choose an obedient mate who was content to remain in the background."

Sally ground her teeth together. She was getting tired of hearing about Roke's imaginary mate.

"She sounds perfect," she gritted.

He shook his head, his lips twisted in a rueful smile. "Instead my mate is a beautiful, impulsive, unpredictable witch who has made me jump through hoop after hoop since she claimed me."

Sally wasn't appeased. "I didn't mean to claim you."

"But you have, now I need to do whatever necessary to ease your pain." Moving forward, he climbed onto the bed and gently pulled her into his arms. "Tell me how I can do that."

Her brief flare of annoyance melted away as she snuggled against the hard strength of his chest.

A part of her knew this was dangerous.

She'd spent a lifetime learning that she could never depend on anyone. They always failed her. Always disappointed.

And the recent encounter with her father only emphasized that painful lesson.

But she didn't have the energy to be sensible.

She badly needed the comfort of his strong arms and the cool wash of his power wrapping around her like a security blanket.

"You could start with waving a magic wand and giving me new parents," she admitted, the words edged with a bitterness she couldn't disguise. "I'm not fussy. The Borgias had to be better."

"Parents?" She felt his muscles tense beneath her cheek. "As in plural?"

"I just had a close encounter with an alien claiming to be my father."

"Alien?"

"He might as well be. He said . . ." She sucked in a deep breath. She hadn't fully wrapped her brain around the latest bombshell to hit her life. Strange, really. You'd think she'd be used to unpleasant shocks. "He said he's a Chatri."

Roke gave a low hiss, his fingers sliding beneath her chin to tilt her face up to meet his narrowed gaze.

"Start at the beginning."

Still raw from her encounter with her father, Sally instantly bristled at the sharp command.

"That sounded dangerously close to an order."

His lips flattened, but he spoke the words she never thought she'd hear.

"Please, Sally."

She might have smiled if her heart weren't bruised and aching.

"I'm not sure what happened after we were in the portal."

"Did your father open the portal?"

She shook her head, wrinkling her nose. "He said that I did."

He looked more curious than astonished by her revelation. "Is that how you took us to Nevada when I was unconscious?"

"No. An imp opened that one." She was struck by a sudden thought. She'd been so worried about Roke dying that she'd forgotten the sensation of the imp's magic sinking inside her, as if she were claiming it for her own. "Although, I think I must have . . . absorbed how he weaved his magic when he created it," she said slowly.

Roke frowned, trying to work through her babbling. "What imp?"

"It doesn't matter." She didn't want to discuss her weird, rapidly changing powers. Not now. "Once we were in the portal we were separated. You came here and I ended up in an illusion created by my father."

His thumb brushed the line of her jaw. "Tell me about him."

She relished the soothing caress. The mating between her and Roke might be fake, but the comfort he offered her was very real.

As long as he was near, the world seemed . . . right.

"He's beautiful," she said.

A faint smile curved his lips, his gaze sweeping over her face.

"That much I expected."

"No." She gave a firm shake of her head. "Not just pretty, but so beautiful it's almost painful to look at him," she said. "And he smelled like wine."

The silver gaze continued to sweep over her face, as if he was seeing her for the first time.

"So you're the daughter of a Chatri."

Her eyes narrowed. "You don't seem surprised."

"It explains why the fey were going crazy," he murmured. "You're royalty to them."

"So Sariel claimed," she muttered. Roke raised his brows in a silent question. "He said he was the King of the Chatri," she clarified.

His thumb moved to trace her lower lip. "If you expect me to bow to you, you can forget it."

She shivered, remembering the bizarre behavior of the fey over the past few days. She'd survived her entire life by fading into the background.

Being forced to become the center of attention felt like someone had just painted a big, fat bull's-eye on her back.

"I don't want anyone bowing to me." Another shiver. "It's creepy."

Roke's eyes darkened as he felt her burst of fear. "Did he have a purpose in revealing himself to you?"

"Oh yes." Her lips twisted into a humorless smile. "I doubt my father has ever done anything without a purpose."

"Why do you say that?"

"He told me that he'd been captured by some mysterious enemy when the rest of his people left our world and that he was trapped in a portal."

"Trapped?" Roke frowned. "How's that possible?"

"I don't have a clue."

"What did he want from you?"

"He wants me to follow the map on the box and rescue him."

She was still speaking when he gave a decisive shake of his head.

"No."

She lifted her head off his chest, her eyes narrowed with warning.

"It's not your decision, Roke."

"He made you sad," he growled, his hand lowering to circle her throat in a gesture of pure possession. "I can feel it."

"Not sad . . ." She searched for the right word. "Disappointed."

"Why?"

"I spent a lifetime clinging to the hope I had a father out there who cared about me." She gave a sharp laugh. "So stupid."

He scowled, leaning down until they were nose to nose. "You're not stupid, my love. Never that."

"Fathers who care don't abandon their children." She breathed deeply of Roke's scent. Cold steel and raw male power. She'd been furious with him in Nevada, even permitting Zoe's deceitful accusations to cloud her mind with doubts. Now she clung to their bond, using his steady presence to shield her from the pain of dying dreams. "I knew that on some level, but there was still a part of me who wanted to cling to hope. Now I have no choice. Sariel's only interest in me is what I can do for him."

He dipped his head down to press his lips to her temple. "Then why would you want to help him?"

"Because we need him."

He stilled, his mouth resting against her skin. "For what?"

"To break our mating."

* * *

"No."

The barked denial was flying from his lips before he could soften it.

Not that he wanted to soften it.

His entire body hummed with fury at the mere mention of breaking their mating.

Dammit. He'd just gotten her back in his arms. There was no way in hell she was going to get rid of him.

She *belonged* to him.

On a deep, cellular level that wasn't going to be ended no matter what hocus-pocus she might learn from her bastard of a father.

"Again, not your decision," she said, clearly annoyed.

He pulled back, studying her with a brooding frown.

She looked tired, with purple shadows beneath her eyes. Even her delicate face was more pale than normal. Which was the only reason he was struggling to leash his fury at the mere suggestion of breaking their bond.

"What happens to our mating is very much my decision," he managed to say in a remarkably calm voice.

She jutted her chin to a stubborn angle, the damp strands of her hair shimmering with hidden fire in the dim light.

"You want it broken and the only way to do that is to have my father show me how," she said.

His hand slid to her nape, delighting in the satin heat of her skin.

"We can discuss it later," he smoothly assured her, the intoxicating scent of peaches becoming a distinct distraction.

Well, the scent of peaches and the half-naked female body that he craved to have beneath him while he proved that there was no magic that could end the hunger that burned between them.

"Later? You happen to know another Chatri we can ask?" she muttered.

He allowed his lips to graze down her temple to the curve of her ear.

"I have more important matters to worry about."

She trembled, the sound of her rapid heartbeat music to his ears. Her expression might be one of stubborn indifference, but her body was giving him all the encouragement he needed.

"I doubt that your clan thinks there is anything more important." She deliberately reminded him of the torture his clan had forced her to endure. "They hate me."

Or maybe she was reminding herself of why their mating should be broken.

In either case, he wasn't going to let his people stand between them.

"Styx has already made certain they won't dare try to hurt you again," he promised with a harsh sincerity.

The Anasso hadn't been amused when Roke confessed that Sally had been locked away and beaten. Styx, however, had convinced Roke to allow him to deal with the situation rather than letting Roke go postal on them.

Except for Zoe and Dyson.

Roke had taken great pleasure in making that phone call personally.

"How?" Sally demanded, her tone defensive. "They're convinced I've put you under a spell."

"He announced you were under his protection and any vampire who tried to hurt you would suffer his wrath." Roke grimaced. "No one wants that."

Sally shrugged. "Zoe might be willing to risk pissing off the Anasso if it meant getting rid of me."

"I spoke to Zoe." He shook his head as he recalled the female vampire's frantic pleas to be forgiven. He'd underestimated her raw ambition to become his lover. Not just because she desired him, but because she lusted for the power he wielded. Which only proved that he'd been a fool to think he could control destiny. Zoe might have been what he thought he needed, but she could never have been what he truly wanted. Sally was what he wanted. "She and Dyson have been ordered to find a new clan."

Sally's eyes widened in shock. "But—"

"Yes?"

She looked . . . flustered, obviously not having expected to have the roadblock so easily knocked aside.

Then, she swiftly latched on to the next available excuse to keep him at a distance.

"You were the one who was having a hissy fit when I accidentally caused the mating," she accused.

He arched a brow. "Hissy fit?"

"I thought you were desperate to get rid of me."

His fingers trailed down her spine, dipping beneath the towel she'd wrapped around her damp body.

"Maybe I'm used to having you around."

Her breath fractured, her eyes darkening with desire. "You just said you wanted an obedient sheep for a mate."

"I said that's what I thought I wanted." His finger tugged at the towel, loosening it as his lips brushed over her cheek. "I've discovered there are benefits to having an autumn-haired beauty creating passionate chaos in my very boring existence."

"You're just saying that because you don't want me to put myself in danger," she said, her voice thickening, the enticing scent of her arousal perfuming the air.

"I'm saying it because it's true." His tongue teased at the pulse racing at the base of her neck. "And for the record, you're not going to put yourself in danger."

She made a sound of annoyance. "We may be temporarily mated, but you're not the boss of me."

"I just got you back, Sally." With one smooth motion he

had her flat on her back and he was straddling her hips. Holding her startled gaze, he pulled off the towel. "Don't push me."

She sucked in a deep breath. "Roke, what are you doing?"

With tender care he allowed his fingers to trace the prominent line of her collarbone, his cock already fully erect and throbbing to be deep inside her.

It wasn't sex.

It was a critical need to be intimately connected to her. To reassure himself that she was here and that nothing was going to take her away from him.

"Making sure you weren't hurt," he murmured, taking a long minute to appreciate the sight of her spread beneath him.

The glorious gold and red satin of her hair spread across the white pillow. The dark eyes softened with a desire she couldn't deny. Her ivory skin flushing with rising excitement.

"I told you I wasn't," she husked.

With a wicked chuckle he bent down to stroke his tongue over the tip of her rose-tinted nipple.

"Some things I need to see for myself," he murmured, capturing the nipple between his lips until she arched beneath him in pleasure.

"With your lips?"

"Mmm." He kissed a path down her stomach, using his fangs to lightly scrape over her skin. "And other body parts."

She groaned, her hands grabbing the sheet beneath her in a death grip.

"We're discussing how we can break the mating," she breathed, her voice unsteady.

He lifted his head to stab her with a fierce glare. One more word about breaking their bond and he was going to sink his fangs deep into her neck and make certain there was no going back.

There was no doubt in his mind that this was the female fate had intended for him.

"No, you were assuming I'm in a hurry to break our mating and I'm proving we have all the time in the world."

She bit her bottom lip, the vulnerability she struggled so hard to hide softening her expression.

"Because you want to have sex with me?"

"Because I'm not ready to let you go," he admitted with blunt honesty, lowering his head to return to his determined path down her quivering body.

"Oh . . ." She breathed, her body melting as she willingly allowed him to spread her legs and discover the welcome heat of her core. "Goddess."

Clamping his hands on her hips to keep her in place, Roke glanced up the length of her beautiful body, holding her darkened gaze.

"There's a good chance I'm never going to let you go, my love."

Chapter Twenty

Less than a mile from the Anasso's estate, Brandel was settled in a leather wing chair that was pulled close to the roaring fire.

It wasn't as if he needed the heat from the flames despite the chill in the night air, but reading in front of a fireplace suited his current image.

He glanced around the long library with towering shelves and heavy walnut furnishings. He'd arrived in Chicago the night before, drawn by the pulsing fey magic. At the time he'd been too drained to try to slip past the King of Vampires' impressive defenses, and chosen the closest mansion to use as his lair.

It was only now that he had the opportunity to appreciate his surroundings.

The elegant house that was decorated to resemble an English country estate beat the hell out of dank caves filled with obnoxious Oracles. And best of all, he had a full staff of properly trained English servants who were eager to cater to his every need.

Even the sweet little maid who'd given him a professional blow job before breakfast.

They didn't have a clue he wasn't their employer who'd

Brandel killed and stuffed in the pool house that was boarded over for the season. He'd become a perfect replica of the slender, gray-haired businessman with watery brown eyes and a prominent nose.

The stench of the rotting body would eventually blow his cover, but for now he intended to enjoy being surrounded by luxury.

Sipping the cognac that was perfectly aged, he was debating his options of bypassing the layers of security wrapped around the Anasso's lair when an unmistakable vibration in the air warned him that his brief sense of peace was about to be destroyed.

Setting aside the cognac, he was prepared when the uniformed butler stepped into the room, his back poker-straight and his expression puckered, as if he'd just swallowed a lemon.

"There is a Mr. Raith to see you, sir," he said, his toneless voice not able to disguise his disdain for the visitor.

Brandel clenched the arms of his chair.

"Tell him—"

"That you're anxious to speak with your dear friend who has traveled so far just to see you?" a familiar voice drawled as Raith stepped into the room, still clinging to his Adonis form.

Brandel grimaced, understanding his servant's blatant disgust.

Raith had left his halo of golden curls to tumble to his broad shoulders, which were revealed by a sleeveless vest stretched tight over his large muscles and a pair of jeans that had half a dozen rips in the faded material.

He looked like he should be turning tricks on a downtown corner, not visiting a powerful tycoon of business.

Brandel kept his own face expressionless as he met the mocking brown eyes.

"Raith." He waved a hand toward the servant. "That will be all, Fenmore."

The elder man gave a half bow. "Yes, sir."

They waited in silence for the servant to exit the room, shutting the door behind him.

Then, with a motion too fluid for a mere human, Raith gave a toss of his hair and crossed to stand near the crackling fire.

"A butler?" he drawled, speaking out loud. The human servants would be curious if they didn't hear voices from behind the closed door.

Brandel forced himself to relax back in his chair.

He'd known this encounter was coming. He'd just hoped he'd already have his hands on the box when Raith tracked him down.

"I have to find somewhere to hide from the Oracles," he said, pointing out the obvious.

Raith glanced around the library that was the size of most homes.

"This is hardly discreet."

Brandel shrugged. "Our enemies would expect me to be cowering in a dark cave."

Raith didn't look particularly impressed by his logic. "So instead you're hiding in plain sight?"

"You have a better suggestion?"

Raith waved away the question, his eyes flickering to black, the slit of crimson reflecting the nearby flames.

"And that's the only reason you'd settled in this particular place?"

Brandel didn't bother pretending he didn't know what his companion was implying.

"No. I'm still attempting to acquire the box so it can be destroyed."

Raith arched a golden brow. "Destroyed?"

"Of course." Brandel managed a stiff smile. "The Oracles have already discovered that I'm not what I pretended to be. We can't afford for them to realize that we're holding a Chatri captive."

Raith leaned against the mantel, his gaze never wavering from Brandel's guarded expression.

"So—"

"What?"

"This has nothing to do with wanting the box for yourself?"

Brandel stiffened, inwardly cursing Raith's persistence. "I said I intend to destroy it."

"And I'm not convinced of your sincerity," his companion drawled.

"I'm here, aren't I?"

"Yes, but for what purpose?" The air vibrated in reaction to Raith's swelling anger. "To destroy the box or claim it?"

Brandel rose to his feet, pacing toward the heavy walnut desk.

"I don't know what you mean."

"You twice had the opportunity to get rid of the box and yet you failed miserably on each occasion."

"The witch—"

"Yes?" Raith prompted.

"Is more."

"More what?"

Brandel unconsciously frowned. It troubled him he couldn't figure out how the female managed to disrupt his very essence. If it hadn't been impossible, he would have suspected she was somehow gaining power from the box.

"I'm not certain, but there's something strange about her," he muttered.

The vibrations became more intense. "So that's your excuse?" Raith demanded.

"She's an unexpected variable."

"You know what I think, Brandel?"

Brandel turned back to meet Raith's narrowed glare. "What?"

"I think that you could have destroyed the box, but instead you tried to keep it for yourself."

Brandel struggled to hold his human form. "Why would I do that?"

"For the magic," Raith accused. "The power."

Enough.

Raith clearly wasn't going to be fooled. There was no point in continuing his charade.

"You believe you should be the only one with magic?" he instead accused.

Raith straightened from the mantel, his anger shattering the crystal vases that were lined along a top shelf.

"You have an entire world of fey to feast upon," he hissed.

As if a mere fey could remotely compare to what Raith had been gorging on for the past few centuries.

"But none with the magic of a Chatri."

Raith smiled without humor. "We all have a role to play."

"Well, I am weary of my role."

"Fine." Raith stepped forward. "Then return home and I'll send another to clean up your mess."

Brandel refused to back down. He'd devoted centuries to putting his life on the line, always the one who was in danger while Raith remained in the shadows, drunk on Chatri magic.

No more.

He was close. So close. Nothing was going to stand in his way.

"No one will be replacing me."

"Then do your duty."

"I'm done with duty. I want what's mine."

Lifting a clenched hand he sent a concentrated burst of pulses directly toward the smirking Raith. The attack was Brandel's specialty and designed to disrupt his opponent's powers.

Caught off guard, Raith abruptly turned to mist and headed toward the nearby windows.

It wouldn't buy much time.

He would just have to ensure it was enough.

Roke had reluctantly left Sally sleeping in the wide bed shortly before sunset.

He wanted nothing more than to remain curled around his precious mate, pretending the world outside their door didn't exist.

But the unmistakable scent of Cyn arriving at the mansion had him sliding silently out of the bed and taking a swift shower before he was dressed in black jeans and matching tee with his usual moccasins that molded up his legs to his knees. He shrugged on his leather jacket as he headed down the stairs.

It wasn't coincidence that brought the clan chief of Ireland to Chicago.

Roke would wager his left nut that Styx had commanded Cyn to search for a way to break his mating to Sally.

Stepping into the small study, he eyeballed the oversize ancient berserker who was seated in a leather chair as he flipped through a leather-bound book.

On this occasion Cyn was fully clothed, thank the gods, in a pair of faded jeans and a jade green silk shirt that perfectly matched his eyes. His hair was left free to fall halfway down his back except for the front strands that were, as always, woven into tight braids that framed his face.

He glanced up when Roke entered the room, smoothly setting aside the book.

"Hello, Roke. Did you miss me?"

Roke moved to the center of the room, folding his arms over his chest.

"What are you doing here?"

Cyn gave a lift of one broad shoulder. "I'm the leading

expert on fey. And from what I've heard, you're up to your ass in the creatures."

Roke snorted. "If you're such an expert, then why didn't you know that my mate is a Chatri?"

Cyn's lack of astonishment revealed that Styx had already shared the information of Sally's bloodline.

"I have a theory," Cyn informed him.

"I do too," Roke said. "You were distracted by nymph tits."

"They were very nice tits," Cyn pointed out with a reminiscent smile. "But I wasn't distracted."

Roke rolled his eyes, but he inwardly had to admit that Cyn might prove helpful.

As he rightly claimed, he knew more about the fey than any other vampire.

"Tell me your theory."

"Most mongrels—"

"Careful," Roke interrupted, baring his fangs.

Cyn grimaced. "Half-breeds, if that makes you happier."

Roke didn't know if it made him happy, but it sure the hell was better than calling his mate a mongrel.

"Fine," he muttered.

"They tend to come into their powers after they hit puberty."

"Sally is past puberty."

Cyn smiled, the jade eyes darkening with appreciation. "Yes, I noticed."

Roke scowled, the temperature of the room dropping. "Don't notice."

Cyn chuckled, clearly appreciating yanking Roke's chain before he was leaning forward, his expression serious.

"Most half-breeds have a combination of their parents' DNA. One species might be more dominant, but they both exist. But when one of the species possess powers that are overwhelming when compared to the other they do more than just mix bloodlines. They scour away any genetic material until they leave behind a pureblood."

"Like a Chatri and a human?"

"Yes." Cyn rose to his feet, his massive body consuming far more than his fair share of the room. "I would guess that her blood has been slowly altering for years."

Roke gave a shake of his head. He'd been mated to Sally barely a month, but in that time she'd gone from a human witch with a talent for black magic, to a demon who could not only compel a vampire clan chief to do her bidding, but could create a portal to haul three people across the country.

The gods only knew what she would be able to do a week from now.

"Not a bad theory, but her powers have been skyrocketing over the past days, not slowly altering."

Cyn refused to be dissuaded. "It would've taken time for the Chatri blood to fully consume her human half. Especially since she was a powerful witch. But once it reached a critical mass"—he made a gesture of a bomb exploding—"the power would have blasted through her."

Okay. That made sense.

"Does that mean she's fully fey now?"

"She's fully Chatri, my friend," Cyn corrected. "Which isn't at all the same."

Roke shrugged. He didn't give a shit what blood ran through Sally's veins.

"It doesn't matter."

"Of course it does," Cyn protested. "For one thing it makes reversing your mating more difficult. We know very little about the Chatri magic. Lucky for you I've been doing some research and—"

"Stop it," Roke snapped.

Cyn frowned in confusion. "Stop what?"

"The research." Roke paused, concentrating on leashing his anger. Only when he was certain he wasn't going to bring the roof down on their heads did he continue. "Sally is my mate. There will be no reversing it."

"Roke."

"No," Roke bit out. "That's the last word on the subject."

Cyn flattened his lips, obviously fighting the urge to insist that Roke wasn't thinking clearly.

A good thing.

If one more person tried to convince him to get rid of his mate, he was going to . . .

The various possibilities ran through his mind, each bloodier than the next.

As if sensing he was on the brink of snapping, Cyn held up his hands in a gesture of submission.

"Whatever you want."

Roke wasn't stupid. Cyn would continue searching for a way to break the mating no matter what Roke said. They were all certain he would come to his senses and demand the bond with Sally be ended.

So long as they kept their thoughts to themselves, he didn't give a shit.

He understood.

Their mating was eternal.

Just as it was supposed to be.

Giving a shake of his head, Roke squashed his anger and instead concentrated on how he could best use Cyn's presence.

"If you actually want to help, you'll tell me what you know about the Nebules," he at last demanded.

Cyn's eyes widened, easily recalling the glyphs he'd been trying to decipher for Roke.

"Of course," he muttered. "The mist people that were mentioned on the music box. You think the glyph was talking about the Nebules?"

"Yes."

Cyn shook his head, the beads at the end of his narrow braids banging against his chest.

"I thought they were extinct?"

"That was the general opinion."

"What's your opinion?"

Roke didn't hesitate. "I think one is hunting my mate."

Cyn nodded, accepting Roke's fear without question. "Do you know why they would be interested in her?"

Roke paced toward a glass case filled with ancient scrolls. Styx's vast collection of books, scrolls, and artifacts were beginning to take over the McMansion despite Darcy's best attempts to keep them contained.

"I'm not sure, but it seems to have something to do with the music box," he said, his voice harsh with frustration. "A music box that just happens to have a map leading to Sally's father."

"Ah. You think they're trying to find the Chatri?"

"I don't know," Roke admitted, feeling a vast indifference when it came to his father-in-law. "He claims that he's being held captive."

"The Nebule is being held captive?"

"No." Roke turned back to meet Cyn's puzzled frown. "Sally's father."

"Christ." Cyn planted his hands on his hips. "Are you deliberately trying to confuse me?"

Roke stepped forward. He would make it crystal clear.

"I need to know how to kill a Nebule."

"What about the Chatri?"

Roke made a sound of disgust. "As far as I'm concerned he can stay stuck where he is."

A strange expression settled on Cyn's bluntly carved face. "And how does Sally feel about her leaving her father trapped?"

Roke tilted his chin. "I intend to make damn certain she doesn't put herself in danger."

"Right." Cyn's laughter filled the room. "Good luck with that."

Chapter Twenty-One

Sally clutched the box in her hand as she crept down the grand staircase.

She didn't really think she could slip through a household of vampires unnoticed. Even if the house wasn't wired with high-tech security, they would be able to hear her every footstep, her every breath, and every beat of her heart. Not to mention catching her scent from a freaking mile away.

Yeah. There was no sneaking in a vampire house, but she did hope to do some quick research while Roke was otherwise occupied.

Her mate wasn't going to be pleased when he realized she hadn't given up her determination to find her father. She grimaced. *Not pleased,* was the understatement of the century.

He was going to do everything in his power to try to stop her.

Brooding on the upcoming battle, Sally reached the landing and turned toward the hallway leading toward the library before she realized there was a slender figure waiting in a shallow alcove. She came to an abrupt halt, watching the man stroll forward with a wary expression.

He was . . . exotic, to say the least.

She'd never seen hair so red that it glowed beneath the

light of the crystal chandelier. Or eyes that exact shade of emerald. And that outfit . . .

The shirt was a flimsy see-through material to emphasize his surprisingly muscular chest and matched with zebra spandex pants that looked like they'd been spray-painted on him.

All in all, he was designed to capture attention.

"There you are." Without warning the stranger performed a deep bow. "I have been waiting."

She held up a warning hand. "Please, don't come any closer."

Straightening, the man took a deliberate step backward, although he ran an avid gaze over her slender form.

"Forgive me. I just wanted a glimpse."

She resisted the urge to glance down and make sure she was fully covered. It had been less than a half hour ago that she'd dressed in the jeans and Chicago Bears sweatshirt she'd found in the closet of her bedroom. She'd even found a pair of comfortable running shoes.

She knew quite well she was adequately covered.

"A glimpse of what?" she demanded.

"You."

She frowned. "Why?"

"Are you kidding?" The emerald eyes widened. "You must know you're like a goddess to my people."

Sally shivered, wrapping defensive arms around her waist. This whole new gig as the daughter of a Chatri was making her feel terrifyingly exposed.

"Oh. I—" She licked her dry lips.

Perhaps sensing she was on the point of bolting, the creature held up his hands in a gesture of peace.

"Allow me to introduce myself. I am Troy, the Prince of Imps," he murmured, a hint of wicked sensuality sparkling in the emerald eyes. "And you are Sally."

Troy? A portion of her unease faded. This was the imp that Levet had said could help them.

"Did Roke invite you?"

He rolled his eyes, clearly familiar with her mate.

"It wasn't precisely an invitation. He was less than pleased when you didn't arrive in Chicago with him," he said dryly. "He hoped I could help locate you."

Ah. She grimaced. She hadn't actually considered Roke's reaction when he'd arrived in Chicago only to find she was missing.

His response had no doubt been . . . epic.

The poor imp was lucky he was still in one piece.

"I can imagine." She wrinkled her nose. "I should probably apologize for him. Roke can be—"

"Rude, bad tempered, impossibly arrogant?" Troy helpfully supplied.

She smiled with rueful humor. "All of the above."

Troy waved a dismissive hand. "There's no need for an apology. I'm accustomed to leeches. They're all the same." The emerald gaze swept over her pale face with an unnerving intensity. "And to be honest, I wouldn't have missed this no matter how annoying my companions might be. It's . . ." He sucked in a deep breath, his expression bemused. "Remarkable."

Her unease returned. "What is?"

"Your power feels like lightning dancing over me. It's intoxicating." Troy closed his eyes, shivering with blatant pleasure. "I understand why my ancestors would have worshiped you."

Crap. If she'd been any other woman she'd probably be delighted by the thought of being royalty or even a virtual goddess. Who didn't want to be treated as if she were something special?

But she wasn't any other woman.

She was Sally Grace.

The girl who'd survived by being invisible.

"Please don't say stuff like that," she muttered.

Genuine regret touched the imp's lean, too-pretty features. "I'm sorry."

"I'm not used to . . ." She gave a helpless shrug. "Attention."

Troy tilted his head to the side, the crimson braids brushing over his broad shoulders.

"Unfortunate considering you're going to be attracting every fey in the area," he murmured, glancing toward the high, arched windows that framed the double doors. "They're already starting to surround the estate."

"Hell." She shivered, considering the very real possibility of returning to her room and barricading the door. Cowardly? Maybe. Okay. Definitely. She heaved a sigh. A damned shame it wasn't a viable option. "I never wanted this."

Troy offered a rueful smile. "You'll eventually settle into your powers and they won't be so loudly broadcasted. Until then the vampires will keep all but the most persistent away."

She shook her head. "I can't hide here waiting for my powers to settle."

Troy blinked, seemingly surprised that she didn't intend to cower behind Styx's layers of security.

"You have someplace you need to be?"

She hesitated, remembering Sariel's anger when he'd realized that the box he'd bound to her was no longer a secret. He clearly didn't want people knowing that he was trapped.

Then, she gave a shrug.

What did it matter how many knew of his imprisonment if she couldn't figure out how to rescue him?

And Troy, the Prince of Imps, could provide her with far more information than any book she might be able to find in Styx's library.

Holding the emerald gaze, she confessed the truth.

"My father is being held captive. I need to help him."

"Captive?" Shock rippled over the pale face before Troy was abruptly narrowing his emerald gaze. "Wait. Does Roke know about this?"

She tilted her chin, her deeply entrenched sense of independence instantly outraged by the question.

"Roke is my mate, not my keeper."

Troy snorted. "He's a vampire."

"Yeah, I had noticed."

He studied her stubborn expression before giving a slow nod of his head.

"Very well," he said, his tone implying she was playing with fire. Something she didn't need pointed out. "Do you know where your father is?"

"No." She held up the box. "This is supposed to lead me to him."

Troy stilled, his gaze attached to the box that shimmered with magic.

"May I approach?" His voice was low, reverent.

She gave a nod. "Yes."

With slow steps, Troy crossed the marble floor, halting when he was a few inches from her.

"I've never been near a defaro when it's connected to a Chatri," he murmured.

Defaro. Sally frowned, her fingers unconsciously stroking the box.

"Is that what this is called?"

"Yes. I have several in my collection."

Her lips twisted into a rueful smile, wondering if fate had crossed her path with Troy just when she needed him, or if her father had somehow manipulated her yet again.

And did it matter?

She pushed aside the niggling worry to brood on later.

"Can you read the glyphs?"

"Only a few." Troy lifted his head to meet her steady gaze. "Why?"

"I need to figure out how to decipher the map," she said. "Until then I can't do anything to help my father."

"You don't need to read the glyphs to follow the map."

She glanced at the box, searching for something besides the glyphs that might be a map.

"I don't understand."

"The glyphs will lead you in the right direction without being able to read them."

She made a sound of irritation, holding the box toward the imp.

"Show me."

Troy held a slender hand over the box, careful not to touch the wood that glowed with her father's power. Leaning down he spoke a foreign word that resonated deep inside her.

The box grew warm in her hand and Troy stepped back. "Keep your eye on the glyphs and walk across the room," he said, waiting until she'd reached the double doors before speaking again. "Now this way."

She walked back toward the imp, her breath catching as she turned the box over to discover one corner had changed colors.

"This glyph is glowing brighter."

"Northwest," Troy said. "It's leading you in the right direction."

Sally frowned. "So it's like a game of hot-hot-cold?"

Troy blinked. "I never thought about it like that, but yes, it's similar."

"That doesn't seem very efficient," she muttered. "Why not draw a map like a normal person?"

"Security."

She furrowed her brow. "Glowing glyphs don't seem particularly secure."

"They only glow when you're holding the box," Troy explained, reaching to gently take the box from her hand. "Watch."

The second her hand left the box, the glyph returned to its previous color.

"Oh." She reached to take back the box, too distracted to notice the sudden drop in the temperature. "So I just wander around the countryside following the glowing box?"

"No. Way. In. Hell," a familiar voice warned as Roke stepped into the foyer.

Roke knew he was handling Sally all wrong. It didn't take a genius to know that the one certain way to make her do what he didn't want her to do was to tell her she couldn't do it.

But dammit, she was making him nuts.

Why would she even think about trying to help a father who considered her nothing more than a means to his escape?

And that's exactly what she was plotting.

Why else would she be with the damned imp learning how to use the map on her box?

Moving forward, he pointed a finger at Troy. "Leave us," he growled.

The imp gave a toss of his crimson braids, but blowing a kiss in his direction, he turned to sashay down the hallway.

With a sound of disgust, Roke moved to stand in front of his mate, matching her glare for glare.

"Are you having fun tossing around your orders?" she demanded.

"Not particularly." He reached to touch her cheek, hiding a rueful smile at the scent of scorched peaches that filled the air. "Have you had dinner?"

"Don't change the subject," she snapped.

He leaned until they were nose to nose. "The only subject

I care about is why you're so determined to put yourself in danger."

She stepped back, a mutinous frown pulling her brows together.

"I can't just pretend my only family isn't being held prisoner and that he needs me."

His fingers slid beneath her chin as he held her wary gaze. "I'm your family."

"Only because I forced a mating on you."

"No." He pressed his thumb to her lips, angered by her insistence on dwelling on how the mating had started. It was meaningless. "Don't say that."

"It's true."

"It isn't. This . . ." His lips twisted as he struggled to find the word that expressed his volatile reaction when he'd first caught sight of her in Styx's dungeon. "Attraction between us started before we mated."

She shook her head, but he didn't miss the abrupt sizzle of awareness that heated their bond.

She recalled their first meeting as vividly as he did.

"You didn't even know me," she tried to protest. "I was a prisoner that you resented even being near."

His thumb stroked her bottom lip. "It's true I resented you, but not for the reason you think."

"You didn't want to babysit a witch."

His lips twisted. That's what he'd told himself. And anyone else who would listen.

He was supposed to be impervious to his emotions.

"The minute I caught sight of you, I was captivated."

She made a sound of disbelief. "You were a complete jackass."

"True." He could hardly deny his fierce attempt to reject what was happening to him. "I spent several centuries convinced I'd purged my baser instincts. It was an unpleasant shock to have that belief shattered by a tiny scrap of a female with a smartass mouth and enough power to turn me into a newt."

She rolled her eyes. "That doesn't sound captivated."

"I couldn't get you out of my thoughts no matter how I tried," he continued, his brooding gaze sweeping over her delicate features. That beautiful face had been seared into his brain the moment he'd caught sight of her, tormenting him with a craving to possess her that refused to leave him in peace. "And when I found that damn fairy bringing you a tray of food I nearly ripped out his throat. No one was allowed to take care of your needs but me." He gave a rueful laugh. "I knew I was in trouble from the start, but I couldn't stay away."

A hint of yearning softened her dark eyes, as if longing to believe his confession. And then, abruptly, she was giving a shake of her head, clearly preparing to change the subject.

"Roke . . ."

He swooped down to plunder her mouth with a kiss that stole her words. Her hands instinctively lifted to clutch his shoulders, her lips parting in astonishment. Only when he felt her tremble in answering need did he reluctantly lift his head to study her flushed cheeks.

"That's better."

"What are you doing?" she husked.

"You're going to say something I don't want to hear," he confessed.

She made a choked sound. "And you think kissing me is going to stop me from saying it?"

His gaze lingered on her soft lips, his body reacting with predictable enthusiasm to having her near.

"I was hoping for a distraction."

She jutted her chin to a stubborn angle. "That's not going to change my mind."

His hand cupped her cheek. "What will?"

"Roke, I have to do this."

He growled deep in his throat, frustration slamming through him.

"I still don't understand why," he hissed through clenched teeth.

She met his smoldering gaze, silently pleading with him to understand.

"You're not happy with Zoe, right?"

He went rigid at the mere mention of his former clanswoman. "If she has any sense of self-preservation she'll be careful not to cross my path," he snarled.

"But if she was in danger you would rush to her rescue, wouldn't you?"

His frustration amped up another notch, cracking the marble floor beneath their feet.

"It's not the same," he mulishly insisted. "Zoe has been a part of my clan for a very long time."

"She is your duty," she insisted. "Just as my father is my duty."

He was shaking his head before she finished. "You don't even know for sure he's your father."

She blinked, as if startled by his words. "Why would he lie?"

"This could be a trap."

Her hand lifted to lightly touch his cheek. "There's only one way to find out."

He rolled his eyes toward the heavens, knowing he was once again defeated by a tiny female witch with velvet brown eyes and an annoying habit of twisting him around her little finger.

"Shit."

Chapter Twenty-Two

Seated behind his desk, the King of Vampires tapped an impatient finger on the glossy surface.

"I don't like this," he muttered, his gaze tracking Roke as he paced from one end of the priceless carpet to the other.

Roke curled his hands into tight fists. He'd left Sally less than a quarter hour ago, unable to sway her stubborn determination to go in search of her father.

"I can't say I'm particularly happy about it either, but Sally refuses to listen to reason," he admitted, wondering if this was fate's way of laughing at him for assuming he could choose a meek, easily trainable mate.

Styx gave a resigned shake of his head. "She's a woman on a mission."

"A ridiculous mission."

Styx winced. "You didn't tell her that, did you?"

Roke continued his pacing, grimacing at the memory of his mate's angry response to his attempt to dissuade her from charging into danger.

"Not in so many words," he muttered.

"Ah." There was a wealth of censure in Styx's voice. "A tactical mistake, amigo."

Roke sent his king a glare. "Thanks, but your words of wisdom come a little late."

"Do you want me to lock her up?"

His lips twisted in a humorless smile. He was desperate, but there wasn't a chance in hell he was going to try to physically restrain Sally. Each time she'd been caged, it had destroyed something inside her.

Besides, he knew that she wasn't entirely wrong.

Something was going to have to be done to get the Nebule off her trail.

"Yeah, because that worked out so well the last time," he pointed out dryly.

Styx shrugged. "Just a suggestion."

"Would you lock Darcy up?"

"I tried once."

Roke came to an astonished halt, regarding his companion in disbelief.

Darcy might be a peace-loving vegetarian, but she was also a pureblooded Were who could do some serious damage when she was pissed.

"What happened?"

Styx pulled back his lips to expose his massive fangs, his hands landing on the desk as if he was being tormented by an unpleasant memory.

"She slipped away and damned near became the Queen of Weres instead of vampires."

Roke grimaced. Thank the gods he hadn't been around when Darcy had disappeared on Styx. The resulting meltdown had no doubt been the stuff of nightmares.

Turning his thoughts back to his mate, Roke gave a fatalistic lift of his shoulder. There was nothing he could do but accept the inevitable.

"I can't stop Sally. I can only try to protect her."

Styx nodded, slowly rising to his feet. "How can I help?"

Roke considered for a minute. There was no point in

taking any of his brothers on his journey. The Nebule not only had his nasty poison darts that could kill a vampire, but Brandel's ability to turn into mist meant that they were virtually worthless in a battle against the creature.

How did you kill mist?

"You could encourage the Oracles to step up their search for Brandel," he suggested, not surprised when Styx grimaced.

No one wanted to deal with the Commission.

"I'll do my best."

Roke nodded. It was all he could hope for.

"Cyn has promised to discover how we can kill him, but until then we'll be vulnerable if he attacks."

"What about the fey?" Styx asked. "It's going to be difficult to sneak around when you have a parade of fairies following your every footstep."

It was a problem that Roke had already considered. Beyond all the attention the fey would attract, he wasn't in the mood to trip over a sprite or nymph every time he turned around. Besides, the adoring groupies were truly freaking out poor Sally.

"Troy is supposed to be spreading the word that Sally is to be left in peace until further notice," he said.

"You trust an imp?"

"I don't trust anyone, but he's at least cleared away the horde that was surrounding your lair."

"Troy did that?" Styx glanced toward the window, a wry smile curling his lips. "And here I thought my fearsome reputation had been responsible for their flight."

Roke grunted. "Not even the threat of your anger could dislodge them. The creatures are nothing if not tenacious."

"Are you taking Troy with you?"

A shudder of horror raced through him at the mere thought. "Good God, no."

There was the sound of the door being shoved open before the stench of granite filled the air.

"Why would he need an imp when he already has a kicking side?" a French accented voice demanded as Levet stepped into the study along with Sally.

"Sidekick," Sally corrected, her gaze warily watching Roke's immediate reaction to the gargoyle's implication he was going along for the ride.

"No," he growled.

Her lips flattened at his stark refusal to even contemplate being stuck with the pest.

"We need him."

"Why would we possibly need that"—he pointed toward the smirking Levet—"lump of granite?"

Levet stuck out his tongue. "Bah."

Sally made a sound of impatience. "If the demon is capable of changing shapes, we need someone who can use his sense of smell to warn us if he is near."

Roke scowled, instantly offended. "I'm capable of smelling the demon."

Levet ran a claw over his tiny snout. "But you do not have my superior senses."

Stepping forward, Roke intended to toss the annoying gargoyle from the room only to be halted by Styx.

"I hate to agree with the gargoyle, but he does have a better nose," the king said.

Roke sent him a disgusted frown. "You just want to get rid of him."

"There is that," Styx agreed, his smile mocking.

"Enough." Sally threw her hands in the air, turning to head back toward the door. "I'm going. You can come if you want. Otherwise, stay here."

Roke was swiftly in pursuit. "Dammit, Sally, wait."

"Call if you need backup," Styx called.

Roke stomped down the hall, following his irritated mate and her aggravating gargoyle companion.

"Backup, my ass."

Sally glanced toward the vampire seated behind the steering wheel of the Land Rover. He didn't look happy. In fact, his grim expression and narrowed glare suggested his mood was downright foul.

He hadn't said a word since he'd commanded Levet to take a back seat and they'd headed in a northwest direction at a speed that made her hair stand on end.

Partially her fault, she ruefully admitted.

Since making the decision to try to rescue her father she'd been questioning her sanity.

Did Sariel really deserve her concern?

It wasn't as if he'd ever given a damn about her. How many times had she'd been imprisoned without her father bothering to help?

Why put her life on the line for him?

She had plenty of excuses, some of them quite reasonable, but no genuine answer for why it was suddenly so imperative for her to release Sariel from his prison.

Was it any wonder that Roke's impatient announcement she was acting like a fool had scraped against her raw nerves?

Clearing her throat, she tried to break the ice. "Are you going to sulk for the entire trip?"

His gaze remained locked on the highway that was thankfully empty of traffic.

"Yes."

"That's your answer? Yes?"

"Yes."

"What do you want? An apology?"

"I want you to just once listen to reason."

Well, fine.

She'd tried.

"You didn't have to come," she muttered, grimacing as the temperature dropped to near freezing. "Well, you didn't," she pointed out with a shiver.

His gaze at last slashed in her direction. "You can't expect me to be happy that you're deliberately putting yourself in danger."

"I'm going to be in danger until I find my father and give him back the box," she said. "Until then the demon is going to be hunting me no matter where I might try to hide."

His jaw tightened, but he didn't bother to argue. Which meant he'd already accepted she couldn't hide forever. He was just being an ass because he was scared for her.

"We could have destroyed it," he countered, his tone more stubborn than convinced they could actually harm the box.

"Highly doubtful," Levet chimed in from the backseat. "The spell that is placed on the—"

"Shut up, gargoyle," Roke snarled.

Levet sniffed. "My next road trip will be strictly leech-free."

"Thank the gods," Roke muttered.

Sally ignored the two as the upper glyph on the box pulsed a sharper shade of gold.

"It's shining brighter," she muttered.

Roke frowned, glancing at the glowing glyph with blatant suspicion. "What does that mean?"

Sally bit her bottom lip. "I assume that we must be getting closer."

"Already?"

Sally shared Roke's wariness. She didn't know where she expected to find her father, but it wasn't less than an hour north of Chicago.

"I know, it seems—"

"Too good to be true?" Roke finished for her.

"Yes."

Levet abruptly poked his head between them, his snout wrinkled as if catching a bad scent.

"Not so good."

Sally turned her head to meet the gargoyle's worried gaze. "What is it?"

"I smell demon," Levet warned.

"Shit." Roke grabbed his phone off the dash and punched in a number before pressing it to his ear. "Cyn, I need that info on killing the Nebule, pronto." There was a brief pause before he was shoving the phone into his front pocket. "Perfect," he muttered.

"What did he say?" Sally demanded.

Roke pressed the accelerator to the floor, his knuckles white as they gripped the steering wheel.

"The only known way to kill the bastard is with the power of a Chatri."

Of course that was the only way.

It couldn't be something simple like ripping out his throat or putting a stake through his heart.

"We have to get to my father."

"*Oui.*" Levet's wings created a mini-windstorm. "And you might want to hurry."

"What the hell do you think I'm doing?" Roke muttered.

There was a tense moment of silence as they hurtled through the darkness. Then, a mist was forming in the air between Roke and Sally.

"*Sacrebleu,*" Levet squeaked as Roke slammed on the brakes, nearly sending the tiny creature through the front windshield.

Sally was moving before the vehicle came to a complete halt, shoving open the door and hitting the ground in a desperate attempt to outrun the demon.

A wasted effort.

She'd taken less than a step when the air in front of her

began to vibrate, pulsing through her with enough force to send her to her knees.

She moaned, feeling the full impact of the demon's powers.

The first time he'd attacked she'd been partially protected by her magical shield. The second time, he'd been focused on Roke.

Now she realized that she didn't have a damned way to protect herself from a brutal, excruciating death.

Glancing up, she watched as the mist solidified into the form of a chubby Miera demon that Brandel had used before.

"Give me the box," the Nebule demanded, his black eyes that were slit with crimson glowing with a spooky hunger.

She clutched the box to her chest, shaking her head. "No."

The demon held up a hand, his brown robes hanging unnaturally still despite the brisk autumn breeze.

"Give me the box or die."

He wasn't bluffing. Already the agonizing vibrations were ramping up, damaging vital organs as they swept through her.

"Sally, give him the damned thing," Roke snarled, crawling toward her with blood dripping from his nose and eyes.

Sally hesitated only a second before she threw the box directly at the demon.

What choice did she have?

She might have increased in power over the past weeks, but her insides were turning to goo. She didn't know if that was something she could survive.

And once she was dead, she didn't doubt for a minute Brandel would use his poison on Roke and maybe even poor little Levet.

Catching the box in a chubby hand, the demon gave a maniacal laugh before he was blinking out of sight.

Sally slumped forward, her nose nearly touching the ground as the savage pain slowly receded.

Oh . . . crap.

Who knew the sensation of her innards repairing themselves could be almost as brutal as having them squished in the first place?

A cool hand brushed her nape, offering a welcome comfort.

"Are you hurt?" Roke asked, his voice thick with his own pain.

She forced herself to straighten, meeting his anxious gaze with a rueful smile.

"Nothing that won't heal."

With a grim expression, Roke shrugged out of his leather jacket, then with one sharp tug he ripped off his T-shirt to gently clean the blood from her face.

His own injuries were rapidly healing, the blood flaking off him to leave his face as starkly beautiful as ever and his dark hair as smooth as silk.

She smiled without humor. She'd just managed to destroy any hope of finding her father, and her mind was consumed with the knowledge Roke looked breathtakingly perfect while she probably looked like she should be in the emergency room.

Maybe her brain had been squished along with the rest of her soft organs.

It seemed the only logical explanation.

Once satisfied he'd cleaned off the last of the blood, Roke wrapped his arms around her, his touch careful not to jar her aching body.

She blinked back her tears, knowing how much it cost him not to vent his angry frustration at how close she'd come to dying.

It was evident in the tiny quakes that shook his body and the frantic kisses he was pressing to the top of her head. But, with uncharacteristic restraint, he kept his emotions tightly leashed as he murmured comforting words and his hands stroked down her back in a soothing motion.

She didn't know how long they continued to kneel on the ground, her body slowly healing as she leaned heavily against Roke's chest. Eventually, however, she became aware of the sharp breeze that cut through the material of her sweatshirt and the scent of granite that assured her Levet was near.

With an effort she lifted her head and glanced around the empty countryside. Her brain still felt fuzzy, but she knew that she had to think.

She might have lost the box, but that didn't mean that she'd given up on her plans to rescue her father. There had to be another way to find him.

The thought barely had time to form when Roke was barking out a curse and dragging her from the box that reappeared on the ground mere inches from her knees.

"*Voilà,*" Levet cried, waddling toward them. "I told you Sally could not rid herself of the box. The spell has bound it to her."

Far less impressed with the rematerializing act, Roke had his phone out and pressed to his ear.

"Styx, we need backup. You can locate us with the Land Rover's GPS," he snapped. "Send someone who can't be hurt by the poison the demon carries." Pulling Sally to her feet, Roke backed them away from the highway. "Help is on the way."

Sally frowned, not doubting Styx's ability to round up any number of warriors who weren't vampires, but fairly confident that they would never reach them in time.

It wouldn't take the demon long to figure out what happened to his prize.

"Shouldn't we run?" she asked.

Roke shook his head. "I want my hands free the next time he shows up."

Levet gave a snap of his wings. "He's coming."

Sally tilted back her head, feeling nearly overwhelmed by the surge of guilt.

Dammit. She should never have allowed Roke or Levet to come with her.

She'd known this was dangerous.

She'd even known that there was a good chance the demon would be hunting her.

But she'd never dreamed he could locate her so swiftly. She'd somehow assumed she'd be able to reach her father before he could track her down.

Now she deeply regretted not waiting until Roke was distracted and she could have slipped away alone.

"Roke," she breathed, her voice raw.

"I know."

He captured her face in his hands, kissing her with a fierce intensity that made her knees tremble. It was far too short, as he lifted his head to study her with eyes that glowed a brilliant silver in the moonlight.

"Do I get a kiss?" Levet intruded into the moment. "A hug?"

Roke snorted, dropping his hands so he could move back and prepare for the coming attack.

"Just be ready, gargoyle," he growled.

It was a warning that shook Sally out of her lingering stupor and with a muttered curse she reached into her pocket to pull out the tiny amulet she'd prepared before leaving Styx's lair.

She'd come up with a crazy idea for how to hurt the demon. It was nothing more than a theory that was as likely to get her killed as to actually help, but it seemed an appropriate time to give it a try.

It wasn't like she had any actual spells that could hurt the creature.

There was a strange hum in the air seconds before the Nebule made his dramatic return. Immediately, he lunged toward the box that Sally had left on the side of the road.

At the same time, Roke lunged forward, knocking into the

demon with enough force to send them both tumbling to the ground.

There was a high-pitched scream from Brandel as Roke sank his fangs deep into his throat, ripping through the flesh with a savage fury.

Sally scurried forward, kicking the box toward Levet who scooped it up and took off with a flap of his delicate wings.

The demon could obviously track the box, but Sally hoped to keep him from disappearing with it long enough to do some damage.

She was forced to skip backward as the demon threw Roke off him and tried to surge back to his feet. Roke growled, using his claws to rip through Brandel's spongy flesh.

The demon cursed and the eyes flashed with a black and crimson fire as he gained his feet. At the same time, the air began to fill with the vibrations that threatened to destroy them.

Roke grunted as the wave hit him first, but refusing to concede defeat, he flowed upward, managing to slice a gaping wound through the creature's chest. There was another wave of vibrations and, hissing in frustration, Roke managed to wrap his arms around Brandel's waist as he was being forced to his knees by the pain.

Sally held the amulet in her hand, hurrying toward the back of the demon while he was distracted by Roke. Then with a muttered prayer, she leaped forward, wrapping her arms around his neck as she pressed the amulet against his oddly elastic skin.

Brandel jolted in shock as the magic flowed over him, trying desperately to dislodge Roke's ruthless hold so he could turn and attack Sally.

"Oh no you don't, witch," Brandel snarled, lifting his hands to grab Sally's wrists. "Not this time."

Debilitating pain jolted down her arms, aiming straight for her heart. She groaned, desperately breathing the spell that would lock the demon into his current form.

"Dammit, Sally, what are you doing?" Roke growled, staggering to his feet.

"His physical form can be hurt," she gasped, not sure how long she could last. "We can't let him turn to mist. The amulet will hold him and you kill him."

Comprehension flared in the silver eyes and with a roar that sent the nearby wildlife stampeding in terror, he attacked with a flurry of fangs and claws.

Brandel jerked, clearly able to feel physical pain as he was being ripped open by an infuriated vampire. Even the hideous jolts he was sending through her began to lessen, as if he were losing strength.

Still, he refused to die.

Yanking a dagger from the top of his moccasin, Roke stuck it deep into the demon's chest, carving it open as he searched for a heart.

Sally shuddered, beginning to feel her amulet running out of juice. There was only so much magic that could be contained in the small medallion and it was being swiftly drained.

Crap. This wasn't working.

Cyn had been right.

They needed the magic of a Chatri.

Magic that flowed in her blood, a voice whispered in the back of her mind.

Was it possible she had the power to kill the Nebule?

Sariel claimed her humanity had been scoured away to leave her a pure-blooded Chatri.

Now seemed as good a time as any to discover if he'd been telling the truth.

The sooner the better, she abruptly realized, sensing Brandel's body was beginning to melt beneath her fingers.

"He's turning," she warned through gritted teeth.

"Then let go of him and run," Roke growled.

She shook her head, trying to block out the pain and panic and Roke's furious commands to leave.

She could do this.

It was her birthright.

Her legacy.

Searching deep inside herself, Sally reached for the magic she unconsciously kept locked away.

It was the same magic that had allowed her to enchant Roke. And to create a portal.

The warm, brilliantly colored strands of magic that flowed through her like music.

"Sally, what the hell?" she heard Roke mutter, his voice edged with something that might have been shock.

"I can do this," she murmured. "Trust me."

The world seemed to fade away as the warmth burst past her barriers and filled her entire body. Distantly she could feel Brandel shuddering as she held him tight against her body, and hear Roke calling her name. She was even aware of Levet returning to land on top of the Land Rover.

But she was drowning in the heat and magic that was swelling up until it threatened to burst out of her.

"Roke, get back," she hissed, unable to stem the tide.

"No, I won't leave you," he snapped, typically determined to play the hero.

"I can't contain it." She held his wary gaze, willing him to obey her command. "Get back."

Chapter Twenty-Three

Roke stumbled backward, blinded by the light that surrounded his mate. Dammit. He didn't know what was going on, but he had to get Sally away from the damned demon.

Regaining his balance, he narrowed his gaze and forced himself to stare into the painful glow.

It took a second to realize that the light wasn't just shimmering around Sally. It was actually spilling out of her, as if the sun was captured inside her and couldn't entirely be contained.

He froze in shock.

God almighty.

With her autumn hair floating on an unseen breeze and her eyes glowing with a pure ebony, she didn't look entirely real.

She was . . . magnificent.

A beauty beyond his comprehension.

Giving a sharp shake of his head, Roke struggled to think beyond the dazzling, near destructive sight of his mate. He'd worry about her sudden ability to glow later. For now all that mattered was fleeing from the seemingly indestructible Brandel.

Pronto.

Shifting his attention toward the demon who Sally continued

to hold around the neck, Roke prepared to launch another attack. He'd even taken a step forward when he realized that Brandel wasn't fighting against Sally's hold.

In fact, his black, crimson-slit eyes were stretched wide and his pudgy face frozen in an expression of horror.

Was the light hurting him?

It was impossible to tell with a creature who didn't have a solid physical form.

Muttering a curse, Roke clutched his dagger and took another step forward. There had to be some way of disabling the demon long enough to get Sally away.

Brandel made an odd noise as the light burned even brighter, the heat becoming nearly unbearable.

"Roke, stay back," Sally hissed between clenched teeth.

He scowled. Did she truly expect him to stand aside and watch her fight the demon on her own?

Meeting the dark gaze that blazed with the unearthly light, he was forced to accept that was exactly what she expected.

His fangs ached, his entire body trembling with the fierce need to leap into the battle, but he leashed his primitive instincts.

This wasn't Sally being stubborn. Or trying to assert her aggravating independence.

In this moment she was a warrior giving commands that were meant to be obeyed.

Feeling as helpless as a damned dew fairy, Roke forced his feet to carry him backward, his gaze locked on her beautiful face until the light grew so bright it surrounded her and the petrified Brandel behind an incandescent aura.

Christ. He couldn't see her.

The earth shook beneath his feet, the nearby highway buckling beneath the stress of his brutal terror. Then, when he knew he couldn't stand and watch another second, there was a sizzle in the air followed by an explosion of heat that sent him flying.

Roke plowed into the side of the Land Rover with enough force to crush the passenger door, but ignoring his broken ribs and punctured lung, he untangled himself from the twisted metal.

"Sally," he roared, surging to his feet to discover his mate lying on the ground.

He hissed in shock as he caught sight of the terrain that had been flattened and charred by the explosion. In several spots the grass had been seared away to leave nothing but blackened dirt. And in other places deep gouges scarred the landscape.

Holy shit. It looked like ground zero with Sally collapsed in the center.

Stark fear clutched his heart as he hurried toward his mate. At a distance she appeared unhurt, but he needed her in his arms.

Nearly at her side, Roke grimaced as he leaped over the large, greasy spot of . . . sludge. Christ, was that all that was left of Brandel?

Roke knelt on the grass that remained unharmed around Sally's body, gently wrapping her in his arms and pulling her against his chest. The brilliant light had faded, but her skin remained warm to the touch and the scent of peaches saturated the air, reminding him of the power she had so recently wielded.

Not that he gave a shit that she'd just proven she was one of the most dangerous creatures to walk the earth. All he cared about was holding her tight as his senses swept over her, searching for injuries.

Finding no wounds, he frowned as he studied her pale face and the shadows beneath the heavy fringe of her lashes. Had she burned herself out with such a large burst of magic?

And if she had, what did he do to help her?

"Sally?" he urged softly, relief shooting through him as her lashes fluttered up to reveal her dazed eyes.

"Roke?"

"Are you hurt?"

"No," she instantly denied. "Just drained. I'll be fine."

His hand wasn't entirely steady as he smoothed a strand of golden red hair away from her face.

"What the hell happened?"

She wrinkled her nose, her lashes lowering to shield her eyes. Almost as if she couldn't meet his gaze.

"I'm not entirely sure. The magic just—"

"Exploded?"

"Yeah, something like that." She pulled herself out of his arms, silently taking in the devastation that surrounded them. "The demon?" she at last demanded.

Roke rigidly squashed the need to pull her back into his embrace. She was obviously rattled by her . . . volatile surge of magic.

He got it.

Although it'd been centuries since he'd been a foundling, he could still remember his shock the first time his powers had manifested and he'd collapsed a tunnel on his head.

It'd taken him hours to crawl out of the rubble and a few decades to become comfortable with his destructive talent.

"There," he said, pointing toward the pile of grease, determined to make her proud of what she was becoming.

She shuddered, rising to her feet to take a step away from the charred remains of Brandel.

"That's all that's left of him?"

"That's it." He kept his tone light as he straightened to stand at her side. "You were quite impressive."

"She was brilliant," Levet pronounced, waddling forward to offer the box to Sally. "Truly *magnifique*."

Sally clutched the box in a white-knuckled grip, still staring at the scorched ground that surrounded them.

"We need to return to Chicago," Roke abruptly announced.

Ridiculously, Sally frowned at his announcement. "Why?"

"You're tired."

She shook her head. "No."

Growling with impatience, he moved to stand directly in front of her, his hand cupping her cheek.

"You can't lie to me, Sally," he reminded her. "I can sense your weariness."

"I want to be done with this."

His brows drew together, his shoulders squaring as he prepared for yet another battle of wills.

"The demon is dead. What does it matter if you continue your search tonight or next week?"

"We don't know if he was the only demon after the box," she said.

"All the more reason to return to Chicago until you can recover your strength."

She reached up to grasp his wrist, pressing his fingers tighter against her face as she studied him with a pleading expression.

"Roke, we can't move forward until I've dealt with my past," she said softly.

"Move forward. Or move on without me?" he demanded, revealing his greatest fear.

She closed her eyes, sucking in a deep breath. "This has to be done."

For a crazed minute he considered the satisfaction of tossing her over his shoulder and hauling her back to Styx's lair.

Or better yet, his own lair, where he could spend the next several centuries convincing her that the past didn't matter.

Then, with a painful effort, he lowered his hand and stepped back.

Sally had made her decision to save her father. Nothing, not even his dubious charms, was going to change her mind.

"Gargoyle," he snapped, grabbing his leather jacket off the ground and pulling it over his naked torso.

"*Oui?*"

"Return to Chicago and inform Styx what has happened."

The tiny demon wrinkled his snout, his hands on his hips. "What if you have need of my skills?"

Roke raked an impatient hand through his hair. "Do you want to fight whatever had enough power to trap a Chatri?"

"Ah." The gray eyes widened at the mere thought. "I should perhaps return so the vampires do not worry where you have gone."

"Good choice," Roke said dryly.

Levet moved to take Sally's hand, pressing her fingers to his lips.

"*Au revoir, ma belle.* Return to us swiftly."

Sally smiled with a forced confidence. "I intend to do my best."

Roke's growl trickled through the air. Sally didn't need to do her best. It was his job to make sure she was kept safe.

"Are you ready?" he demanded.

She nodded. "Yes."

Roke glanced toward the gargoyle. "Tell Styx to keep his phone on."

"*Oui.*"

In silence, Roke led Sally to the Land Rover, waiting for her to climb over the driver's seat since the passenger door was trashed. Then, settling in his seat, he started the engine and turned the vehicle onto the highway.

As the silence continued, Roke covertly studied Sally's tense profile.

Was she worrying about the danger of trying to rescue her father? Or was she still brooding on the tidal wave of magic she'd so recently unleashed?

Whatever her thoughts were, they were sending frissons of unease through their mating bond.

"Why do you keep looking at me?" she at last spoke, her expression troubled.

"I like looking at you." He smiled wryly. "I like touching you even better."

"It's not that," she said, refusing to believe his teasing words. "Are you—"

"Sally?" he prompted as she struggled to share her dark thoughts.

"Are you scared of me now?"

He frowned at her abrupt question. "What are you talking about?"

She bit her bottom lip. "My powers are becoming dangerous."

"You've always been dangerous, my love," he drawled, recalling the moment he'd caught sight of her.

He hadn't stood a chance.

"Yeah, but I wasn't a nuclear bomb waiting to explode," she muttered.

Ah. So it was her combustible magic that was troubling her.

"Your powers will be unstable until they plateau," he said, his tone matter of fact. "Once that happens you'll gain command of them."

"What if I hurt you before I gain command?"

He was caught off guard by her question.

She was worried about him?

That was . . . unexpected.

Did that mean she was beginning to care for him? Genuinely care for him and not just because of their bond?

He latched on to the faint hope with a desperation that was downright pathetic.

"You won't," he assured her.

The dark eyes smoldered with frustration. "You don't know that."

"I trust you."

Her fingers tightened on the box, her tension a palpable force in the air.

"Roke, maybe it would be better if I did this alone."

He slammed on the brakes, sending the vehicle skidding onto the shoulder.

Sally gasped in surprise, her eyes widening as he reached across the seat to grasp her arms. He dragged her forward until they were nose to nose.

"Don't ever say that again."

Sally had heard the phrase "tugging the tail of a tiger," but she'd never actually given it much thought.

Now she knew exactly what it meant.

Roke's power blasted through the confined space, making the vehicle tremble and the windows frost over.

He was clearly pissed by her suggestion, which, as far as she was concerned, was totally unfair.

Hadn't he seen what she'd done to that demon?

For God's sake, the Nebule had been reduced to a weird glob of tar.

Okay, she wasn't sorry that she'd killed the demon. He would certainly have squashed her without a second thought.

But it wasn't as if she'd targeted Brandel and released her power to destroy him. She hadn't even known she *could* destroy him.

The magic had simply crashed through her barriers, filling her with a heat that was so intense she couldn't contain it.

If Roke hadn't stayed back, he would be a tiny pile of ash.

A thought that twisted her gut with a savage pain.

She couldn't let that happen.

Even if it meant finishing her quest on her own.

Not that her steely-eyed mate appeared to be in the mood to be reasonable.

As usual he looked like he wanted to bite something.

Preferably her.

"Roke—"

"No," he interrupted, refusing to listen to reason.

Typical.

She heaved a frustrated sigh. "You are without a doubt the most stubborn creature I've ever met."

The silver eyes narrowed. "Have you looked in a mirror lately?"

She jutted her chin. She wasn't stubborn. She was . . . determined.

Completely different.

"There's no reason for you to put yourself at risk," she pointed out, ridiculously aware of the press of his slender fingers into her flesh. Now wasn't the time to be remembering how those fingers had explored her body with exquisite dedication only a few hours before. "He's my father and it's my duty to release him, not yours."

"You're my duty," he growled, unexpectedly kissing her with a stark need that stole her annoyance. "And my pleasure," he murmured against her lips. "Without you, I can't survive."

"Stubborn," she breathed in resignation.

His lips brushed softly against hers before Roke was abruptly pulling back, his gaze locked on the box that abruptly flared with light.

"Sally?"

"This is the place," she muttered.

"Here?" He scowled. "It's way too convenient that we'd stop at the precise place we need to be."

Sally sympathized with his suspicion. It *was* way too convenient.

But she was beginning to understand that she wasn't actually chasing her father, but rather finding a location that would allow his portal to align with this world.

It was fluid.

Holding Roke's gaze, she waited until he muttered a low curse and slid out of the vehicle. Sally was quickly crawling out to stand beside him, no longer looking out of the box as she could feel the magic calling to her.

"This way," she murmured, stumbling through the overgrown culvert that ran beside the road before making her way to the clump of oak trees at the edge of a field.

"I don't like this." Roke followed behind her, his disapproval crawling over her skin with a sharp chill.

Pretending she didn't have a sulking six-foot-plus vampire on her heels, Sally walked between the trees, breathing deeply of the scent of moss and rich earth.

Was that the magic?

Her silent question was answered when an unmistakable tingle heated her blood.

"Here," she said, stopping abruptly in the center of a small clearing.

Coming to a halt at her side, Roke continued to scan the shadows between the nearby trees, his muscles coiled to strike.

"Now what?"

"I'm not sure." She leaned down to place the box at her feet, her heart leaping as a shimmering became visible in the air directly in front of her. "Oh."

Unable to detect magic, Roke scowled in confusion. "What?"

"I see it."

"See what?"

"The opening to the portal."

She took a step forward only to be halted by a ruthless grip on her upper arm.

"What are you doing? You can't just charge in there," Roke snapped. "If your father is being held prisoner, then there must be guards."

Tilting back her head, she met his seething gaze. "Waiting here isn't going to change that."

"Fine." He reached to pull a gun from the holster at the small of his back. "Send me in and I'll deal with the guards."

"I can't."

He scowled. "Can't or won't?"

She waved an impatient hand. "I'm not entirely sure how it works, but we'll need my magic to lead us to my father. Even if I could get you into the portal without me, you would be wandering around blind."

He didn't like it, but Roke grudgingly accepted she was right.

"Dammit."

She stepped toward the iridescent opening. "Let's go before I lose my nerve."

"If I thought that was a possibility, I'd tie you to the nearest tree," he muttered.

She rolled her eyes. "You're such a . . . man."

"Is that an insult?"

"Absolutely."

Taking a deep breath, Sally waited for Roke to place a hand on her shoulder before she took the final step through the mist and entered the portal.

Instantaneously she was surrounded by a kaleidoscope of colors that swirled around her in a dizzying dance.

"Oh," she breathed.

His fingers tightened on her shoulder. "Can you see something?"

"Strands of beauty," she said, sensing they were moving through the portal.

"Are you screwing with me?"

"The magic is filled with the most beautiful colors," she said, trying to explain her fascination. This magic was different from her human spells, or even the magic used by the traditional fey. This was richer, fuller . . . lethally addictive. "It's hypnotizing."

He kept his voice low as he muttered his own opinion of

magic, his jacket brushing her spine as he pressed close behind her.

Leaning back, Sally allowed herself to briefly enjoy the cool power that wrapped around her.

It felt so natural.

Even vital.

As if she'd become so accustomed to the sense of this vampire being nestled deep inside her that she instinctively depended on his unwavering strength.

It was a dangerous realization, but she wasn't in the mood to worry about it.

Not when there was a good chance she wasn't going to survive the night.

On that cheery thought Roke suddenly stiffened, a growl rumbling in his chest.

"I smell wine."

She caught the scent a mere second after Roke. "Father," she breathed, straightening to try to peer through the swirls of magic.

"There's something else," Roke muttered.

She was distracted from his warning as her father's voice filled her head.

"Sally."

Turning, she watched as the strands of magic parted to reveal Sariel lying on what looked like a dirt floor.

The air was squeezed from her lungs as her gaze took in the sight of his motionless form drenched in a sickly green glow. He was as beautiful as he'd been in the meadow with his golden hair spilling over the ground and his pale features so perfect they might have been carved in marble.

But as she studied his elegant form she detected the white robe was now a grimy gray and so frayed it barely covered him while his silver headband had become tarnished.

"There he is." She hurried forward, only to run headfirst

into an invisible wall. "Damn." She rubbed her abused nose. "There's a barrier."

"At last," her father purred inside her head. "Come to me, my daughter."

She ignored Roke's frown, speaking out loud. "I can't get past the barrier."

"Release your powers," Sariel urged. "They will join with mine."

Her powers?

She grimaced, not overly enthusiastic at the thought of releasing the torrent of uncontrollable magic when she didn't have a clue what would happen.

She could potentially crush the portal and kill them all.

Or lose control and hurt Roke.

Still, what choice did she have?

With a slow nod she held her hand toward the barrier, allowing herself to concentrate on the magic that had so recently proven to be lethal.

"Sally, what are you doing?" Roke rasped, grasping her wrist as she began to glow with a golden light.

"Joining my powers with my father," she murmured, her gaze remaining trained on her father.

Was there a hint of a glow around his unmoving body?

"Dammit. This could be a trap."

She turned her head to meet his worried gaze, her expression pleading.

"I'm sorry, Roke, but I have to try."

His lips parted, no doubt to continue the argument, but with a hiss of warning he was spinning to the side, his fangs fully exposed.

"Something's coming." He paused, using his senses to search what was nothing but darkness to him. "Brandel."

Sally flinched, forced to remember the greasy spot that was all she'd left of the demon.

"He's dead."

"No loss," a voice drawled as a large, bronzed male began to form from a black mist.

Sally's eyes widened as the creature solidified.

Completely naked the stranger had the face of a Greek god with a halo of golden curls. His velvet brown eyes flickered to reveal slits of red that proved he was related to Brandel. Not that there seemed to be any love lost.

"The bastard had become too greedy for his own good," the stranger murmured, smiling at Sally's shock.

"Sally," her father's voice cut through her sudden burst of fear. "Concentrate on your powers."

Licking her lips she glanced toward her mate. "I have to free Sariel."

His lips flattened with disapproval, but he gave a nod as he pulled out his dagger and stepped around her.

"I'll keep him distracted."

She swallowed the lump in her throat. "Be careful."

Chapter Twenty-Four

Roke took a swift inventory of his enemy.

He dismissed the bulky muscles and image of power in the naked body. The demon was a shape-shifter. He could assume whatever form he wanted.

Besides, a Nebule didn't need physical strength.

They had far more lethal skills.

What he instead concentrated on was the unmistakable arrogance etched onto the too handsome features and the complete disdain for Sally's attempt to rescue her father.

The demon believed himself far superior to his unexpected intruders.

And that was his weakness.

Pulling out his dagger, Roke shifted to the side, not halting until the demon's back was turned toward Sally.

Now all he had to do was keep the bastard talking until his mate could complete her task.

Or kill them all in the attempt.

"You're wasting your time," the Nebule taunted, stifling a yawn.

Roke tested the edge of his blade with his thumb. "You think?"

"A human witch can't break through the barrier and you can't kill me, leech."

Not by the flicker of an eyelash did Roke reveal his surprise at the demon's words. So, he didn't realize that Sally was Chatri. Or that she was Sariel's daughter.

Interesting.

He smiled, waving his dagger toward the naked body.

"This is the best you can do?" Roke mocked, deliberately prodding the male's ego.

It was the most certain means to keep him from wondering what was happening behind him.

The demon frowned. "Are you referring to my body?"

Roke snorted. "You can take any form you want and you end up looking like a porn star?"

"The fey are attracted to beauty." The male ran a loving hand over his six-pack. "Like a vampire I use my charms to lure my prey."

Roke arched a brow, studying the demon with icy disgust. "You're nothing like a vampire."

"Of course I am," the male argued, clearly obsessed with the belief he was somehow comparable to a vampire. Inferiority complex? A smug smile curved the creature's lips. "I even fuck my dinner while I'm draining away their life. Tell me that your climax isn't better when it comes at the exact moment your prey dies in your arms?"

Roke hid his grimace.

He wasn't a prude. Hell, he'd done things that would make a nymph blush. But he'd never been a fan of death-by-sex.

"So why not drain the Chatri you captured?" he asked. "I assume he would have more magic than a regular fey."

"He's necessary to keep the portal open between our worlds," the Nebule readily answered, his arrogance enjoying the opportunity to brag.

His words reminded Roke of the imp's explanation that a portal couldn't be closed while the fey was still inside and just that quickly the kidnapping of Sariel made perfect sense.

"This is your only way to travel to our dimension?" he asked, although he already knew the answer.

The red slit in the dark eyes flashed with fury. "The Chatri did their best to isolate us, denying my people the magic we so desperately need."

"Need?"

"Need. Crave." The demon waved aside the distinction. "It's all the same."

Over the demon's shoulder Roke became aware of a steadily growing light. Sally had found her magic, but it still wasn't bright enough to be at full strength.

He had to keep the demon talking.

"So you kept the Chatri imprisoned so your people could have ready access to their drug of choice?" he scoffed, not having to fake his disdain.

The Nebule were bottom-feeders who had to steal the powers of others.

"It's a very profitable arrangement," the male admitted without shame.

"And what was Brandel's role?"

"He was to keep a watch on the Commission."

That explained why the bastard had been posing as an Oracle.

Roke's pretense of interest suddenly became very real.

"Why?"

"All formal petitions came through him, so he could make sure to destroy any complaints by the fey that they had family disappearing." He eyed Roke as if expecting him to be suitably impressed with their cunning. "We couldn't allow the Commission to come snooping."

He had to admit they'd been clever.

It was no wonder they'd gone undetected for centuries.

The glow became brighter, an unmistakable heat sizzling through the air.

Roke stepped forward, determined to keep the demon's attention focused on him.

"Why was he after . . ." He bit back Sally's name. "The witch's box?"

"Box?" The male looked momentarily confused. "Oh. The defaro was connected to the Chatri; we couldn't allow the magic to be recognized." The bronzed form became misty around the edges, as if his temper made him lose command of his form body. "He was supposed to destroy the damned thing."

"But he changed the rules?"

The demon curled his lips in a sneer. "He wanted the magic for himself."

And speaking of magic . . .

The glow abruptly became a flood of light that could no longer be hidden.

"If he wanted the magic, then why take it directly from the source?" Roke asked, not surprised when the demon jerked toward the prison holding the Chatri.

"Sariel is mine," the Nebule growled.

"And Sally?" Roke taunted, angling himself to attack the demon, while keeping an eye on Sally as the magic spilled from her skin and surrounded her with a blinding aura.

Beyond her, he could see a more muted glow that had to be coming from her trapped father.

"She's a witch," the male muttered. "Just a witch."

Roke snorted. His mate had never been just a witch.

She'd always been a rare, dangerously enticing female with powers far beyond a mere mortal.

"You're not any smarter than your friend," he taunted.

"No." A murderous fury twisted the Adonis features.

"He's mine."

* * *

Sally's mouth went dry as Roke move toward the Nebule demon.

This wasn't how she envisioned this moment.

She was supposed to have hunted down the prison, rescued her father, and swooped away like Wonder Woman. Only with smaller boobs.

And in the end she would have . . . what?

Proven she was worthy?

To whom?

Herself? Her father? Roke?

Not that it mattered.

She wasn't Wonder Woman.

She was a terrified witch who couldn't control her own magic and she'd managed to put Roke smack-dab in the path of a demon who could kill him before they could get out of the portal.

Trying to ignore the fear that raged through her, Sally instead concentrated on the powers that remained locked deep inside her.

"It's not working," she muttered from between clenched teeth.

"Patience, child," her father's voice echoed through her head.

"We don't have time for patience," she snapped. "Roke can't hold off the Nebule forever."

She sensed her father's confusion that Sally would even consider Roke's welfare.

"Your vampire is capable of taking care of himself."

"He's vulnerable to the demon's powers."

"This is our only opportunity," her father chided. "You must free me."

She grimaced at the man's self-absorption.

Okay, he'd been imprisoned for a very long time. She got that.

But, so far he hadn't revealed even a hint of concern for her or her mate's danger.

She gave a shake of her head, resisting the urge to glance in Roke's direction. She had to concentrate on freeing her father so they could all get the hell out of there.

"That's what I'm trying to do," she said, pressing against the invisible wall as she tried to tap into seething powers that just waited to be released. "The barrier won't let me through."

"It was specifically designed to repel my magic, which is why I've been unable to escape."

She frowned at the explanation. "Then why did you think I could help if my magic is the same as yours?"

A faint glow became visible around her father's prone body and Sally felt an answering heat begin to spread through her veins.

"Because they will cancel one another out," Sariel assured her.

As if that answered everything.

Her frown deepened. "I don't understand."

"Once we synchronize our powers they will work as one."

She could almost feel the pulse of his magic as it struggled to align with her own. A faint glow beginning to spill from beneath her skin.

"But it will still be the same power," she said, needing to understand what was expected of her. How else could she use her powers to help?

"Exactly." There was a patronizing edge to her father's voice. "While it is forced to keep you from passing through, it will not be able to sense as I slip out."

Sally briefly hesitated before giving a nod. "I suppose that makes a weird sort of sense."

The glow around her father brightened, his power battering into her.

"You must trust me."

A laugh of disbelief was wrenched from her throat. From

what she knew of this man he'd deliberately seduced her mother, allowing her to leave with her mind stripped of memories so she could have a child whose only purpose was to return and save him.

It was hardly the reunion story designed to give her a case of the warm fuzzies.

"Trust you?" She gave a shake of her head. "I have no reason to trust you."

"I am your father."

"No. You were a sperm donor."

She sensed his astonishment at her blunt accusation. "You are blood of my blood."

"Sally, you've been recognized," Roke's fierce voice sliced into her dark thoughts and she glanced to the side to see the Nebule was staring at her in horror.

Oh hell. How could she have allowed herself to be distracted for even a nanosecond?

Watching Roke move to stand between her and the demon, Sally turned back to her father, desperation clawing through her.

"Tell me what to do," she hissed.

Sariel's frustration sizzled through the air. "I cannot synchronize our magic if you will not allow me in."

"I'm trying."

"There is a wall you keep around you."

Sally clenched her hands. Of course she had a wall. She'd been trying to protect herself for as long as she could remember.

How else did she survive a childhood of neglect followed by years of being hunted like an animal?

Trust was the enemy.

Now she bit her bottom lip until the blood flowed as she struggled against her most deeply ingrained instincts. She'd kept herself cut off for so long it was no simple matter to simply lay herself open.

There were no tangible walls. Nothing she could physically get ahold of and tear down. Instead she had to mentally *will* herself to stop fighting against the press of her father's magic.

Something that she discovered was much easier said than done.

Sweat dripped down her spine, her heart racing with fear. Blessed goddess, she felt like she was being smothered.

This was never going to work, she realized with a stab of dread. She couldn't do it.

It was at last the sound of Roke's grunt of pain as he was attacked by the Nebule that shook her out of her swelling panic.

She could do it, because she had to do it.

If not for her father, then for Roke.

The same surge of adrenaline that had released her powers against Brandel pumped through her blood, allowing the magic to expand through her.

"That's all I can do," she managed from between clenched teeth.

Her father's magic began to weave through her, intruding in a way that made her stiffen before he gave a startled hiss.

"You've actually mated with the vampire?" he demanded. "Unacceptable."

Her teeth were gritted against the need to shove out the unfamiliar invasion.

"Is it really important right now?"

"His claim on you is interfering," Sariel complained, his tone almost . . . peevish. "Can you convince him to release you?"

She grimaced.

Not only was it an impossible request, but she was fairly certain in Roke's current mood he'd kill her father before he'd release his claim on her.

"No."

The magic continued to weave with hers, a slow and surprisingly painful process.

"You are making this more difficult than it needs be," her father accused.

There was another groan from Roke and Sally banged her hand against the invisible barrier.

"I'm going to make it impossible if you don't hurry up," she warned.

The glow around her father spread outward, his hair floating as if on a breeze she couldn't feel.

"You lived too long as a mortal." The disgust in Sariel's tone assured Sally that wasn't a compliment. "It is why I discouraged our people to mate with lesser beings."

Anger exploded through her.

Was he kidding? She'd risked Roke's life, not to mention her own, to try to rescue him. A man who was nothing more than a stranger. And all he could do was complain?

Jackass.

"And yet you were quick enough to mate with a mere human when it suited your purpose," she rasped.

"My other children are not nearly so quarrelsome," Sariel complained. "They understand that I am to be given the proper respect."

All thoughts halted as her world tilted to an unexpected angle.

His words shouldn't have been unexpected.

The fey had the same low birthrate of most demons, but when you had an eternity of sex, there were bound to be a few children.

But after a lifetime alone, the casual mention that she had brothers and sisters had thrown her seriously off-balance.

"I have siblings?" she asked, hating the yearning she couldn't keep from her voice.

"Of course."

There was a grunt as Roke landed only inches from her feet, his face covered with blood and his skin ashen.

"Sally, I'm running out of tricks," he growled, flowing back to his feet and launching himself back at the Nebule who was desperately trying to get his hands on her.

Dammit, dammit, dammit.

She was going to get Roke killed if she didn't get Sariel out of his prison.

"Father, finish this," she hissed.

"Press your hands against the barrier," he commanded, the glow around him becoming a blinding light as he slowly began to levitate off the ground.

Sally pushed her palms flat against the invisible wall, silently urging Sariel to hurry.

It was taking too long. Too long.

The vibrations that seemed to be the Nebule's most lethal weapon was filling the portal, sending Roke to his knees and making Sally cry out as the destructive jolts of pain slammed into her.

Feeling blood trickle down her cheeks, she grimly kept her hands pressed to the barrier, averting her face against the brilliant light that threatened to sear her eyeballs.

The scent of fermenting wine filled the air as the barrier trembled beneath her hands. Then, with a blast that sent her tumbling backward, the wall shattered and the light blasted through the tunnel.

"At last," her father said aloud, his voice triumphant as he allowed the light to fade and he revealed his physical form.

He was once again the godlike creature from the meadow.

His golden hair flowed over his shoulders, held back by the silver band that was no longer tarnished. His face was chiseled perfection and his amber eyes shimmered with shards of jade. Even his robe had returned to its flawless white satin.

With a low groan, Sally was on her feet and glancing toward

her mate who had his arms wrapped around the Nebule as it continued to pummel him with waves of deadly vibrations.

"Roke."

She started forward only to be halted when her father grabbed her shoulder.

"Do not be a fool. You've been weakened," he chided, his voice so rich and compelling she had to battle against the urge to gaze at him in dazzled wonder. "The Nebule could hurt you."

He was right, damn him.

She hadn't even noticed how much energy Sariel had drained from her to destroy the barrier. Not until she realized her knees were threatening to buckle and her eyes weren't entirely focused.

"Then help him," she commanded.

"Why?" Sariel demanded in genuine confusion. "The Nebule can rid us of the pesky vampire and then I can put an end to the Nebule. Far more efficient."

"I don't want to be rid of the vampire," she snapped. "If you won't help, then I will."

Meeting her death glare he gave an impatient click of his tongue. "Very well." With a liquid grace, the Chatri moved forward, stepping around Roke as he directly confronted the Nebule. "Stay out my way, leech. Raith and I have unfinished business."

Chapter Twenty-Five

Sariel reveled in his freedom as he moved forward, his power flowing through him.

For years he'd been held prisoner by the lowest scum of a demon.

Him. The King of the Chatri. The leader of the ancient fey who had been feared and respected by all.

It was a disgrace that he would be forced to bear for the rest of his very long life. But he could help to ease the shame by destroying the Nebule as slowly and painfully as possible.

"Stand aside, leech," he commanded, his gaze locked on the bastard who'd dared to hold him captive. "Raith and I have unfinished business."

The vampire peeled back his lips to reveal his fangs as Sariel swept past him.

"Happy to fucking meet you, too," he growled, forcing himself back to his feet. "And you're welcome."

Sariel glanced over his shoulder. "For what?"

"For coming to your rescue."

Sariel waved a dismissive hand. Did the leech actually expect him to appreciate his presence?

Absurd.

"I knew my daughter would come," he said, forgetting the vampire as he turned to meet Raith's horrified gaze.

"Daughter?" The creature shook his head. "That's impossible. The Chatri have retreated from the world."

Sariel eyed his enemy with cold anticipation. "I am the King of the Chatri. My blood can create gold out of dross."

"But . . ." The Nebule hissed in sudden fury. "The witch."

"Yes." Sariel's smug smile hid his initial shock when he'd first felt the witch's spell that had reached even through the barrier.

Her desperation for a child had not only drawn his attention, but it'd given him the perfect solution to escaping from his prison.

If she wanted a baby, he would give her one.

A very special one.

The air trembled as Raith's goat eyes smoldered with a slit of crimson.

"I should have tracked her down and killed her."

"I knew in time your arrogance would be my eventual means for escape."

Raith tried to covertly back away. Did he think Sariel would actually allow him to escape?

"You call me arrogant?"

"I call you a fool." Sariel held up his hand, cold anticipation bubbling through him like the finest nectar. "Now you will pay."

"No." Holding out his hands, Raith went to his knees. "We can work out a bargain. I have acquired a fortune over the centuries."

Sariel took satisfaction in the sight of his captor pleading for his life.

A pity he couldn't take the creature to his homeland. It would be far more satisfying if he could prolong the Nebule's torture for several centuries rather than a handful of minutes.

Unfortunately, the spells he'd woven around the entrance to the lands of the Chatri had been specifically created to kill a Nebule who dared to trespass.

"You have nothing I want," he informed the pathetic demon.

"You don't know that." Raith paused, clearly trying to think of something that might tempt a Chatri. "I've collected priceless gems and magical artifacts," he at last offered.

Sariel considered less than a heartbeat.

It was true that Chatri were addicted to collecting wealth. Only dragons could claim larger hoards of gems, precious metals, magical artifacts, and knowledge. And as king, his hoard was larger than any other.

The temptation to increase his wealth wasn't something he would have dismissed so easily if he hadn't been plotting for years to destroy this creature.

Focusing his power to a narrow band, he directed it to wrap around the kneeling demon. Like a lasso of light that seared into the Nebule with intense pain.

"All I want is your death."

"Why?" The demon shuddered, his human form desperately trying to disintegrate to escape the searing magic. "It will give you nothing."

"You're mistaken." Sariel smiled, taking full pleasure in watching the golden glow slicing through the spongy flesh of his tormentor. How many hours had he devoted to imagining this precise moment? Thousands and thousands. His smile widened as he deliberately allowed his magic to burn brighter, increasing the pain. "Killing you is a priceless treasure."

Raith screamed until his voice came out in a hoarse plea. "What about your people?"

Sariel heard the sound of his daughter urging the vampire away from his power that was spilling through the portal. Not that he cared what happened to the leech.

It would be far better if he died at the same time as the Nebule.

"What about them?" he demanded, his tone revealing his lack of concern.

There was no means for the demon to hurt his people.

"I have them hidden," the Nebule warned, his voice a mere thread of sound. "They will die if you kill me."

Sariel frowned. Captured?

Abruptly he realized Raith was referring to the kidnapped fey that he and his partner kept in a holding pen somewhere in the portal.

He waved a dismissive hand. "They're not my concern."

"But . . ." The words were forgotten as another scream was wrenched from the Nebule, his flesh slowly melting beneath the heat of Sariel's magic.

With a ruthless precision honed over centuries of battles, Sariel amped up his magic notch by agonizing notch.

The Nebule pleaded and cursed and threatened until he could no longer speak. Instead he tumbled forward, his body twitching with a pain that was unimaginable.

Sariel allowed it to linger for nearly an hour, his fierce need for retribution only partially fulfilled when the creature abruptly burst into flames. Within seconds there was nothing left of Raith but a greasy pile of sludge.

Walking forward, he passed a hand over the blackened pile, wrapping a layer of magic over Raith that would prevent his people from collecting his remains and giving him a proper burial.

He might be dead, but his soul would remain trapped in this spot for all of eternity.

"I suppose that shall have to satisfy me," he murmured, turning to find his daughter clutched in the arms of the vampire. "You killed his partner?"

She gave a wary nod. "Yes."

"You make me proud," he informed her, knowing that his

words of praise would be worth more than the finest jewel to his offspring. "Only the most powerful Chatri could destroy a Nebule single-handedly."

She frowned, not seeming to appreciate how rare and precious it was to receive his praise. Some of his people had devoted decades of labor just to earn a faint nod of approval from him.

"It wasn't single-handed," she protested, glancing toward the vampire.

"Fah." Sariel sniffed. His daughter's bond with the vampire was something he needed to break. The sooner the better. "A leech couldn't be of assistance."

The vampire flashed his fangs. "I really don't like you, fey."

Fey? He was Chatri.

Sariel squared his shoulders. "Trust me, the feeling is mutual."

Sally continued to frown, seemingly impervious to the male sniping.

"What did he mean?" she abruptly asked.

Sariel turned his attention to her tense face. "Who?"

"The Nebule."

"Ah." He forgot the vampire. This was a proper response for a true Chatri. "You wish to claim his treasure?" He offered a gracious smile. "It is yours if you desire it. You have earned a reward."

Her brows snapped together as if offended by his generous offer.

"No, I don't care about treasure."

Impatience flared through him. What was wrong with the female?

"Of course you care," he told her. "You are my daughter. We are judged not only by our beauty, but by the wealth we have accumulated."

She snorted, indifferent to his careful explanation. "Then I'm destined to be low man on the totem pole."

"You have a totem pole?" he demanded in confusion.

She shook her head. "No. What I mean is that I don't care how you judge me."

Sariel stiffened. Among his people such a response could have the offending person thrown into the dungeons, if not killed outright.

"You're tired so I forgive you for your heresy," he said stiffly. "We should leave this place."

The vampire tightened his arm around Sally's shoulders. "That's the first intelligent thing you said."

Sally grimly dug in her heels. "What about the people the Nebule mentioned?"

Sariel arched a brow. "People?"

"He called them *your* people."

"Oh." Sariel shrugged. He'd already forgotten the Nebule's desperate attempt to avoid his painful death. "Raith and his partner would capture a group of fey and keep them imprisoned until they could arrange an auction on their world."

"Where are they?"

He gestured behind him. He'd heard the screams of the latest prisoners just before Sally's timely arrival.

"Somewhere in the portal."

"Can you find them?" she pressed, ignoring the glares of her vampire.

"If I wanted to." He curled his lips. "Which I most emphatically do not."

"Why not? You're their king."

He clicked his tongue, running his hands down the rare silk of his gown.

"I am King of the Chatri," he corrected.

"And the fey are still your people," she ridiculously insisted.

He peered down the length of his long nose. A gesture that would have sent most of his court scurrying in fear.

"I sense you have some expectation of me."

Not only did his daughter not scurry, she stepped away from her vampire to stab him with an impatient glare.

"I want to find the fey and take them back to our world." Roke and Sariel spoke in unison.

"No!"

Sally planted her hands on her hips, refusing to be quelled by the two men who were studying her as if she'd gone nuts.

And maybe she had.

It wasn't like she could explain why rescuing the fey was important.

They were, after all, mere strangers.

But over the past weeks, Roke had taught her that she could no longer hide.

Not from her enemies. Or the world.

Or even herself.

She didn't know who she was becoming, but she wanted it to be someone who could be proud of the choices she made.

Someone who could walk down the street with her head lifted high, not cowering in the shadows.

"I'm not leaving without them," she announced in stubborn tones.

"Sally." Roke cupped his fingers beneath her chin, tilting her head to meet the stunning silver of his gaze. "I didn't like your insistence on rescuing your father."

"Understatement of the century," she muttered.

His expression was grim as he no doubt battled the urge to toss her over his shoulder and force her to leave.

"But I understood that you felt it was your duty," he continued.

"It was," she agreed.

His thumb stroked the line of her jaw. "Now that you've done what was necessary, we have to get out of here."

She wanted out of there as much as Roke and her father.

The swirling lights of the portal were making her dizzy and the weird smell of the smoldering Nebule remains was turning her stomach.

But she knew that if she gave in to Roke's urgings, she would never forget that she'd sacrificed the lives of others because she couldn't be bothered to save them.

"And leave behind innocents?" she asked, holding Roke's gaze.

"You made sure that no more fey will be captured," he rasped. "You've done enough."

Her father couldn't resist intruding into their conversation.

"As much as I hate to agree with the leech, he is right."

She stepped around Roke to meet her father's bored gaze. "So you intend to just abandon them to an eternity of being trapped in hell?"

He blinked at her unexpected attack. "It's doubtful they will survive an eternity."

"Good Lord," she breathed. She was quickly discovering her father was a coldhearted narcissist who rarely considered anything but himself. Still, the knowledge he would easily abandon people who considered him a god was a breaking point as far as she was concerned. "Fine," she rasped, moving before either man could react. "I'll find them myself."

She had taken less than two steps when Roke was at her side, his hand on her arm.

"Sally, you're not thinking clearly," he said, the words setting her teeth on edge.

She sent him a scowl. "Don't tell me what I'm thinking."

He growled in exasperation. "Why would you risk your life for a bunch of fey you don't even know?"

"And if they were vampires?"

They both knew the answer.

Roke was a clan chief who was programmed to do whatever necessary to protect his people.

Not that he was going to concede defeat gracefully.

"Don't do this," he said in low, urgent tones.

"Roke, you aren't going to condemn those poor demons to a life of misery." She lifted a hand to press it against his cool cheek. "It's not who you are."

He covered her fingers with his hand, his expression somber. "I would abandon everyone and everything if it meant protecting you."

"Listen to your leech, my child," her father urged. "The worth of the fey is negligible when compared to you."

Sally made a sound of disbelief as Roke flashed his fangs toward Sariel.

"You're not helping."

The Chatri sniffed. "I speak the truth. We need to get her out of here."

Sally narrowed her gaze. "Leave if you want, but I'm going to find the prisoners and free them."

Brushing past a frustrated Roke, Sally headed down the portal.

What had started as a mere obligation was now a full-blown quest.

"Stop her," her father called from behind her.

Roke snorted as he moved to walk beside her. "Obviously you've never been mated."

Sally heaved a faint sigh as Roke grabbed her hand, threading their fingers together.

She'd known he wouldn't leave her.

Until the mating was broken he *couldn't* leave her.

Which meant she was putting him in danger yet again.

"I'm sorry," she said softly.

"Don't be." His lips twisted with resignation. "You're right."

"I am?"

"We can't leave the fey stuck here." He glanced over his shoulder, making certain his words would carry. "And since the mighty king can't be bothered to take responsibility, it looks like we'll have to rescue his people."

"This is absurd," Sariel called, his seething anger filling the portal with a shimmering heat.

"No shit," Roke muttered.

There was a stir of air before the King of the Chatri was brushing past them.

"This way," he commanded, holding up a slender hand as he shifted the swirling strands of magic to curve toward the right.

In spite of her annoyance with her father, Sally found herself fascinated by his manipulation of the magic.

She could almost . . . see . . . how he was loosening the weaves to tug them in the direction he wanted.

In time she was fairly certain she could learn to do the same thing.

Now, however, she was more interested in why her father was altering the portal.

"What are you doing?"

"Searching for the prisoners. Raith said they were hidden. You will never locate them without my assistance." Sariel sent a chiding glance toward Roke. "Clearly you are not a suitable mate or she would have learned to obey your orders."

Sally's brief fascination was replaced by a surge of outrage as she glanced toward her mate.

"Obey?"

Roke arched his brows. "Hey, you're the one who wanted to rescue him, not me."

She heaved a sigh. "Don't remind me."

Chapter Twenty-Six

Roke stood at the window of Styx's library, watching as Sally helped Troy load the last of the terrified fey into the black SUV with tinted windows.

They'd returned to the elegant lair on the outskirts of Chicago just before dawn and tumbled into the nearest bed in exhaustion.

When he'd awoken hours later he'd intended to keep Sally secluded in their rooms to discuss their future.

Well, first he had intended to peel off her clothes and taste her from her strawberry-tinted lips to the tips of her tiny toes before spreading her legs and driving deep inside her welcoming heat.

Then, he had intended to turn her over and repeat the process.

But after that, he'd had every intention of convincing her that it was time they return to his clan in Nevada.

Moving to stand beside him, Styx shoved a brandy snifter in Roke's hand, sipping his drink as the line of SUVs pulled down the long, sweeping drive.

"You did a good thing," he murmured as they watched the fey departing.

Roke shook his head.

It'd taken Sariel less than an hour to track down the prison and smash through the walls to expose the two dozen fey who were huddled in terror.

Fairies, imps, sylphs, sprites, nymphs, and the rare Sylvermyst had been reluctantly coaxed out of the portal and then to Styx's lair where Troy had been waiting for them.

Eventually they would be reunited with their families who no doubt had been convinced their loved ones were dead.

"It was Sally," he corrected with a wry smile. "She's a better person than I am. If you want the truth, I'd have left them there."

"She's your mate," Styx said as if that explained everything. "It's your instinct to put her safety first. Just as it's her instinct to soften your rough edges."

Taking a sip of the aged brandy, Roke slid his gaze toward the towering Aztec at his side.

"Is that what Darcy does?"

"Absolutely."

Roke snorted, amazed Roke could say that with a straight face.

"Your edges are still lethally rough," he pointed out.

Styx gave a shift of his shoulder, emphasizing the large sword that was strapped to his back and the gun holstered beneath his left arm. The Anasso had declared that as long as his lair was filled with strangers, he wasn't going to take any chances.

Roke fully agreed with his caution.

"Maybe, but she makes me consider other people's feelings," Styx said.

Roke grimaced. "Good God."

"I know." Styx polished off his brandy and set aside the snifter.

"And it doesn't bother you?"

A smile that would have shocked most of the demon world suddenly softened Styx's dark features as he thought of his mate.

"On the contrary, she has made me a stronger leader than I would ever have been without her."

The simple confession made Roke wince. He understood. Too late. But he understood.

"That I believe."

Way too perceptive, Styx sent him a questioning glance. "What about you?"

Roke frowned, watching as Sally joined her father to stroll across the wide gardens.

She looked unbearably young in her faded jeans and loose sweatshirt, her hair pulled into a ponytail. Next to her, the golden-haired Chatri wearing his spotless white robe carried with him an aura of timeless age.

It was an effort not to rush after them as they moved out of sight.

"What about me?" he asked in distracted tones.

"Do you still believe Sally will weaken your position as chief?"

Roke set aside his glass and shoved his fingers through his hair, turning to meet his friend's curious gaze.

"Christ, I'm such an ass."

"No argument from me."

Roke dropped his hand, his lips twisting at the memory of his smug certainty that he could plot out his life as if it were a battle plan.

"I actually thought I could control who would be my mate."

"A damn good thing we can't," Styx growled.

"You're right." Roke shuddered at being stuck with the woman of his dreams. "I would've ended up with a spineless fool who was too timid to speak her mind, or worse, a power-hungry bitch like Zoe who would have made me miserable within the first year of our mating."

Styx's dark gaze searched his disgusted expression. "So you're satisfied with Sally as your mate?"

Roke hissed in shock. "What the hell kind of question is that?"

"A very reasonable one."

With an effort, Roke resisted the urge to punch his friend in the face.

He was pissed, not insane.

"You wouldn't think so if I asked you if you are satisfied with Darcy."

Styx was unrepentant. "My mating to Darcy wasn't caused by a spell gone wrong."

"Any mating is a result of demon magic no matter whose magic it might be," Roke snapped.

He didn't want to be lectured as if he were too stupid to know what he wanted, or needed.

"You know that it's not the same," Styx said.

Roke swore in frustration. "What do you want from me?"

"Sariel will soon be leaving to join his people."

Roke didn't try to hide his relief that the arrogant bastard would soon be out of his hair.

Not only had Sariel broken Sally's heart by admitting he had no interest in her beyond what she could do for him, but he'd selfishly lured her into danger to save his ass.

The sooner he disappeared, the better.

"Thank the gods."

"Yeah. You get no argument from me," Styx groused, having endured Sariel's litany of complaints from the size of his bedroom to the food he was served. Apparently, Styx's lair wasn't a suitable setting for his Excellency, the King of the Chatri. "But, he's the one who has the knowledge and the power to remove Sally's spell."

The windows rattled beneath Roke's blast of anger. "No."

Styx slammed his fists on his hips. "Roke, you need to think about this."

"It's done." Roke slashed his hand through the air. "End of story."

The Anasso refused to back down. "It might not be. Have you considered the possibility that you might eventually meet your true mate?"

There was no hesitation. "Sally is my true mate."

"You won't know that for certain unless you break the spell," Styx pressed.

Roke shook his head. He didn't need to break the spell to know the truth.

Sally was so deeply ingrained inside him there was no possibility the bond with her could ever be broken.

"I told you, no."

"If she's your true mate, then you can finalize the bond in the more traditional way."

Roke folded his arms over his chest, not about to confess that he had every intention of finalizing the bond as soon as he could get Sally alone.

The mere thought of sinking his fangs deep into her flesh and tasting the peach-scented blood . . .

Christ, he was fully erect just imagining the explosive pleasure.

Turning back toward the window, Roke instinctively searched for his mate who was traveling past the garden and out the fences that protected the grounds.

Where the hell was she going?

"We can't be certain that trying to break the spell is safe," he muttered.

Styx hesitated, clearly considering the danger to Sally for the first time.

"You think it might hurt her?"

"We have to be careful." Roke placed a hand on the window, not happy his mate was out of sight. "She's just coming into her powers. They're too unstable to screw around with."

"This might be your only opportunity," Styx warned, sounding frustrated by Roke's growing distraction. "Once the Chatri leaves there won't be anyone here to teach Sally how to break the spell."

Roke hid his smile of satisfaction.

He didn't want anyone teaching Sally how to break the spell.

"The decision has been made."

Styx allowed a punishing trickle of his power to slam into Roke. Not enough to damage him, but certainly sufficient to gain his attention.

"Have you made the decision for Sally as well?" he demanded.

Roke was caught off guard by the question. "What the hell is that supposed to mean?"

"Did you ask her if she wants to continue the mating?"

"Why wouldn't she?"

Styx gave him an are-you-shitting-me look. "Your clan did try to kill her."

A cold, unnerving fear trickled down his spine.

He couldn't dwell on all the reasons Sally might decide he wasn't worthy to be her mate. Not when he knew the scales weren't weighted in his favor.

"I promised Sally that it would never happen again," Roke swore.

Styx's expression abruptly softened and he reached out to grasp his shoulder.

"Talk to her, amigo," he urged. "It's only fair."

Roke scowled. "Maybe I don't want to be fair."

Sally walked beside her father in silence as they left the manicured lawns of Styx's estate to the narrow band of trees that were beyond the high fences that concealed the house from its distant neighbors.

She wasn't sure why Sariel had asked her to stroll with him. He'd made it fairly obvious he hadn't been pleased by her insistence on freeing the imprisoned fey. Or by her refusal to listen to his warnings that the vampires were dangerous beasts who were destined to betray her.

Somehow she'd assumed he would simply disappear. No good-bye. No thank you for saving his life.

Which made this strange encounter even more awkward.

"I assume you will soon be returning to your people?" she asked, feeling a sudden need to break the silence.

"*Our* people," he corrected, halting so he could turn to study her with his amber gaze. "And yes, I must join them."

She cleared her throat, still not comfortable with the idea she was some sort of powerful Chatri. Even worse, the poor creatures they'd released from the Nebule prison had been so determined to show her their gratitude they'd spent the entire day spreading word of her heroism throughout the fey world.

Already there were piles of gifts outside the gates to Styx's driveway and several dozen fairies hoping for a glimpse of her and her father, the King of the Chatri.

It was enough to make any woman long to lock herself in her bedroom and throw away the key.

Especially if that bedroom included a silver-eyed vampire who could make her shiver with the demanding pleasure of his lips and the sweet invasion of his hard body that made her arch in need.

She licked her lips, resisting the urge to tug at the neckline of her sweatshirt as a hot flash nearly boiled her alive.

Holy crap.

With an effort, she slammed the door on the image of Roke spread naked on her bed.

It was just . . . creepy when she was standing next to her father.

She forced a stiff smile to her lips. "Will you be coming back here?"

"That's a question I will consider," he murmured.

"So . . ." She licked her dry lips. "I suppose this is good-bye."

Expecting Sariel to take advantage of her farewell, she was startled when he reached to take her hand in an uncomfortable grip.

"It need not be."

She glanced down to where his slender fingers held hers. "No?"

"You could come with me."

She struggled to follow the bizarre conversation. "To your home?"

"That is where you belong. With me."

Okay. This was so not what she was expecting.

She shook her head. "It's a kind offer, but my place is here."

A hint of impatience rippled over his painfully beautiful face.

"You have no desire to meet your family?"

She sucked in a sharp breath as he hit her at her most vulnerable spot.

A lucky shot? She didn't think so.

Her father was clearly a masterful manipulator.

"You've spoken to them?"

"Of course."

"Tell me about them," she requested, her voice nearly lost on the chilled breeze.

"You have four sisters who are all princesses. Three are married to suitable Chatri males and the fourth will be married as soon as I return," he readily answered. "There are also two brothers who are in line for the throne. They are currently training to become leaders of their own houses."

His words were no doubt intended to tempt her into traveling to his home. Unfortunately for him, they only reminded Sally of the difference between herself and her siblings.

Princesses? Princes?

She would be a joke.

Feeling Sariel's piercing gaze, she ducked her head. "I'm nothing more than a stranger to them."

"You rescued me from the Nebule. You would be a hero to them." His voice was coaxing. "They will no doubt compose songs and poems in your honor."

Sally grimaced in sheer horror. "No thanks."

The perfect features tightened, as if he was irritated by her response.

"Then what about your family?" he insisted.

"What about them?"

"Among the Chatri nothing is more important." He chose his words with care. "Would you deny them the opportunity to meet you?"

Sally couldn't deny a pang of regret.

She'd been so alone for so long, always secretly dreaming she would find a place to call home.

Now that she was actually being offered one, it was unbearably wrenching to turn her back on it.

"I'm not truly family," she whispered.

His grip tightened on her fingers. "What do you mean?"

"I'm a half-breed," she reminded him. "I doubt the princes and princesses would be happy to have me pop out of the proverbial closet."

With his usual arrogance, Sariel shrugged aside the inevitable horror at her arrival among the coldly aloof, shatteringly beautiful Chatri.

"They will accept you."

A sad, wistful smile tugged at her lips. He was king. He could probably force his people to bow and scrape before her if that's what he commanded.

But he couldn't make them think of her as anything but an interloper.

There mere thought made her shudder.

"I'm looking for more than gruding acceptance," she told him softly.

He frowned. "I don't understand."

She smiled wryly. "I know."

He hesitated, his supreme confidence faltering as he studied her in exasperation.

Had he expected her to leap for joy at his invitation?

Probably.

"Tell me what you desire."

She turned to glance toward the house they'd left behind. She could see no more than the roof, but it didn't matter. She didn't need to see the sprawling mansion to know that Roke was inside.

Unconsciously she lifted a hand to rub it against the center of her chest, directly over heart.

"Love."

Sariel studied her in confusion. "Love?"

The word was clearly unfamiliar to her father. Perhaps the Chatri considered messy emotions beneath them.

But Sally didn't.

She'd devoted years to futilely trying to earn her mother's love. And then even more years trying to pretend it didn't matter.

Why shouldn't she be blessed with the happiness other people took for granted?

"It's what I've wanted my whole life," she admitted. "And I'm not going to stop searching until I find it."

Sariel studied her with a steady amber gaze, the scent of intoxicating wine filling the air.

"Does the vampire love you?"

Sally grimaced.

Her father certainly had a way of striking where she was most vulnerable.

It was a question that she'd refused to consider.

She'd told herself that any emotions Roke might or might not feel for her were nothing more than a result of the unwanted mating. And that once she'd reversed her spell, he'd walk away without a backward glance.

But while she hadn't consciously allowed herself to

nurture dangerous hopes, a few had managed to creep beneath her defenses and lodge themselves deep in her heart.

A part of her desperately wanted to believe that when the mating was at last broken, Roke would feel more than relief. That he would . . .

She bit her bottom lip, trying to leash her fantasies.

It wasn't fair to Roke. He'd already sacrificed so much for her. How could she expect him to fall in love with the woman who'd bewitched him, bonded him, and then nearly gotten him killed a dozen times?

And she knew him well enough to realize that if he suspected leaving her would break her heart, he would feel guilty. Or worse, try to pretend he wasn't desperate to get away from her.

"I'm not certain." She was careful to keep the yearning out of her voice. "I know he cares, but how much of that is a result of the mating and how much is genuine affection is impossible to know."

"Not impossible," he assured her.

She met the amber gaze. "You can remove the spell?"

His pale, beautiful face gave no indication of his inner thoughts. "It's a simple enchantment spell but because your powers were surging at the time, they triggered his mating instincts."

Sally grimaced. She hoped her powers would level off soon. The goddess only knew what disaster she might create next time.

"What happens if you remove it?" she asked.

"You'll know the truth of his heart."

She nodded at his blunt words.

It's what she wanted. No, wait. It wasn't what she *wanted*. The thought of Roke leaving was a sharp, jagged pain that threatened to destroy her.

But it was what she needed.

What they both needed.

There was only one question that had to be answered first. "Will it hurt Roke?"

"No." Her father's lips flattened in disapproval. "Unfortunately."

She ignored Sariel's lack of enthusiasm for her mate. The two males were way too alpha not to strike sparks off each other.

She had far more important things to worry about.

Drawing in a deep, painful breath, she squared her shoulders.

The spell had to be broken.

It was the only way Roke could be free to choose the future he wanted, not the one she'd inflicted on him.

"Then do it," she said before she could lose her nerve.

A smile that bordered on smug curved her father's mouth. "Only if you agree to visit my home."

Sally snatched her fingers from his grip, stepping back with a deep scowl.

She should have suspected her father's help wouldn't be freely given.

He no doubt invented the Trojan horse.

"No way."

Sariel's expression remained calm, his fingers absently smoothing the sleeve of his pure white robe.

"I said visit, not stay."

She told herself to walk away. Hadn't she just convinced herself she had no place among the Chatri?

Besides, she didn't trust this man.

If he wanted her to travel with him to her homeland, then there had to be an ulterior motive. And she doubted it had anything to do with ending her mating with Roke.

But even as she told herself to turn around and return to Styx's lair, her feet refused to move.

Instead she remained frozen in place, her curiosity overcoming her common sense.

"Why?"

He paused, his amber gaze lowering to where tiny flowers were beginning to bloom along the edge of his bare feet.

It was the most amazing sight.

"I am beginning to realize that I have not been the father you wish me to be," he at last said, the stiffness of his tone indicating how hard it was to concede he might not be perfect.

She jerked her gaze up to study his carefully composed expression.

"That's not your fault."

And it wasn't.

Sariel was the leader of people who obviously didn't put value on emotions. He couldn't have known how desperately she wanted a father who could fill the dark void in the center of her heart.

"Given time I believe we can create a better understanding of one another," he persisted.

Sally frowned. Was he being for real?

Could he truly want . . . an understanding? Whatever the hell that meant.

"Why would you want that?"

Another awkward pause. "It is difficult for me to admit, but it's possible we have become too isolated as a people."

She remained suspicious. Who could blame her? So far Sariel had been clear that she'd been created for one purpose. And it wasn't to be his loving daughter.

"I thought that was the whole point of leaving here?"

He shrugged. "It was, but after meeting you I believe there's something to be said for variety. And for—"

"What?"

"And for having a connection to the world beyond our borders."

She sensed he had a point. She just couldn't figure out what it was.

"What sort of connection?"

His gaze abruptly lifted, the amber eyes shimmering with hints of jade.

"You."

"I'm not sure I understand."

He seemed to search for the proper words. "You could be a diplomat between our world and this one."

She jerked in shock.

A diplomat? Her?

It was a career she'd never considered.

She had no skill with languages, no personal charm, not to mention the fact she tended to become a smartass when she was feeling defensive.

Not the sort of characteristics that would win friends and influence people.

On the other hand, she was one of the rare few who possessed the blood of a Chatri who was also of this world.

That did make her . . . unusual.

"Oh."

Sariel held her gaze. "Would you like that?"

"Yes." Sally widened her eyes in surprise as she felt an unmistakable surge of anticipation. She might not fit among the Chatri, but she could offer them something no one else could. "Yes, I think I would."

"Good." With a triumphant smile he grasped her hand. "Let us go."

It was the abrupt burst of colors that warned Sally her father meant to leave immediately.

She tried to tug her hand free, but this time her father refused to loosen his grip.

"Wait—" she protested, but it was too late.

Already the swirls of magic were dancing around her, sucking her into the portal and away from Roke.

Chapter Twenty-Seven

Leaving Styx to deal with his endless duties as Anasso, Roke headed directly into the moon-drenched gardens.

He wasn't intending to stick his nose into Sally's private meeting with her father. That would be . . . wrong, wouldn't it?

But, if his lazy stroll happened to take him in the same direction of his mate, then he couldn't help if he happened to overhear their conversation.

A fine plan that was interrupted by the blond-haired berserker who almost instantly joined him near a marble fountain.

Cyn had proven to be invaluable help when they'd arrived at Styx's lair with a gaggle of terrified fey. While Troy had been busy contacting the family members of the recently returned prisoners, Cyn had not only revealed a surprising kindness as he'd urged them to their various rooms, but he'd also managed to contact several local fey who brought food and clothing that were specifically designed to make the nearly comatose fey feel at home.

He was dressed similar to Roke in faded jeans and tight black tee, although Cyn chose shitkickers instead of Roke's knee-high moccasins.

As usual he'd braided the front strands of his long hair and tied them off with metal beads, while he had his favorite dagger strapped to his upper leg and a handgun holstered on his hip.

Never let it be said Cyn didn't know how to rock the screw-with-me-and-die vibe.

They walked in silence until they neared the marble grotto in the center of the garden.

"So you'll be returning to your clan?" Cyn abruptly demanded.

Roke grimaced. It was a discussion he'd been putting off.

"Once Sally is comfortable with the idea," he said.

Cyn sent him a knowing glance. "You think that might be a problem?"

"I'm not sure."

"What if it is?"

Roke shrugged. His decision had been made.

"Then I hand the position to Kale. He's a competent leader who I trust to protect my people."

Cyn came to a sharp halt, a blatant horror etched onto his bluntly chiseled features.

"You would walk away from your clan?"

Roke stopped beside his friend, folding his arms over his chest.

"Without hesitation," he admitted. "Nothing is more important to me than making Sally happy."

Cyn gave an exaggerated shudder. "Better you than me."

Roke laughed. Only weeks ago he'd been nurturing a sense of outrage at being stuck with Sally as his mate for all of eternity.

Even when he'd known in the depths of his heart that he was never, ever going to allow her to escape.

Fate seemed to have a peculiar sense of humor.

"Your mate is out there," he warned his friend. "And chances are you'll find her when you least expect it."

"Don't be trying to curse me." Cyn made a hasty sign to ward off evil. "I'm a vampire who fully embraces his freedom."

Roke smiled wryly. Well wasn't that the truth?

"By freedom you mean big-busted nymphs?"

Cyn waggled his brows. "Or fairies. Or sprites. I'm not choosy."

"No shit." Roke rolled his eyes. "Will you be leaving for Ireland?"

"Aye. I . . ." The vampire frowned as Roke went rigid and his power shook the ground. "Roke?"

"Goddammit," Roke growled, racing toward the nearby gate as fear exploded in the pit of his belly. "Not again."

Cyn kept pace beside him, pulling his gun as Roke's temper shattered the marble benches to dust.

"Tell me what's going on," the clan chief commanded.

Roke could barely speak, a dark panic threatening to cloud his mind.

"Sally."

"She's hurt?"

"She's gone."

Cyn was wise enough to avoid the stone archway as it crumbled into a pile of rubble, instead following Roke as he smoothly vaulted over the high fence and headed into the nearby woods.

"Gone where?"

"I don't know," Roke snapped, his senses spreading through the neighborhood for any hint of his mate. "She was here one minute and gone the next."

Cyn muttered a low curse. "Could it have been a portal?"

"Yes." Roke skidded to a stop, bending down to touch the ground that was still warm from the magic. "Here."

Cyn closed his eyes as he tested the air. "The Chatri."

"Goddamn that bastard." Roke straightened, wishing he'd left the King of the Chatri trapped in the Nebule's prison.

He'd known as soon as he'd met the arrogant ass he was going to be trouble. "He stole my mate."

Cyn shifted his feet, looking uncomfortable. "Roke, you can't be sure."

Was he kidding? Roke shook his head.

"There are no other scents beyond Sally and Sariel. He had to have been the one who took her."

"I'm not suggesting he wasn't the one who formed the portal."

Roke narrowed his gaze. "Then what are you saying?"

Cyn grimaced. "Maybe it wasn't a kidnapping."

Common sense warned Roke that his friend had a point. It wasn't, after all, the first time that Sally had disappeared. Hell, it wasn't even the second time.

But he wasn't currently listening to common sense.

He was listening to his heart that whispered Sally wouldn't abandon him.

Not without speaking to him first.

"Sally wouldn't have left me."

Cyn carefully considered his words. Wise vampire.

"Sariel is her father."

Roke shook his head. "He's a selfish bastard who destroyed her dreams of finding a family who actually cared about her."

"Still, family is family," Cyn pressed, speaking words that Roke didn't want to hear. "Especially to a young woman who never had one."

No. Roke wouldn't doubt her.

He had to believe that she'd been taken against her will.

It was the only way to keep a grip on his sanity.

"She wouldn't have left," he stubbornly insisted. "Not without telling me she was going."

Cyn tempted a swift, painful death. "She did before."

Roke gave a low growl.

Enough.

He wasn't going to waste time arguing. Not when Sally was being taken farther and farther away from him.

"She was forced," he muttered, yanking his dagger from beneath his leather jacket before he was running through the trees with fluid ease.

There was a startled sound behind him before Cyn was racing to catch up.

"Where the hell are you going?" he rasped, his gaze scanning the thinning trees for any potential danger.

"I can feel her."

Cyn scowled. "Feel her?"

Roke slammed his fist against the middle of his chest. "Here."

"You've lost your mind, buddy," Cyn muttered as they hit the street and Roke picked up his pace until they were traveling too fast for the human eye to follow.

"Maybe." He really didn't give a shit. Still, as eager as he might be to risk his life, he wasn't nearly so ready to put Cyn in danger. "Return to Styx and—"

"No way," his companion interrupted, continuing to scan their surroundings with a wary gaze.

Roke frowned. "This isn't your fight, Cyn."

The vampire kept his gun at his side, clearly determined to play the role of bodyguard.

"It is now."

Roke rubbed the aching void in the center of his chest. His connection to Sally remained steady, but it was . . . muffled. As if something or someone was trying to hide her.

It didn't take a genius to know who that might be.

"Why?" he demanded of his companion.

"Obviously, you need me."

Roke snorted. It wasn't often that anyone dared to imply

that he was anything but fully competent at taking care of himself.

"I do?"

They reached the outskirts of the chichi suburbs, and Roke veered toward the empty farmlands, barely noticing the lesser demons who scattered in terror at the sight of two powerful vampires on the hunt.

"If Sally is with the Chatri then you need someone who has a basic knowledge of the fey," Cyn explained. "So it's me or Troy, the Prince of Imps."

Roke grimaced. The only thing worse than traveling with the ridiculous imp would be another road trip with the gargoyle.

"This could be dangerous," he warned. "I'm not Sariel's favorite person."

"Hard to believe," Cyn said dryly.

"He might fight to keep Sally," Roke pointed out.

Not that he truly hoped he could convince Cyn to return to Styx's lair. Telling the berserker that there was danger involved was almost a certain guarantee he'd be first in line.

Cyn didn't disappoint.

Smiling with irrational anticipation, Cyn ran his tongue down the length of one massive fang.

"All the more reason you need me."

Roke did.

Although he didn't know if Cyn's knowledge of fey would actually help when it came to the mysterious Chatri, he was a powerful warrior who could slash his way through a horde of trolls without batting an eye.

"I owe you one," he said.

"Aye, you do," Cyn agreed. "Don't think I won't collect."

When Sally was young, she was addicted to fairy tales. What lonely little girl who was raised by a neglectful mother in bleak, isolated cabins wouldn't dream of a world where beautiful people twirled through elegant ballrooms dressed in shimmering gowns and sparkling jewels? And where handsome princes tumbled into love with Cinderella even if she was a gawky, introverted witch instead of a pretty princess.

But dreaming of fairy tales and actually being dumped into one were two very different things, she quickly discovered.

She was still struggling against Sariel's hold when they'd stepped from the portal into a large foyer with massive chandeliers and walls painted with exquisite murals.

Which meant she was completely unprepared for the swift arrival of her sisters and brothers who'd welcomed their father home with a stiff, but seemingly genuine happiness at his return. That had been followed by an endless line of Chatri who viewed their king's arrival with varying degrees of pleasure.

All of them were, of course, breathtakingly beautiful with hair that ranged from pale gold to brilliant red and lean, elegant bodies dressed in silk robes that were heavily embroidered with priceless jewels. And all of them eyed her with a blatant curiosity that made her want to crawl behind the nearest fluted column and disappear from view.

There was none of the disapproval she'd been expecting, but it was still unnerving being the center of attention.

Her discomfort only grew as they were whisked away to a banquet hall that was twice the size of most football fields and filled with long rosewood tables and high chairs carved by the hand of an artist. The tableware was made of gold and crystal that reflected the magical balls of light that danced near the coved ceiling.

Once they were seated several dozen fairylike servants dressed in modest robes entered with trays laden with fruit and freshly baked bread and bowls of honey.

Sally had dutifully eaten, unwilling to become even more of

a spectacle, but as the meal had ended and several musicians had settled in the balcony at the far end of the hall to fill the air with an exquisite melody, she'd become increasingly loud in her demand that she be returned to Roke.

Sariel smiled, promising that she would soon be allowed to speak with him even as he had lifted a hand toward Fallon, one of her sisters, and insisted the female take Sally to her rooms so she could bathe and change her clothes while her new rooms were being prepared.

Swallowing her angry words, Sally had little choice but to follow the beautiful female through marble corridors. Her father might be a powerful king, but in many ways he acted like a child. The more she insisted to be returned to Roke, the harder he would dig in his heels.

She would obviously have to pretend she was content to remain until she could find some way to escape.

Or at least contact Roke.

Fallon took several side corridors, making Sally wonder if there was any end to the sprawling palace, and then they entered a set of rooms that made her breath catch.

There was a delightful warmth in the delicate tapestries that covered the walls and the thickly cushioned furniture that was built for comfort rather than to impress. A cascade of water spilled through a wide crack in the flagstone floor, lined by flowers with vivid blooms in shades from crimson to brilliant sapphire.

It was as if a tiny meadow had just appeared in the center of her room.

Even the attached bathroom was filled with fragrant blooms that surrounded the sunken bath where Sally quickly washed and pulled on a satin gown that had genuine emeralds sewn into the neckline.

She suspected the casual beauty of the rooms was a reflection of her half-sister who lacked the rigid decorum of the others.

Returning to the main living room, Sally briefly put aside her gnawing need to speak with Roke and studied the female who was her sister.

It was a given she was beautiful.

Her hair was the color of a sunrise; gold brushed with hints of pale rose. Her eyes were rich amber with flecks of emerald. And her ivory features were so perfect they didn't look real.

But there was a genuine friendliness in her smile as she moved toward Sally and gently placed a delicate gold chain around her neck that held a flawless pendant.

"There," she murmured in satisfaction, stepping back to inspect Sally's appearance. "You look beautiful."

Sally wrinkled her nose. "I appreciate the words, but we both know I'll never make the ranks of beautiful. Especially not here." She shook her head as she remembered the crowd of females who looked like they should have wings and halos. Only angels should be that gorgeous. "If I was vain, I would have slit my wrists the moment I arrived."

A shadow darkened Fallon's amber eyes. "Physical perfection is tedious."

Sally snorted. "Says the female who can claim physical perfection."

"You have captured far more attention than I have ever received."

"Yeah." Sally shuddered. That sort of attention she could do without. "Because I'm a freak."

Fallon absently strolled toward the windows where the glow of the sun bathed her in a golden light. Sally frowned. Not out of envy, although she was female enough to feel a pang of regret that she would never be able to compete with such stunning beauty, but at the realization that time obviously moved differently here.

When they'd left Chicago it'd been ten o'clock in the evening.

So had they gone back in time or forward?

Or did the sun never set here?

She needed to find out.

Fallon slowly turned back to meet Sally's curious gaze. "No, it's because you're . . . alive."

Well that was true enough. She was most certainly alive, although it'd been a close call on more occasions than she wanted to remember.

"No thanks to my parents," she agreed with a wry smile. "No one's more surprised than I am that I survived their separate efforts to get me killed."

"Oh, it's not that. We had no idea that Father had—"

"Created a mongrel?" she helpfully supplied.

"Created a sister for us."

Sister. Sally tested the word in her mind. It felt . . . strange. But terrifyingly wonderful.

"Then I'm confused," she said. "You said you were surprised I'm alive."

"No, we're fascinated by the life force that shimmers around you."

Sally blinked. "Oh."

"You're a vivid burst of energy that is nearly blinding," Fallon continued. "We have all become too complacent with our existence. We drift from day to day, barely noticing that we have forgotten to live."

Sally tried to be sympathetic. Not easy when she'd spent most of her life being hunted like an animal.

"A peaceful existence can't be all bad."

"Peace is different from stasis," Fallon pointed out, her calm demeanor not entirely disguising a bone-deep frustration that gnawed deep inside her. "We have forgotten the thrill of not knowing what will happen next. The breathless excitement of passion. The beauty of a future filled with endless possibilities." She smiled with a wistful yearning. "For us, you are a breath of fresh air."

Sally moved toward her sister. She might not fully understand how anyone could not be content growing up in a family that at least seemed to care for one another and surrounded by such beauty, but she better than anyone understood that outward appearances meant nothing.

"Fallon, are you not happy here?" she asked softly.

The young female heaved a faint sigh. "I will admit that I have longed for the opportunity to travel away from our homeland."

That didn't seem such an outrageous dream. Unless females weren't allowed to travel away from their family?

Many demon societies were still obnoxiously dominated by males.

"Have you discussed this with your fiancé?" she cautiously probed. The last thing she wanted was to stir a mutiny between Fallon and the crimson-haired warrior who she'd introduced as her soon-to-be mate.

Fallon instantly shook her head. "He would not understand."

"He would if he loves you."

"Love?" Her sister looked baffled by the mere concept of a love match. "Our marriage will be the joining of two powerful houses. Nothing more. The Chatri no longer seek their true mates."

Sally tried not to grimace.

She was beginning to understand her sister's desire to travel away from paradise.

What woman wouldn't want a fling before being forced into a loveless marriage that was destined to last an eternity?

"That's terrible," she muttered.

Fallon shrugged. "It's our tradition."

"But . . ." Sally forgot what she was going to say when the chime of a bell echoed through the room. "What's that?"

Her sister stiffened, her teeth gnawing on her lower lip with a nervous gesture that was identical to Sally's habit.

"You must swear not to tell anyone," she at last said, her voice so low Sally could barely hear her.

Sally nodded, deeply curious. "I swear."

Hurrying across the room, Fallon locked the door before moving to a heavy tapestry that was hung on a far wall.

"Watch this."

Fallon tugged aside the tapestry and pressed her hand against the paneled wall. There was a faint glow around her fingers before a hidden door slid open.

Sally raised her brows in shock. "A secret room?"

Fallon nodded, motioning for Sally to follow as she stepped through the door.

Intrigued, Sally swiftly trailed behind her sister, not certain what to expect.

Probably a good thing since she would never have guessed it would be a barren room that had been carved from pure stone. There were no windows, but fairy lights danced in the shadows of the low ceiling, revealing the numerous wooden bowls that had been carefully arranged on the stone floor.

Each bowl was a different size and made from a different wood, but they each held a shallow pool of water.

"Wow." Sally gave a bemused laugh. "It's like the Batcave."

Fallon frowned. "The . . . ah. *Batman*. That is a human television show, is it not?"

"Yes." Sally studied her sister in surprise. "How did you know?"

"My talent is to scry beyond our homeland," Fallon said. "I have long been intrigued by your world."

Ah. That explained the bowls. Sally had a basic ability to scry, but she needed an anchor to direct her, like a strand of hair to connect her to the person she was searching for. Not to mention the fact that it drained her to the point of exhaustion to maintain one search.

She shook her head in wonder at the images that flickered nonstop on the surface of the water in each bowl.

The amount of energy each scry must be sucking from Fallon was staggering, but she didn't look the least affected.

Amazing.

"So why the secrecy?" she asked, knowing she'd be eager to display such talent.

Fallon's smile faded. "My . . . fiancé disapproves of my interest."

"Oh, I'm sorry."

Fallon tried to pretend indifference. "It doesn't matter."

It did, of course. But what could Sally say?

She didn't know enough about her sister's relationship with her fiancé to offer any advice.

"What is the beeping?" she asked.

Fallon moved toward a large bowl in the center of the floor. "Someone is near the entrance to our homeland. I made a warning device."

Very clever. A damned shame she felt she had to hide her talents.

Absently joining Fallon, Sally glanced down at the bowl, her heart slamming against her ribs as she caught sight of the dark-haired vampire with pale silver eyes and a fierce expression.

"Roke," she breathed, a stark longing to be with her mate sending her to her knees. "Can he get through?"

Fallon shook her head. "No. Not without a Chatri to open a doorway." She pointed a slender finger toward the large blond who stood at Roke's side in the middle of a field. They looked like they were arguing. "This is your vampire?"

Sally shook her head. "The other one."

"Then who is his companion?"

"His friend Cyn," she said, too distracted to notice her sister's odd tone. "I have to go to him."

She surged back to her feet, but before she could return to the outer room, Fallon was grabbing her arm.

"No."

Sally hissed with impatience. Roke was near. She had to get to him.

"Look, it's been great to meet you, but Roke has sacrificed everything for me," she said, trying to tug free. "I'm not going to allow him to think that I just abandoned him."

Fallon maintained her grip, her expression somber. "If you leave here to go to him, it will give Father the right to kill him."

A cold chill lodged in the pit of her stomach. "Kill him?"

"You are a princess," Fallon said, not seeming to remember that Sally was a mongrel. "No man who hasn't been formally approved by her family is allowed to touch you."

Sally's eyes narrowed as she remembered her father's determination to bring her here. He must have realized that once he had her in his homeland she would be caught between a rock and a hard place.

"So this was a setup," she snapped. "If I leave, then I put Roke in danger. If I stay, he can't reach me. Damn Sariel."

Fallon's fingers tightened on her arm. "I have a plan."

Sally struggled to think past the red haze of anger that clouded her mind.

"What?"

Fallon glanced back toward the images dancing on top of the water.

"You can't go to the vampire, but I can bring him to you."

Sally sent her sister a suspicious frown. "And lead him to certain death?"

"No," Fallon protested in shock. "Bloodshed is forbidden here. Not even the king is allowed to strike out in violence."

"Oh." Sally bit her bottom lip. "So once he's here—"

"He would be safe."

Sally's lips parted to demand that Fallon do whatever necessary to protect Roke, only to falter when she caught sight of the grim determination etched onto her sister's pale features.

"What about you?"

Fallon squared her shoulders, looking every inch a dignified princess.

"I can take care of myself."

"Fallon—"

"Please," she interrupted Sally's protest. "Let me help."

Sally hesitated before giving a slow nod. She hated the thought of allowing her sister to do something that might get her in trouble. Or worse. But, she had to get word to Roke.

The goddess only knew what he would do if he discovered he couldn't open the doorway.

"What do you want me to do?" she at last asked.

"Join Father in the throne room," she urged. "I will bring Roke to you."

"You're sure?"

Fallon smiled with . . . was that anticipation?

"Never more so."

Chapter Twenty-Eight

Roke paced the center of the field, a murderous fury boiling his blood.

After running at full throttle for the past seven hours, he'd at last homed in on his missing mate.

She was here.

He could feel her.

Hell, he could even catch the scent of peaches.

But he couldn't get to her.

It was as if she was sharing the same place, but in a different dimension.

"Roke?" Moving to block his restless path from one end of the field to the other, Cyn studied him with a puzzled expression. "What are we waiting for?"

"She's here," Roke muttered.

Cyn glanced around the clearing that was hidden in the middle of the Canadian national park.

"In the middle of an empty field?"

Roke hissed in frustration. "I don't know how to explain it, but she's close."

Cyn nodded. "The doorway to the Chatri homeland must be near."

"How do I open it?"

His companion hesitated before giving a shrug. "I don't know that you can."

That was not the answer Roke wanted.

He didn't care what he had to do, he was getting back his mate.

"There has to be a way," he snarled.

"We'll figure it out, I swear," Cyn said, attempting to soothe. "But we need to consider a place to stay for the day. Dawn is less than an hour away."

Cyn thought he would leave?

When he'd finally pinpointed her location?

Hell, no.

"She needs me," he stubbornly insisted.

"Then you have to make sure you stay healthy enough to rescue her."

Roke rolled his eyes. "When did you turn into a mother hen?"

"When . . ." The large vampire's words dried up as there was a sparkle in the air less than a few feet away and a female figure suddenly appeared. "God almighty. It's an angel," Cyn croaked.

Roke had to admit the stranger did look angelic.

Her long, burnished gold hair surrounded a face so delicately carved it would make an artist weep in delight. Her eyes were faintly slanted and the color of amber with unexpected glints of emerald.

As she moved forward the silk of her white gown caressed her tall, slender body causing the large rubies that were sewn along the hem to glisten like fire in the waning moonlight.

Definitely angel material.

Immune to her beauty, Roke stepped forward, struggling not to wrap his fingers around her neck and demand answers.

"Where's Sally?" he rasped.

The unknown female glanced toward Cyn who had his gun pointed directly at her heart.

"If you'll put away your weapons I'll take you to her," she promised, her voice a brush of velvet over his skin.

"Fine." Roke took a step forward even as Cyn placed a restraining arm across his chest.

"Wait," he growled, keeping his gun pointed toward the female Chatri. "How do we know this isn't a trap?" He glared at the woman. "If you have Sally then bring her out here."

She folded her arms, calmly ignoring Cyn as she held Roke's gaze.

"If I do, the warriors will destroy you."

Cyn muttered a curse at the implication he could be bested. The female clearly knew very little about male pride.

"They could try," he snarled.

Again, the female ignored him.

"Once you're within our homeland they can't touch you," she promised. "Will you come with me, vampire?"

"No, he damned well won't. Not until we know—"

"Cyn," Roke sharply interrupted, glowering at his friend.

"What?"

"Back off."

Cyn growled as he lowered the gun, his muscles clenched as if he were expecting a full-out attack.

"I don't trust her."

Roke stepped around his bristling friend. He didn't trust the female, either. But it wasn't as if they had a whole lot of choice.

"Take me to Sally."

She gave a dip of her head. "Follow me."

Turning, she disappeared into the strange sparkle of lights and Roke was quickly hurrying to join her.

"Roke."

He glanced toward his companion who remained stubbornly at his side as they stepped through the entrance to the portal.

"I know, but this might be my only chance to find Sally."

"You had better hope this isn't a trick, fairy," Cyn growled at the back of the female Chatri. "Your people might not shed blood in your homeland, but I'm quite willing."

"Barbarian," she muttered.

"Berserker, thank you very much," Cyn informed her, his fangs fully exposed.

"What the hell is wrong with you?" Roke asked.

Cyn was always a lethal warrior, but he wasn't usually so touchy. Especially not with a beautiful woman.

The clan chief grimaced, as if realizing he'd been acting out of character.

"She . . . troubles me."

Roke studied his friend's tense expression. "Hmm."

There was the sensation of the air pressure shifting, then they were out of the portal and standing in a hallway lined with glossy wooden floors and marble walls nearly hidden beneath the climbing ivy.

Roke and Cyn both hissed at the golden sunshine that peeked through high windows. Dammit. They had to be in a dimension that ran on a different time. Thankfully the angle of the sun meant that the glow hit high on the wall, leaving the actual corridor in shadows.

"We must be swift," the female warned, taking off at a brisk pace.

Roke ignored Cyn's icy disapproval, allowing himself to be led from one hallway to another.

Eventually they became wider with more marble and gilt, not to mention a few passing Chatri who stared at them in startled dismay.

"Mother of gods, I've never felt so out of place in my life," Cyn muttered as they tried to ignore the elegantly dressed men and women who looked as if they were headed to some fancy-ass ball.

"No killing," Roke muttered as Cyn ran his fingers over

the blade of his dagger, eyeballing a male who flared his nose as if he'd just smelled something nasty.

Cyn shook his head. "You don't know anything about having fun."

Sally pinned a smile to her lips.

Seated next to her father on the high dais, she struggled to concentrate on the formal speeches being offered in celebration of her father's return. Even if her nerves weren't shredded as she waited for some sign from Fallon, she would hate being put on display.

If being a princess meant sitting on an uncomfortable throne so a group of strangers could gawk at her, she'd be happy to give the privilege to someone else.

Immediately.

Perhaps sensing her growing distress, Sariel leaned sideways to awkwardly pat her hand, which clenched the arm of the chair.

"I told you that my people would be happy to welcome you, child," he reminded her.

Despite being furious with her father, Sally couldn't deny a rueful pleasure. He was doing his best to make her feel at home.

"I've been happy to meet them as well. Especially my sisters and brothers," she said, keeping her voice low so it wouldn't carry. "But you promised I would be allowed to contact Roke."

Sariel's lips flattened. "In time."

"He's going to be worried about me."

Her father abruptly changed the conversation. "Tell me what you think of Lasko?"

"Who?" she asked in genuine confusion.

Sariel nodded toward the young man standing near a

marble column, his beautiful features carved with an inbred arrogance that made Sally grimace.

"He's the eldest son of the Sonesel House."

She sent her father a horrified glare. "You're not trying to play matchmaker, are you?"

He shrugged. "Once I break your mating you will be free to choose another male. Lasko is not only wealthy and a powerful warrior, but his house is a rival to ours. Such an alliance would be highly beneficial."

She snorted. "Beneficial to whom? Not me."

The amber eyes held a hint of censure at her flippant tone. "To all Chatri."

She rolled her eyes. It seemed her father just couldn't resist trying to use her to his own advantage.

Not that it mattered.

There was only one man who would ever be her mate.

"Thanks, but no thanks," she said. "I have no plans to play Juliet."

Sariel frowned, obviously not a fan of Shakespeare.

"I don't understand."

"I'm not interested in Lasko even though I'm sure he's a fine man," she clarified.

"There are others," her father began only to be interrupted by a flurry of soft gasps and a few cries of fear from the back of the room. Slowly Sariel rose to his feet. "What is the disruption?" he demanded.

The crowd slowly parted to reveal Fallon as she moved forward with two large vampires flanking her.

Sariel went rigid, a flush of anger staining his pale cheeks.

"Fallon, explain yourself."

Fallon flinched, but with remarkable courage she met her father's furious glare.

"Sally's mate was anxious to be reunited with her."

Indifferent to her father or the chattering crowd, Sally

launched herself off the dais and directly into Roke's waiting arms.

She breathed deeply of his familiar scent, tears streaming down her face as he buried his face in the curve of her neck.

"I have you," he murmured, running a comforting hand down her spine. "And I'm never letting you go again."

"Leave us," her father bellowed, and Sally glanced up to watch in surprise as the Chatri scurried out of the room, along with Fallon who pulled a stubborn Cyn through a side door.

Once alone, her father moved to stand directly in front of them.

"How dare you trespass in my home, leech?"

Roke tucked Sally behind him as he faced her father without fear.

"I've come for my mate." His power fractured the floor beneath their feet. "I'm not leaving without her."

Her father ignored the display of strength. "She came here to end the mating."

She felt Roke tense at the soft words, his brows drawing together as he glanced toward her.

"Sally?"

Sally resisted the urge to deny the accusation. This was too important to screw up.

"Sariel has promised to break the spell," she admitted.

The pale eyes darkened with a hurt he didn't bother to try and hide.

"That's why you left?"

She glanced toward her father. "Can we speak in private?"

The king parted his lips to deny her request, only to hesitate when he read the unmistakable threat in her eyes.

He'd already crossed a line when he'd brought her to his homeland without asking. If he pressed her on this, there was a good chance she was never going to forgive him.

He made a sound of disgust. "Very well. I will allow you a

few moments." He pointed a finger at Roke. "But know this, vampire, you are in my territory. Here you will obey my rules."

Sally laid a finger against Roke's lips, preventing him from spewing his angry words. Only when her father had disappeared behind the thrones did she lower her hand.

"Someday," Roke muttered.

Turning so she could face him directly, Sally laid her hand on his cheek, the ache in her heart easing as his power settled like a cloak around her.

"I didn't mean to disappear," she told him.

He peered deep into her eyes, as if searching for the truth. "Then why did you?"

"My father requested that I become a sort of diplomat between the Chatri and our world."

Her words caught him off guard. Lucky for him, he didn't share his personal opinion of the offer. It was enough that his lips curled with blatant repugnance.

"And you said?" he asked.

She held his gaze. "I said, yes."

He carefully hid his reaction. "I see."

"Next thing I knew I was here," she continued her story.

The pale eyes blazed with silver fire. "Here and asking for our mating to be broken."

She stroked her fingers down his cheek to trace the stubborn line of his jaw.

"The *spell* to be broken."

"Why?"

She released an unsteady sigh, forcing herself to speak the painful words.

"Because you deserve the opportunity to find your true mate."

He grabbed her fingers that she was stroking down the line of his throat and pressed them to his lips.

"I have found her," he snapped.

It's what she hoped for with every fiber of her being, but

she couldn't risk that someday he would be denied the female destined to be at his side.

"You don't know that."

He wasn't happy. "Christ, what do I have to do to prove it to you?"

"Allow my father to break the spell."

"No."

She frowned, baffled by his refusal to even consider her request.

"If you're so confident I'm your mate, then why are you being so stubborn about the spell?"

His thumb rubbed against her inner wrist, the air prickling a sharp chill.

"I have no doubt you're my mate."

"But?"

There was a short hesitation, then with obvious reluctance, he admitted what was bothering him.

"But, I can't be certain I am *your* mate."

Sally stared at him in confusion. "Isn't it the same thing?"

"Not necessarily." He lowered her hand, turning her arm over so he could push up the sleeve of her gown and reveal the crimson marking. "When a vampire's mate is of a different species there's no guarantee that they will be similarly committed." His fingers brushed over the sensitive tattoo, sending a jolt of lust straight through her. "Do Chatri even have true mates?"

She stepped closer, her gaze lowering to the sensual temptation of his lips.

"It doesn't matter."

She could feel his rising arousal as her gaze remained on his lips, his fingers continuing to caress her arm.

"It doesn't?" he asked, his tone husky with need.

"No." She smiled as she caught a glimpse of fang. Ah, her gorgeous, sexy, utterly exasperating vampire. "Because I love you."

He blinked, looking as if he'd just been hit upside the head with a shovel.

"You . . . you love me?"

Sally chuckled. Dear goddess. Did he think that she melted for every man who touched her? Or risked her life to take him to his own people when he was injured? Or was willing to suffer the agony of losing him to make sure he never regretted being her mate?

"Irrevocably, madly, and for all eternity," she swore, going on her toes to press her lips to the corner of his mouth.

He gave a low groan. "Sally."

She pulled back to study his expression, which remained wary. "Is that all you're going to say?"

"You're certain?"

She hid a smile at his vulnerable plea for assurance. This wasn't the aloof, I-am-an-island vampire she'd first met. Her heart swelled with the love she could barely contain.

"Roke, I don't need a spell to be committed to you," she murmured, planting tiny kisses over his cheek. "You've had my heart since you brought a tray of buffalo wings to my prison cell."

"And apple pie," he reminded her in thick tones, his arms wrapping around her waist to haul her tight against his body. "Don't forget the apple pie."

She chuckled, her lips finding a sensitive spot just below his ear.

"I'll never forget anything, you aggravating vampire."

There was a swish of satin before her father returned to the room, his mood stormy as he caught sight of them embracing.

"That is enough privacy," he snarled. "It is time to end this mating."

Pulling back, Sally held Roke's gaze. "Trust me."

Chapter Twenty-Nine

Roke didn't like this.

He didn't want to break the mating. And he most certainly didn't want Sally's pain-in-the-ass father to be the one to remove the spell.

The bastard might use his magic to convince Sally that she no longer loved him.

Loved him.

He grimaced as Sally's soft words whispered through her mind.

She told him that she loved him. And then she'd asked him to trust her.

What else could he do?

"Fine," he muttered, glaring at the king as he approached. He silently swore he would kill the man if he did anything to alter Sally's feelings. "Remove the spell."

Sally suddenly pulled out of his arms, glancing toward the distant door where a handful of Chatri were trying to peek through a narrow opening.

"Wait," she muttered.

"Second thoughts?" Roke asked.

"No, but I'm tired of being gawked at." She shuddered. "I want to do this in private."

"We can go to your rooms," Sariel pronounced, turning to head with dignified pace toward a small door behind the dais. "They have finished being prepared."

Roke placed an arm around Sally's shoulders as they followed in his regal wake.

"You have rooms?" he demanded, not liking the thought of her having a permanent place that was anywhere but at his side.

"This is my daughter's home, of course she has rooms," Sariel retorted.

"Her place is with me at my lair," he growled.

The king glanced over his shoulder with an accusing expression.

"Among people who tried to kill her?"

Roke felt the familiar stab of guilt. "That was . . . a mistake. They will honor her as my mate."

Sariel sniffed in disdain. "Here she is a princess."

Roke clenched his teeth. There was no answer to that.

She was a princess here. And while he knew his people would grow to adore Sally, they hadn't made it easy for him to convince her that his lair was going to make some fantasy dream-home.

It was Sally who at last broke the silence as they walked down yet another marble hallway with dark red roses circling the fluted columns.

"There's no reason I can't assist Roke with his duties as chief and be a diplomat for the Chatri."

Both men were swift to offer their protests. "But—"

"That wasn't open for debate." She effectively slammed the door on their objections.

Roke smiled. This was his feisty little witch.

"Bossy," he teased.

"That's right." Her dark eyes held a wicked amusement. "I am woman, hear me roar."

They paused before a set of double doors and Roke

glanced down at her pale, vulnerable face, needing to know if she truly meant that she could face returning to his people.

"You're willing to travel to Nevada?" he asked softly.

She smiled, holding up a hand that had destroyed a Nebule demon with pure light.

"I think I can hold my own now."

He nodded, in full agreement. He didn't doubt she could make even the most powerful vampire regret screwing with her. But he didn't want her to think for a second she had to worry about protecting herself in her own home.

"True, but there will be no need." He paused, making sure she knew he spoke the absolute truth. "That, I promise."

Sariel threw open the doors and gestured them inside. "Let us be done with this," he snapped.

They entered a room that was a schoolgirl fantasy.

The walls were made of mirrors that reflected the overhead chandelier, giving the image of tiny diamonds dancing in the air. The floor was a polished wood and in the center of the room was a massive bed with a pink canopy.

Roke grimaced. He felt like he'd been shoved into an oversize dollhouse.

Unaware that his choice of décor proved just how little he knew about his daughter, Sariel held a hand over Roke's head.

"Don't move."

Roke bared his fangs, immediately feeling a strange heat surge through his blood.

It wasn't the intense blast of power that had knocked him unconscious when Sally had first enchanted him, but there was no mistaking something was happening.

At last the man dropped his hand and stepped back.

"Is the spell gone?" Sally demanded.

"Yes," Sariel answered.

Shrugging out of his leather jacket, Roke allowed it to drop to the floor as he turned over his arm.

They watched in silence as the crimson tattooing slowly faded. Roke choked back a curse, able to feel the King of the Chatri's smug satisfaction.

Lucky for the jackass, he didn't have time to boast before there was a tingle beneath Roke's skin and the mating mark returned, even more vivid than before.

With a fierce surge of satisfaction, he lifted his head to meet Sally's dark gaze.

"I told you that you were my mate."

She slowly smiled. "And you're always right?"

He was barely aware he was moving before he had her wrapped in his arms, the feel of her soft curves making him instantly hard.

"Always," he assured her.

"Sally," her father snapped.

Roke lowered his head, his gaze intent on Sally's flushed face.

"Go away, Sariel," he growled.

There was a gasp of disbelief. "This is my home."

Sally stroked her hands over Roke's chest. "Father, please," she murmured, clearly distracted.

With a huff, the king marched toward the door. "We will speak later."

"Much later," Roke warned.

Neither noticed the door slamming as Sariel made his dramatic exit, each too intent on the other and the intense emotions that were exploding through their bond.

There was relief and joy and the ever-present desire.

And love.

A stunning, how-did-I-ever-survive-without-this love.

"My mate," Roke murmured, yanking off her sweatshirt so he could savor the sight of his mark branded into her inner arm.

It might not have been the typical mating that occurred between vampires, but it was just as real.

And just as lasting.

"Yes," she breathed, a brilliant smile curving her lips.

He pulled her back into his arms, burying his face in her hair.

"Don't ever leave me again."

"Never," she swore, her hands exploring his chest with a growing insistence.

Roke's fangs pulsed in perfect tempo with his fully erect cock.

He'd denied his deepest hunger for so long.

Now he was being consumed by his most primitive instinct.

"I need—"

"Roke?" she prompted as he lifted his head to study the heat staining her cheeks.

He needed to watch her expression. He couldn't bear to frighten her.

She'd had more than her fair share of unpleasant surprises.

"I need to taste you," he said.

Her expression was more curious than wary as she considered his words. "You want to bite me?"

"More than you could ever possibly imagine," he growled.

Slowly she tilted her head to the side, exposing her slender neck.

"Then do it."

He quivered, nearly overcome with lust.

"You're certain?"

She grabbed his face and urged it toward her throat. "Now, Roke."

He didn't need another invitation. Hell, he couldn't have resisted another minute if there'd been a stake pressed to his heart.

Exposing his fangs, he struck at the base of her throat, sinking deep into her flesh.

Pleasure exploded through Roke as her blood hit his tongue, the taste finer than any aphrodisiac.

"God. You taste of peaches," he muttered, his entire body shuddering with desire. "My favorite."

"Oh . . . yes," Sally groaned, her hands roughly tugging at his T-shirt.

"Sally?" he said and pulled out his fangs, carefully licking shut the tiny wounds.

"I need you naked."

His cock gave a twitch of approval, trying to bust through the zipper of his jeans. But his brain hadn't forgotten they were in Sariel's territory. Who knew when the bastard might decide to return?

"What about your—"

Sally managed to wrangle the shirt over his head, her fingers moving to attack his jeans.

"Less talk, more action," she commanded.

With a sinful chuckle, Roke gave in to the desire that thundered through him.

If anyone tried to interrupt them, he'd personally rip out their throats.

Leaning down he scooped Sally off her feet and headed for the pink monstrosity of a bed.

"I think I've managed to create a tyrant," he murmured in full approval.

Sally didn't know how much time had passed when the sound of yelling woke her from her pleasant dreams.

Untangling herself from Roke's possessive arms, she slid off the bed and pulled on her satin gown.

"What the hell is going on?" her mate demanded, looking delectably sexy with his dark hair rumpled and his silver eyes still dark from their most recent bout of lovemaking.

"I'll find out," she promised, heading across the room.

She was pulling open the door when Roke was standing beside her, fully dressed and with a massive dagger clutched in his hands.

She rolled her eyes.

Vampire speed.

She'd never get used to it.

"Not alone you won't," he muttered.

Together they moved down the hallway, finding her father headed in their direction, his robe flowing and his golden hair floating as his power swirled around him.

Sally instinctively grabbed Roke's hand as she viewed Sariel's expression of pure fury.

"Father, has something happened?" she cautiously asked.

"That . . . vampire."

Sally frowned before she realized he must be referring to Roke's friend.

"Cyn?"

"He disappeared." Sariel glared at Roke. "With my daughter."

Roke blinked in bewilderment. "Which daughter?"

"Fallon."

"Oh." Sally hid her grimace.

Not that her father was in any mood to notice. He was already weaving his magic to create a portal.

"When I find him I will destroy him," he swore, barely waiting for the opening to form before he was disappearing through it.

On impulse, Sally stepped into the edge of the portal even as Roke tried to wrap his brain around the unexpected disaster.

"Why would Cyn take your sister from her home?" he muttered. "He can be self-indulgent, but he would never put a female in danger."

Sally wrinkled her nose, well aware that her sister was probably responsible for Cyn's unusual behavior.

"It's possible Fallon asked him to help her leave."

"Oh . . . hell," Roke muttered, reaching in his pocket to pull out his cell phone. "This is bad. I should call Styx and warn him."

She reached to grab his wrist. Even if a cell phone did work in this dimension, she wasn't about to unleash the King of Vampires on her sister. It was bad enough she was being hunted by their father.

Fallon had put herself in danger to reunite Sally with her mate.

She would do what she could to allow her sister a taste of the freedom she so desperately craved.

"Or we could allow Cyn and Fallon the opportunity to escape while we travel to your lair."

"*Our* lair," Roke automatically corrected.

"Our lair," she agreed, holding his gaze. "What do you say?"

He glanced around the empty hallway. "Can we get out of here?"

She tugged him toward her. "I stepped into the entrance of the portal my father created when he took off in a huff. It remains open."

"Ah." He gave a soft laugh as the swirl of magic danced around them. "Well played, my clever witch, well played."

She went on her toes to press a lingering kiss on his mouth.

"Let's go home."

Please turn the page for an exciting sneak peek of
BLOOD ASSASSIN,
the next book in Alexandra Ivy's Sentinels series,
coming in January 2015!

SENTINELS

The history of the Sentinels was mysterious even among the high-bloods.

Most people knew that there were two sects of the dangerous warriors. The guardian Sentinels who possessed innate magic. They were heavily tattooed to arm themselves against magical attacks, as well as any mind control, and were used to protect those high-bloods who were vulnerable when they were forced to travel away from the safety of Valhalla.

And then there were the hunter Sentinels. They had no magic, but they were equally lethal. Hunters were used to enforce the laws of Valhalla, and since they were able to "pass" as human and capable of moving through the world undetected, they were used to track down high-bloods who might be a danger to themselves or others.

It was also well known that both sects of Sentinels were stronger and faster than humans, with an endurance that was off the charts. And both were trained to kill with their hands as well as most known weapons.

But that was as far as public knowledge went.

How they were chosen and how they'd become the protectors of the high-bloods were closely guarded secrets.

No one but Sentinels knew what happened behind the thick walls of the monasteries where they were trained.

Chapter One

One glance into the private gym would send most humans fleeing in humiliation.

What normal male would want to lift weights next to the dozen Sentinels?

Not only were the warriors six feet plus of pure chiseled muscles and bad attitudes, but the very air reeked of aggression and testosterone-fueled competition.

Hardly a place for the weekend jock trying to battle the bulge.

It was, however, the perfect place for the Sentinels to work off a little steam.

The vast gym was filled with mats, punching bags, and treadmills. And, at the back of the room, there was a row of weight machines where the baddest of the badasses was currently bench-pressing enough weight to crush a mortal.

Fane looked like he'd been sculpted from stone. A six-foot-three behemoth, he had the strength of an ox and the speed of a cheetah. A result of the natural talents that came from being born a Sentinel, and the fact he'd been honed from his youth to become a weapon.

He was also covered from the top of his shaved head to the

tips of his toes in intricate tattoos that protected him from all magic.

The monks who'd taken him in as a young child had trained him in all the known martial arts, as well as the most sophisticated weapons.

He was walking, talking death.

Which meant very few bothered to notice the dark eyes that held a razor-sharp intelligence or the starkly beautiful features beneath the elegant markings.

Something that rarely bothered Fane. For the past decade he'd been a guardian to Callie Brown. All people needed to know about him was that he would kill them the second they threatened the young diviner.

Now, he . . .

Fane blew out a sigh, replacing the weights on the bar so he could wipe the sweat from his naked chest.

Three months ago Callie had nearly died when they'd battled the powerful necromancer Lord Zakhar, and during the battle she'd fallen in love with a human policeman. Or at least Duncan O'Conner had been passing as human. Turned out he had the extra powers of a Sentinel as well as being a soul-gazer, which meant he could read the souls of others. He was perfectly suited to take over the protection of Callie.

Fane's hand absently touched the center of his chest where he'd once felt the constant connection to Callie. They'd transferred the bond last week, but he still felt the strange void that was wearing on his nerves.

He needed a distraction.

The thought had barely passed through his mind when a shadow fell over him and he glanced up to discover a tall, lean man with copper-tinted skin and ebony eyes. Wolfe, the current Tagos (leader of all Sentinels), had a proud, hawkish nose, with heavy brows and prominent cheekbones that gave him the appearance of an ancient Egyptian deity.

It was a face that spoke of power and fierce masculinity.

The sort of face that intimidated men and made women wonder if he was as dangerous as he looked.

He was.

Just as arresting was the shoulder-length black hair that had a startling streak of gray that started at his right temple. There were whispers that when Wolfe was a babe he'd been touched by the devil.

Something Fane fully believed.

Swallowing a curse, Fane tossed aside his sweaty towel. Damn. This wasn't the distraction he'd been wanting.

Wolfe was dressed in jeans and a loose cotton shirt with the sleeves rolled up to his elbows. He had his arms folded over his chest and was studying Fane with an expression that warned he wasn't pleased.

Around them the gym went silent as the other Sentinels pretended they weren't straining to overhear the potential confrontation.

"I heard through the grapevine you've taken a position as a trainer," he said. That was Wolfe. Always straight to the point.

Fane scowled. It'd been less than twenty-four hours since he'd made the decision to seek a position as a trainer in a monastery halfway around the world. How the hell had word spread so fast?

"The grapevine should mind its own business."

The ebony eyes narrowed. "And I shouldn't have to listen to gossip to learn when one of my Sentinels is leaving Valhalla."

Fane met his Tagos glare for glare. "I have no direct duties here, at least not anymore. I'm allowed to return to the monastery without clearing it with you."

The air heated. Sentinels' body temperature ran hotter than humans', and when their emotions were provoked they could actually warm the air around them.

"Don't be an ass. This isn't about duties, I'm worried about you."

Oh hell.

This was exactly what Fane didn't want.

He'd rather be shot in the head than have someone fussing over him.

"There's nothing to worry about. You know that I was a trainer for years before coming to Valhalla. I'm simply returning to my brothers in Tibet."

"You've just endured the removal of a long-standing bond. A traumatic experience for any guardian," the older man ruthlessly pressed. "And *we're* your brothers, you thankless son-of-a-bitch."

Fane gave an impatient shake of his head. Wolfe was a hunter Sentinel, not a guardian, which meant he could never understand the truth of the bond.

"I know what you're thinking, but you're wrong."

Wolfe slowly arched a brow. There weren't many who had the chutzpah to stand up to him.

"What am I thinking?"

"Callie and I never had a sexual relationship."

"Did you want one?"

"No," Fane growled. "Jesus Christ. She was like a sister to me. She still is."

The dark gaze never wavered. "And it doesn't bother you that she's with Duncan?"

"Not so long as he treats her right." Fane allowed a humorless smile to touch his lips. "If he doesn't . . . I'll rip out his heart with my bare hands."

Wolfe nodded. They both understood it wasn't an empty threat.

"Good," the Tagos said. "But that wasn't my concern."

Fane surged to his feet, his tattoos deepening in response to his rising temper. It was barely past noon, but it'd already been a long day.

"Does this conversation have an end in sight?"

Wolfe stood his ground.

No shocker.

The man *always* stood his ground.

"The past decade has been dedicated to protecting Callie. Now you're going to have a void where the bond used to be. It's going to make you . . ." He paused, as if sorting through his brain for the right word. "Twitchy."

"Twitchy?"

Wolfe shrugged. "I was going to say as mean as a rabid pit bull, but that would be an insult to the pit bull."

There was a snicker from the front of the room. Fane sent a glare that instantly had the younger Sentinel scurrying from the gym.

He returned his attention to his leader, his gaze narrowed. "And fuck you, too."

"I'm serious, Fane," Wolfe insisted, standing with the calm of a born predator who could explode into violence in the blink of an eye. "You need to take time to adjust."

Fane grimaced. "Don't tell me your door is always open so we can chat about our feelings?"

"Hell, no." Wolfe shuddered. "But I'm always available if you need a partner who isn't terrified to spar with you."

"Ah, so you're offering to kick my ass?"

A hint of a smile softened Wolfe's austere features. "And to offer you a place at Valhalla. I'm in constant need of good warriors." The smile faded. "Especially after our battle with the necromancer. We lost too many."

Fane ground his teeth at the sharp stab of loss that pierced his heart. During the battle against the necromancer they'd lost far too many Sentinels. Many of them brothers that Fane had served with for decades.

And while the threat of death was a constant companion for warriors, they rarely lost so many at one time.

It had left them dangerously weakened.

"All the more reason for me to train the next generation," he pointed out.

Wolfe refused to budge. Stubborn bastard.

"Someone else can handle the training. These are dangerous times. I need experienced warriors."

Smart enough to avoid ramming his head into a brick wall, Fane instead changed the conversation.

"Did you find any information on the Brotherhood?"

Wolfe muttered a curse at the mention of the secret society of humans who had been discovered three months ago. Like many norms they held a profound hatred toward "mutants," but they were far more organized than most. And more troubling, they possessed a dangerous ability to sense high-bloods merely by being in their presence.

They were a new, unexpected complication.

The zealots might be nothing more than a pain in the ass. Or they might be . . . genocidal.

"Nothing useful," Wolfe admitted, his tone revealing his barely leashed desire to pound the truth out of the bastards.

"I can do some digging at the monastery if you want," Fane offered. "Their library is the most extensive in the world. If there's information on the secret society, it will be there."

"Actually I have Arel working on gathering intel."

Wolfe nodded his head toward a young hunter Sentinel who was running on a treadmill. The overhead lights picked up the honey highlights in Arel's light brown hair and turned his eyes to molten gold. He looked like an angel unless you took time to notice the honed muscles and the merciless strength that simmered deep in the gold eyes.

He also had the kind of charm that made women buzz around him like besotted bees.

Including one woman in particular for a short period of time.

His hands unconsciously clenched.

"Arel?" he ground out.

Wolfe made a sad attempt at looking innocent. "Is that a problem?"

"He's young." Fane forced his hands to relax, his expression stoic. He'd lost his right to make a claim on any woman years before. "And he has no magic," he continued.

Wolfe deliberately allowed his gaze to roam over Fane's distinctive tattoos. "Which means he has a shot at infiltrating the group if we decide they're going to be a danger in the future. Something that would be impossible for most of us."

Fane couldn't argue.

Although guardian Sentinels had the benefit of magic, as well as the protection of their tattooing to avoid spells and psychic attacks, they did tend to stand out in a crowd.

Understatement of the year.

Arel, on the other hand, looked like a kid fresh out of college.

"It's risky," Fane at last muttered. "We don't know how powerful this Brotherhood is."

Wolfe lifted a shoulder. "He's a Sentinel."

"True." Fane tried to dismiss the problem from his mind. Soon enough he would be in the seclusion of the monastery and the dangers of the world would no longer be his concern. Right? "It sounds like you have it covered. I'll send you more warriors when they've completed their training."

"Dammit, Fane . . ." Wolfe bit off his words as the atmosphere in the gym abruptly changed.

Both men turned to discover what had happened.

Or rather . . . who . . . had happened.

"Shit," Fane breathed, a familiar ache settling in the center of his chest at the sight of the beautiful female who sashayed into the room.

Serra Vetrov had the habit of changing the atmosphere in rooms since she'd left the nursery.

Hell, he'd seen men walk into walls and cars drive off the road when she strolled past.

An elegantly tall woman with long, glossy black hair that contrasted with her pale, ivory skin, she had lush curves that she emphasized with her tight leather pants and matching vest that was cut to reveal a jaw-dropping amount of her generous breasts.

Her features were delicately carved. Her pale green eyes were thickly lashed, her nose narrow and her lips so sensually full they gave the impression of a sex kitten.

Although anyone foolish enough to underestimate her was in for an unpleasant surprise.

Serra was not only a powerful psychic, but she was a rare telepath who could use objects to connect with the mind of the owner. Over the years, she'd used her talents more than once to find missing children or to track down violent offenders.

On the darker side, she could also use her skills to force humans, and those high-bloods without mental shields, to see illusions and could even implant memories in the more vulnerable minds.

Still, it wasn't her dangerous powers that made grown men scramble out of her path. Serra had a tongue that could flay at a hundred yards and she wasn't afraid to use it.

Wolfe sent Fane a mocking smile. "It appears I'm not the only one who listens to the grapevine. Good luck, amigo."

Turning, he strolled toward the cluster of Sentinels who were watching Serra cross the gym like a pack of starving hounds.

Bastards.

Serra kept her head held high and a smile pinned to her lips as she marched past the gaping men. She was female enough to appreciate being noticed by the opposite sex.

Why not? But today she barely noticed the audible groans as she took a direct path toward her prey.

She felt a tiny surge of amusement at the thought of Fane being anyone's prey.

The massive warrior was two hundred fifty pounds of pure muscle and raw male power. He was also one of the rare few who was completely impervious to her ability to poke around in his mind.

Which was a blessing and a curse.

A blessing because it was impossible for a psychic to completely block out an intimate partner, which was a distraction that would make any lover cringe. There was nothing quite so demeaning as being in the middle of sex and realizing your partner was picturing Angelina Jolie.

And a curse because Fane was about as chatty as a rock. His feelings were locked down so tight Serra feared that someday they would explode.

And not in a good way.

Or maybe it would be good, she silently told herself, gliding to a halt directly in front of his half-naked form.

There weren't many things worse than watching all emotions being stripped away as you approached the man you'd loved for the past two decades.

Especially when she was a seething mass of emotions.

She wanted to grab his beautiful face in her hands and kiss him until he melted into a puddle of goo. No. She wanted to kick him in the nuts for being such a prick.

Maybe she'd kick him and then kiss it better.

To make matters worse she was on a lust-driven adrenaline high.

Just standing next to his half-naked body coated in sweat made her heart pump and her mouth dry.

God. She was so fucking pathetic.

Accepting that her companion wasn't going to break the awkward silence, she tilted her chin up another notch.

Any higher and she was going to be staring at the ceiling.

"Fane," she purred softly.

His dark gaze remained focused on her face, resisting any temptation to glance at her skimpy vest. Of course, if it hadn't been for the rare times she'd caught him casting covert glances at her body, she might suspect he hadn't yet realized she was a woman.

"Serra."

On the way to the gym she'd practiced what she was going to say. She was going to be cool. Composed. And in complete control.

Instead the fear lodged in the pit of her belly made her strike out like a petulant child.

"You're leaving?"

He gave a slow dip of his head. "I'm returning to Tibet."

The fear began to spread through her body, her hands clenching at her sides. "Did you ever intend to tell me?"

"Yes."

"When?" she snapped. "On your way out the door?"

"Does it matter?"

Oh yeah. He was definitely getting kicked in the nuts.

"Yes, it damned well matters."

He remained stoic. Unmoved by her anger. "What do you want from me?"

She lowered her voice. It wasn't that she gave a shit that they had an audience. Living in Valhalla meant that privacy was a rare commodity. But she had some pride, dammit. She didn't want them to hear her beg.

"You know what I want."

Something flared through the dark eyes. Something that sliced through her heart like a dagger.

"It's impossible," he rasped. "I'll always care for you, Serra, but not in the way you need."

She should walk away.

It's what any woman with an ounce of sense would do.

But when had she claimed any sense when it came to this man?

Instead she stepped forward, bringing them nose to nose. Well, they would be nose to nose if he didn't have six inches on her.

"Liar."

He frowned, the heat from his body brushing over her bare skin like a caress. Serra shuddered. Oh God. She'd wanted him for so long.

It was like a sickness.

"A Sentinel doesn't lie."

She snorted at the ridiculous claim. "Maybe not, but you can twist the truth until it screams. And the truth is that you've always used your duty to Callie as a shield between us."

His fists landed on his hips, his eyes narrowing at her accusation. "My duty was more than a shield."

Okay. He had a point.

His bond with Callie had been very real.

But that didn't mean he hadn't hidden behind his obligation as a guardian.

"Fine." She held his gaze. "And now that duty is done."

He was shaking his head before she finished speaking. "My duty to Callie is done, but my duty to the Sentinels remains."

She clenched her teeth. It was true most Sentinels never married. But it wasn't against any rules.

Niko had just returned to Valhalla with a wife who promised to be a valuable healer, and Callie had married Duncan who'd recently become a Sentinel.

It might demand compromise and sacrifice on both sides, but it could be done.

So why was Fane so unwilling to even give it a try?

"I assume that's going to be your new excuse?" she forced between gritted teeth.

Without warning his expression softened and his fingers lightly brushed down her bare arm.

"Serra, I don't need an excuse," he said, the hint of regret in his eyes more alarming than his previous remoteness. She was used to him pretending to be indifferent to her. Now it felt like . . . good-bye. Shit. "I've never made promises I can't keep," he continued, his tone soft. "In fact, I've been very clear that you should find a man who can give you the happiness you deserve."

For one weak, tragic moment she allowed herself to savor the brief touch of his fingers. Then her pride came galloping to her rescue and she was jerking away with a brittle smile.

She would endure anything but his pity.

Hell no.

"Very generous of you."

He grimaced at her sarcastic tone. "I know you don't believe me, but all I've ever wanted was your happiness."

"And you assume I'll find it in the arms of another man?" She went straight for the jugular.

The hesitation was so fleeting she might have imagined it. "Yes."

She leaned forward, infuriated by her inability to read his mind. Dammit. Just when she needed her talents the most she was flying blind.

Was this how humans felt?

This maddening helplessness?

It sucked.

"It won't bother you at all to know that I belong to another?"

"I will be . . ." He took a beat to find the right word. "Content."

"Bullshit," she breathed, unable to accept he was actually prepared to walk away from her.

"Serra—"

"Look me in the eyes and tell me you don't want me."

He refused to be provoked. Worse, that pity continued to shimmer in his dark gaze. "I'm not going to play games with you."

"Because you can't do it," she snarled. "You want me. You're just too much a coward to do anything about it."

"Find another, Serra," he warned, a muscle in his jaw bulging as he reached down to grab his towel and stepped around her. "Be happy."

Her heart screeched to a painful halt. "Where are you going?"

He hesitated, but he refused to turn around. "To pack."

She glared at the broad back covered in swirling tattoos. God. He was destroying her.

Did he ever care?

"When are you leaving?"

"In the morning."

Not giving her the opportunity for further discussion he simply walked away, his shoulders squared and his head held high.

"Bastard," she breathed.